AR

PRAIRIE AVENUE

by Arthur Meeker

NEW YORK

ALFRED · A · KNOPF

1949

THIS IS A BORZOI BOOK,
PUBLISHED BY ALFRED A. KNOPF, INC.

To ROBERT MOLNAR

Prefatory Note

THE author would like to express his thanks to the library staff of the Chicago Historical Society, who have cheerfully and tirelessly helped him make his researches. He is also indebted to various people for communicating memories of a period long before his own, and for the loan of letters and other documents: particularly to his aunts, Mrs. James R. Walker and Mrs. David S. Cook; to his friend, Mrs. Robert W. Hamill; and, above all, to his father and mother, Arthur and Grace Murray Meeker.

The author was born on Prairie Avenue and lived there until he was twelve. His parents were not born there only because the street had not, in the sixties, been really developed; they were, however, both brought up in the neighbourhood and were steeped in its lore, which in later years they loved to recall. The book could not have been written without them.

Prairie Avenue is a novel and, like all novels, is a mixture of fact and fiction. None of the characters is meant to be a portrait of any actual Chicagoan, living or dead; the author has, both intentionally and unintentionally (as a novelist must), scrambled houses and people, births and marriages, divorces and deaths, so that (he hopes) it would be a very wise descendant indeed who could match his ancestors to the histories belonging to them.

Contents

BOOK I: 1885–1886, *page* 3

BOOK II: 1895–1896, *page* 143

BOOK III: 1904, *page* 245

EPILOGUE: 1918, *page* 297

PRAIRIE AVENUE

Book 1 : 1885-1886

> *"The sunny street that holds the sifted few . . ."*
>
> OLD CHICAGO SAYING

Chapter 1

THEN it's decided," said Mrs. Ramsay. "Ned is to spend the winter with Hiram and Lydia in Prairie Avenue."

"Oh, I suppose so," said Mr. Ramsay. "I suppose there's nothing else for him to do."

Ned did not speak. He went on standing where he was with his back to the room, looking out the window at the cold slanting sleet, the rows of cable-cars clanging past, and the jumble of horses and carriages, and foot passengers carrying umbrellas, that filled State Street on this rainy afternoon in late November. He knew well enough what lay beneath the resolute cheerfulness in his mother's voice, nor did he need to turn in order to ascertain that her bright black eyes were shining with unshed tears, and that his father was pulling his long sandy moustache, as always in moments of perplexity or dismay.

Indeed, Ned told himself he had been sure all along that it would end like this. The holiday in Chicago had been too good to last: no limit had been set to their pleasures and expenditures—dinner one night at the Richelieu and, the next, at the Grand Pacific Hotel, with a box at McVicker's or Hooley's to follow. Mr. and Mrs. Ramsay had embarked on their round of festivities with an air of feverish and almost furtive enjoyment that, Ned could tell from past experience, betokened a looming

3

disaster. Their "good time" must be nearly over; one of the "bad times" was obviously about to begin.

Ned was accustomed to bad times. What was new and disturbing was that, for once, apparently, he was not to be allowed to share it.

He waited, after his parents' remarks, until he felt he could command his voice sufficiently to use it without a tremor. Then he said slowly: "Where will you and Papa go?"

"That's not settled yet, darling," Mrs. Ramsay replied. "Papa isn't sure . . . New York, or perhaps back to Europe for a while . . . If Uncle Hiram can manage to help us . . . and he will, I know he will—he *must!* Anything else would be too bad to be true . . . Very well, Robert, I'll not say a word more. But the point is, Neddy, we'll probably be travelling most of the winter, and your father and I are agreed you're getting too old for that kind of thing. You were twelve in September; there's the question of your schooling, you know; it's time you were thinking of preparing yourself for college. Then you ought to have more of a proper home life than Papa and I are able to give you just now. You've not been so strong as we'd like to see you since that siege of pneumonia last winter in Vevey. So Papa and I believe it would be much better for you to settle down here for some months of study and quiet. You'll not mind it too much, I hope, my own boy?"

Ned released the thick tassels on the dark green rep curtains, which he had been fingering as if his life depended on it, and wheeled suddenly to face the room. As he did so he caught an instant vision of what was before him, as though it were a scene in one of the plays he'd been seeing all week: the square, sombre private parlour at the Palmer House, with its heavily carved walnut "suite," and the liver-brown marble mantel draped in a fringed green plush lambrequin, above which hung a coloured reproduction of "The Horse Fair" by Rosa Bonheur. A monumental bouquet of proud red roses stood on the round centre table next a box of candy from Gunther's:

4

these were his father's contributions to the family's comfort—
as the sewing-basket and litter of novels and magazines were
his mother's—and were as invariable as the splendid gardenia
in Mr. Ramsay's buttonhole, the mingled odour of expensive
tobacco and Florida Water that heralded his presence. Under
the cruel radiance cast by the flaring gas-jets in the bronze
chandelier the Ramsays themselves appeared somewhat di-
minished—little Mrs. Ramsay, in her black feathered toque
and close-fitting Newmarket (she had just returned from a
shopping trip to Gossage's; there were still drops of rain flashing on her fur collar), fidgeting about the floor; plump Mr.
Ramsay sitting dejectedly with his knees apart in an armchair
beside the round table, all unaware of the luxury surrounding
him or, indeed, of anything save his own depressing thoughts.
(Had it been just that morning Ned had seen him fussily
bounteous, over-spending right and left in his determination
to have only the best?)

"I'd much rather go with you, Mamma."

Ned had understood from the first that it would be impossible. He would not fight the family's decision, and knew they
knew it, too. Still it seemed important to go on record . . .

"I'm sure you would, darling." Mrs. Ramsay's smile became
brilliantly unconvincing. "And your Papa and I should much
prefer to keep you. But this time it seems . . . Uncle Hiram's
been very kind . . . Aunt Lydia, too, of course. They propose
to take you right into their home like one of their children.
You remember Uncle Hiram, don't you, Neddy?"

Ned nodded.

"Naturally, it's been years since you've seen him. But he's
always been good to us—never forget that. If it hadn't been
for my brother . . . When you were a baby and we lived in
Prairie Avenue, too, he was very fond of you. Why, in a way
it'll be a kind of homecoming, won't it? After all, you were
born in his house—only it wasn't his house then, but Papa's
and mine."

"I remember the house," said Ned, "better than Uncle Hiram. It was tall and thin, all yellowy stone, with high front steps and a peaked roof."

"Aunt Lydia's changed the inside a good deal," said Mrs. Ramsay, with a sigh. "That was only to be expected. But I'm certain you'll be very comfortable there. And your cousins will be company for you—Tom and Porter, and little Almira. I saw the boys last night when Papa and I went to call. They're regularly grown-up—sixteen and fifteen, I think they said— and they go to the Harvard School, where you'll be sent as soon as Doctor Mallard decides you are strong enough. But Almira's about your age—eleven and a half, Aunt Lydia told me—you ought to have plenty of pleasant times with her and her friends."

Ned fixed his round green eyes on his mother.

"Did you see her?"

"No, dear; she'd just gone to bed when we got there. But Aunt Lydia spoke of her so nicely, and said she was so pretty and good-tempered."

"She was dreadfully stupid when I saw her last," Ned pronounced gravely. "We were sent into the yard to play after lunch, and she *wouldn't* pretend Uncle Hiram's cane was an Arabian charger."

Mrs. Ramsay laughed tolerantly.

"Well, but that was a long time ago, and no doubt she's improved a lot since then."

Ned did not think so, but it seemed useless to insist on the point.

"When must I go to Uncle Hiram's?"

Mrs. Ramsay glanced inquiringly at her husband, who had not spoken since his first statement of opinion.

"Why, I hadn't thought . . . It depends on Papa and . . . and one or two other things. Let me see, this is Wednesday, isn't it? I expect by the end of the week, unless . . . Oh, Neddy, it's not what we hoped for, but I'm afraid it's the best we can

6

do, this year! Say you'll be happy, my darling! We'll write to each other often, often . . . and perhaps in the spring . . ."

Mrs. Ramsay stopped her frightened fluttering, her ceaseless clasping and unclasping of her hands, long enough to fling her arms round her son. Ned felt her tears warm on his cheek.

"I'll be happy, Mamma," he said quickly.

At this, Mrs. Ramsay clasped him still more closely than before, while Mr. Ramsay roused himself from his lethargy to thump the boy on the back, and produced a half dollar to provide the afternoon's entertainment. Ned had been promised a trip to the "Battle of Shiloh" in the Panorama Building. Now, to his satisfaction, he found himself bidden to include the "Battle of Gettysburg" as well—though it would cost another dime—with a ride home in the Wabash Avenue cable-car and the whole remaining quarter his to squander as he liked.

"Your mother must take a little rest," said Papa. "I'd go with you myself, but I've an important appointment with your uncle at the Chicago Club. Be sure to be back by six o'clock: we've got stalls for *The Mikado* and I thought it might be amusing to dine in the gold room at Kinsley's tonight."

Ned and his father took their departure together. Mrs. Ramsay kissed them both: Ned was adjured to keep his umbrella aloft, not to speak to strangers, and to come straight home without loitering; while Mr. Ramsay was besought to wear his rubber overshoes and to remember all that Hiram had done for them.

"I'll not need my rubbers, my love," declared Mr. Ramsay; "I'm taking a hansom-cab." (That was a flicker of expiring grandeur, as everyone knew the Chicago Club was just across the street.) "And I'm not likely to antagonize Hiram Stack—there's too much I need him to do for me."

Ned's parents exchanged a lingering look, which showed more plainly than words how serious their situation must be. Not that there hadn't been words, too, plenty of them. Ned reflected, as he bade Papa good-bye on the corner and plunged

7

into a sea of dripping umbrellas, that what he most appreciated in his family was their disposition to treat him as a reasonable being. They never talked deliberately over his head. Whatever the subject, from the war with King Thebaw of Burma to the choice of a luncheon *entrée,* he was urged to take part. Better still, when they were worried, they didn't pretend not to be: it went a long way towards reconciling him to the separation to feel he had been told the truth about its necessity. . . . How cold it was, and how damp and murky the air! Getting dark already at half past three. And people walked so fast and pushed so hard. Ned had forgotten, in his years away, how noisy and rude they were in Chicago. Grasping his own umbrella firmly, he breasted the jostling throng, a small, slight figure in his plaid ulster cut like a man's; cap pulled low over the straight, silky brown bangs; wide-open eyes vague and unfocussed as he fixed his attention on the problem of Papa and Mamma.

Yes, they had always told him the truth, always made him feel that he counted with them more than anything. Perhaps they had been so much overjoyed at having a son, after ten years of childless marriage, that it never occurred to them their delight in his company might not be matched by his corresponding delight in theirs. At all events, Ned was deeply attached to them both; his love was so great that it never occurred to *him* the life they led was peculiar, all studded with agitations and accidents as mysterious as they appeared to be unavoidable.

The trouble was, Papa sometimes was rich, and sometimes was poor. The change could come—frequently did—over night. Mamma had more than once tried to explain. . . . It had to do with stocks and bonds, and the bewildering operations of the Board of Trade. There was a place called the Wheat Pit, where "Bulls" and "Bears" did battle. Ned was too old now to imagine, as he had done as a little boy, that animals actually fought with one another. He understood that men

8

were buying and selling grain, and that his father was one of the men, though Papa was rarely present in person—his broker attended to that.

But grain went up, and grain went down. When it went down, strangely enough, the Ramsays were rich. After one of Papa's lucky deals they would spend a winter at the Holland House, or a summer in Saratoga Springs. They might go travelling for months—hire a villa in St. Augustine, tour Europe with a courier in a private *diligence*. (Ned's acquaintance with continental *hôtels de luxe* was vast and detailed.)

On the other hand, when grain went up, they were poor. Ned knew as much about cheap foreign *pensions* as he did about Palace Hotels: the boarding-houses of New York's and Chicago's shoddy West Sides were no less familiar than the *pensions*—for often catastrophe arrived so rapidly and completely that they hadn't the price of a steamer ticket.

When grain was down, Mrs. Ramsay had fine gowns and jewelry, a French maid to dress her, and a stylish carriage and pair. Ned would be given a pony, all the toys he could play with, all the books he could read. Sometimes he was sent to the best school in town, but this in the long run proving impracticable—since he was liable to be removed at a moment's notice—a series of tutors were engaged, with instructions to "pick up where the boy had left off."

When grain was up, these luxuries vanished. Tangible property was sold or simply abandoned; the maids and tutors scuttled off; and Ned, to his secret gratification, was told to continue a kind of education-by-reading by himself, "till things are a little more settled, my dear."

It was not restful, but it had not been dull.

Ned never asked himself why other children did not live the life he did; why the Ramsays' fortunes alone appeared to be linked to the troubling, unpredictable Bulls and Bears. He had not even minded the absence of friends—for casual acquaintance with unnumbered page-boys and porters could hardly be deemed to have supplied the lack. He had been content as long as he could share what befell Papa and Mamma.

Lately, though, it had seemed as though grain had been up more than usual. The bad times came closer together; this week at the Palmer House had been the first spent in such surroundings in almost two years, the first in five the Ramsays had been in Chicago at all.

Ned had an idea that the prolonged absence from the city they called home had something to do with Uncle Hiram. When the going was hard, Uncle Hiram, of course, had helped them out again and again. Equally of course—though Papa and Mamma hadn't said so—Uncle Hiram disapproved of his brother-in-law's business career. It was significant that, during the current visit, neither Mr. nor Mrs. Stack had come to call. Nor, as far as Ned knew, had the Ramsays been asked to dine at the tall yellow house in Prairie Avenue. That alone would have warned him of sulphur in the atmosphere, even if Papa's own actions—his absentmindedness, his nervous affability, the constant trips downstairs to the broker's office in the lobby— had not already given the show away.

At intervals all afternoon Ned's thoughts recurred to his father's financial affairs. Even the sanguine allurements of the famous panoramas could not wholly distract him. He prayed that things might turn out better than he feared, and also— though without much hope—that somehow it might be arranged for him to stay with Papa and Mamma.

However, he was not really greatly surprised when he got back to the Palmer House, at half past five in a freezing rain, to find the parlour a scene of wild confusion.

It was scarcely necessary to ask what had happened. Papa and Mamma, one gathered, were leaving almost at once. They were taking the evening train to New York and sailing on Saturday on the "Umbria." The place was crowded with trunks and boxes: Mamma, who unfailingly rose to emergencies, was packing with a kind of concentrated fury, assisted by a puzzled but interested chambermaid and her own Thérèse, a sharp-faced Belgian whom Ned privately suspected of having purloined more than an equitable share of his mother's gloves and ribbons. Papa, at a desk in the corner, was vainly trying to marshal his forces to dash off a series of last-minute notes. The door-bell rang continually; porters and bell-boys came and went; bills were presented. . . . In the midst of the hubbub two waiters appeared with champagne in a bucket and an elaborate dinner no-one had time to eat.

"We'll telegraph before sailing," said Mamma, bonneted and cloaked for flight; "and of course, darling, I'll write you our plans the moment Papa and I have any. I can't tell where we'll be in New York, for I don't know myself, and besides there are reasons . . . Oh, Neddy, I can't bear to leave you like this! We'll not even have time to take you down to Prairie Avenue. But Uncle Hiram has promised to fetch you. All you've to do is stop here till the carriage calls for you. It'll be quite all right, won't it, Robert? The management understands . . ."

"I don't know why they shouldn't," said Papa, with a gloomy glance at the platter of *filets mignons aux truffes* curdling in its gravy. "We've paid for the rooms till tomorrow."

It was Papa, after all—though he'd said so little—who had the last word. Cutting short his wife's stream of tearful goodbyes, he called Ned to him and put his hand on his shoulder.

"You're taking this like a man, son," said Papa, in a choked, gruff voice, "and I'm proud of you. It won't be for long, I warrant you. We'll be back before you've had time to miss us, as merry as grigs and on top of the world again. Before we go I'd like to say . . . I want to tell you . . ."

He hesitated, blew his nose; then unexpectedly thrust his hand into his waistcoat pocket and drew out his fat, shiny gold watch—his best watch, Ned knew, the one with Grandfather Ramsay's initials on it and the handsome gold penknife with three blades that served as fob on the other end of the heavy link chain.

"Here you are, Ned; I can only do little things for you now."
Ned started to protest, but Papa waved him away.

"Nonsense, my boy—it'll be yours some day, anyhow. Give
your mother a kiss . . ."

There was no time for tears, even if Ned had been inclined
to them. Before he quite realized it his parents were gone, in
a final flurry of hugs and parcels and farewell messages, and
Ned was alone in the square parlour (which seemed suddenly
much too big for him), holding the watch and the penknife
that were all that was left of Papa and Mamma.

For a few minutes he continued to sit where he was, fiddling
gently with the massive gold links, and taking some comfort
in touching them; for they seemed almost like part of his father. Then, philosophically, he nibbled some cheese and biscuits (the *filet mignon* was cold), sampled a bottle of claret
(it was hardly worth while opening the champagne), and
languidly investigated an impressive, though partially melted,
iced pudding before ringing to have the meal removed.

After that, there was nothing to do but return to his chair
by the round centre table with the bouquet of festive red roses
—were they fading a trifle?—and wait with as much assurance
as possible till the Stacks came to fetch him.

Thérèse appeared to inquire, with an injured air, if Monsieur Ned desired anything. She detested children, Ned in particular (Ned was aware), since his suspicions concerning the
gloves and ribbons had not been lost on her. Still the child
looked so little and lonely, all by himself, having been as good
as cast off by his unnatural parents . . .

Ned shook his head valiantly, and Thérèse, tossing hers,
retired to her own quarters, there no doubt to assemble and
appraise the results of the week's depredations.

Ten minutes later, by Papa's gold watch, Uncle Hiram's
carriage was announced.

Ned felt afterwards that his departure from the Palmer
House had been agreeably dignified. Descending to the lobby,

he distributed quarters, as he had often seen his father do, amongst all the servants who seemed to expect them, and marched out under the *porte-cochère* to find the Stacks' black shiny brougham drawn up at the Monroe Street entrance.

It had grown somewhat misty, but the rain was coming down harder than ever. Tim, the coachman, white-haired and ruddy, with a face like a benignant baboon's, looked black and shiny, too, encased in rubber from head to foot.

"I brought the brougham, Master Ned, 'stid of the cowpay," said Tim, in as matter-of-fact a tone as if they had been meeting daily, "for fear there'd not be room enough for yer boxes an' things. Is this all the luggage ye've got?"

Ned nodded as he stepped in, wishing only that the unsympathetic Thérèse might have seen him and that he had worn his other, and better, hat.

"Yer uncle's at a meeting at the Commercial Club," Tim continued, adjusting the rug round his passenger's legs, "an' yer aunt has company"—he pronounced it "coompany"—"but I doubt not ye'll see the both of them before ye go to bed."

Ned nodded again; he could not think of anything to say.

Tim sprang up on the box with surprising agility, seized the reins, chirruped to the horses—a fine pair of bays with long bushy tails—and the carriage splashed slowly out into the mainstream of Wabash Avenue.

It was very dark inside the brougham. Ned had at first a feeling of total eclipse; then he grew accustomed enough to the faint light filtering through to inspect the interior, which smelled of moth balls and was impressively grand, with grey broadcloth upholstery, a cut-glass vase for flowers, and cream-coloured fringed silk shades on the two small square windows. There were round silk bobbins attached to the shades that, when pulled, caused the latter to run up and down on their cords. Resisting a strong temptation to play with the bobbins, Ned composed himself in the middle of the bench, and tried deliberately to recall as much as he could of his uncle and aunt and their children.

Uncle Hiram, who was always referred to in the papers as the "well known lumber merchant," he had heard a great deal about; but, oddly, it was hard to picture his face. Certain aspects of his personality remained: his gold-bridged *pince-nez* on their black ribbon, the luxuriant brown side-whiskers, the droll way his double-chin dipped into his high wing collar when he lowered his head. . . . Of Aunt Lydia, Ned remembered simply that she was tall and stately, with reddish hair and a perennial smile. Almira reappeared as a fat little girl in yellow pigtails who was no good at imaginary games (the only kind Ned cared for). The boys, on the other hand, might be seen almost too clearly: they would have been just old enough, five years ago, for their good opinion to have mattered supremely—and that, Ned was dismally sure, he had never had. He could summon to mind with painful vividness the pair of square, scornful pink faces, the wide grinning mouths and resolute chins—but was Tom the dark one and Porter the blond, or t'other way round?—; relive, as though it were yesterday, the flat disdain with which they'd received his shocking admission that he didn't play baseball and had never learned how to swim.

Ned's liveliest misgivings centred, not unnaturally, round Tom and Porter Stack. Probably the best to be hoped for was that they'd feel too old now to bother about their young cousin.

But there was not time to worry much: upon reaching Michigan Avenue Tim headed the bays south along the row of smart hotels and shops that filled the right side of the street. On the left, the strip of park, the railway, and the lake were an undefined void, broken only by the dark looming shapes of Battery D Armory and the great Exposition Building. As they proceeded, the shops and hotels gave place to houses standing in blocks or, occasionally, detached in their gardens. At Park Row railway and lake were left behind; houses closed in on both sides; at Sixteenth Street they travelled east through a shabbier neighbourhood, past the intersection with Indiana. Then, suddenly, the houses grew bigger and grander, the elm trees taller, the gardens more spacious, and they were in Prairie Avenue.

Ned had seen it most often by daylight and in summer, when the elms were in leaf and the great piles of brick and stone basked proudly in smoky Chicago sunshine. On this wet November night the prospect was gloomy. It was exceedingly cold and damp; a fog-horn kept sounding its sad minor thirds as a reminder that the lake must be near. It was also very dark: street-lamps glimmered wanly through the mist, barely reflected in the pavement's black streaming river; and few lights showed in the houses, which seemed wrapped in chill seclusion. A minute later, Tim slowed the horses' clip-clop and turned their heads through an entrance between spiked iron gates. The brougham came to a halt at the foot of a flight of high stone steps that looked quite familiar.

"Here ye are!" shouted Tim.

He clambered down from the box and opened the door for Ned with a flourish.

Ned got out slowly and stood at the bottom of the steps, feeling rather shy. Unlike its neighbours, the tall yellow house was sparkling with lights from attic to basement, but in the circumstances this was hardly reassuring—hadn't one been told that Aunt Lydia was giving a party? Should he ring the bell? Or would it be better to wait till Tim . . . ?

Before Ned had time to make a decision the door was flung open by a rosy-cheeked maid in cap and apron, and he found himself ushered inside.

After the cold emptiness of the street the paneled hall seemed pleasantly warm and bright. All the gas-jets were lighted and there were flowers about, mostly cheerful yellow chrysanthemums in pots. The room was full of furniture: Ned thought he recognized some of the pieces, particularly a massive carved black walnut highboy with a mirror to match and a tall grandfather clock with a gold face like the sun. The double doors on the right that led to the parlour were shut. Behind them someone was playing the piano, a gay rhythmic refrain Ned—who knew a good deal about music—identified as a Chopin mazurka.

"Yer uncle's not home yet from the club," said the maid, who was plump and black-haired and spoke so softly and liltingly that it sounded like singing. "An' the company's still here. But wait now till we see . . ."

Without warning the music stopped and the parlour doors burst open, revealing a glimpse of rose and gold under the glittering crystal chandelier. Instead of the brilliant assembly Ned had imagined within, the figures of a single lady and gentleman emerged.

The lady came first. She was in evening dress, a wonderful gown of primrose yellow velvet all winking and twinkling with gold passementerie. She was very tall and had very bright brown eyes; chestnut braids were arranged coronet-fashion round her shapely head. Her jewelry, too, was gold—a necklace and diadem of beads—and two bracelets shaped like serpents with emerald-and-diamond eyes twined about her bare white arms.

As for the gentleman, who was also tall and also in evening dress, Ned had no time to make a detailed examination, so wholly engrossed was he by the radiant apparition before him.

"Bless me!" exclaimed the lady, in a deep, warm, slow voice Ned remembered at once (and was never thereafter to forget), "it's Ned! . . . Rob's and Katie's boy, you know," she flung over her shoulder to her companion, who had remained standing on the threshold to the parlour. "Why—what a brave little man we have here!"

Stooping, she held out her arms, heedless of her nephew's dripping ulster and of his slight recoil (for Ned was not sure he liked being a "brave little man"), and folded him in a perfumed embrace.

16

"Welcome, my darling, to Prairie Avenue!" said Aunt
Lydia Stack.

Chapter 2

ALTHOUGH Aunt Lydia professed herself delighted to see
him, Ned was not invited into the parlour. After introducing him to Mr. Terriss, the tall gentleman in
evening dress, she declared that her nephew must be exhausted
and dispatched him upstairs with the black-haired, rosy-
cheeked maid, who was ordered to give him some cocoa and
biscuits.

"I sent the children off to bed half an hour ago," said Aunt
Lydia. "They begged to wait till you came, but this is a school
night, you know—you'll see them all in the morning."

She kissed Ned again, and smiled and waved her hand to
him as he climbed the red-carpeted stairs.

Ned smiled back, a trifle faintly. He was really not tired; it
was hardly half past nine, and Papa and Mamma often let him
stay up till ten if he liked—even later, if they went to the
theatre. Nor was he in the least hungry. However, he guessed
at once that Aunt Lydia was not used to being opposed, so he
followed Mary Kelly, as the maid told him she was called, to
the large back bedroom on the third floor, where Tim had already deposited his luggage.

"Yer cousins Master Tom and Master Porter have the front
room," said Mary Kelly. "Ye're to share the bath with them.
Miss Almira's on the floor below, next Mr. and Mrs. Stack. She
moved down last spring; this used to be her room; I hope
ye'll like it."

Ned looked about him and decided that he did, very much.

It was a high-ceilinged chamber furnished rather quaintly in bamboo; the exotic note was further emphasized by the wall-paper, an all-over pattern of palms and tropical creepers dotted by bright-coloured, improbable-looking birds. (Ned wanted to ask what kind they were, but it seemed certain Mary Kelly would not be able to tell him.) There were two good-sized windows: one on the side where the garden was, the other at the back, which must overlook the railway and lake. The scarlet silk curtains were drawn; an oil-lamp was lighted on the bed-table, and a fire laid in the grate under the black marble mantelpiece.

Mary Kelly turned up the lamp and then lighted the fire, though the room was not cold. The cedar sticks blazed up at once and began to snap; they gave off a woodsy sweet smell.

"Fires," said Ned seriously, "are very expensive."

He was thinking of various disputed items on the bill at European hotels. But Mary Kelly threw back her head and laughed.

"Bless yer heart, yer uncle can well afford it! Hasn't he all the logs in the world he wants?"

While Ned was divesting himself of his outdoor garments and unpacking his bag, she fetched the cocoa and biscuits. Ned did not like to refuse them; besides, it was pleasant to sit in front of the fire, glancing round at items of interest. There was a large Viennese painted urn on the mantel (Perseus rescuing Andromeda), flanked by two handsome china parrots, as bright-coloured as the birds on the wallpaper and no less ornithologically incorrect.

Mary Kelly stood and watched him, laughing again at his surprise when the biscuits turned out to be sugar cookies shaped like baby chickens with currant eyes. She was decidedly one of the pleasant things in the room, with her fresh complexion, good-humoured smile, and soft, shining hair folded like sable wings under her cap. Ned would have liked to prolong the interview by questioning her about his cousins, but as soon as he had finished the refreshments Mary Kelly picked up the tray and bade him good night.

"Ye'll not want to unpack yer big box till tomorrow, I'm thinking? . . . The bathroom's just across the hall; I've left the gas on for ye. I suppose ye can undress yerself. Well, then, breakfast's at seven, an' I'll call ye a half-hour beforehand. Sleep well, Master Ned."

Although he knew it was unnecessary—possibly even foolish, in view of the startlingly early rising hour—Ned felt he could not go to bed until he had stowed his clothes away in the wardrobe and found places for his principal treasures: the pictures of Papa and Mamma on the bureau, his few books in the bookcase (evidently Almira's, judging by its innocuous and improving contents); his cherished small ivory clock, with a replica of the Lion of Lucerne on top, on the bedside table, where he could hear its comforting tick during the night. When he was undressed he pulled back the curtains that screened the rear window, threw up the sash, and stared out into the darkness. The air was still penetratingly damp; the foghorn went on moaning somewhere out on the water. It was too dim to see much: there was the Stacks' back-yard, and the back-yard of the corresponding house on Calumet Avenue. Beyond them was nothing but a black smudge, where Ned knew the lake and the railway were. As he stood there shivering, in spite of the warm woolen robe he wore over his nightshirt, there came a sudden rumbling and roaring, the house shook till the glass in the windowpanes and the bookcase squeaked protestingly, and a great fire-breathing dragon rushed screaming by to disappear in a cloud of smoke and molten cinders.

Ned was excited. He waited a few minutes to see if another train would pass. But soon he was shivering too hard to stand in the window any longer. It was too cold even to say his prayers on his knees. Hopping into bed, he turned out the lamp, burrowed beneath the fat red silk quilt, and gabbled a series of perfunctory supplications his mother had taught him in French.

Here was the moment he had been dreading all evening. But somehow it wasn't so bad as he'd feared. This had undoubtedly been the strangest day he had ever lived through, but it was ending better than it might have done. He thought over all that had happened since morning. It seemed that the Ned Ramsay who had breakfasted with his parents at the Palmer House—toying with his omelette because there were griddle-cakes and maple syrup to follow, and lamenting that the sleet storm would prevent their trip to the Lincoln Park Zoo—could not be the same as the Ned Ramsay lying between rose-scented sheets in the queer, pretty room with the bamboo furniture and birds on the wall. A spasm of loneliness tore through his heart as he remembered Papa and Mamma speeding away from him, perhaps in the very train he'd just seen. But the pain was happily fleeting. He believed their promise that soon they'd come back. Meanwhile there was plenty to amuse him in his new surroundings.

Drowsily Ned watched the firelight flicker and listened to the tick of the little ivory clock, and to the faraway sound of the piano below. He had forgotten that Aunt Lydia played the piano. This was not Chopin, though, but something wild and insistent that floated upstairs on successive waves of emotion, all alike and yet all different, too. What could it be? . . .

Suddenly out of the past, for no apparent reason, he recalled the first time he'd seen Aunt Lydia Stack.

It must have been—oh—years ago, he'd been standing in the window of the front room of some house in Chicago: very likely this one. His mother was with him. They'd seen a woman approaching in the street, a woman tall and handsome and heavily furred; for it was winter and snow lay thick on the ground. With a peculiarly unhurried gait she walked nearer and nearer, head high, lips vaguely smiling, till she was opposite the window where the Ramsays stood. Then she

20

paused, bright in her green-plumed bonnet against the snow, to nod and wave her hand before pursuing her stately way down the avenue; and Mamma said quickly: "Wave back at her, Neddy; that's your Aunt Lydia, darling." (But *why* had she added, half under her breath: "I wish to Heaven she'd stub her toe and fall into the gutter!"?)

It was still quite dark next morning when Mary Kelly came to wake Ned. He had slept well all night, having been more tired than he'd realized. Now he dressed as quickly as possible, shuddering at the grey gloom outside and wishing the fire had not burned itself to ashes. After that, he ran downstairs, guided by a heartening smell of coffee to the dining-room.

The dining-room was the room Ned knew best in the tall yellow house, probably because most of his visits had been at mealtimes. Like the hall it was paneled in sombre oak, but it would always have been gloomy, as the principal windows looked north and were shadowed by the house next door. The huge polished oak table was surrounded by high-backed crimson velvet chairs on casters: a bronze gas lantern descended on a long cord from the ceiling to make a pool of light over the centrepiece of ferns in their low silver dish. By its uncompromising beams the Stack family was revealed at breakfast: Uncle Hiram at the foot of the table (the head was empty), Tom and Porter on his right, and on his left Almira, with a vacant place between her and her father.

From the hall outside Ned had heard the sound of voices and a cheery clatter of cutlery, but directly he appeared there fell a hush; his cousins stopped talking and eating, as if by clockwork, and turned their faces silently towards the figure on the threshold. Uncle Hiram, who had finished his coffee and retired behind the *Tribune* with his cigar, lowered his paper, peered through the smoke to see what was the matter, and then cleared his throat with a loud *"Ahem!*—Good morning, my boy. Children, where are your manners? Get up and speak to your cousin at once!"

Three high red chairs were pushed hastily back (they were so top-heavy that Porter all but overset his), and three right hands were offered Ned in turn. Almira said: "Good morning," in a clear treble. Tom and Porter muttered something that sounded like "Har yuh, Ned, glad t'see!" Ned replied politely: "How do you do?", wishing that it had not somehow a chillingly formal ring. There was a general settling down, and Mary Kelly brought another bowl of porridge.

The conversation, however, did not recover its pace and volubility. Ned was frankly afraid of the boys, who had grown so much taller that they were almost like men, though with an embarrassing number of arms and legs. They still had square, pink faces, still looked much alike (Tom *was* the dark one, after all); in the circumstances Ned was thankful that, after their perfunctory greeting, they gave full heed to their bacon and eggs, and to an elliptical argument between themselves concerning some projected excursion to Washington Park, which involved numerous "Prime sport's" and "Bully for you's!", as well as Porter's plaintive, recurrent "Joe don't *need* to come, I tell you, but t'won't be half the fun if he don't!"

If they had been alone together, Ned felt he might have talked to Almira, who looked reassuringly much the same as five years ago. (She had grown, too, of course, and her pigtails were a taffy-brown instead of yellow.) But she kept her head modestly bent over her plate, confining her stolen side-glances to those moments when Ned's attention was fixed elsewhere.

It would have been wounding, if Ned had not speedily surmised that a peremptory warning must just have been issued not to discuss the latest Ramsay collapse—and what else, one wondered, could his cousins possibly be thinking of, today of all days?

Uncle Hiram, as if understanding that he himself was to blame for the tension, laid his paper aside, with the air of a duty to be done, and adjusted his *pince-nez* on their black silk ribbon to a more comfortable angle. He was a big man, full

22

and impressive of figure, with thick curly hair and a wealth of side-whiskers a little too brown to be natural. Many years older than his sister Mrs. Ramsay, he had aged a good deal since Ned had last seen him: his bulldog face, even squarer than his sons', was lined and leathery; the two folds of skin that ran from his nostrils to the corners of his mouth had deepened perceptibly; and surely that high winged collar contained yet another chin? . . . Uncle Hiram had the immense dignity of a man of substance accustomed to being obeyed on the instant. His voice was slow and rather awful; even when he smiled his lips revealed a frightening number of teeth (there, again, like a bulldog). Only the eyes, dark and bright like Mamma's, made Ned feel unreasoningly at ease with his formidable relative.

With plodding thoroughness Mr. Stack put his nephew through the conventional catechism concerning his tastes and pursuits. "How did you sleep, my boy? . . . Good, good; delighted to hear it. A bit weak in the chest, your mother tells me. Let's hope a winter in Chicago will set that right. Our climate's severe, but undoubtedly healthy. Doctor Mallard thinks well of it. How are you getting along in school? . . . What? Not been to school lately? Hem! Hem! Sorry to hear it. Been tutoring, I suppose? . . . What? Not tutoring either? Well, your aunt, I believe, has made arrangements with Doctor Locke at Grace Church to have his assistant, a young man named Leslie, come over each morning for the present. He's an excellent scholar, I hear, and of course an exemplary Christian. I dare say a little religious instruction may not come amiss, eh?"

Ned murmured that he was sure it would be nice, and that his uncle and aunt were very kind.

"Not at all! Not at all! There's no need to thank us in any way, shape, or form. I hope you'll be happy and prosper, Ned. Naturally, it will take you a little time to get used to our ways. You've been, I can't help thinking, unfortunate up to now, spending so much time abroad. There's rilly nothing to Europe, and so I've told your parents a hundred times. Even New York has a certain levity in the atmosphere. Where have you been stopping in New York, my boy? . . . Ahem! They do you very well at the Holland House, very well indeed. I rather wonder your father . . . Still hotel life's unsuited to young people. The want of regular hours . . . unwholesome amusements . . . Well, that's no matter now. Keep your eye on your book and do as you're bid, and I doubt not you'll serve as an admirable example to your graceless young cousins."

Almira giggled self-consciously. The boys looked somewhat abashed, but were saved the trouble of answering by a shrill whistle in the street. Porter, with a rapid "Papa-may-I-be-'scused?", pushed back his chair so violently that, this time, it did crash to the floor; righted it clumsily, and turned to his brother. "There's Joe. You coming, Tom?"

Tom, reddening slightly, replied that he was waiting for someone; whereupon Porter gave a derisive hoot as he ran into the hall and started scrambling his school-books together. Almira laughed and clapped her hands, exclaiming: "It's Carrie Mallard—Tom's sweet on her!" (These were almost the first words Ned had heard her speak.)

Uncle Hiram rose with an air of heavy displeasure and bade his daughter mind her own business. At the door Mary Kelly was waiting with her master's tall hat and fur-trimmed overcoat, which he donned as if the rite had an intrinsic importance. Then, more imposing than ever, he laid a benevolent hand on Ned's shoulder.

"Good-bye, my boy. Here's a dollar for you—the same weekly allowance I make my own children. If there's anything you want and don't get, don't hesitate to ask for it. 1817 Prairie Avenue's your home now, God willing, for as long as you need it to be."

Ned thanked his uncle, wondering what the latter would say if he knew that Papa had sometimes let him spend that amount in a day. Mary Kelly opened the door: Uncle Hiram strode out on the threshold and slowly descended the yellow stone steps to where Tim was waiting with the coupé to drive him to his office in the Montauk Block and, later, to the great lumber yards of Stack and Company, over on the south branch of the river. In the grey winter's dawn Ned, stepping outside, saw carriages standing in front of other lighted houses along the block; more figures like Uncle Hiram's, high-hatted and portly, were getting into them. The air felt bitterly cold. Leafless elms looked black against a sooty sky, from which a few snowflakes were reluctantly falling. Ned was moved by the scene, though he could not have told why.

While he was standing at the top of the steps, drawing quick breaths of the raw, smoky air, Almira, who had scampered away after breakfast, reappeared wearing her brown winter coat and hat, with a fur tippet and muff to match, and announced that she was going to take Ned for a walk.

"I don't have to go to school today; Mamma says I may stay home for once, 'cause you've just come and t'wouldn't be polite to leave you the very first morning. And Mr. Leslie's not coming till noon; I asked to make sure. Mamma says you've to study only an hour a day till you're stronger. I wish *I* was delicate. What have you got wrong with you?"

"I don't know," confessed Ned, rather embarrassed. "Nothing much, really. I get lots of colds in winter."

"Oh, is *that* all?" Almira, having obviously suspected some lurid ailment, looked disappointed. "So do I. So does everyone in Chicago, I guess. Well, fetch your coat, why don't you? You haven't a cold today, I hope!"

As they set forth Ned eyed his cousin with shy inquiry; she stared back at him, seriously but with perfect good-humour; suddenly they both burst out laughing for no reason at all, and were friends.

Now they had plenty to say to each other. Almira's silence in the house had apparently been caused by awe of her father;

she seemed ready to answer all Ned's questions. (If she asked none of her own, that was probably because she could not think of any to ask.) Their first errand was to explore the garden, really just a yard separating the Stacks' house from the next one to the south. The grass was sere and lifeless, and the shrubbery along the path looked spindly without its leaves. There were two trees in the garden, both leafless too. "This one's a horse-chestnut," said Almira consequentially. "They're very rare." "Not in France," objected Ned. But Almira only opened her blue eyes wide and remarked that they weren't in France now.

As the stables lacked interest without Tim and the horses, Almira proposed a walk "round the block," which turned out to be the grand tour from Eighteenth Street to Twenty-Second, and home by Calumet Avenue along the lake and the railway tracks.

It was much lighter; the lamps had gone out; behind their ornamental stone copings and spiked iron fences the big houses on the avenue, so aloof and unfriendly last night, had resumed their daytime air of dignified comfort. Were there more of them than before? Ned, taking cognizance of changes in the neighbourhood, thought that there must be: the copings were almost continuous now and most of the vacant lots he remembered had vanished, though here and there a frame cottage remained, simple survivor of an earlier day. (It was hard to imagine that, fifteen years ago, the settlement had scarcely existed; yet Ned had often heard Papa say that when he and Mamma had moved there, after the fire of '71, Prairie Avenue was little more than a cow-track across sand dunes shaded by cottonwood trees.)

The houses were of all sizes and shapes, and their styles were as varied as their building materials. Ned, his eyes newly sharpened by his European travels, saw for the first time that they were designed after foreign models. A balconied Venetian *palazzo* stood next a German gingerbread house with gargoyles

26

on the roof, while a red brick Queen Anne mansion, a Byzantine fortress, and a Renaissance castle (all fancy grey stone embroidery) made an oddly assorted trio over the way. What seemed peculiar to Chicago were the high flights of steps leading to the front doors—most of the residents entered half a storey above the street level—and a certain stodgy plethora of decorative detail. (If five chimneys were good, ten were better.) Ned did not know what was wrong, but felt it without knowing and liked his uncle's tall yellow house, which was unpretentiously of no style at all, best of the lot.

Briskly the children marched—it was too cold to loiter—along the soft limestone sidewalk, their breath rising in twin puffs of vapour as they moved. Save for a postman making his solitary round, they had the street to themselves. The lords of Prairie Avenue had ridden forth to war, and it was too early for their ladies to be on their way to market. Between Twentieth and Twenty-First Streets Almira halted a moment in front of the biggest place they had yet seen. This was a French brownstone *château* that reminded Ned a little of the Grand Opera in Paris. Its entrance was flanked by pillars, its *porte-cochère* supported by sculptured nymphs; the roof soared, a wilderness of chimneys and fretted iron-work. Everything about this splendid property seemed to be in scale. The fence enclosing it was twice as high as any other; the garden was larger, the trees more numerous; there were marble statues scattered on the lawn, a sundial and a fountain; a glass hot-house bulged importantly between the main building and spacious dependencies at the rear.

As the children paused to admire so much ordered magnificence a flock of slate-blue pigeons sailed through the murky air to settle, with great fluttering and rustling, among the chimneys on the roof. The postman was climbing the brownstone steps; in response to his ring an immensely dignified Negro in uniform came to the door to receive a packet of letters.

"I don't remember that house at all," said Ned.

"Of course you don't," said Almira, waving cheerfully to the Negro. "It was built only last year, after the old one burned down. The Kennerleys live there. Mrs. Kennerley's Mamma's best friend, and I'm in the same class at Dearborn Seminary with Celia. She's got two brothers, too, same as I have: Roscoe, the younger, is a horrid little wretch—he's only five—but Sonny Kennerley's 'most thirteen. I like him pretty well, and he's in love with me."

Ned stared; Almira had made the statement in the same placid, unconcerned tone with which she might have declared that Sonny Kennerley was fond of limedrops. Ned knew something about the Kennerleys, who were friends of his family, too. Abner Kennerley, the "Grocer King," was supposed to be the richest man in Chicago. It would have been interesting to pursue the subject of romance, but Almira switched it suddenly, as they reached the corner of Twenty-Second Street, where the skating-rink was, by remarking that nobody lived south of here and they might as well go back before they froze to death.

On the return trip along Calumet Avenue—where they stopped twice to watch trains and Almira got a cinder in her eye—Ned gathered a good deal of useful information concerning the Stacks. For instance, Aunt Lydia never, it seemed, got up for breakfast (that accounted for the empty place at table). She had it on a tray in her room . . . "No, not upstairs; that's where Papa sleeps. She sleeps there sometimes, but her own room's downstairs behind the parlour. Mamma's delicate, too. Doctor Mallard don't like her to climb."

Uncle Hiram, according to his daughter, thought of nothing but his business. He was always taking trips south to see to his lumber companies in Mississippi. Mamma never went with him. She didn't seem to mind being left, though. Mamma had so many friends. She paid a call on Mrs. Kennerley every single morning, and in the evening people paid calls on her. Even when Papa was out or away, she was never alone. Mr. Ken-

nerley often came, and lots of other gentlemen. There'd be a
fire in the parlour, the pink-shaded lamps were all lighted, and
Janet, the "upstairs girl," brought in tea and little cakes.
"Then sometimes, you know, in the evening there's music . . ."
Ned interrupted to say that he knew it—last night he'd heard
his aunt at the piano.

"Oh," said Almira, as if he'd said something stupid, "that
wasn't Mamma playing—that was Uncle Rock."

"Uncle Rock—who's he? Is he my uncle, too?"

And Almira replied, still more loftily, that he wasn't *anybody's* uncle. "He's just Mamma's friend, Mr. Terriss, the
lawyer. His office downtown is right next Papa's. He gives us
lovely presents at Christmas and birthdays, and he told us to
call him Uncle Rock, so we do."

When they got home Mary Kelly met them in the hall with
a message that Mrs. Stack would like to speak to the children.
Ned followed his cousin through the rose-and-black-walnut
grandeur of the parlour to a pair of folding doors at the back,
which, he seemed dimly to recall, in his parents' time had led
to the library. (But the library now was confined to a small
antechamber adjoining the dining-room: it was clear that
neither Uncle Hiram nor Aunt Lydia cared for books.) Almira
tapped on one of the doors, and a deep, warm voice, as smooth
as cream, said: "Come in!"

Aunt Lydia's room, all green and white and gold, must,
Ned thought, be the prettiest in the house. A great canopied
bed filled one corner; in another, under the marble mantel, a
hot coal fire was hissing and glowing. Next the fireplace, in
its basket tied with a taffeta bow, lay an enormous white cat
with emerald eyes. The muslin-draped dressing table stood in
the window overlooking the garden; it had a triple mirror
and was littered with gold toilet articles and an assortment of
Bohemian glass jars and flasks and little boxes. Aunt Lydia,
clad in a wonderful frilly dressing-gown, sat in front of the
table, gazing intently at her image in the glass. Her chestnut

hair rippled over her shoulders, so full of ardent lights that it gave the effect of sunshine on this grey winter's day. Janet was braiding it. At least, Ned supposed it must be Janet: the maid had a screwed-up brown nut of a face and frowned near-sightedly as she bent to her task.

For a moment Ned feared Aunt Lydia was frowning, too, the mirrored eyes were so fixed and expressionless. She made no attempt to speak; it seemed an age that the children stood there, while Janet's deft fingers went on plaiting and poking and pinching and devising. Not until the last shining satin coil was looped into place did she turn in her chair; as she did so her face resumed by degrees, like the sun slowly rising, its habitual look of bland good-humour.

"There! *That's* done!" said Aunt Lydia. "Ned, child, how are you? Is my little girl looking after you properly?"

Ned replied that indeed she was; they'd just come in from a walk.

Aunt Lydia shivered as she looked out the window.

"Brr! Aren't you frozen? What a dreadful day! I think it must be going to snow. I know just what you're going through, poor lamb, missing your mother and father too badly and feeling as homesick and lost as a cat in a strange garret— though some cats like it here, as I dare say you've noticed. (Janet, don't forget Alexander's saucer of tea: *two* lumps of sugar this time, if you please.) Did your uncle tell you Mr. Leslie is coming at twelve? I spoke to the young man myself; he seemed pleasant enough as curates go, but a little too pur-poseful for my taste. Don't, whatever you do, let him give you too much homework. Homework's such a horrid waste of time. And I'm sure you've always your nose in a book anyhow —you look like a scholar to me. Doctor Mallard is anxious for you to get plenty of rest and outdoor exercise, you know. Al-mira, what have you planned for this afternoon?"

Almira, who had been staring round-eyed at Janet's opera-tions—just as if she'd never seen her dress her mother's hair before—shifted uneasily from one foot to the other and mumbled that Phronsie Wagstaff was giving a birthday party.

Aunt Lydia raised her fine black brows.

"Phronsie Wagstaff! And who is she, pray? (Stand up straight, dear, and don't shuffle your feet; it makes me nervous.)"

Almira muttered, still more uneasily, that Phronsie was in her class at school—she was a regularly splendid girl—her family'd just moved to town from Cincinnati.

"Oh, yes," said Aunt Lydia, her brow suddenly clearing, "I know who they are; I've heard Uncle Rock mention them. But, darling, don't they live at Twenty-Ninth Street? You know how your Papa and I feel about your going 'way out there. Must you really . . . ?"

"Then you'd rather we didn't?" said Almira meekly.

Aunt Lydia shrugged her shoulders; she was busy choosing a pair of kid gloves from a drawerful Janet had presented for her inspection. "Suit yourself, baby; you know I never interfere with your pleasures. Only I should think you might find something more amusing for your cousin on his very first day. If it were summer, there'd be plenty to do, what with swimming and sailing and riding and baseball. Oh, summer's the time for young people in Chicago! As it is, I hardly know . . . you might go skating after lunch. Do you skate, Ned?"

"Yes," said Ned, thankful to be able to tell the truth without flinching; "pretty well, I think. I took lessons last winter in Vevey."

"Well, have you skates with you? . . . But how stupid I am! Why should a boy go wandering round the world with a pair of iceskates in his trunk? Here, wait a moment . . ."

Aunt Lydia stood up deliberately, flinging aside the frilly robe to reveal her white wool walking-dress all sewn with little gold buttons. She was so tall and so perfectly formed that, in spite of the stiff, cramping lines of her basque and bustle, Ned was reminded of a statue of Juno he'd seen in the Tuileries

31

Gardens. "Janet, my new cape and bonnet, and the sable stole, please. And hand me my purse. There, my boy; I'm sure you can buy what you need in Twenty-Second Street with that. Almira, be good—I'll see you both later. Aunt Corinne and I are lunching down town and going to Mr. Stoddard's lecture at Central Music Hall. We'll drive home by the rink and pick you children up: then, if you decide you really want to go to the Wagstaffs', I've no objection."

Ned started to protest that Uncle Hiram had already given him a dollar, but Aunt Lydia checked him with an admonishing gesture, slid into the cloak Janet held for her, kissed the tips of her fingers, and sailed out—not by the door to the parlour, but through a smaller one at the back concealed by beaded *portières*. There was a sound of steps descending; then the door below closed with a click. In the silence left by her going the coals in the grate hissed loudly. The great white cat got out of its basket, stretched itself, and followed its mistress out of the room. A minute later, Aunt Lydia reappeared outdoors.

"Where is she going?" demanded Ned, running to the window. "And who's Aunt Corinne?"

"That's Mrs. Kennerley," Almira answered. "I told you, Mamma goes to see her every day."

Her bright brown eyes fixed on some point in the middle distance, her lips vaguely smiling (but was it really a smile? Or was her customary expression arranged to *look like one?*), Aunt Lydia picked her way serenely along the garden path towards Prairie Avenue. As Ned watched her he remembered again the first time he had seen her: why did everything she did seem interesting and faintly mysterious? He was puzzled, also, how a creature who presented the superb embodiment of health could possibly be "delicate." But most of all he wondered why his mother ever had wanted anyone so bewitchingly amiable to fall into the gutter.

Chapter 3

THE afternoon was half over by the time Almira and Ned got to the skating-rink. Mr. Leslie, a mild-mannered but methodical young man, had kept his pupil a quarter of an hour over time, while he attempted to clarify the cloudy perplexities of compound fractions. In consequence lunch was served late, much to the servants' annoyance; and directly after lunch Mary Kelly asserted Mrs. Stack's orders were that Master Ned was to rest for at least forty minutes.

The delay was disappointing. In his haste Ned recklessly bought the first pair of skates he tried on; then, naturally, fell prey to gnawing regrets that troubled him all the way back from Mr. Tompkins's shop. But after all, though the light was already beginning to fade a little, the rink was still crowded when they arrived.

The ground was quite white in the vacant lot on the corner of Twenty-Second Street, for it had snowed hard for an hour: the air swarmed with flakes tossed hither and thither on a wind too wild for the Prairie Avenue pigeons. (Only a solitary sea-gull blown across from the lake dared measure its strength against the blast.) In the middle of the lot the grey square of ice was alive with skaters of all ages and sizes, most of them wearing bright-coloured caps and jackets. Ned caught sight of Porter at once; a moment later Tom flew by, on his arm a tall, russet-haired girl who, one supposed, must be Carrie Mallard.

Almira, puffing and blowing, put on her skates with some difficulty and hobbled out on the ice. She was still a novice and kept clutching the back of a rickety chair and squealing in mingled exhilaration and dismay. Ned glided easily after her, hoping he looked as composed as he felt.

"Why don't you let go that old thing," he suggested, "and strike out for yourself?"

But Almira only shook her head and squealed more loudly. "I don't dare! I don't dare! What if I should fall?"

"Why, then, you'll fall, I suppose," replied Ned. "T'won't hurt you a bit. Don't be silly; you can lean on me if you like; see, it's really quite simple."

To encourage her he executed a neat turn, congratulating himself that despite lack of practice his skill had not left him. It would have been dreadful to look awkward before those big boys; besides, there was satisfaction in demonstrating his superiority, in one field at least, to the cousin who, with her undoubted kindness, had maintained a slight air of patronage all day.

Poor Almira, her cheeks as red as apples, made heroic efforts to conquer her wobbling timidity; but it took Ned a long time to persuade her to circle the rink just once on his arm, and no sooner had they got back to their starting point than she besought him to leave her.

"I don't want to spoil your fun. Anyway, here's Maudie; she's learning, too; we can try it a while together."

The latecomers found themselves suddenly surrounded by a whole group of the younger skaters, including Florence Harper, a pallid, hatchet-faced child in spectacles and a green plush coat; merry Maud Mallard, who looked like a pocket-edition of Carrie; and her brothers, Joe and Jamie. Joe was a burly big boy; Jamie, a puny small one; but all the Mallards were sandy and snub-nosed, freckled and friendly.

To her friends in general Almira made the portentous announcement: "This is my cousin Ned Ramsay, who's come to live with us. He's delicate."

Florence said: "Oh!" and shrugged her shoulders. Maud said: "Hello!" and grinned. Jamie grinned without saying anything; and Joe remarked: "Delicate, eh? He don't look it, do he?"

"I'm *not,* really," demurred Ned, blushing indignantly, and sure that this was no moment for the interesting drawn look he sometimes assumed before sympathetic adults.

As if to prove his earnest disclaimer, he cut a furious figure eight and returned to the group breathing frosty defiance.

Joe whistled. "The young 'un can skate! Tell you what, Ned: I'll race you to the end of the rink and back—what say?"

"Oh, but that's not fair!" cried Maud; and Florence added: "Everyone knows Joe Mallard's the best skater in town."

Ned hesitated, inwardly quailing. But he knew there was nothing else for it: he'd *have* to agree. Defeat in the circumstances would be perfectly honourable. He swallowed the lump in his throat and nodded.

"All right!" said Joe.

Jamie screamed, in a high, piercing voice: "On your marks —get set—*go!*"

They were off in the teeth of the biting wind, the other skaters laughing and exclaiming in good-natured excitement as they made way for the contestants.

Tears sprang to Ned's eyes: his breath came in gasps; but he kept his face set on the goal. There was no time to look at his rival. The rink was barely a hundred yards long: before he realized it he had reversed and come scrambling back as fast as he could to slide gasping to the ground, a full length ahead of Joe Mallard.

Shouts of approval rang out: Almira, her face bright scarlet with cold and emotion, hopped up and down, still holding tight to her chair, and shrieked like a railway engine.

Ned picked himself up in a daze and dusted the snow from his coat and mittens.

Joe was waiting for him on the ice.

"All right, kid," he said, holding out his hand. *"You're* all right, too, you know!"

Ned felt his cheeks burning; he wished momentarily he

were anywhere else. But then reassurance lapped over him in a comforting wave: he had wondered all morning, and worried not a little, how he, who had never had any friends of his own age, would get on with Almira's. Apparently, without planning it, he had hit upon the quickest means of winning their esteem. For a minute or two he was engulfed by a vociferous throng. (Only Florence Harper, whose idol had fallen from his pedestal, hunched her thin shoulders in disgust and skated off with a female crony.)

As he disengaged himself, half diffident, half delighted, from the ranks of his admirers he caught sight of a new boy standing a little apart from the rest. The boy was very dark; he wore a red knitted cap with a tassel over a tangle of jet-black curls, and had a pleasant, eager, lively expression.

When he saw that Ned was staring at him he skated up and laid his hand on Ned's arm. Close to, it was easy to see that, though he was a good deal the taller and stouter of the pair, they were about the same age.

"Jolly for you!" said the boy. "I wish *I* could've done that. You *can* skate, can't you? Congratulations!"

He smiled broadly, showing flashing white teeth in his handsome brown face. Ned felt something indescribably warm and harmonious flowing between them, but before he had time to do more than smile in return the boy in the red cap saluted and vanished in the crowd.

Ned had no idea who his new acquaintance might be, but just then he heard the Harper girl say in a spiteful whisper to her crony: "If that isn't just like Sonny Kennerley—always buttering up a stranger!"

To cover his mounting confusion he struck out by himself, circling the rink with his hands in his pockets and trying to look unconcerned.

It was growing darker now; the flakes came down faster and faster. Still there seemed to be just as many skaters as before.

36

Perhaps they were loath to go, realizing that too heavy a snowfall must soon cut short their revels. As Ned pressed close to the bank he became conscious of a slight commotion on shore. A stout woman with untidy hair straggling from beneath a poke bonnet was pursuing a little girl in a blue velvet coat. The little girl was on skates, which hampered her movements; but she was agile enough to evade her would-be captor; as soon as she reached the edge of the rink she gave a tinkling laugh and sped to the centre in one long, rapid slide. The stout woman, obviously afraid to follow her charge any farther, clucked her dismay and burst into a torrent of French.

Ned paused, amused by the comedy. But soon he saw that the woman's fears were well grounded. The little girl in the blue velvet coat was no finished performer. Once the impulse was spent that had sent her spinning onto the ice, she was at a loss, wavered this way and that, trying to balance herself with her arms. (One hand was encased in a miniature ermine muff, a preoccupation which seemed to add to her troubles.) She glanced over her shoulder in search of help; muttered "Bother!" quite audibly once or twice; but made no attempt to return to the bank, where the stout woman was now running up and down, wringing her hands and wailing: *"Célie! Reviens vite, je t'en prie! Ne te hasarde pas toute seule sur la glace!"*

Ned skated up and said politely: "Can I help you?"

The little girl did not answer at once. She said "Bother!" again, made several more unsuccessful efforts to gain her balance; then, finally, accepted the hand Ned was proffering, and smiled.

Ned's heart gave a throb. He did not know what had happened to him, but he was instantly sure that the little girl in the blue velvet coat was the most marvelous being he had ever beheld.

She was a very pretty little girl indeed, with hair of spun

gold (so pale it was almost spun silver), a roseleaf complexion, and eyes of a strange, cold blue that reminded Ned of the deep, pure waters of Lac Léman at Vevey. Her smile, too, was strange: slow to come and slow to go, it lighted up her face with a breathtaking radiance, but brought her no nearer: she seemed as remote from the world about them as a frost princess in some northern fairytale.

For a minute they stood holding hands in silence. Then the little girl said, in a light, cool voice exactly right for the frost princess:

"Thank you very much. I shan't fall. I know how to skate, really; it's just that I was in such a hurry to get away from Mademoiselle I didn't wait to fasten the buckles properly. They're too loose. I wonder . . . do you think you could . . . ?"

Ned was already kneeling. "Can you manage to stand while I do it? Wouldn't it be safer to sit on the bank?"

The little girl shook her golden curls, powdered with snow, and laughed.

"That wouldn't be safe at all. Mademoiselle'd catch me and make me go home."

"Very well, then," said Ned, bending once more to his task. "Lean on my shoulder; it won't take a minute."

He was perspiring in spite of the cold. But the frost princess looked as if she were used to being waited on. She surveyed her cavalier calmly and said: "You're Ned Ramsay, aren't you?"

"Yes; how did you know?"

"I saw you come with Almira."

"Is she a friend of yours?"

"We go to school together. I'm Celia Kennerley, you know." Ned was not surprised; he felt he'd guessed it all along.

"I thought you might be, when I heard your governess call you Célie."

"I saw you race Joe Mallard, too, and beat him," continued Celia reflectively. "You skate awfully well, don't you?"

"Well, I ought to," replied Ned. "I've had lots of practice in Switzerland. I was in school last year in the hills above Vevey, where they have ice all winter long."

"Oh!" said Celia. "No wonder, then." There was a pause. "But I do think you skate better than any boy I ever met." Another pause. . . . "The minute I saw you I wanted to skate with you. Did you know that? That's why I ran away from Mademoiselle. She tried to get me to wait for my brother. But I wouldn't." Still another pause . . . "Well, what do you say, Ned Ramsay? Now that I'm here, will you skate with me?"

Ned straightened up and wiped the moisture from his brow.

"There you are," he said, in a queer, hoarse voice that did not sound like his own. "They're all right now, I think."

Celia frowned.

"You haven't answered my question."

Her voice was still distant and cool as the snowflakes that fell all around them. She scarcely looked at him while she spoke. Yet Ned was so choked by emotion that he hemmed and ha'd, utterly unable to find the words he wanted. "Why . . . why . . ."

Suddenly, with a burst of desperate courage, he held out his hand, as he had done at the beginning of their interview. Celia once more gave him hers; it was so minute, even in the thick white wool mitten, that she seemed more than ever like a fairy. Then she laughed again, this time very gently.

"Come along, Ned!"

Off they flew in the gathering dusk . . . Celia was right: she could skate well enough, with unusual lightness and grace. At the same time she possessed no such skill as her companion, and appeared, oddly, to expect everyone else to keep out of her way—*she* would not voluntarily deflect her own course by a hairsbreadth.

Ned guided her without seeming to. On land he'd never have dared be so bold, but ice was his natural element. He heard the voices of the other children, the clink and scrape of their skates, as if in a dream. Even the strident plaints of the stout woman floundering about in the snow went unheeded. ("Don't pay any attention to Mademoiselle," ordered Celia. "*I* don't have to!") He was conscious of no-one but the golden-haired frost princess in the blue velvet coat, with one tiny hand in her ermine muff and the other clasped confidingly in his.

What brought their flight to an end at last was the arrival of a smart coupé drawn by two prancing black horses that rolled down the avenue and pulled up abruptly at the corner. A lady's face appeared at the window of the coupé, but even before she began calling out in a high, sweet voice Celia dropped Ned's hand with her favorite exclamation of "Bother!" and flitted away without a word of farewell.

Ned, however, was by no means resigned to being forsaken thus unceremoniously. Still under the spell he, too, quitted the rink, observing how Mademoiselle pounced on her prey, pulled off her skates, and shooed her towards the carriage, without young Miss Kennerley's losing for an instant her attitude of unassailable hauteur. The door flew open; Celia was stuffed through it summarily. Within, Ned perceived Aunt Lydia, beaming and gracious, on the far side of the back bench, beside her a small woman swathed in sables. There was a moment of confusion, a babble of feminine voices; then Aunt Lydia, who must have recognized her nephew, said something to her companion, and Celia was allowed to get out and say good-bye to Ned, which she did in rather perfunctory fashion.

Ned was also presented briefly to Mrs. Kennerley. He was given a black-gloved hand hardly larger than Celia's to hold; caught a fleeting glimpse of a pair of enormous, melting, dark eyes and a melancholy smile.

"Thank you," said the high, sweet voice, "for being so good to my little girl."

Celia was snatched up again, the door slammed, and the black horses trotted off, leaving Ned, disconsolate, to watch the carriage slowly vanish in the twilight and the whirling snow.

That night the whole Stack family met for the first time at the dinner-table.

It was a more sociable occasion than breakfast. Uncle Hiram, who had driven home from the lumber yards about six o'clock, appeared rosy and refreshed after a nap. Almira and her brothers looked almost unnaturally tidy and smelled strongly of Jean Marie Farina soap. But the lightening of the atmosphere, Ned decided at once, was principally due to Aunt Lydia. Attired as though for a party in a fine brown velvet gown, there seemed to be something festive in her manner as well; it was as if a cheerful lamp had been lighted at the head of the table.

In the comfortable glow of her presence her children's tongues were unloosed: secure from their father's possible disapproval, they chattered away about anything that interested them. Aunt Lydia listened indulgently to Tom's and Porter's conflicting views on the rival pugilistic merits of Frank Burke and John L. Sullivan, and received, with apparent pleasure, a voluble account from Almira of Ned's prowess at the skating-rink. ("That's splendid, dear; I'm so glad for you.") Ned's ears burned as he heard his cousin's whole-hearted praise, though he was touched by her unselfish pride in another's success; he was also surprised to find that evidently she bore her mother not the slightest ill-will for driving off with Mrs. Kennerley and forgetting all about Phronsie Wagstaff's party.

Aunt Lydia proved equally sympathetic to her husband's circumstantial recital of his dissatisfaction over the luncheon menu at the Chicago Club—"The oyster bisque wa'n't fit to eat: now *this* is perfection: my compliments to the cook!"— and his unexpected defeat, after lunch, at poker at the hands of "old man Cobden, who don't know enough to come in when it rains." And she talked a good deal herself, describing her trip to market and Mr. Stoddard's lecture about Mary, Queen of Scots, a charity board meeting and the latest news of the war in the Balkans, with a kind of purring imperturbability. It was all the same, whether she spoke of the sufferings of Mary Stuart or the price of coffee at Tebbetts and Garland's, the creamy voice flowed on; she was no more moved by blood-curdling reports of Bulgarian casualties than by Jane Mallard's quarrel with Dora Harper about arrangements for the Christmas celebration at the Erring Women's Refuge.

Dinner proceeded to its appointed close unmarred by the faintest discord. Directly it was over Tom and Porter excused themselves on the plea of home-work to be done. Almira also had home-work to finish from the night before, but she begged so earnestly for a few extra minutes downstairs that she was allowed to follow her parents and Ned to the parlour, where Mary Kelly had lighted the fire and turned up the lamps in their rose-coloured shades.

Uncle Hiram settled himself with the evening paper in his favourite easy-chair. Aunt Lydia, on the pink sofa by the fire, produced her needle and embroidery hoops. And Ned was just wondering whether it would be rude if he asked permission to fetch a book, when the door-bell rang and Janet thrust in a supercilious head with "Mr. Kennerley's compliments, and if Mr. and Mrs. Stack were at home, he'd be pleased to come in to see them."

Abner Kennerley seemed to bring a breath of keen winter air into the warm relaxed clime of the pink-shaded parlour. He stood for an instant in the doorway, his face rosy from the cold, brushing the snowflakes from his thick wavy hair and moustache. Uncle Hiram got to his feet and greeted the visitor heartily. Aunt Lydia had not moved from the sofa; Ned admired the graceful way her flowing velvet sleeve fell back from her rounded white arm as she raised it.

The children were next brought forward. Mr. Kennerley

shook hands with Ned, and patted Almira's head as he asked whether she were a good girl (without waiting to hear her answer). Once this formality had been complied with, they were both completely forgotten, though Almira whispered to her cousin that, if they did not keep perfectly still, Mamma would remember to send them upstairs.

The conversation that ensued was not especially stimulating to young people. It was conducted at first chiefly by the gentlemen, Aunt Lydia restricting her contributions to an occasional query or word of assent—she never disagreed with either of them—while her smile increased momently in brilliance, as though the lamp were turned higher and higher. Ned did not know which subject he found duller, the fluctuations of the stock market or the political sins of President Cleveland. He was, however, interested in Mr. Kennerley, and not only as Celia's father. As soon as he'd seen him he felt he'd seen him before; Papa and Mamma had often talked about him; perhaps, though, it was merely the frequency with which the Grocer King's likeness appeared in the papers that made his face so familiar.

Everyone in Chicago knew Abner Kennerley. The smart red delivery wagons of Kennerley and Company, pulled by matched pairs of dappled grey horses, were as ubiquitous as Marshall Field's green ones. His name was just as ubiquitous as the wagons, prime mover of a hundred business enterprises, head of innumerable lists of bank directors, and social and charitable committees. One of the sights most proudly pointed out to strangers was the tall, erect figure in a beaver-lined topcoat driving a Goddard buggy down Michigan Avenue to his office in the Kennerley Block.

He was the most satisfactory celebrity the city had ever had because, as Papa sometimes said, he obviously liked being a celebrity. Even people who did not know who he was were impressed by his slender, wiry grace; the fine-drawn aquiline features; the beetling black brows that contrasted so strangely with blond hair and a moustache greying fast at fifty; the ice-blue eyes as cold as little Celia's, but cutting and ruthless instead of calmly self-absorbed. Only his voice, light and high-pitched, with a slight Yankee twang to prove he'd been born in Vermont, sounded a querulous note disappointingly out of key with Abner Kennerley's air of regal assurance.

This querulousness persisted, although he and his host were in perfect accord, and despite Aunt Lydia's determination to pour oil on waters even before she made sure they were troubled. So mild and uncontroversial a topic as the weather served to provoke an outburst of petulance. It was, said Mr. Kennerley, a devilish cold night; the snow was beginning to pile up in drifts in the streets. He reported the papers' prediction that a blizzard was on its way from Colorado as if it were coming on purpose to spite him.

Aunt Lydia's eyes sparkled.

"I love winter," she said. "There can't be too much snow for me. But I'm grateful for a carriage in this weather. If the Lord had intended me to walk, why didn't He give me four feet?"

"By the bye, how did you like my wife's new coupé? I understand you were out driving with her this afternoon."

"Oh, it was beautiful—quite the most elegant thing I've ever beheld! What taste! What charming appointments! I vow I'm really quite jealous. Hiram, do you be sure to notice Corinne's carriage the next time she uses it. I'm sure, if you ordered one like it from Brewster at once, you could get it for me for Christmas—that is, if Mr. Kennerley don't mind our copying him?"

Mr. Kennerley replied at once that he'd be exceedingly flattered; he wished only that Mrs. Kennerley had cared as much for her present. Of course, she was born in Charleston,—it was natural for her to miss the southern sunshine and flowers—but truly, with Corinne, the matter had become an obsession. "I've seen her scream and stamp her foot the minute the snow

44

starts to come down, and sometimes, if we've a spell of hard frost, she'll go to bed and stay there for a week. T'isn't reasonable! She's got the finest furs money will buy, and a stableful of good English horses—she's only to say what she wants."

Aunt Lydia changed the subject diplomatically by asking if the Kennerleys were going to the Cinders subscription dance next week at Martine's Academy. The Stacks were not. "I'd like it, of all things; but Hiram says we're too old to dance any more. I'm nearly thirty-six, you know—can you believe it? I don't feel a day older than I did when first we came to live in Prairie Avenue—and that was the year after the fire, when the Cinders were started."

"You don't look a day older, either, my dear," said Uncle Hiram gallantly; and Aunt Lydia gave him a radiant smile.

Mr. Kennerley sighed. "Ah, if I could but get Corinne to agree with you! Not that I care for dancing myself; I haven't time for folderols and frivolous diversions. But it strikes me we owe it to the community to show ourselves occasionally in public. One can't mope at home with the children and servants every night in the week."

"Corinne is an exquisite person," declared Aunt Lydia; "a poet at heart. She's too fine for this coarse modern world. I can't tell you how much her friendship means to me; I admire her more than anyone I know."

Mr. Kennerley eyed her gratefully.

"And *I* can't tell *you* how much I appreciate your spending so much time with my wife. I'd be eternally your debtor if you could manage to persuade her to take part in some of your activities. I know she's not very strong; but couldn't she join a board or two, for the look of the thing?—the Orphan Asylum, say, or the Home for the Friendless?"

Aunt Lydia shook her head.

"I've tried to get her to do it again and again, but she just laughs and says she belongs in the home herself. Dear Corinne —always so witty!"

45

"In fact, she don't care at all for society," continued Mr. Kennerley, airing what was evidently a long-established grievance. "She wouldn't join the Fortnightly when she was asked —I had to lead the grand march at the Charity Ball without her last year—and only the other day she tore up our invitation to the game dinner at the Grand Pacific Hotel without saying a word to me about it. If it hadn't been for my secretary's forethought, I'd not have got there myself."

"Corinne is so sensitive," said Aunt Lydia meditatively. "She thinks the South Side women don't like her. I tell her they don't like *me* either—what does it matter? I never have cared much for women."

"Women," remarked Uncle Hiram, "are a great waste of time unless you are married to 'em; and if you *are* married, they haven't time to waste on you!"

Aunt Lydia slapped her husband's wrist, crying out playfully that he was a horrid tease to hector her so. But Mr. Kennerley unsmilingly stuck to his point: "Dear Mrs. Stack, you will do what you can to help me, won't you? If you can't inveigle Corinne into mending her ways, no-one in Chicago can." And Aunt Lydia, serious once more, promised that she would renew her best efforts. She was devoted to Mrs. Kennerley; there was nothing she'd be loath to try for her sake.

Then, as if feeling another change of subject was indicated, she switched her attention brusquely to the children, who had been sitting unobserved in their corner since Mr. Kennerley's entrance. For no discoverable reason Almira, much to her confusion, was coaxed to recite a poem in French; and as soon as the recitation was over Aunt Lydia insisted on consulting Mr. Kennerley's opinion of the arrangements she had made for Ned's tuition.

Mr. Kennerley seemed rather bored by Almira's performance. (Perhaps, though, it was merely that he didn't understand French.) On the other hand, when it was Ned's turn to be thrust into the limelight, he fixed his disconcerting blue gaze full on the boy; darted a series of questions at him concerning his travels and scholastic attainments; inquired his age; and asserted that he himself had been just twelve years old when he went to work at Jabez Wilson's market in South Water Street at four dollars a week. (Twelve years later, he'd bought out his employer.) Would Ned be going into business one of these days with his Uncle Hiram?

Ned blushed and squirmed, conscious that this was no opportune time to confess his ambition to write novels as good as Mr. Dickens's when he grew up. Uncle Hiram muttered, not quite under his breath, that he hoped at any rate poor Katie's lad would have sense enough not to follow in his father's footsteps. Aunt Lydia finally brought the scene to an end by exclaiming that Ned was going to be a scholar, she was sure of it—but he'd never progress as he should if he didn't get enough sleep—it was past nine o'clock, time for all good little people to be tucked in their beds! Whereupon Ned and Almira found themselves dismissed as abruptly and inexplicably as they had been brought forward.

Aunt Lydia gave them each a kiss, and a caramel from the silver filigree dish on the centre table. She must have forgotten, Ned thought, that Almira had her lessons yet to get; but Almira herself had not forgotten: as soon as the children joined Tom and Porter in the schoolroom she produced her books and went methodically to work.

Ned, whose slender tasks could well be kept for the morning, amused himself in desultory fashion with the "Youth's Companion" till Mary Kelly summoned the younger ones to bed.

He had hardly got to the top of the third storey stairs when he heard Uncle Hiram's heavy tread on its way to the second. Leaning over the banisters, he peered down through the stair well to note that the lights were still lighted below, and the murmur of voices went on behind closed doors in the pink-shaded parlour.

Chapter 4

I<small>T DID</small> not take Ned long to grow accustomed to his new life.

He had, it was true, a few bad hours on the Monday following his arrival, when his mother's first letter came. Even before he opened the envelope the sight of the familiar flowing writing upon it brought back the past, particularly the recent past, in a rush of vivid and painful memories. Mamma wrote on the eve of sailing, from New York but not from the Holland House; the fact that she felt it necessary to conceal their address was the measure of the Ramsays' calamitous fall from security. The letter itself said little: Ned's parents both were well and hoped their son was, too; Papa was very busy, but sent his love with Mamma's; they trusted that their next might contain a full account of their plans for the winter. . . . The same post had brought a second letter from Mamma, this one inscribed to her brother. Ned had not dared ask what was in it, but the contents must have been mournful, judging from Uncle Hiram's sober look as he read it, the pensive sigh of "Poor Katie!" with which he tucked it away in his inside coat pocket.

Ned cried himself to sleep that night, with his envelope under his pillow. However, he told himself reasonably next morning, it would be several weeks before he could hear from his mother again. In the meantime there seemed little point in attempting to whip up a grief that must be endured the whole winter through. Besides, Mamma did not want him to grieve. She had bade him expressly be as happy as possible, and to try his best to make himself a cheerful and accommodating member of his uncle's household.

As a matter of fact, in less than a fortnight Ned began to feel he had lived with the Stacks for years rather than days.

This was partly because the family had accepted the new recruit promptly as one of themselves, with the utmost good-will but without making a tiresome fuss over him. But also no doubt that interesting novelty, unvarying routine, exercised gradually an almost hypnotic effect.

Every week-day, at least, was precisely the same in the tall yellow house, and—one could not help supposing—in all the other houses in Prairie Avenue.

It started, for Ned, at half past six as Mary Kelly entered his room bearing an armful of kindling wood. (This was by special order of Aunt Lydia, who was resolved that her nephew should not catch cold during the severe winter months.) As time went on Ned became used to the queer early rising; now, when the maid opened the door, like as not he'd been awake for some minutes already, snuggled warm under his quilt as he listened to the scrape of Tim's shovel clearing a path to the stable. For the snow continued to fall every day; it was packed down so hard in the streets that it deadened the other commonest early morning sound, the clip-clop of horses' hooves along the pavement; the horses themselves often were hitched to sleighs rather than carriages.

Breakfast with Uncle Hiram and the cousins was always the same, too. The young people ate rather fast and talked with their mouths full. Uncle Hiram ate slowly but perseveringly, and talked between mouthfuls—that is, when he was not engrossed in his newspaper. He seemed to feel it his duty to present a series of conversational scraps to his children, amongst whom Ned was of course now included. Yet his mind was palpably elsewhere; in Aunt Lydia's absence he was seldom altogether aware of what went on around him.

Almira and her brothers did not care. (Ned soon made the discovery that the comparative silence of the first day had been caused by their shyness of *him*.) They disappeared, directly they'd finished their food, with a rush and a clatter; while Uncle Hiram's leavetaking, if less precipitate, was quite as punctual.

After a day or two Ned had assumed, at Mary Kelly's suggestion, the office of holding his uncle's coat. He had been bashful about it, and Uncle Hiram at first had not seemed to notice the substitution; then suddenly, one morning, he'd smiled and said: "Thank you, my boy"; and Ned felt repaid.

It came to be his custom, also, to wave good-bye from the top of the steps as the coupé drove off: someone, he thought, ought to do it—and who else was there? Uncle Hiram looked surprised the first time it happened, but he waved back; and after that Ned never omitted the ceremony.

When his uncle was gone he went back into the hall and shut the front door. Somehow the atmosphere inside had changed. It had been purely masculine, pervaded by the smoke of Uncle Hiram's cigar, dominated by his grave, booming baritone and the raucous young voices of Porter and Tom. Now, subtly, the man's house had become a woman's; from upstairs and down rose a gentle hum of feminine activity. Mary Kelly sang as she cleared away the breakfast dishes and started washing up in the pantry. Ned could hear her calling down the shaft of the dumb-waiter to Mary Murphy, the cook, busy with *her* washing up in the basement kitchen. Up on the second storey Janet made the beds and dusted floors energetically. Miss Watson, the seamstress, was in the sewing-room cutting out patterns for a set of new pinafores for Almira. . . . Although the presiding genius remained in seclusion, hers was the hand in control: nothing, it appeared, could happen at 1817 without her blandly passive coöperation.

Yes, the house was Aunt Lydia's—but it was Ned's as well. He was alone; he would be alone all morning, till the noon symphony of factory whistles warned him of Mr. Leslie's impending arrival. There was no-one to bother about what he did, which suited him exactly. The slight touch of pathos implied by his solitary state—one recalled the child left behind in the "Pied Piper" poem—exactly suited him, too.

First, of course, he had to get his lessons. He might have done them in the evenings, when his cousins did theirs. But how delightful it was to trifle with "Chatterbox" or the latest "St. Nicholas," while Tom and Porter puzzled their brains over Cicero's "Orations" and Almira fretted at the tedious intricacies of Square Root and Long Division! And, after all, Ned's tasks were soon disposed of. Arithmetic was the one troublesome subject: History he found interesting; he'd read most of the books in English Literature already; and as for French, his constant care was to keep Mr. Leslie from discovering how much less he knew than his pupil.

When home-work was finished Ned was supposed, unless it were snowing too hard, to take a brisk walk "round the block." On these expeditions he clung obstinately to the route he and Almira had taken the first day together. (Why was it dangerous to venture farther?) Soon it grew so familiar that he recognized every crack in the sidewalk and recalled, without conscious effort, the copings that were fun to walk along —balancing the while with one's hands—and those others that were no good at all, either because they were sharp-edged or had fences on top.

Ned could tell by instinct where he was likely to meet Mr. McGregor, the postman, and on which corner the "fresh fish" cart might be found. He learned when the ladies Aunt Lydia knew would be starting to market: grim old Mrs. Cobden stalking down the steps of her Gothic palace to lead the procession; haughty Mrs. Harper (Florence's mother) issuing, with the tread of an Empress, from the rough-hewn Romanesque prison next door; plump, motherly Mrs. Mallard, the Doctor's wife, always breathless with haste, as if to make up for the greater distance she had to travel from Calumet Avenue to the Twenty-Second Street shops.

The ladies bowed to Ned, and he bowed in return, raising

his hat with a flourish he'd copied from Papa. (He also bowed to black Edna, Mrs. Kennerley's maid, who went shopping instead of her mistress, accompanied by Benjy, a pop-eyed pug puppy.) In time he felt they really were his friends, although they seldom spoke to one another. Stranger still, the houses they lived in came to seem friendly, too—even the ugliest and most forbidding of them. But none of these, naturally, had as much fascination as the Kennerley mansion, though Ned's reasons for lingering in its vicinity had little to do with its architectural preëminence.

After Ned got back from his walk his aunt sent for him. Generally she was sitting, as he and Almira had seen her the first day, in front of her dressing-table; and that was how, in later years, Ned best remembered Aunt Lydia, wearing the frilly robe, with her hair pouring over her shoulders in a magnificent chestnut cascade. He felt that Aunt Lydia must be very proud of her hair: she seemed purposely to prolong the hour at the looking-glass, and gazed bemused at her image all the while Janet was busy constructing the coronet of braids. (In a queer way Ned was proud of it, too; he was sure that none of the other Prairie Avenue ladies could rival what was so truly a crowning glory.)

Aunt Lydia always smiled as her nephew came in, and gave him a kiss. She asked how he'd slept, then bade him be seated on the ottoman in the window.

They were never entirely alone, for Janet was there; but Janet spoke so rarely that, when he grew up, Ned could not recall the sound of her voice. Not infrequently, too, Mary Murphy sued for admittance, to plan the day's menus with her mistress.

Ned was interested by Mary Murphy, although she was neither so pretty nor so pleasant as the other Mary. She had a frizzy head and a long, glum upper lip; a caustic tongue and a voice like a tragic viola. She said "yez" for "you" and "thim" for "them": when Ned asked her colleague why, Mary Kelly shrugged her shoulders and replied: "Sure, she was born in County Wicklow, the creature!"—which left him as much in the dark as ever.

Mary Murphy was a professional pessimist. She looked defeated before she began to speak; inquired "What will yez be havin' for dinner tonight?" as if there were not a single valid idea left in a barren and profitless world; and appeared gloomily pleased to announce that "thim last potatoes weren't worth eating; the fish man hadn't wan single lobster; an' brown sugar is out, ma'am, an' Mr. Tebbetts says he can't promise us anny at all before the first of the year."

Aunt Lydia declined to be downcast. The inferior potatoes could be returned, couldn't they? Mr. Stack really liked buttered crab better than lobster. And if there wasn't any sugar to be had in the shops, Mr. Kennerley, she knew, would be glad to send some over from his warehouse. In her relaxed and dilatory fashion Aunt Lydia was an admirable housekeeper. Though she might be the last of her circle to get to market, somehow she managed to secure most of the prizes. Butchers were persuaded to save her their best cuts of meat; grocers, their choicest out-of-season delicacies; and as Mary Murphy dealt with this provender with the hand of a master, it was universally admitted that no-one in Prairie Avenue set a finer table than the Hiram Stacks.

Ned often could not remember after the interview just what he and his aunt had talked about. It was Aunt Lydia's manner, rather than anything she said, that established them on an intimate footing. Young as he was, Ned was made to feel that she recognized him as a man. She deferred to his judgement as she would not have done to Almira's. . . . "Will it snow today, my dear, do you think?" And, "How do you rate Mr. Leslie's French accent?" On the other hand, she might consult his taste, as if he had been a daughter. One could not imagine her asking Tom and Porter what they thought of her new striped polonaise, or whether she should wear the red toque or the mauve Princess bonnet to the St. Luke's Aid Society.

As a rule she opened with a perfunctory inquiry after his health. ("How are you, Ned? Feeling stronger, I hope?") Ned could not but feel that if he'd replied he was dying of a galloping consumption, Aunt Lydia would simply smile her genial smile and say: "I'm delighted to hear it, my dear." Nor was it her policy to delve too deeply into her children's activities, though if they'd something agreeable afoot, she was pleased to be told of it.

In return she was apt to give Ned a sketch of her day. Aunt Lydia had always enough to do, but never too much. There'd be a meeting of the Fortnightly, or one of her charitable committees—perhaps nothing more exciting than a fitting at Weeks' and her indispensable call on "Aunt Corinne." Whatever her plans, she was charmed by them; Ned would scarcely have been astonished if she had started to purr, like the fat white cat dozing beside the coal fire.

The scene ended as deliberately as it began. When Aunt Lydia rose to go she lingered to pat Alexander, dawdled as she drew on her gloves, called a few parting instructions over her shoulder to the scowling Janet, and then—more often than not—slipped back to press a final violet-scented kiss on Ned's forehead before sailing out by her private staircase and door.

She was gone for the day. . . . Ned's solitary lunch was the worst trial he had to bear, for Mary Kelly rushed him through it, irritated, as even the best-tempered servants invariably are, at having to serve a meal that had not previously formed part of her duties.

Rest after lunch was another trial; but things began to look up when the young Stacks came home from school.

The first week was not over before Ned found himself, unexpectedly, growing fond of Almira. She was no more sprightly and imaginative than she had ever been, but her disposition was amazingly even, and she was ready for anything that came along: running three-legged races, building a snow-man at the Mallards', or bobsledding breathlessly down the street hitched on to the grocer's wagon. Moreover, her patronizing air melted away as soon as there was nothing left for her to explain to her cousin; Ned quickly assumed the dominating rôle, never to relinquish it, and she followed him loyally like a real younger sister.

While the cold spell lasted most of their afternoons were spent at the skating-rink. There Ned established, to his abiding astonishment, that Almira's friends were disposed to accept him as heartily as the Stacks had done. He told himself diffidently that doubtless his skill as a skater accounted for it. Only Florence Harper held aloof from the welcoming chorus; and that, in the circumstances, was not to be wondered at: she had, Almira told Ned privately, been "terribly stuck-up" ever since her family had had a telephone put in last fall. But it was hard to go on being shy with the bouncing Mallards, who were forever issuing wholesale invitations to play in their yard, and whose mother thoughtfully kept a barrel of Winesaps and a bottomless crock of gingerbread cookies just inside the back door.

Ned made some progress, also, in his acquaintance with Sonny Kennerley. It was odd about Sonny: Ned admired him and would have liked to know him better, not only because he was Celia's brother. Yet somehow they had not much to say to each other. After their opening smiles conversation was apt to lag. Was that because Sonny, for all his charm, was secretly nervous and unsure of himself? He was always attempting to play the affable leader, without being sure how to set about it.

Ned's one great disappointment was that he had not seen Celia again. She never once came to the rink; and when he plucked up courage—hoping his voice sounded properly casual —to ask where she was, Sonny replied that she was kept in the house by a bad cold. Ned haunted the Kennerleys' neighbourhood after that, but he did not know which was Celia's room, and no vision of distant blue eyes and blond curls rewarded his patient vigils.

Uncle Hiram's return, in the late afternoon, brought the man's world and the woman's, so strictly separate all day, into conjunction at last. "Where is my wife?" he'd call as he came in the door; and Aunt Lydia was always waiting, beautifully dressed, in the parlour to greet him. The Stacks sometimes dined out: if they did not, Uncle Hiram might walk to the Calumet Club after dinner; if he stayed home, he went to bed early.

Aunt Lydia was then left alone by the fire in the glow of the pink-shaded lamps—but not for long. Six nights out of seven she entertained callers. "Uncle Rock" Terriss came at least every other night, and Mr. Kennerley, very nearly as often; there were others Ned did not know.

At these times the children were expected to keep out of the way. Almira and her brothers worked with their eyes on the schoolroom clock: not for worlds would they have opened the parlour door, but they knew that at ten precisely Janet would appear from the pantry with her tray of tea and little cakes— and a well-timed raid from above was generally successful in carrying off plunder. Ned read his magazines, yawning a little, except on the evenings Uncle Rock spent at the piano: *then* he'd sit on the stairs as long as he was allowed to, enraptured by the player's masterful way with the "Tempest" Sonata, a Chopin Etude, or the strange new music one hadn't a name for. He did not even care for the little cakes; when Mary Kelly came to tell him it was time to go to bed, it was hard to struggle back to reality.

The week's routine was varied twice only: on Monday afternoons Aunt Lydia, garbed in her best, cardcase in hand, ordered Tim and the carriage and drove forth to pay calls north of the river. And on Tuesdays, equally resplendent, she sat behind the silver tea-urn in her own parlour, while the North

Side ladies visited their friends in the fashionable districts of Prairie and Calumet, Indiana and Michigan Avenues.

On Sundays breakfast was later and grander, with sausages and buckwheat cakes as well as eggs and bacon and beefsteak and potatoes. Midday dinner was grander still, so stupefying that Uncle Hiram slept half the afternoon away behind drawn blinds, and even the children felt heavy and unfit for mental or physical exertion.

Between these immovable feasts they attended Sunday School, and then joined their elders at morning service at Grace Church on Wabash Avenue. Ned rather enjoyed the ritual, which was Episcopalian and therefore, from the Ramsays' Presbyterian point of view, decidedly frivolous, with candles and flowers and endless jumping up to sing, short traditional prayers, and a not-over-lengthy sermon by old Doctor Locke, who'd been there for years.

Uncle Hiram wore a frock coat and a collar even higher than usual; Aunt Lydia, a gown and bonnet quite as elegant as those she displayed at mundane affairs, but more discreet in hue—just as her refulgent smile was tempered to an exquisite half-radiance for God.

The young people sat in a row, looking preternaturally neat and good, trying to spy out their friends without seeming to do so. Ned was delighted to observe that the Kennerleys' pew was just across the aisle from the Stacks', but on the first two Sundays after his arrival Mr. Kennerley and Sonny occupied it alone: Celia, of course, was laid up with her cold; Roscoe was too young to stay after Sunday School; and Mrs. Kennerley, for some reason of her own, did not deign to put in an appearance.

On Ned's second Monday in Prairie Avenue Aunt Lydia announced at the dinner-table, with an air of slightly spurious brightness, that the dancing class was about to begin again.

Porter gave his usual derisive whistle; and Almira laid down her knife and fork and cried, all in one breath: "Miss-Jenny-and-Miss-Lucy-Kirk-oh-Mamma-must-I-go?"

"Well, dear," said her mother tolerantly, "to tell the truth, I'd been thinking a little of sending you to Bournique's this year for a finishing course, and I'm still not sure but what in the spring . . . But the Kirks are very nice women and they've had very hard lives. Besides, Aunt Corinne is so fond of them; it gives her such pleasure to do what she can . . ."

"Oh, *Mamma!*" said Almira.

Porter gave another whistle and volunteered the information that Joe Mallard had said he'd be gol-derned if he'd go to that sissy class again to please Mrs. Kennerley or anyone else.

"Joe Mallard will do what his mother tells him," said Uncle Hiram, frowning, "just as you will, Porter, and you, too, Almira."

"I suppose Porter *is* a little old for it now," said Aunt Lydia, rather hastily; "but I thought that perhaps Ned . . ."

It was Ned's turn to stop eating, while a sick sensation invaded his stomach.

"I don't know how to dance, Aunt Lydia," he protested. "I mean, truly, I've never had any lessons."

"Then it's high time you began, my dear. And I'm sure you'll enjoy meeting the young people of the neighbourhood in an informal and intimate way. After all, you've not lived here always as my own children have."

"Mamma," said Almira earnestly, "Ned knows all the people he wants to *already*. And he'll never learn anything from those awful old maids. Miss Lucy can't even keep time on the piano, and Miss Jenny does nothing but mince about and look at herself in the glass and say: 'Children, remember your manners—bow to your partners—now a great big splendid curtsy, *please!*'"

"Oh, dear, that's not quite fair," said Aunt Lydia. "I know the Kirks are rather old-fashioned, but Aunt Corinne was saying only the other day Miss Jenny had brought back a lot of lovely new steps from her trip to New York. And she and Celia are so careful in making up their list, it's really an honour to be asked to the Kennerley ballroom."

Ned's heart gave a leap. What a fool he'd been to forget that of course Celia would be there! He couldn't admit the real reason for his change of heart, but he refused, much to Almira's disgust, to second her repeated attempts to discourage the plan, and ended the discussion by saying quite meekly (though he knew it meant incurring the charge of currying favour with grown-ups). "I don't mind trying it if you think I ought to, Aunt Lydia."

From Monday's point of view the whole project appeared comfortably remote. However, Ned suffered a certain recurring malaise all week, which rose to a sharp pitch on Saturday afternoon, when he was dispatched to his room after lunch instructed to don his best suit, a blue serge trimmed with an objectionable amount of black silk braid. He spent half an hour tying and retying his bow tie—resisting an impulse to seek Mary Kelly's friendly assistance—and another lengthy period attempting to flatten his hair completely by copious applications of water.

Meanwhile Almira, still loudly dissenting, had been led away by Aunt Lydia, to reappear presently looking like a large and expensive doll in stiff white lace and a broad blue sash, her hair released from its customary pigtails and twisted by Janet's deft fingers into a wealth of glistening taffy-brown shaving curls.

To Ned's surprise her attitude had likewise undergone a transformation: she was now twittery with pleasurable excitement and could hardly wait to hop into the carriage that had been ordered, on account of a sudden snow flurry, to convey the children the block and a half to the Kennerleys'. She was not even upset by her mother's last-minute defection, seeming content with the latter's assurance that she meant to run in and look at them later.

As the brougham rolled up under the brownstone *porte-cochère* Ned wondered if he were going to be actively ill.

Johnson, the butler, impressive in his black livery and white cotton gloves, opened the door.

Ned had thought a good deal about the Kennerleys' house, and even made mental plans of it; but in none of his fancies had he foreseen the great octagonal hall, with its twin fern-banked marble fountains flanking the circular staircase. He gained a swift impression of a setting as darkly sumptuous as wedding-cake: there were tapestries and tasseled *portières,* Persian carpets and heavy gold mirrors, a bewildering array of ornaments of porcelain and bronze and ivory and beaten brass—all revealed by the lurid beams of an immense stained glass Moorish lantern that swung from the ceiling. Other chambers probably equally magnificent opened in every direction, but there was no time to explore: Johnson was waving them towards the passage that led to the ballroom, through which floated festive strains of music.

"They've begun without us!" Almira exclaimed in consternation. "I *told* Mamma they would."

Ned stared, more surprised than ever.

"I thought you didn't want—" he began; but Almira hadn't waited to hear him; she was half way along the passage already.

Abner Kennerley was justly proud of his ballroom, the only one in the city not relegated as a kind of afterthought to the top storey, but planned as an integral part of the reception rooms of the house. It was lighted by crystal chandeliers, whose frivolity did something to counteract the sombre effect of maroon velvet walls. Thirty gilt chairs lined the length of shining parquet; at the farther end, on a raised platform enclosed by a railing, sat a row of indulgently smiling mothers. Ned recognized Mrs. Mallard and the beautiful Mrs. Harper and, although she was nobody's mother, old Mrs. Cobden, who was surveying the scene through a critical lorgnette. (She was generally supposed to "say things," Almira had told him, if she were not asked to even the simplest neighbourhood gatherings.) A dark little woman in scarlet Ned knew must be Mrs. Kennerley, as she wore no hat and appeared largely preoccupied by her efforts to keep young Roscoe from dropping a collection of toys on the dancers' heads.

On the main floor in one corner Miss Lucy Kirk, a depressed middle-aged blonde in a blue taffeta bustle and turquoise bangles, was heavily engaged at the piano; while her younger sister Miss Jenny, determinedly lively in mustard green, superintended the gyrations of fourteen couples of Prairie Avenue's most select young people to the prancing measures of the *Esmeralda Galop*.

Ned halted in the doorway and looked to Almira for guidance: what were they to do now?

Almost as they entered the music stopped, the dancers clicked their way to their seats, and Mrs. Kennerley came flying down the steps from the platform to greet the newcomers in her fluting southern voice.

"How are you, Ned? I'm delighted you're here. Almira, child, what made you so late? And where's your dear mother?"

Almira explained that they had had to wait for Tim and the horses, and added that Mamma had said she'd be over later.

Miss Jenny then pounced on the children with a scream, asserting, in accents as languidly unmistakable as Mrs. Kennerley's, that Almira had grown six inches since last year, she surely had and was this her cousin Ned Ramsay, who had come all the way from Switzerland just in time to attend our little class? Almira must take him round the room *directly* and introduce him to every one of her dear young friends, so that he'd feel at home.

"He knows them all now, Miss Jenny," said Almira coldly. "He's been living in our house more'n two weeks."

She grasped Ned's hand and led him to a pair of unoccupied

chairs at the end of the row next Florence Harper and Jamie Mallard.

Ned was grateful to Almira for rescuing him; he could not help clinging to her a little and extracting her promise to dance with him as often as she could, and in no circumstances to abandon him to the clutches of Miss Jenny, to whom he had taken an instant and violent dislike.

Under the attentive eyes of so many adults conversation flickered feebly. The girls whispered together across their partners or stared at one another's frocks and ribbons; the boys sat silent, gloomily conscious of their own unwonted elegance. It was almost a deliverance when Miss Jenny blew her whistle —which she wore on a long silver chain attached to her belt —and bade the gentlemen rise to find their partners for the schottische.

There was a scraping of chairs and a clatter of heels on the bare floor. "Don't leave me!" begged Ned in agony. "And what in thunder *is* the schottische?"

"Oh," said Almira cheerily, "it's just about the same as the polka. You remember—I showed you how to do it last night. There's nothing to worry about. Get up, though, and make a bow like the rest of them, or Miss Jenny'll be after you. There! That's right. Now come along, don't be bashful. There's no need with *me*."

Ned soon found, to his gratified amazement, that Almira was right—their practice at home had removed the worst obstacles. He was hardly a graceful dancer, but he passed muster well enough to escape the unfavourable notice of Miss Jenny, who was far too busy chasséing up and down the room with her "one-and-two-*ah*-one-and-two!" to detect any but the most flagrant flaws in technique.

When the music stopped again he sank back into his chair in a gentle perspiration of relief.

Of course, he could not dance every dance with his cousin. Soon Almira tripped away from him in the knowing grasp of Sonny Kennerley, and Ned bowed to Maud Mallard, who was fortunately next to him, to ask the pleasure of her company for the waltz.

The waltz, of which Almira had also taught him the rudiments, went about as well as the schottische; and after that Ned was fairly well launched.

Only one increasing regret spoiled what enjoyment he might have derived from the afternoon, and that was that he did not dare ask his young hostess to dance with him. He had been vividly aware of her ever since his arrival. In fact, he could feel where she was without turning to look at her. But it was hard not to look at Celia Kennerley, who was certainly the prettiest girl in the room, in rosy clouds of tulle and a pair of distractingly dainty pink satin slippers. She wore a diamond necklace; her unbound hair fell over her shoulders in a fluffy cascade utterly unlike Florence Harper's string-like locks or Almira's manufactured ringlets.

In imagination he rose a dozen times to claim her, but somehow each time his courage failed.

Celia seemed indifferent to his neglect. She had waved to him and Almira from a distance when they first entered the room; once when they passed each other on the floor she gave him a fleeting, impersonal smile. This reserve raised a wall between them, which Ned was powerless to break down. He brooded upon the dilemma so constantly that he grew absent-minded, and came to himself to find a hush fallen over the room, Miss Jenny's reproachful eye upon him as she tartly observed: "The music will not begin until *every* lady has found a partner."

Ned stumbled to his feet to seek the one unappropriated damsel, Miss Florence Harper, who was biting her nails, very nearly in tears.

"M'ave the pleasure of this dance, Florence?"

"Oh, I suppose so," replied Florence, crimson with annoyance. "But honestly, Ned Ramsay, if my mother weren't here,

I'd as soon slap your face as not, I declare to goodness I would!"

This was no propitious mood in which to take the floor, and the dance they embarked upon, the varsoviana, was unluckily not amongst those in which Ned had received schoolroom coaching. He stepped upon Florence's feet almost immediately; they soon collided heavily with Joe Mallard and Celia (of all people!), and were thereupon forced to a series of covering, shuffling manoeuvres in the corner, in the hope of avoiding Miss Jenny, while every other couple in the ballroom glided by them with odious fluency and Florence affirmed, in a wrathful half-whisper, that he was the very meanest and stupidest boy she'd ever met and cross her heart and hope to die if ever she danced with him again.

When the dance ended there was an interval during which Johnson and Job, the footman, passed trays of lemonade and sponge cake. Aunt Lydia still had not appeared. Mrs. Kennerley, after seeing that Miss Lucy and Miss Jenny and the ladies on the balcony were properly served, descended from her perch and fluttered about the room to chat with her children's friends. Ned saw Mrs. Cobden and Mrs. Harper exchange looks and shrugged shoulders over what they evidently considered a sad want of decorum. He would have liked to talk to his hostess when she stood beside him—there was something indescribably wistful in her eyes, as if she'd have asked nothing better than to sit down and be one of them—but he was too much upset by his recent mischance to chat at all readily, and Florence kept her sulky silence intact save for an occasional sniff. After a minute or two Mrs. Kennerley moved on, and presently slipped out of sight.

Miss Jenny then blew her whistle and announced archly that the next number would be Ladies' Choice.

There was an outburst of giggles, and a great tossing of curls and rustling of ribbons, as the feminine half of the assembly rose to its opportunity. Florence, of course, was gone

in a trice—doubtless to pre-empt her favourite Joe Mallard—
that much was a blessing. Ned glared fiercely at his pumps
and tried not to care that he was sure to be the last boy chosen.
After all, who would want to dance with him *now?* The best
to be hoped for was that Almira might sacrifice herself for the
sake of cousinly loyalty, or kind-hearted Maud take pity on
his isolation. He could hardly believe his senses when he heard
a cool small voice saying: "Don't be silly, you're going to waltz
with me!"—and looked up to see an exquisite figure in rose-
coloured tulle curtsying demurely.

Blushing bright red, he jumped up and stammered a few
words—he'd no idea what.

Celia was, as always, perfectly self-possessed. She did not
reproach him for his neglect, but gave him a smile as demure
as her curtsy and laid her hand on his shoulder as Miss Lucy
thumped out the opening bars of the *Valse de la Kermesse*
from *Faust.*

Ned was in Heaven—but alas! for a few moments only.
Even as he clasped Celia carefully to his bosom (she looked
so delicate and fine that one was reluctant to touch her) he
knew he would never be equal to the test. His nascent abilities,
which had proved sufficient for his previous partners (always
excepting the acidulous Florence), could not sustain him now,
when he had most need of them. Oh, why hadn't Mamma
made him take dancing lessons?

He blundered unhappily through a few revolutions, while
Celia with what Ned felt was angelic patience endeavoured to
match her steps to his. But it was no good. Suddenly she
stopped in the middle of the floor and shook her golden head:
"You can skate, Ned Ramsay, but you can't dance a bit!"

"Where—where are we going?" faltered Ned. "You daren't
leave the room like this. What will Miss Jenny say?"

"Oh, daren't I, though?" Celia laughed airily. "I s'pose I
can do what I want in my own house. I'd like to see Miss
Jenny or anyone else try to stop me. Come on!"

Ned did not repeat his mistake of questioning her, but followed his partner down the passage to the entrance hall, where the music, deadened by two sets of velvet *portières,* reached them only faintly.

The children faced each other beneath the sinister splendour of the Moorish lantern: Ned puzzled but acquiescent—apparently the only way of getting on with Celia was to give her her head—Celia smiling complacently, as if this were what she had all along intended to have happen.

"Well!" she said finally. "That's better, isn't it? I don't blame you for getting mixed up when Miss Lucy plays so like a pig. Aren't she and Miss Jenny just awful?"

"Yes," replied Ned, with simple fervour. "I think they're the worst I ever saw. Why does your mother . . . ?"

"Oh," said Celia contemptuously, "Mamma don't care a pin for them. They come from South Carolina and so does she, but she never knew them there and they're not really friends. She takes them up just to make Papa mad—he can't bear the sight of them, you know. But don't let's waste time talking about ninnies like the Kirks. Come on!"

This time Ned felt emboldened to ask their destination. Celia opened her star-like eyes very wide: "Why, I'm going to show you the house, of course!"

The tour of inspection did not take long, because his guide was indisposed to loiter. She was absolutely sure what she wanted to do. In turn they visited the dining-room and the various parlours, while Celia rattled off their principal attractions and pointed out the difference between Bird's-eye maple and Circassian walnut. In the library she indicated the finest sets of books; she knew, without looking at their labels, the names and prices of all the pictures in the picture gallery—from "Sheridan's Ride" to "A Sunset in Holland"—and could tell which ones Papa had picked up at a Calumet Club show for a song, which imported at vast expense from New York or Europe.

66

The information was offered in a glib monotone; there was no vanity in Celia's performance; it was only as if she were saying: "This is what we are and how we live—you might as well know the whole story, so you can make the best of it."

Ned was both impressed and depressed: never had his love appeared so distant, so hopelessly beyond his humble reach.

Only when they approached the conservatory—which had been saved till the last—did Celia show a flicker of personal interest. Under the glittering dome, all silvered with frost from without, she ceased her mechanical explanations, drawing long breaths of the humid air as if it were her natural element. Gravely she tiptoed from blossom to blossom: Ned noticed that it was chiefly the orchids and camellias she cared for, waxen and cold in their scentless perfection.

In the middle of the glass-house they came upon an aviary, gay with bright-coloured tropical finches that reminded Ned of the wallpaper birds in his bedroom. They flew about in an aimless way and kept up a shrill, incessant twittering.

He would have liked to watch the tiny creatures for a little, but again Celia was loath to linger.

"The birds aren't mine, they're Mamma's," she replied indifferently to Ned's question. "I don't care much about them— they screech all the time instead of singing properly. Some of them come from Java and some from South America. They don't live long—Papa's always complaining how much it costs to replace them, but he *will* do it."

On the way back they encountered a solitary stroller in a scarlet dress, flitting as aimlessly as the finches amongst the palms and flowers. Mrs. Kennerley did not seem surprised to see them; she even nodded her head in approval when Celia said she had been showing Ned round. "All the same, darlings, I think we'd better go back now, don't you? The class must be almost over; we don't want poor Miss Jenny to think we've deserted our duty."

"Don't we, Mamma?" said Celia; and her mother laughed and kissed her and said she was a naughty girl.

In the ballroom couples were forming in a row to march out sedately to Miss Lucy's lack-lustre version of the *Marche Militaire*. Celia took Ned's hand; they managed to slip into line without attracting attention. Ned saw that there were many more mothers on the platform than there had been, and even a few fathers. The front row remained as before, with the belated addition of Aunt Lydia. The ladies all were smiling: Mrs. Mallard proudly, as befitted the possessor of four solid contestants for the honours of the day; Mrs. Harper, with the fixed, impersonal graciousness of the professional beauty; Mrs. Cobden's grimace was no less alarming than one of the gargoyles on her Gothic roof. But it was Aunt Lydia, befurred and beplumed, on whom Ned's glance rested. She, too, smiled, lifting her head a trifle as she chatted with Mr. Kennerley, who bent courteously over her chair. What was there in her expression that recalled irresistibly the white cat Alexander, as it had looked that morning, when Janet was bringing its saucer of cream?

Chapter 5

AT CHURCH next day Ned was pleased to see Celia and her mother as well as the men of the family in the Kennerley pew. It was an odd time for them to have chosen to come, for the weather was dreary and dark, with a cutting wind on the corners: Uncle Hiram had ordered Tim to fetch the Stacks home instead of telling him, as he usually did, that they would walk back for the exercise. ("I'm fighting for a waistline, Tim," was his invariable formula; and Tim would cackle with laughter as if he'd never before heard the little joke.)

Celia was wearing a set of chinchillas, which perhaps was responsible for her unusual sobriety: whatever the reason, she sat perfectly still and refused to turn round, no matter how hard Ned stared. Mrs. Kennerley, as splendid in purple as she had been yesterday in red, seemed on the contrary possessed by a spirit of impish perversity. She was as restless as Celia was quiet, fidgeting in her seat, snapping the clasp of her reticule, rustling the leaves of her hymn-book during the sermon, constantly readjusting the long mauve veil that fell·from her toque besprinkled with violets. And when they rose to sing she contrived, by a gesture or two, to sketch a droll parody of her tall husband's uncompromising stiffness.

She had smiled at Ned, who occupied the aisle seat, upon first coming in. Now, in the middle of the offertory, she startled him by turning all the way round to show him a bag of sugarplums she had hidden in her muff and giving him a mischievous wink.

Ned was nonplussed. If he winked back, Uncle Hiram and Aunt Lydia might be terribly angry; if he didn't wink, Mrs. Kennerley would suppose he meant to snub her advances. In his perplexity he half smiled, half frowned, blushing and hanging his head as he cursed himself for a fool. Mrs. Kennerley betrayed no annoyance; she laughed aloud as she slipped to her knees for the final benediction, much to the dismay of her immediate neighbours.

Outside in the street she appeared with Sonny and Celia and begged permission of her dearest Lydia to take Almira and Ned home with her to dinner. Mr. Kennerley, it developed, had an unexpected business engagement that would keep him away for most of the day; they'd be dying of boredom by themselves; besides, Celia had a wonderful new magic lantern her father had given her, which she was anxious to display for her friends' enjoyment.

Ned glanced quickly at Celia, who echoed her mother's invitation, but in a half-hearted manner. She was discouragingly distant—it seemed that yesterday had never been.

Aunt Lydia acceded graciously, as she did to all Mrs. Kennerley's requests. "Dear Corinne . . . hospitality itself . . . you'll not let my little people be tiresome, I beg you."

On the way home Mrs. Kennerley walked between Ned and Celia, swinging hands with them both. She asked the former to call her Aunt Corinne as the Stacks did: "If your mother's away this winter, you'll need all the extra relatives you can get!" Ned agreed, feeling, he could not tell why, that this queer little creature made him think of Mamma, and miss her, far more than kind, urbane Aunt Lydia had done.

Sunday dinner, so decorous at the Stacks', was an uproarious performance at the Kennerleys'.

Ned could not help wondering what the meal would have been like if Mr. Kennerley had been there. The huge mahogany dining hall seemed an incongruous setting for levity, with its massive furniture, ponderous silver plate, and row of family portraits on the wall (mostly Beauchamps from Charleston, Celia had said: Papa hadn't, as far as she knew, any ancestors). Even the bowl of fat pink roses on the table looked dignified. But Mrs. Kennerley, who had kept on her hat (that in itself was sufficiently bizarre), sparkled and giggled: criticized the soup, sent away the fish, jumped up in the middle of the turkey and vegetables to scatter breadcrumbs on the window ledge for the pigeons—all the while pouring out a stream of outrageous remarks.

No-one was spared save her two young guests. She made fun of herself, teased the children, twitted the servants unmercifully—Job exploded into fits of gay African glee, and even grave Johnson had to retire rather suddenly behind the tall Spanish leather screen. Nor was her absent husband exempted: "Papa's pulling off one of his clever deals today, my dears. Shouldn't we all be very proud of him? Now perhaps we can afford a box for the German opera next month. Your father's a wonderful man . . . when you think that only a few years ago he was no better than the corner grocer . . ."

Sonny and Ned laughed continually. So did Almira, a little as if she were ashamed of herself. Celia alone stayed scornfully mute. Her eyes were as hard and glittering as a pair of blue diamonds, and she exchanged disparaging glances across the table with Mademoiselle, who, although understanding only half what was said, looked flurried and frightened and excused herself as soon as the ice-cream was served to prepare for her afternoon off.

The extraordinary repast ended at last with a wholesale distribution of bonbons (Ned had never before had as many of these as he wanted); Mrs. Kennerley was then called away by a message from her maid Edna.

It seemed peculiarly quiet after she had gone. Nobody knew quite what to say. Sonny fetched the magic lantern, which they had decided to set up in the hall, since Mr. Kennerley was not at home to object. Celia arranged the slides according to her own very definite tastes, and the four children spent a pleasant, somewhat subdued half-hour with "The Beauties of Italy" and "Famous Scenes from American History."

All went well until Roscoe appeared with his young Irish nurse and demanded a share in the entertainment. Having just got up from his nap, he was full of energy and could see no reason why he should not play with his sister's new toy. "Let the little darlin' help," the nurse advised. "He won't do a mite of harm, Miss Celia."

Celia tossed her head. "He's much too young, you know he is."

Roscoe was a stolid child, with a stubborn trick of repeating his wishes over and over till people were apt to give way to him, just to shut him up. After he had begged, twenty times in succession, to be allowed to put the slides in, Celia shrugged her shoulders. "Very well, then, but mind you don't drop them!"

Roscoe was too much interested and too plodding of habit not to heed her warning. On the other hand, being unable to read, he got half the pictures upside down, much to Celia's disgust.

"Oh, Roscoe, do take care—how could the Bay of Naples look like that? Can't you see which is sky and which is ocean?"

"See here, old fellow," said Sonny kindly, "let's you and me do it together. I know it seems funny, but to make them come right on the screen you have to push 'em in what looks like the wrong way."

Roscoe shook his blond head. "Don't care. I like 'em better upside down."

"Oh, Ros, you *can't!* See here, I'll show you. D'you mind?"

Roscoe did mind, very much indeed. He shook his head again, and when Sonny attempted to touch the box containing the slides the little boy set up a roar.

Celia stamped her foot. "There, now, I knew what'd happen! Babies always ruin everything. Nora, for goodness' sake, take him away this instant minute, or I'll tell Mamma it was all your fault. I can't stand spoilt brats!"

"*Ain't* a brat!" cried Roscoe.

He went on bawling, Celia scolding, Sonny and Nora making ineffectual efforts to calm the tumult; while Ned and Almira sat still and close together, uncomfortable as children are when their friends get into a scrape, but thankful the comparative darkness enabled them to keep out of it.

Mrs. Kennerley came running downstairs to take charge of matters in her spirited way.

"There, there, baby! Please stop your noise. Celia, don't tease your little brother. No, I don't care to hear whose fault it was or anything about it. Nora, it's time for Roscoe to go for his walk. It won't hurt him, even if it is snowing a little. I tell you what the rest of us will do: let's play tag, shall we?"

There was no resisting such infectious gaiety. At her lively bidding the lamps were lighted again, the magic lantern and screen cleared away, and soon all troubles were forgotten in a brisk game of Puss-in-the-corner.

The big, gloomy hall rang with merry shouts and laughter. After the first moment of utter amazement it seemed natural for Mrs. Kennerley to be playing, too: she was scarcely taller than Almira; had it not been for her long dress and her piled-up black hair, she might easily have passed for a little girl.

Sonny was "Puss," in full flight after his mother, when there came a sound of steps outside the front door, the bell rang peremptorily, and Johnson admitted two men to the vestibule.

Sonny stopped suddenly. "I think someone's coming."

"Never mind—never mind—I dare you to catch me!" cried Mrs. Kennerley.

Although Sonny failed to continue the chase, she flew the whole length of the room, her long purple skirts whipping after her. As she looked back to see why she was not being followed the tip of her train caught on the leg of a small table and upset it. The table itself did not break, but a lamp that was standing upon it, a tall column of alabaster with a beaded crystal shade, went crashing down in splinters just as Mr. Kennerley opened the vestibule door.

"My dear Corinne, surely you've not . . ."

Mrs. Kennerley faced her husband defiantly at the foot of the staircase, her bosom rising and falling in a series of little gasps. In spite of her recent exertions her face was very pale; her black eyes looked enormous; under the violet toque her hair was wildly dishevelled. For an awful moment nobody spoke. Then she stamped her foot in a tantrum as Celia might have done.

"I don't care—I'm glad I did it! It was a horrid old thing— you can buy a dozen more just like it—a hundred, for all I know! I only wish it had been something you really set store by. So there! I—oh!"

Turning on her heel, she picked up her skirts and ran rapidly upstairs. They could hear her voice in the distance, piercing and unmodulated as a guinea-fowl's: "Glad—*glad,* I tell you . . ."

It was impossible not to admire Mr. Kennerley's deportment in a crisis. He showed neither surprise nor resentment; rang for Job to sweep up the fragments of stone and glass; and then addressed his companion quietly: "I think, Mr. Somers, we shall be quite undisturbed in the library."

Ned had only one wish, and that was to get out and go home as soon as possible. He suspected that Almira shared it, but that she also felt, as he did, that they could not leave their friends now. As it was he was grateful to his kind little cousin for proposing a round of Authors, one of the few card games permitted on Sunday. By common though tacit consent they quitted the hall for the front parlour; each of the four, it seemed, was making an effort to forget what had happened.

It was not easy. Mrs. Kennerley appeared no more, but the fear that she might come down again was hard to dismiss. Moreover, though Ned did his best not to listen, it was obvious that the scene going on in the library was a disagreeable one. The stranger did most of the talking. He seemed to be protesting; his voice sounded loud and angry; but it was Mr. Kennerley's cold, courteous tones that reached them most plainly through the closed door: "You should have thought of that, sir, when I approached you last year . . ." And, "I'm not in business, Somers, for my health alone. . . ."

A few minutes later Johnson announced that Mr. and Mrs. Stack were at the door, on their way home from a sleigh ride in Grand Boulevard. It was snowing quite hard and they thought that perhaps . . .

Ned and Almira said good-bye politely. Sonny smiled and said he hoped they'd come over soon again. Celia gave them her hand in unsmiling silence.

As they were leaving they saw Mr. Kennerley's caller coming

out of the library: Ned never forgot the sick, white despair on his face.

In the sleigh Aunt Lydia, bundled in furs, accosted them affably: "Well, darlings, did you have a good time?"

Of all the strange things that had happened that afternoon, Ned thought it the strangest when Almira, her eyes serene as summer lakes, replied: "Oh, yes, Mamma, *lovely!*"

That night the Stacks, never particularly observant of emotional states in the young, were further distracted by plans for a dinner-party. Uncle Hiram and his wife entertained with reasonable frequency, but it happened that now, owing to an untoward combination of circumstances, they found themselves indebted to most of the members of their immediate circle.

"We'll have the Kennerleys, of course," said Aunt Lydia, "and the Cobdens; the Harpers, the Mallards, and Annie Trask to balance Rock Terriss—unless, my dear, you'd prefer me to ask Mrs. Rankin? They tell me she's starting to go out again. After all, her husband *was* president of one of our biggest banks, and she's still very rich; I like to put my best foot forward with Corinne."

Uncle Hiram remarked that that might be so, but old Joshua Rankin was as dead as a door-nail and his widow was a confounded disagreeable woman. On the other hand, Mrs. Trask (who was Mrs. Mallard's sister) was a general favourite; she played an excellent hand at cards; and he supposed it was to be Progressive Euchre after dinner?

Aunt Lydia agreed, resignedly, that it was: the Harpers and Mallards played five nights a week; and only yesterday Mrs. Cobden had announced she and Hezzy intended to learn the game: if they didn't, they'd hardly be asked out to dine all winter. Now would Hiram be good enough to speak for three brace of ducks at the club? Or did he think prairie chickens . . . ?

An animated argument ensued. It took most of the rest of the evening to determine the menu; Ned marvelled at the importance his uncle and aunt attached to food: never had Papa and Mamma, in their palmiest days, so endlessly hashed over the respective merits of quail and canvas-backs, a prime roast of beef versus saddle of mutton with hot jelly sauce.

The dinner was set for Tuesday week. On the Monday before the house was subjected to a strenuous cleaning; the Marys and Janet went about with their heads tied up in dusters; the place smelled of soapsuds and wax and furniture polish all day.

On Tuesday morning Uncle Hiram, keys in hand, descended to the wine cellar to choose the Chablis to go with the oysters, the sherry to flavour the soup, the Mosel and claret, champagne and port. Mary Kelly received her master's instructions with respectful gravity, and bore each bottle tenderly away as if its contents had a sacramental significance. They then repaired to the silver safe on the stairs, which was opened by a secret spring.

Meanwhile Aunt Lydia, rising somewhat earlier than her wont, was equally busy in her own departments. Happily the Christmas holidays had begun, so Ned and Almira were able to watch her writing her gilt-edged place and menu-cards, and selecting the linen and glass and china—much grander than those ordinarily in use. Lunch was served on a card-table in the library; later, the children were permitted to peep into the dining-room, where the familiar oak table, elongated to unfamiliar dimensions and covered with a lace-embroidered banquet cloth, proudly bore its shining freight of crystal and silver and crested Crown Derby. All was complete, from the beaded pink silk shades on the candles to the mounds of peppermint and wintergreen patties in their Sheffield plated shells. Aunt Lydia, frowning a trifle, bent gingerly forward to incline at a more graceful angle a spray in the vast centrepiece of maidenhair and Jacqueminot roses. Then she retired to rest from her labours till six, when Mr. George would appear by appointment to dress her hair. (Ned wondered how Janet felt about being supplanted.)

But, on the whole, by far the most interesting place to be was the kitchen, where Mary Murphy had been toiling since dawn to produce the miracles described so alluringly in French on her mistress's menus.

It was, for Almira and Ned, at any time a rewarding port of call. There was always a faint but agreeable sense of peril about the trip down—for if one took the wrong turning in the dark basement passage one tumbled into the cavernous furnace-room instead. Once having arrived in safety, however, the atmosphere was unfeignedly cheerful. The tea-kettle sang on the stove; a pleasing assortment of spice cakes and sugar cookies was sure to be offered, together with vivacious small-talk and glimpses of Prairie Avenue from an unconventional point of view. ("That's the second pair of boots Mrs. Harper's had on since lunch"; or, "It must be raining harder than it looks—McGregor's pants are all streakéd.")

Like most dictatorial and temperamental women, Mary Murphy showed to best advantage on her own home grounds. Today, in spite of her extraordinary duties—or perhaps on account of them: she was artist enough to rise to the occasion —her spirits were almost ebullient. Positively she smiled as she beat eggs for her cake and assured the dubious Almira that "lobsters *like* being biled—what else would they be good for, the creatures?"

There was no doubt she and Mary Kelly, who presently joined the party, were stimulated by the presence of Bridie, the "company" waitress, a lively red haired girl whose tongue was as nimble as her fingers were deft.

Bridie got about a good deal, and naturally had much valuable information to impart. Ned and Almira were as fascinated as the Marys by her graphic account of a woman she knew who'd been cut half in two by a cable-car, and lived to tell the tale. She had also in her current repertory a fine line of blood-curdling anecdotes concerning the recent Apache massacres, and was wonderfully knowledgeable about the children from Newark who'd been bitten by a mad dog and were being sent to Paris to take Doctor Pasteur's treatment.

"They do be saying it's a new disease they're catching: *hydryphoobia* t'is called," said Bridie, cutting brown and white bread for cucumber sandwiches with incredible rapidity. "The butler at Cobdens' told me all about it last night. If what he says is true, they'll be bleeding at the eyes an' frothing at the mouth an' rolling on the floor in fits, so they will, unless they let this outlandish French doctor try his black arts upon them. Sure, I'd rather die at home in me own comfortable bed than risk a sea vyidge this time of year, with goodness knows what kind of deviltry at the end of it."

"I heard Mamma talking about it with Papa the other day," contributed the round-eyed Almira. "That's why they won't let us have a puppy for Christmas. I teased and teased, and got Tom and Porter to tease, too; but Papa says it wouldn't be safe. Do *you* think it isn't safe, Bridie?"

"Sure," replied Bridie, now paring radishes at unparalleled speed, "what would a poor innocent puppy do half as bad as those heathens in Paris? Haven't there been dogs on earth since the days of Adam an' Eve, an' did we ever hear of hydryphoobia till those wicked doctors invented the thing? With their finding this kind of gerrum an' that kind of gerrum, it soon won't be safe for a body to venture forth on the street!"

The Marys clucked their approval; but Ned felt he had to say: "I think the germs were always there. It's just that people hadn't names for them before."

"An' much better when they hadn't," Bridie retorted smartly. "Least said's soonest mended, with gerrums. Ye leave them alone an' they'll leave *ye* alone, Master Ned."

"Well," said Mary Kelly, after a short pause, evidently feeling the conversation had taken too serious a turn, "aren't we going to have a bit of music this afternoon? Come on, Murph, give us a song while we're waiting for the kettle to bile!"

"Oh, Mary, do sing!" cried Almira; and Ned added his persuasions to his cousin's.

Mary Murphy required a great deal of coaxing. This was also part of the programme. She pretended that she was hoarse; that she didn't know any songs; that she hadn't a minute to spare; that the whole idea was so much foolishness. All the while, however, as her audience well understood, she was preparing for her performance. There was something irresistibly comic in the contrast between her long, doleful face and the jaunty ditties she liked to sing. Finally she flung back her head and emitted a kind of howling cadenza before beginning:

> *"T'was at a fancy ball last night*
> *I was the fairest belle;*
> *Among the nice young fellers was*
> *An eighteen-carat swell . . ."*

There were innumerable verses tracing the course of true love, each ending with the refrain:

> *"He won my heart and won my hand*
> *While dancing in the waltz!"*

After this brilliant success there was a pause for refreshments, which somehow tasted better than they did in the dining-room. Ned, looking back later on his winter in Prairie Avenue, decided that never had tea been so hot and fragrant, buttered toast so meltingly delicious, as in Mary Murphy's kitchen. Neither she nor Mary Kelly objected—as Aunt Lydia did—if one blew upon the liquid, or poured some out in the saucer; it was also the cosy custom to dip bits of cake in the cup.

Conversation grew gradually more intimate as Bridie, surpassing her former efforts, gave them a pungent review of neighbourhood eccentricities. It was absorbing to hear that old Mr. Larned on the corner spoke Potawatomi with his half-breed hired man; that Mrs. Rankin's help were allowed nothing but newspapers to spread on their bedroom floors; that Mrs. Harper donned a fresh nightgown every night and a new set of underclothes every morning, and kept one maid busy doing nothing but changing ribbons. "That reminds me, Miss Almira, which dress will yer mother be wearing tonight—the yellow velvet or the voylet brocade?"

"Neither one," answered Mary Kelly. "She's got a new one just home from Weeks's—white bangoline silk with a jacket to match all embroidered in seed-pearls: t'is a gorgeous thing."

"Ah," said Bridie, wagging her head, "there's not a better dressed lady on the block than Mrs. Stack. She's elegant entirely. It's lucky yer papa owns all o' them lumber woods, me dear, for it must cost him a pretty penny to have her turned out like a queen."

"We'll sit on the stairs, Ned, when the guests start coming in," said Almira. "That's what Tom and Porter and I always do. I love to watch the ladies in their pretty, shiny evening dresses. I wish they came to see Mamma more often, not only just when they're 'specially asked. Why don't they call all the time the way they do on their other friends?"

Ned saw the Marys exchange a look; but it was Bridie who replied: "Sure, yer mother has plenty to do, child, besides stopping at home an' twirling her fingers round a tea-cup."

"Yes—but so have other ladies," said Almira. "And she's got all the gentlemen callers she wants. Florence Harper says it's 'cause ladies don't like Mamma. They only come here when their husbands make 'em, and they wouldn't do that only Papa's so rich they have to. She says her mother told her so."

The looks increased in intensity.

"Well, well!" exclaimed Mary Kelly, "what foolishness will we be hearing next? Whyever wouldn't the ladies in Prairie Avenue be liking yer mother, Miss Almira, dear?"

"Why," said Almira, in her high, clear tones, "Florence says her mother told her it's 'cause people don't know where she came from. Aunt Corinne's bad enough, she says—but at least everyone's heard of her folks; there isn't a more 'ristocratic family in the South than the Beauchamps. But nobody knows who the Porters were."

"Mrs. Harper's a great one to talk," snorted Bridie. "Old Harper's as common as dirt. T'was only a few years ago his wife had to send him to dancing school to learn him to take off his hat in the parlour an' not to eat his victuals with his knife. As for Mrs. Harper, for all she's grown so grand an' buys her clothes twice a year in Paris, her own name was Clancy an' she was born on the *West Side!* Yes—an' I could show ye the very house she lived in—shanty's more like it— where her poor old father went on living till the day of his death. Mended chicken-coops he did, the creature, an' made whisky unbeknownst on the back premises. I don't know which the old devil was worse at, for he never turned an honest penny in his life."

There was a silence, while all present contemplated these striking statements. Then Mary Kelly said soothingly: "Mrs. Harper's just jealous, dear, because she's not so popular with the men as yer mamma is. An' Florence Harper has no right to go repeating such tales. People like that are no better than them nasty gerrums Bridie was telling us about. If I were ye, I'd forget the whole thing like a good girl."

"But it's true," persisted Almira, flushed and unhappy. "I mean, I don't know who Mamma's folks were. Do you, Ned? All I know is, she came from the country, somewhere in southern Illinois. She was an only child, and both her father and mother are dead—which is why we haven't any grandparents, 'cause Grandpa and Grandma Stack died years ago, too—I guess they'd be 'most a hundred if they were living now."

"Why, what more do ye want to know?" cried Bridie; but Almira, not far from tears, could not stop.

"Florence says her mother says no-one has any idea where Papa picked her up. He just took her to church with him one Sunday, and there she was! But some people think she was a *waitress in a hotel.*"

For a moment it was impossible for anyone to speak. Finally Bridie collected herself to remark, with studied lightness: "An' what's wrong with being a waitress, I'd like to know?"

Poor Almira turned scarlet. "Oh, Bridie, dear, I didn't mean . . ."

Mary Murphy, who up to now had said nothing at all, rose like a thundercloud from her seat at the head of the table. "That's enough o' such nonsense! I'm ashamed of yez all. Thim that listens to trash are no better than thim that invents it—which well yez know, Miss Almira. Now out o' my kitchen, the lot of yez! I've no time for anny more such goings-on. *Whoosh!*"

The group dispersed precipitately. With an air of virtuous unconcern Bridie began washing up. Kind Mary Kelly took Almira upstairs to wait for Mr. George, who had promised to make her a wig for her doll. And Mary Murphy, still muttering angrily, returned to her saddle of mutton.

Ned, having nothing particular to do, drifted into the servants' dining-room to run through the magazines, some of which had been sent down from the library; others, generally more diverting, were supplied from less orthodox sources. To-day, however, not even Mary Kelly's Dream Book could hold his interest. Almira's strange revelations had started him thinking. He was struck not so much by her blurting them out— one had always known she could not keep anything to herself for more than a few minutes—as by her choice of confidants.

As for the news itself, it was true that Aunt Lydia seemed as rootless—though apparently also as flourishing—as one of the Kennerleys' orchids. It *was* queer that she never spoke of her family, or told tales of her childhood and youth, the way other people's mothers did. Ned had supposed, up to now, that it wasn't deliberate reticence, but merely that she had not much time to entertain her children. He himself knew only that she was so much younger than Uncle Hiram that she might have been his daughter instead of his wife; ten years younger even than Mamma. His mother had often told him how, when Grandpa Stack died, her brother had gone west to seek his fortune, leaving her, a half-grown girl, with Grandma Stack in the old home in Albany. It had been several years before he'd saved enough money to send for them: when they finally joined him, Mamma was on her wedding journey with Papa, but Uncle Hiram was still a bachelor.

They'd all lived together in Ontario Street, till the Fire burned them out and they moved down to Prairie Avenue. By that time, though, Uncle Hiram must have been married, for the Fire had been in '71, and Tom was already sixteen past. But when or how Aunt Lydia had appeared on the scene, Ned had no idea. Perhaps his parents' silence was more significant than any explanations could have been. . . .

In the midst of his cogitations Bridie's loud voice, pitched high above the clatter of pots and pans, floated out of the kitchen: "'T'is a pity the poor innocent baby should be bothered by such low, sneaking stories. But indeed, me dear, many's the time I've wondered how long it would be 'fore the childern . . ."

Mary Murphy opened the oven door, and then slammed it shut so violently that Ned lost the end of the sentence. Bridie's voice, however, cut through the noise again a minute later: "Truth to tell, *I* always heard he found her in a *house*. . . .'

This seemed anti-climactic: where else, Ned asked himself, would people be likely to meet? But the din round the stove had increased to such terrifying proportions that he judged it prudent to slip upstairs without returning to the kitchen.

After a schoolroom supper—whose comparative plainness would be made up for later by a sophisticated selection of tidbits—Ned and Almira kept watch in the latter's bedroom window till the first carriage stopped at the door, and then scampered downstairs to survey the arrivals. Almira had learned from experience, she said, precisely how far one might safely venture without being seen from below; she was, Ned soon saw, in her usual spirits. He was beginning to understand that, for his cousin, to express an emotion was to free herself from it.

In quick succession the guests streamed in, the men in swallow-tails under their topcoats, the women in long rustling gowns with lace pinned to their heads. Aunt Lydia's "half past seven for a quarter to eight" meant just what it said; no-one, it was clear, cared to risk spoiling Mary Murphy's culinary triumphs. Each time the double doors to the parlour opened Ned caught a glimpse of his uncle and aunt standing in front of the fire. Presently the polite murmur from within swelled to a steady hum. . . .

The Harpers were almost the last to appear. Mr. Harper turned on the threshold to call an order to his departing coachman, while his wife, superb in rose velvet and pearls, sailed up to the hall glass and posed as she patted her straw-coloured tresses and adjusted her ribbons. Ned, recalling her unkind insinuations about her hostess as retailed by Almira—even if Almira herself seemed to have forgotten them—wondered if she were nervous about making an entrance. But the beauty gave her invariable pretty, chiming laugh as she passed into the parlour ahead of her husband; and Aunt Lydia, one perceived, held out her hand with her changeless welcoming smile.

"Now they're all here but the Kennerleys," said Almira. "Aunt Corinne's often terribly late. I can't think why, with all those maids to dress her. I guess she just don't start in time."

Eight o'clock had struck on the gold-faced grandfather clock, and Mary Kelly had twice been in to announce dinner,

when at last the bell rang once more. Bridie opened the door
for Mr. Kennerley, who hurried in alone and stood frowning
a little and biting his lips as he pulled off his gloves. It was
the first time Ned had ever seen him even slightly ill at ease.

"Good evening, Bridie. I wonder if I might speak to Mrs.
Stack a moment?"

Before the maid could answer him the parlour door flew
open and Aunt Lydia, gleaming and glittering in the white
silk and seed-pearls, her chestnut hair all laced with diamonds,
glided through it.

"Abner, what's wrong?"

Her voice was short and sharp, and sounded almost vexed.
But Mr. Kennerley, bowing over her hand, had recovered his
poise.

"Madam, I offer you my sincerest apologies. I was detained.
Corinne—my poor wife was taken ill unexpectedly. I fear she
won't be able—"

"Nothing serious, I hope?"

Aunt Lydia knit her lovely brows, at once full of tender
concern for her friend.

"No—oh, no—just a sudden sick headache. You know those
spells of hers. It developed at the last minute; there wasn't even
time to warn you by note. I hardly know how to make her
excuses. I'm afraid we've upset your table arrangements. In
the circumstances it might have been more tactful of me to
have remained at home. But I wasn't sure. I thought perhaps . . ."

"Dear Mr. Kennerley," said Aunt Lydia, smiling—and it
was only then Ned remembered she had first called him something else—"I should never have forgiven you if you hadn't
come to my party. I'm deeply distressed that Corinne should
be suffering; please give her my love and tell her I'll call for
news of her health in the morning. Now shall we go in to
dinner?"

She summoned her guests, who filed into the hall two by

two save for Uncle Rock, bringing up the rear. Aunt Lydia, still smiling composedly, laid one hand in his keeping, the other in Mr. Kennerley's, and tailed the little procession into the dining-room.

On the stairs a dull period of waiting had now to be endured. It was no longer possible to see what was happening, nor to hear more than a confused roar of voices . . . "They always make such a racket," Almira grumbled, "directly they start to eat." But she deemed it unwise to desert their post. "Bridie knows where we are, and she'd better not forget us—she'd better *not,* that's all I can say!"

Tom and Porter, who had scorned to remain on guard with the "little ones," nevertheless seemed to scent from afar when it would be well to appear; they came clattering down from the schoolroom just as Bridie, flushed and breathing heavily, hove into sight with her tray.

"Why, lookee here, Tom—lobster salad, and ice-cream with chocolate sauce—my favourite, by thunder! Have some, my boy?"

Tom declared he didn't mind if he did.

Almira set up a wail.

"That's not fair—Bridie meant it for *us!* You haven't been waiting the way Ned and I have."

"Bridie's my friend," said Porter, with a broad wink. "Aren't you, Bridie? You wouldn't let a fellow starve, I guess?"

"Sure, there's enough for the whole bunch," said Bridie expansively. "It's Murph has the generous hand. Don't ye fret, Miss Almira: if ye want anny more, ye've only to come to the pantry after the company's left the table."

For some little time the only sounds to be heard were the scrape of a spoon on a plate, or an occasional appreciative sigh.

"The ice-cream's not *quite* so good as last time, I think," said Almira reflectively. "Mary must have forgot to put peppermint in the sauce."

"Tastes prime to me," said Tom; and Porter added: "I

only wish we lived at Mallards'. Joe says they serve Roman punch in the middle of dinner and ice-cream at the end, so it's like having *two* desserts."

"Mamma says Roman punch is common," remarked Almira, dipping her round little cocoanut cake in what was left of the sweet.

"Common or not, t'would suit me first rate," said Porter. "Come on, Tom, there's no use hanging round here any longer. Let us know, infants, if there's more grub. Otherwise—leaving you to guzzle . . ."

"Porter's manners are awful," complained Almira, after her brothers had gone. "I don't see why he's so rude—we didn't eat a scrap more than him and Tom, only we'd be ashamed to gobble it up the way they did."

She disappeared, just the same, in the direction of the pantry as soon as Aunt Lydia's little troop of ladies had tinkled and trailed their way across the hall.

Ned stayed where he was, largely because he could not think what else to do. Eventually he found it possible to descend a good deal lower on the stairs, now that the danger of a sudden irruption was past; from his new vantage point he had a view of the dining-room, where the gentlemen were clustered about the host's end of the table to enjoy their coffee and cigars and a glass or two of Uncle Hiram's celebrated port. As Ned saw them then, so he was to see them, and one or two others, many times that winter, though it was not until years afterwards that he came to realize the significance of the group: here were some of the men who had helped make Chicago.

The conversation was not attractive to a child. Ned's life with his parents had made him able to follow an adult train of thought more successfully than his cousins, but there was nothing in the English elections, the effect of the Servo-Bulgarian war on the stock market, or the obscure and irritating policy known as "Bimetallism" to hold his attention.

He was more interested in the speakers as individuals. Of

them all, only the two professional men were negligible personalities: jolly, florid Doctor Mallard agreed with everyone on principle, and quiet Uncle Rock seemed aloof, idly tracing imaginary circles with his finger on the table-cloth. Huge old Mr. Cobden sat on Uncle Hiram's right, his shaggy bison's head sunk on his massive chest; he had an odd habit of knocking his cigar-ash off continually to emphasize his points. Opposite him was little Mr. Harper, the great dry-goods merchant, with his Irish monkey-face (rather like Tim's, thought Ned—only Tim was better looking!) and his anxious desire for preëminence. Uncle Hiram's natural gravity was just as impressive; he was more deliberate of tongue than his friends, but set them right frequently as he conceived it his privilege to do; and his laconic "Rilly!" or, in extreme cases, "Rilly and truhly!" expressed not so much surprise as impatience; it was a kind of conversational treading water till he could get in control himself.

Abner Kennerley, erect, acute, and elegant, spoke less often than the rest; that, it seemed, was merely because he knew so well what he thought that nothing anyone else said could possibly make any difference to him. And when at last he did grow voluble, there was no mistaking the imperious certainty of his manner.

The talk had turned, as it often did, to real estate. Mr. Harper maintained, with vigour, that the North Side was the coming part of town. "Can't see it any other way. Before the Fire it always was the best residential district; bound to be again some day."

Mr. Cobden thrust his stout thumbs in his waistcoat pockets and glared at him through a cloud of blue smoke.

"*We* don't live there!"

"No—but danged if we won't be moving up soon! Mark my words, Cobden, and don't be ornery too long. Remember what happened to the West Side: a few years back warn't it supposed to be due for a boom? Now it ain't possible to give away lots on that side of the river. We were all caught short there, I reckon."

"*I* wasn't!" Doctor Mallard gave his usual cheerful laugh. "Hadn't the money to invest you fellows had. Sometimes it pays to be shy of cash, you know."

"Don't see it, Holland; don't see it at all!" boomed Uncle Hiram. "The North Side's all right. Very pleasant little spot, if you care for country life. But it's too far away from the centre of things. You can tell for yourself what the transportation companies think of its future: with our cable system running all over the place, there's still nothing but horse-cars up in No-man's-land. Am I right, Hezzy?"

"Yes, sir! Prairie Avenue's the spot to be. Suits me to a T. Fine street—convenient to everything—all our friends in the neighbourhood. Why, it'd be exile now to move anywhere else!"

"*Now,* I grant you!" Mr. Harper stuck to his point, tapping his half-empty wine-glass irritably. "But now ain't forever. If we've learned anything from the past, it's that nothing stays the same very long in Chicago. That's why we chose to come here in the first place, I guess. All of us were born somewheres else, but we came this way because we saw it was the land of opportunity and we were looking for a chance to spread ourselves a bit. It's plain mulish obstinacy to try to buck the tide! I tell you, it's running against us. When we moved south we made a mistake in not moving a whole lot farther; then we could have afforded to sit tight. As it is, we're much too close in. Handy, sure—but it's too damn dirty—and the dirt's getting worse all the time with Hezzy's engines dropping cinders all over our gardens and a mess of new factories springing up every year. What's the use of buying fine pictures and furniture, if they're covered with grime in a month? I tell you, my wife's getting sick of it, and I'm getting sick of it, too. We're looking at property up the other side of Pine Street, and I've half a mind in the spring . . ."

"You're crazy, Hol, plumb crazy!"

Mr. Cobden brought his great hairy fist down on the damask cloth with a force that made all the glasses ring affrightedly and caused even Ned to jump in his nook on the stairs. "Hiram agrees with me. What do *you* say, Abner? You've been as dumb as an oyster up to now, but that don't mean you han't an idea or two. What's *your* opinion of Prairie Avenue?"

"*My* opinion?"

Ned leaned forward to gaze at the speaker, whose measured, well-bred tones contrasted oddly with his colleagues' rougher voices. "I can give it to you in one short sentence, gentlemen. By the terms of my will, drawn up just a fortnight ago, it is stipulated that the Kennerley house cannot be sold on no matter what pretext for one hundred years. That's what I think of the value of property on Prairie Avenue."

"Ha, you see!" exclaimed Mr. Cobden; and Uncle Hiram clapped his friend on the back with a heartfelt "Rilly, Abner, you don't say! Glad to hear it, old man!"

"At the same time," Mr. Kennerley continued, holding up his hand to show that he was not finished yet, "there's nothing more short-sighted than to put all one's eggs in one basket. We've made our fortunes by guessing beforehand what the public was going to want, and providing it. Cobden's railroads bring people here; I feed them; Hiram will sell them the wood to build houses with. But whatever our special lines are, we're all in the business of land speculation—and a very profitable business it is. I've lots all over the city, and I intend to go on buying all over the city. The West Side's not finished, Holland. It will come back some day for industrial purposes. And doubtless you're right in saying the North Side is set for some sort of development. Nothing's surer in Chicago than that nothing is sure. But I'm willing to stake my name and reputation as an investor on the future of the very section where we are established. I've built my home in Prairie Avenue; I live here, and I expect to die here; and, if I'm not much mistaken, my children and grandchildren will live here and die here, too."

Somehow, when Abner Kennerley got through with a subject, there was little more to be said. As the group showed signs of breaking up Ned sped upstairs to avoid being caught. At the top of the first flight he paused for breath just as Mr. Kennerley came out of the dining-room prepared to depart. "I hate to go, Hiram, but my wife isn't well."

"I understand perfectly, my dear fellow; only sorry Mrs. Kennerley's not feeling herself. I'll go tell Lydia you want to slip along quietly."

Uncle Hiram vanished; and by the time Aunt Lydia appeared Mr. Kennerley had put on his topcoat and taken his hat and gloves from Bridie. He said a few graceful words, expressing his pleasure in the entertainment and his regret at being obliged to quit it so early. Aunt Lydia murmured that he was very kind; she was sorry, too, and sent her dear love to Corinne.

There was nothing in the least remarkable about their dialogue. It was pure chance that Ned, leaning over the banisters, saw Mr. Kennerley press a small folded scrap of paper into his hostess's hand as he left. Aunt Lydia took it without a word, read what was written on it, and then stuffed it carelessly into her vanity-case. Bridie had already gone; no-one but Ned witnessed the action. He was also a witness of the extraordinary transformation that took place in his aunt; it was as if she had received a sudden charge of electricity, running from the top of her shining crown of braids to the tips of her pearl-embroidered slippers. With her head held high and her face flaming with colour, Mrs. Hiram Stack returned to her guests in the parlour.

Chapter 6

ON CHRISTMAS EVE Ned received a letter from his mother. Owing to storms on the Atlantic it had been over a fortnight in reaching him; the envelope was postmarked San Remo; Mamma enclosed a view of the waterfront, with rows of bushy palms against a blue Italian sky. Ned had never been in San Remo; he realized, with a pang, that it was the first time he had had to picture his parents in an unfamiliar scene.

But at least for the moment his homesickness was eclipsed by an intense feeling of relief, for Mamma also enclosed a ten-dollar bill. He had been wondering all week, with growing anxiety, how he was ever to manage to buy any presents. Careful as he was, a dollar and a half was all he'd been able to save from his allowance. It was out of the question to ask for more: even if he gave the servants only a quarter apiece, that would leave a niggardly fifty cents for everyone else. The girls in Almira's class at the Seminary had been busy for the last month manufacturing calendars and blotting-books to bestow on their friends and relations, but Ned thought the results smacked too plainly of the scissors and paste-pot to be worthy of serious consideration.

The afternoon was half over before he could slip away from the house, clasping his precious greenback in one mittened fist. It had been a sunny day, but the west wind was so cold and dry that it took one's breath away. Ned ran most of the three blocks to Mr. Tomkins's and arrived with his nose and ears tingling. It took him an hour or more to make his purchases; he wanted to savour the lordly sensation of being in funds for all it was worth.

Mr. Tomkins could afford to let his young customer take his time. Business this year had been unusually brisk, but naturally now the rush was over: Ned inspected the counters in company only with the Kennerleys' Edna and two or three "Micks" from the other side of Michigan Avenue—a gang perennially at odds with the Prairie Avenue "Swells."

Luckily the holiday spirit seemed to have imposed a temporary truce. No untoward remarks were passed as Ned and his ragged competitors priced snow shovels and toy locomotives, though the former could not help wondering what such obvious paupers were doing there at all. His final selections included a bronze paper-knife for his uncle, a bottle of *eau de cologne* for his aunt, and a set of miniature dishes decorated with garlands of roses and pansies for Almira. The boys would be harder to please, but it appeared safe to offer a few foreign stamps for their collections.

It was a strong temptation to spend his last remaining dollar on a Japanese vase—blue, with grey and white storks—; but Ned turned away with a sigh and a shake of his head: Celia's affections were not for sale, and it was only too likely that she would be embarrassed, or even annoyed, by an unexpected tribute.

When he finally emerged with his precious bundles the sun was starting to set, and the lamps had already been lighted along Twenty-Second Street. It was bitterly cold. There seemed to be nothing to breathe; Ned gasped after the warmth inside, and stood on the door-step, wrapping his scarf more tightly round his throat and eying a little fearfully the unusual number of Micks on the sidewalk.

Perhaps he should not have been surprised: wasn't it, he asked himself, the custom on Christmas Eve the world over for poor children to press their noses against the glass, pathetically admiring treasures far beyond their reach? And hadn't he often, in more affluent days, begged coins from Papa and Mamma to apportion amongst them? This time, however, the Micks had an object in view: a small woman in a long dark fur coat, who came out of Bartlett's drug store on the corner of Indiana, carrying a large paper bag. In spite of the fading light and the plumed bonnet that partly covered her face Ned recognized Mrs. Kennerley. He wondered what she was doing in this neighbourhood without her carriage, and what she had in the bag; but he soon saw—and so did the Micks. Quickly she began tossing candies right and left, like a farmer's wife feeding chickens.

"Here—here—here!" Her voice was high and wheedling, again like a farmer's wife. But the Micks did not need to be coaxed. With business-like promptness they scrambled for largesse, wasting no breath on words.

Ned wondered what would happen next. Mrs. Kennerley was drifting along the pavement, as haphazard, apparently, as a butterfly. Now she darted into a cake-shop next to Bartlett's; she was gone for only a minute, but during it the crowd of ragamuffins received several additions.

This time she reappeared laden with buns. As she began once more distributing goodies a ray from one of the street lamps struck her face; it looked little and pinched from the cold, quite expressionless, with enormous black caverns where her eyes must be. "Here—here—here!" . . .

Suddenly she wavered across the street, paying no heed to the traffic. The Micks moved with her, shuffling silently, bent with terrible fervour on accompanying their Lady Bountiful to the end. Clearly she was headed for Mr. Tompkins's. Grasping his bundles more firmly, Ned vanished in the shadows before Aunt Corinne could see him.

He said nothing at home about his expedition, and fortunately everyone was too busy to ask where he'd been.

Ned frankly had dreaded Christmas without his parents, but Aunt Lydia rose to the occasion with extraordinary zest. One had not expected it; it would have seemed more in character for her to dismiss the whole business with a smile and an amiable "Do what you like, children, as long as I'm not bothered."

On the contrary, as soon as dinner was over, leaving Uncle Hiram with his newspaper by the fire, she led the young people into the library, where Tim had that morning set up a splendid aromatic spruce. Since she could no longer pretend, said Aunt Lydia, that even Almira believed in Santa Claus, it was best to extract as much fun as possible out of trimming the tree.

And it *was* fun—Aunt Lydia made it so. Ned had never seen her in such spirits: she laughed continually over anything and nothing, hummed scraps of Christmas hymns as she sorted the pretty, sparkling ornaments; her eyes were bright with mischievous secrets; even her deep red gown, with clusters of holly at the waist and on the shoulder, seemed to reflect her holiday mood.

Almira and Ned, hanging gold and silver moss on the lower branches, were enchanted; and the older boys, after asserting loudly that they were too old for such nonsense, were soon cajoled by their mother into lending a hand. She admired extravagantly Porter's symmetrical disposition of the candles; persuaded Tom that only he was tall enough to fasten in place the wax angel that hovered on silver horsehair wings just above the treetop. When the task was finished she allowed them to light up for a few minutes to enjoy the fruits of their labours, instead of insisting, as most grown-ups would have done, that tomorrow would do as well.

"Come, Papa, see how pretty it is!" she cried; and when Uncle Hiram had let himself be led in and had said: "Yes, yes—delightful, my dear!" without really looking at all, she scolded him playfully and declared that as a punishment *he* should read "The Night before Christmas" when they hung up their stockings at the parlour chimney. She went off to bed finally singing "O Little Town of Bethlehem." . . .

Even more uncharacteristically, she woke almost as early

95

as the children did, so that there was no agonized waiting to open the stockings, as Ned had assumed there must be. The presents were lavish and highly satisfactory. It might have been Janet who'd chosen them (as Almira told Ned was generally the case); but Aunt Lydia appeared to know all about them and to have seen to it that everyone got what he or she most wanted.

After breakfast there was a scramble to dress for church; after church the tree was lighted, Uncle Rock and various cousins arrived, and there were presents all over again.

The John Stacks drove up from Kenwood; the Harvey Stacks, beyond driving distance, had taken the train down from Evanston with their twelve-year-old twins Caroline and Geraldine (whom the Hiram Stack children dubbed Lanoline and Vaseline). There was a great deal of kissing: Ned, as a novelty, was also subjected to patting and pinching, and to arch exclamations of "Haven't seen you since you were *so* high!" or, "Do you remember your Cousin Penelope, dear?"

He found it hard to decide whom he most disliked, flaxen-haired, fluttery Lanoline and Vaseline—like a pair of timorous white rabbits—or Cousin John and his wife Cousin Gertrude, who were stuffy and elderly, and made tiresome mistakes: Uncle Hiram, for instance, was given a box of the wrong kind of cigars, and Ned found himself opening a set of "Lulu's Library," surely more appropriate for Almira. . . .

Aunt Lydia, however, went on smiling and being lovely to everybody. She even clasped to her bosom in ecstasy a copy of "General Grant's Memoirs" presented by Mrs. John Stack, though it had been in the house for weeks and Ned had once surprised her apparently lost in its pages, with something by Ouida artfully slipped into the middle.

Dinner lasted for hours. It seemed a small eternity from the soup to the walnuts and raisins and glasses of sweet cider that Uncle Hiram always demanded on holidays. Ned was hardly able to move when they left the table. It was again a very cold

day, but he felt there was nothing for it but to ask permission
to go for a walk.

Almira refused to accompany him; she was collecting her
loot to carry upstairs in her new real leather doll's trunk; so
Ned started out alone, in the teeth of a cruel west wind. In a
forlorn attempt to elude its violence he cut straight across to
Calumet Avenue. The view was limitless across the flat, grey,
steaming lake, but about as cheerful as a scene at the North
Pole. No one was abroad in such weather; there was no living
thing in sight except a few discouraged gulls—and even they
looked glued to floating blocks of ice.

Ned thrust his hands deep in his pockets and trudged
valiantly south, fighting the tears that were trying hard to
come. Hoping to outstrip the homesick feelings he'd kept at
bay so long, he walked a good deal farther than he'd planned,
well beyond Twenty-Second and the boundaries of the familiar world, out to the empty fields and cow pastures round
Fortieth Street.

Just as he was about to turn back he caught sight of a
woman, the only other human being hardy enough to brave
the wintry blast. She was still some distance from him; as he
drew nearer he saw she was wearing a long black fur coat he
had seen before; but even without it Ned was sure he'd have
known Aunt Corinne.

He called out to her as soon as they were within hailing
distance.

Mrs. Kennerley did not answer. She was wandering un-
certainly about an open field, like a bit of tumbleweed blowing
before the wind and then—again like the tumbleweed—halting
here and there for no discernible reason.

Ned felt an impulse to walk by and pretend he had not seen
her. But somehow he could not do it. Leaving the sidewalk,
he picked his way through clumps of bushes covered with
burrs across the rough, partly snow-clad turf.

"Aunt Corinne! It's Ned—Ned Ramsay: can I help you?"

Mrs. Kennerley still made no answer, save to mutter a few unintelligible words. She did not look at him. Her eyes appeared unable to focus; her little face looked whiter and more pinched than ever. But she did not recoil when Ned took her hand—which was ungloved and very nearly frozen—and started leading her towards the road. The strong, acrid smell of whiskey was unmistakable on her breath—and not only on her breath: it seemed to exude from the whole of her person.

She went on muttering all the way back to Prairie Avenue, though fortunately she did not resist Ned's guidance: without it she might well have fallen, for the pavement in this uninhabited district was cracked and uneven.

Ned was thoroughly frightened. He had never before seen a woman drunk. But as long as Aunt Corinne was willing to follow, his duty was plain. It was a blessing no-one was out in the street to observe their strange halting progress.

When at last they reached the Kennerley house he had some trouble in inducing her to mount the long flight of brownstone steps. Once at the top he rang hastily for Johnson, and as soon as he heard someone coming he dropped his companion's hand and ran home as fast as possible.

For a second time Ned kept his adventure to himself. What, after all, could he have said? Much, however, that had been cloudy was made clear by the discovery. He thought about it that night in bed, and pitied Sonny and Celia.

The next afternoon, when he and Almira were asked over to play with their friends, he glanced nervously about as they entered. Mrs. Kennerley was nowhere in sight, and neither Celia nor Sonny spoke of their mother.

While they were walking along the upper hall to the playroom a voice reached them faintly from below, wailing high and fretfully like a sick child.

"What's the matter?" asked Almira, before Ned could stop her.

Celia shrugged her shoulders.

"Mamma's having one of her spells."

The wailing continued. It sounded louder now, and less like a child than the mew of a frightened kitten. Black Edna was soothing her gently: "There, there, Miss Corinne, honey . . ."

"Is she ill?" said Almira apprehensively; and Sonny nodded. "Sometimes the doctor makes her go away."

The next moment Mademoiselle came waddling down the passage, shooed the children into their own quarters, and slammed the door on them with a breathless *"Tenez-vous là, mes choux, et n'en sortez plus ou je vous chasse sur-le-champs!"*

Ned felt older and wiser than ever before in his life.

When they got home that evening they found the household at 1817 as near confusion as so well-ordered a machine could be. A telegram had just come for Uncle Hiram: the largest of his mills in Mississippi was on fire. It was impossible to estimate the amount of damage done, Aunt Lydia told them, as the blaze was still raging; but Papa was leaving by train immediately after dinner.

She seemed deeply concerned, and did what she could to be useful: writing a great many notes, and helping Janet with the packing. Completely disregarding Doctor Mallard's orders, she ran up and down stairs innumerable times; and Ned had to admit it did her no harm, for she came to the table with bright eyes and cheeks only healthily flushed.

Afterwards she insisted on driving to the station with her husband, although he begged her not to, on account of the weather.

Ned was sorry for his uncle, who looked tired and old as he stood in the hall drawing on his fur lined gloves. He and Aunt Lydia often walked arm-in-arm, but as they went down the steps to the carriage he appeared for the first time to lean on his wife.

Two days later, a message arrived from Biloxi: the fire was out, the destruction less than had been feared; but Uncle

Hiram had decided, as long as he was in the south, to make a tour of his various properties; it might be a fortnight before he'd be home.

New Year's Day was cold and blustery: the papers were beginning to speak of the uncommonly severe winter. Ned had almost forgotten what a to-do Americans made about this particular holiday. Having sat up half the night to welcome it in—the children had hardly been able to sleep on account of the din in the streets—they circled the town the following day to drink egg-nog or punch with their friends and acquaintances. At that, asserted Aunt Lydia, it was not so bad as it used to be: in her early married life men would call whether they knew you or not, whereas now they confined themselves to their visiting lists.

Prairie Avenue was in commotion all day. Beribboned baskets were hung at the door to hold calling-cards in those rare cases where the owners were not officially at home, but nearly all the ladies of the neighbourhood kept open house: dining-room tables were laden with good things to eat, and from two o'clock on the street was thronged with vehicles.

Aunt Lydia, dressed in her best, received her friends by the parlour fire. Ned was alarmed to find that, contrary to custom, she expected the young people to help her. Many of the callers were employees of Stack and Company and their families; Aunt Lydia made a great fuss over them, and insisted on the children's doing so, too; it was important, she said, for one never knew when such people might be useful.

As the afternoon wore on more familiar masculine faces appeared in the crowd: these, Almira whispered to Ned, were gentlemen on their way home from the annual reception at the Chicago Club, where they'd been drinking champagne all day. Old Mr. Cobden wandered in with a bright purple nose, closely followed by Mr. Harper and Doctor Mallard, who laughed all the time and were perspiring profusely. The fact that their wives were not with them could for once occasion no comment, since these ladies were amply engaged at home.

Uncle Rock arrived late in evening clothes, having stopped to change after a round of calls on the North Side; he was to stay to supper.

Except for him and Ned and Aunt Lydia, the parlour was empty when Mr. Kennerley entered.

Aunt Lydia looked up without getting up: in her beautiful red Christmas dress she seemed as buoyant and unruffled as if the long hours on parade as a hostess had only refreshed her.

"Happy New Year, my lady; Happy New Year, young Ned! . . . Rock, I think we've met before at the club. . . . Corinne sends her love and greetings by me; she'd have loved to run over herself, but, as you can imagine, the Kennerley house hasn't been precisely deserted today. I've just been able to slip away from my duties myself. Moonlight and the new cutter from Kimball's are at the door; I wonder if I can persuade *you* to play truant for a few minutes and give me the benefit of your opinion of the combination."

Aunt Lydia sighed, and then shook her head.

"I'd love it, of all things. But it's almost supper-time, and Rock and I are going to the opera. The German season opens tonight at the Columbia, you know."

"I didn't know. I don't get about much to such things; they're more in my wife's department. But it won't take long, my dear. I give you my word I'll have you back at any time you say. Do come! It's stuffy by the fire, and if you are going to the theatre, a breath of fresh air will do you a power of good."

Aunt Lydia sighed once more, as if she felt it cool against her hot cheek.

"I'm not even dressed to go out; I'd meant to change for the opera. Rock, would you mind very much . . . ?"

"Good! Then you *will!*" Mr. Kennerley paid no attention to his rival's furious look. "Tell your maid to fetch your warmest cloak. The snow has stopped, but it's a mighty cold night."

Almost mechanically Ned pushed back the parlour curtains and cleared a space with his finger on the frosted glass. The snow had stopped, as Mr. Kennerley had said; it was packed down hard and blue in the street; the sky was blue, too, pricked here and there by a few faint stars; behind the chimney-pots of the houses across the avenue a streak of clear greenish-gold showed in the west. Even through the tightly shut windows the sound of sleigh-bells on the cutter reached them, chiming merrily, as Moonlight trotted away.

Uncle Rock, slumped down by the fire in Uncle Hiram's big chair, broke the silence finally in his quiet, inexpressive voice: "Well, Neddy, that's how it is!"

Ned did not object to the diminutive, otherwise Mamma's sole property. Nobody somehow could ever object to anything Rockwell Terriss did. He was one of those gentle, comfortable people who make themselves felt in a room more by their absence after they have left it. It was hard to tell what Aunt Lydia thought of her friend. She teased him and tried him, commanded him and made use of him shamelessly; but she never refused to see him. Uncle Hiram called him "a soft-meated man. Ought to have been a painter or a writer, or one of those long-haired composer chaps. Damned if I can see why he's such a smart lawyer!" But he, too, seemed fond of him.

The children all liked him better than anyone else who came to the house, and he was there so often that he seemed like one of the family. Ned and he had a particular bond in common: since Uncle Rock had discovered it, he was apt to play, even if Aunt Lydia were not at home. Ned had long ago learned the name of the strange new music that had excited him so much on the night of his arrival; now, if Uncle Rock went to the piano, one knew it would be only a question of time before he'd get to *Tristan und Isolde*. . . .

Tonight there was no chance of a concert. Ned would have liked to say something comforting, but he could not think what to say. It seemed pointless to remark that Aunt Lydia would be back soon; besides—though he hardly knew why—he did not think she would.

"Oh, well," said Uncle Rock, ceasing at last to pull the ends of his pepper-and-salt moustache and looking up with a rueful half-smile, "what's all the fuss about? Your aunt's had a long, hard day, with Hiram not here to help her. I don't wonder she felt she had to get out of the house for a bit. It's only not like her to crowd her appointments; it *is* nearly supper-time, and I'd hate to have her miss the *Tannhäuser* overture."

"Oh, yes," said Ned, who knew about *Tannhäuser*, "so should I."

"I'm taking you and Almira to the matinée on Saturday to hear Alvary in *Lohengrin*," Uncle Rock continued. "I thought that would be what you'd like best, and even the properest parent couldn't object to the plot! What I'd give my eyes for, though, is a performance of *Tristan*. They'll do it in New York, but Chicago's supposed to be too provincial for such adult fare. But if I have to swim across the ocean and back, I'm going to Bayreuth next summer."

Ned knew about Bayreuth also. He plied Uncle Rock with questions concerning the little Franconian town where their hero had lived; presently they were launched on a lively discussion. All through it, however, Ned kept his eye on the white marble clock on the mantel; he felt rather than saw Uncle Rock's eye on it, too.

At seven Mary Kelly peered into the parlour to see if Mrs. Stack were there. At a quarter past she came again. At seven-thirty Almira rattled downstairs.

"Mary says we've got to eat now, 'cause she's going to church. I don't see why Mamma's not home."

Uncle Rock rose all-of-a-piece and gave his shoulders a vigorous shake, as if ridding himself of something.

"I must be off."

"Aren't you staying for supper?" cried Almira. "Your place is set. I thought you and Mamma—"

"No, my dear; thanks very much. I really don't need it. I've been eating all day."

"So have I," said Ned. "I'm not hungry either. Don't wait for me, Almira."

Almira, wide-eyed with astonishment, bounced out into the hall to look for her brothers.

Uncle Rock produced an envelope from his inside breast pocket and took out two slips of yellow pasteboard, turning them over and over in his long, slender fingers.

"Neddy, when your aunt comes home, will you be good enough to tell her . . . ? Perhaps she may want . . . she may think . . . But no, why should she? Never mind, boy; don't say anything at all. That will be much the best."

He tore the tickets once across before casting them away; shook hands with Ned, as if they were men who shared a secret of importance, and quietly left the room.

Ned heard footfalls descending the outside steps in their usual unhurried manner. Then he flew to the basket while a rash scheme rushed unbidden through his brain . . . But how could he manage to get to the Columbia Theater? And how home again, in the middle of the night? What would Aunt Lydia say when she knew . . . ? Besides—decisive factor—the tickets were really too badly torn to pass muster, glue them as he might. He dropped them back where he'd found them and joined his cousins in the dining room.

None of the children was able to eat much. It was true they had been nibbling mince turnovers and pound cake most of the afternoon; however, in Ned's case at least the lack of appetite was not entirely due to dietary indiscretions. He felt unwarrantably depressed, a prey to vague forebodings: had Moonlight run away and upset the cutter in the wide, snowy wilderness of Washington Park?

The others seemed depressed, too. Although they did not say so, it was clear that they were facing an unprecedented situation: certainly their mother had never before been absent without reason from a meal.

After supper they sat in the parlour, with the curtains drawn back and the shades pulled up. Tom and Porter played piquet; Almira, with a resolute air, took up her bronze-leather sewing-box and a piece of rather lumpy crochet-work; Ned pretended to read "Chatterbox." The fact that he alone of the four knew what lay at the bottom of Aunt Lydia's best pink silk scrap-basket was, strangely, the most intolerable burden of all.

It was very nearly nine o'clock when the sleigh-bells jingled to a stop outside the entrance to the tall yellow house. The three young Stacks rushed in a body to the door. But Ned, after determining from his post in the parlour window that the cutter looked perfectly sound and that his aunt was coming in alone, ran upstairs suddenly and did not go down again the rest of the evening.

Chapter 7

EARLY in the New Year Uncle Hiram returned from his trip, looking, against reason, more rested than when he had left; he declared that the change had done him good.

Almira and her brothers went back to school; Ned resumed his studies with Mr. Leslie (which now took nearly the whole morning); Aunt Lydia paid her daily calls once more on Aunt Corinne, and was home as usual in the evenings. Mr. Kennerley and Uncle Rock were her most constant visitors; she saw them alternately rather than together; for some weeks it appeared that the latter was the more favoured of the two. (Perhaps she wanted to make up to him for having treated him shabbily.)

Ned puzzled his brain sometimes about the tangled relations of the Stacks and the Kennerleys. They did not often bother him: nine-tenths of his life was spent in the ordinary occupations and preoccupations of a boy of his age. When he was grown up he used to look back on the events of that winter in Prairie Avenue; it occurred to him then that he ought to have noticed more than he had, wondered more than he did.

Mrs. Kennerley soon recovered from her indisposition. The first time Ned saw her he thought she seemed markedly quieter than before, a little meek and pathetic. Not long after that she invited him and Almira to go to the play with her and her children: they lunched at Kennerley's Restaurant—a popular by-product of the retail store in the Kennerley Block —and before the meal was over she reverted to her old eccentricity of manner. She quizzed the waiters, found perpetual fault with the food; and, because the ices were not being brought quickly enough to suit her, screamed at the top of her voice: "Abner, I complain of the service!"—to the crimson confusion of two railway directors who were lunching with Mr. Kennerley in an adjacent private parlour.

It was a release when they rose from the table. Ned saw Celia stiffen, and felt a quick surge of sympathy; how terrible it must be to have such an impetuous parent! He trembled himself for fear of what their hostess might do at the theatre, but once in her seat she settled down to enjoy Miss Mary Anderson in *Pygmalion and Galatea* as single-mindedly as any of her guests.

As the winter passed Ned's devotion to Celia grew stronger, though it had little to grow on. She accepted his preference for her company as a matter of course. Not infrequently she showed a preference for his: favouring him occasionally at dances, in spite of the awkwardness he never altogether mastered, and always selecting him as her skating partner (but then, that was only too easy to explain).

Gradually he formed the habit of waiting for her to come

out of school. The minutes he spent on the wind-blown corner
of Calumet and Twenty-Second seemed absolutely endless.
A thousand times in imagination he spied the proud little
golden head in the blue velvet bonnet; when at last it appeared
he was so choked by emotion that he could just manage to
speak.

Celia was never the first to leave, and she never left by
herself. Calmly she tripped down the steps, the centre of her
small group; saluted him with a cool smile, and detached herself without comment from her companions. As a special boon
he was permitted to carry her satchel of books, but she did
not thank him for the service; and if for any reason he failed
to come, he was not taxed later with his infidelity.

What was discouraging was that, with Celia, one could not
make any real progress. She might be perfectly charming if
she felt like it, but that augured nothing for the future: the
day after, it was all to do over again.

In February the influenza season opened. Everybody at 1817
caught it. The young Stacks were sent to bed one by one as
they succumbed, but adults made it a point to keep going, no
matter how bad they felt, with the result that the infection
spread rapidly through the house. Aunt Lydia alone escaped
by shutting herself in her own quarters, seeing no-one but
Janet (who brought her her meals on a tray), and maintaining
cheerfully that it was not necessary to be ill, if one took proper
precautions. She refused to go nearer the children than the
crack in the bedroom door, even on the night when Almira
developed a temperature of 104 and was feared by Doctor
Mallard to be on the verge of pneumonia. Ned was amazed
that Almira herself seemed to think it quite natural: *she*
would have been surprised if her mother *had* come, and accepted Mary Kelly's deputy ministrations unresentfully.

But the Stacks were not the only sufferers. Everybody in
the block was coughing and sneezing—and indeed, thought
Ned, with such a climate, why wouldn't they be?

Chicago had a great many different kinds of weather, but as far as he could tell most of the kinds in winter were bad.

If the wind blew from the east, it might be beautifully clear for days, but so raw that part of Lake Michigan seemed to have got into the house. If it blew from the west—as it generally did—the air was so sharp and dry that it hurt going down. (From the north-west, too, came the terrible blizzards that roared across the plains from Canada with no barrier to break their fury.) And if, by some odd chance, there were no wind at all, smoke from the factories settled over the city in a deadly black pall.

If it snowed, the streets were buried almost immediately. If it thawed after that, one waded through slush for days. If instead it got colder, ice stuck to the pavement as a month-long menace. If it failed to snow freshly at least three times a week, what lay on the ground grew so loathsomely dirty that one prayed for a storm.

These unpleasing phenomena succeeded one another in various combinations with bewildering speed, interspersed, it appeared accidentally, by a few mild, sunny days when nothing particularly awful happened.

For all its vagaries Ned loved Chicago, and his own private corner of it, better than he had ever supposed possible. He was not even too much depressed when his turn came to be laid up, for that did not break his contact with the two great primary facts of life in Prairie Avenue—the fierce, exciting, changeable, unpredictable lake, and the bands of steel that bordered it, with their fleet of fire-breathing, cinder-casting monsters flying eternally up and down the shore.

From his bed Ned had a matchless view of both. Although Aunt Lydia neither smoothed his brow with cologne nor sang him to sleep, as Mamma would have done, Mary Murphy's invalid trays were perfection, and good Mary Kelly ran in to sit with him whenever she could be spared from other duties. He really preferred to read to himself; Almira—now convalescent—was ready to play Halma or piquet if his eyes were tired; and towards the end of the week, when he felt strong enough to appreciate it, a handsome box of chocolates arrived from Gunther's: on the card had been scrawled in bold but childishly formed letters: *"Hurry up and get well!—Celia."*

Spring came in the end of March. Spring in Chicago meant that the wind slued round to the north-east and apparently stuck there, for it did not drop, day or night, for many weeks. It was perishingly cold; rain fell in a never-ending deluge; the greening lawns grew soggy, then frankly turned to mud; the lilac buds, burgeoning timidly, got stuck like the wind and refused to unfold into leaves. Everything dripped with moisture: colonies of earthworms writhed in pools in the cracked portions of the sidewalks, or died ignominiously in the gutters—it was too damp even for *them.*

Ned's first outing after influenza took him down town to lunch with his uncle at "the club" (from the fashionable point of view there was only one). They were to meet by appointment in Mr. Stack's office in the Montauk Block. Ned would have preferred a trip to the lumber yards out on the river, particularly as he arrived to find Uncle Hiram had been called to a meeting at the Lumbermen's Exchange. However, the latter's secretary, an earnest young man in gold-rimmed spectacles named Fanshawe, did what he could to amuse his young guest: Ned was allowed to work the wonderful new typewriter, and shown pictures of mills and samples of woods: white pine from Michigan, yellow pine from Mississippi, Indiana walnut and California redwood that really was red.

Uncle Hiram arrived half an hour late with a brief apology, bade Fanshawe call a cab, and proceeded with Ned to Monroe Street. He had apparently meditated this entertainment for some time: "I've been looking forward to having a real visit with you, my boy."

Ned nodded, hoping he did not look nervous: with all his

fondness for his uncle, the prospect of a *tête-à-tête* held undeniable terrors.

He need not have worried. They entered the dining-room to find it quite full and were ushered by the steward to the round table in the corner at which Uncle Hiram usually sat. The lords of Prairie Avenue had a habit of sticking together: of the eight or nine men already seated Ned had met all but two, and those he knew by face and name: stately, benign Ezra Littlefield, whose silver-haired distinction recalled the Duke of Wellington but was equally appropriate to the president of the Illinois Trust; and an ugly, bald little man with shoe-button eyes and mutton-chop whiskers, who looked like an unsuccessful groom and was actually J. C. Bunner, the packer, the richest man in town except Abner Kennerley.

Everyone shook hands with Ned and asked him how he did; he was then entirely forgotten while the gentlemen turned their attention to lunch.

The food was very good, and there was a distracting array of dishes to choose from: Ned only wished that Uncle Hiram and his friends were not in such a terrific hurry: they shovelled in the most elaborate *entrées* as if they had trains to catch, talked with their mouths full, and for the most part disappeared without taking formal leave of the company.

The two main exceptions to this rule were old Mr. Cobden, who preyed on his beefsteak with lingering carnivorous delight, and Mr. Kennerley, rather surprisingly a dyspeptic: bottles and boxes containing pills were laid in a row beside his place, and he contented himself with a small lamb cutlet and an almost ascetically plain baked apple.

If he ate less than the rest, he talked more. Ned had never heard him so voluble: today he waxed vehement against an organization called the Knights of Labour and its leader, one Powderly, who seemed, from what Mr. Kennerley said, to be a despicable character. Many of his strictures concluded with a petulant "I told Harrison straight out what his duty was!"

or, "I said to Oglesby: 'Won't do, my dear fellow, it simply won't do!' "—which puzzled Ned till he realized, with a start, that Mr. Kennerley was referring to the mayor of the city and the governor of the state. . . . He was also very critical of a mysterious division of time known as the "eight-hour day"—how, Ned wondered, could a day have fewer than twenty-four hours?—of which the other men likewise strongly disapproved. "T'ain't sense!" muttered Mr. Harper darkly, shaking his monkey-head with an omniscient air. "Why, next thing you know, our cooks will be banding together and striking for more than five dollars a week!" And Mr. Littlefield added, in his noble *basso profundo*: "The public will never accept the rise in prices, any more than the working-man will accept an eight-hour wage—that's all there's to it, gentlemen."

From matters of public concern Mr. Kennerley switched suddenly to a more personal irritation: Mrs. Kennerley, it appeared, intended to give a party. Nothing unusual in that, perhaps, except that it happened to be Lent, a season when most ladies restricted themselves voluntarily to quilting bees or lectures on Browning. But it was not the fact of the party itself he objected to so much as the choice of the guest of honour: whom did they suppose Corinne purposed entertaining? Why, an actress—some Swedish woman who happened to be singing here at the opera with Mapleson's troupe! Mr. Kennerley did not know her name—he did not want to know it! In his innocence he had imagined, when his wife first made the proposal, that she was planning one of her ordinary afternoons-at-home, with this Madame What-you-may-call-it providing the programme. *That* he could have understood: no doubt the creature had a fine voice; all the Mapleson stars were first-rate; the other night he himself had greatly enjoyed Minnie Hauk in *Carmen*. But—would you believe it?— Corinne wanted to ask her friends to *meet her,* just as if she were a lady! There was to be no music at all, or, if there were, the lion of the occasion would not be expected to supply it.

Mr. Kennerley called his friends to witness: he was a reasonable man, and a broad-minded one—"But upon my word, to be asked to receive riffraff off the streets—for I don't know how else to describe . . ."

There was a general murmur of sympathy. Mr. Cobden cleared his throat and looked up from the carcase of the prairie chicken he was systematically demolishing to say: "Danged awkward, Abner; you have my sympathy, old man!"

Mr. Bunner picked his teeth in perplexity. "I must say, I shouldn't care for it myself. A man ought to be able to buy a picture, oughtn't he, without asking the artist to dinner? And singers and play-actors are a whole lot worse. The men ain't attractive, and most of the women ain't half-way respectable. Why—there's tales I could tell . . ."

Catching sight of Ned's sleek brown head bent over a mocha *éclair,* he subsided prematurely.

"But rilly, Abner, why don't you put it straight up to Mrs. Kennerley?" solicitously inquired Uncle Hiram. "Tell her you've reason to believe she'll regret it—that there's bound to be criticism in the neighbourhood. Ask her at least to postpone the affair until Easter; perhaps by then she'll have forgotten the notion."

Mr. Kennerley sipped his coffee with a slight shudder, as if it were medicine.

"Don't think I haven't tried everything I could think of! The opera will be over in a week: it's now or never, and if you know Corinne, you know which it's to be. Oh, we're in for it! I just felt I'd better warn you gentlemen in advance, so you won't be shocked when you receive your invitations. It won't hurt my feelings a particle if your wives and daughters prefer to stay home, or even if you decide to stay home yourselves. I only wish *I* were a free agent. Forgive me for mentioning such an absurd trifle: what's your idea, Holland, of the chances of a strike at the Pullman works next month?"

Nothing, thought Ned, more plainly showed the disturbance

of Mr. Kennerley's equilibrium than the fact that he cared to hear someone else's opinion on any subject whatever.

Uncle Hiram had another directors' meeting after lunch; but he took Ned down to the door first, bestowed him in a hansom-cab, and gave him fifty cents to pay his fare home.

"Good-bye, my boy," he said. "No need to thank me in any way, shape, or form. I'm glad we were able to have such a good visit together."

For the next few days nothing was talked of but the Kennerleys' party. Invitations were duly received "to meet Madame Sigrid Svenson"; it became known that Mrs. Kennerley had sent them to everyone on her calling list; and Prairie Avenue was split into two camps—those who thought the whole project too improper for words (though that did not prevent their discussing it endlessly), and those hardier souls who, while reserving the right to disapprove, still admitted they intended to go just to see what would happen.

Aunt Lydia, as Mrs. Kennerley's best friend, enjoyed a marked increase of popularity with her female neighbours. Through her agency the pattern became clear by degrees: festivities were to start at four o'clock with a ladies' tea; gentlemen were asked to come in afterwards, on their way home from their offices; and the affair would conclude with a buffet supper. There was to be music, after all, but only incidentally. Aunt Corinne had thought at first of engaging the Misses Zimmermann, who played duets on the zither, or even of Johnny Hand's orchestra, but had finally settled on the Florentine Quartet, unobtrusive but elegant. Towards the end of the week the menu became public, and that, too, was conventionally smart: oyster patties and chicken salad, six kinds of sandwiches, five kinds of cake, and, naturally, ices from Kinsley's.

What Aunt Lydia, out of loyalty, failed to disclose was that the party very nearly did not come off at all, and that for the oddest of reasons: Madame Svenson, it seemed, strongly objected to being entertained. Through her press agent, Signor

Giacetti, she sent a brief unqualified refusal to Mrs. Kennerley's cordial note; it took a deal of parleying, and decisive intervention on the part of Colonel Mapleson himself—no doubt more keenly alive than his recalcitrant star to the necessity of currying favour with Kennerley and Company—before matters were finally arranged.

"The woman shows great good sense," averred Uncle Hiram, when told of this complication on the eve of the event. "Naturally she don't want to mix with her betters any more than they do with her. Can't Mrs. K. take the hint and let the whole thing drop?"

"Oh, my dear," said Aunt Lydia, "if only she *would!* But I'm afraid it's too late. Besides, you know Corinne; opposition merely makes her more determined. Poor darling, my heart bleeds for her! As far as Madame Svenson goes, I believe she's better than most of her sort. Her first husband was an equerry to Napoleon III; she lost him by death, quite respectably; and her second is supposed to be one of the richest men in Sweden. It was *you* told me that, I think, Rock?"

"Was it, my dear?" Uncle Rock, often included in family conclaves, seemed only mildly concerned. "What seems more important to me is that she is really a very fine artist. I thought her *Aïda* delightful, and Wilkins, who writes for the *Times,* says there's a rumour Verdi is composing a new opera for her."

"I might try telling that to Dora Harper," said Aunt Lydia thoughtfully, "though I doubt if it would impress her as much as the equerry. It's no use saying anything to Emmeline Cobden—she's never heard of Verdi! Come early, Rock, if you can; we must do our best to make the thing a success."

"If our poor little neighbour's not disgraced forever, we know whom she'll have to thank for it," Uncle Hiram concluded, kissing his wife's hand as she placed it in his. "You're a good woman, Lydia, and a mighty kind-hearted one. I only hope this time you've not bitten off more than you can chew."

Aunt Lydia laughed, undismayed.

"I rather look forward to a scrimmage. But if there's any biting to be done, I fancy Madame Svenson is quite capable of it. Ah, I wish it were this time tomorrow and all were well!"

The next afternoon, at ten minutes before the appointed hour, she appeared crackling with efficiency in her best brown taffeta and sables, and declared herself ready for the fray. Ned and Almira were to accompany her, at Mrs. Kennerley's particular request; Aunt Lydia said it would never do to hurt Aunt Corinne's feelings, and she allayed their misgivings by saying they might sit in a corner out of everyone's way and not speak unless spoken to—which was all that was expected of children at parties.

They arrived at the Kennerleys' to find the curtains drawn and the house brightly lighted; behind a screen of palms in the hall the Florentine Quartet were already crisply picking their way through the overture to *Martha*.

Mrs. Kennerley jumped up all-a-flutter to greet them. Ned thought she might have been taken for a prima donna herself, in her brilliant orange gown and black beaded Zouave jacket. He saw Aunt Lydia eye her smart French toque regretfully: Prairie Avenue seldom approved of hats in the house; and never by any chance in one's own.

There was no-one else in sight except Sonny, his big, dark eyes brimming with suppressed laughter, and Celia, who looked heartbreakingly beautiful and exquisitely aloof: as usual, she contrived without words to dissociate herself from her mother's activities. In the dining-room Johnson had marshalled his corps of Negro waiters. . . . For a few awful minutes it occurred to Ned that perhaps nobody was going to come to the party. However, four o'clock had hardly struck when the front-door-bell rang, and for the next twenty minutes it went on ringing briskly.

It soon became apparent that curiosity had conquered—or else local society had decided, with Colonel Mapleson, that the

Kennerleys were too influential to snub: the whole of the feminine South Side was there, with a good slice of the North and the possible part of the West as well.

Mrs. Harper presided graciously over the tea-urn at one end of the long table, and Mrs. Cobden was set to pouring coffee at the other. (It had been Aunt Lydia's idea to keep the leaders of the opposition too busy to make mischief.) Johnson and his minions began to pass trays. The Florentine Quartet, having finished with *Martha,* struck up a lively pot-pourri from *Pinafore.* The four children established themselves in a cosy refuge behind one of the fern-banked fountains under the stairs, making occasional sorties therefrom in search of provisions. Gradually the house became filled with a comfortably increasing hum of voices . . . It was, in short, exactly like any ordinary afternoon reception . . . *or was it?*

Ned saw several women near the entrance start perceptibly when the door-bell rang once more, this time with a peculiar peremptory note. Johnson himself went to answer it, and admitted a man and a woman. They halted for a moment on the threshold to the vestibule: an ill-matched couple, for the man was as little and nervous as the woman was large and impassive. He was a swarthy Italian with a greased black pompadour and bright, harmless field-mouse eyes. But it was Madame Svenson who commanded general attention. She was a very tall woman—as tall as Aunt Lydia—big-boned rather than stout, with heavy hands and blunt peasant fingers. She was also one of the blondest persons Ned had ever seen. Her hair was the colour of pale straw; so were her eyebrows and eyelashes. Her square, ugly face was pale; her gown and bonnet were sober grey and devoid of ornament save for some rows of steel-beaded passementerie no harder than her eyes.

She stood where she was, making no effort to advance, raking the crowd with a blankly insolent stare. Then she dropped her lorgnette and turned to her companion with a hunch of her shoulders—the movement was too brusque and convulsive to be described as a shrug: *"Mon Dieu, Giacetti, c'est un Frauenverein!"*

There was an unhappy and hesitant pause. The ladies had all been told that Madame Svenson was Swedish. Naturally nobody was expected to converse with her in her native language; it had been hoped that she might possess at least the rudiments of English. French they were utterly unprepared for: perhaps most of them had studied it at school—but to be asked to be fluent without preparation . . . ! (Where, oh, where was Mademoiselle? And wasn't *Frauenverein* a *German* word?)

Ned cowered behind the stairs, trusting that Aunt Lydia would be too much excited to remember his linguistic prowess. Luckily Aunt Corinne also spoke French. She rushed up to the big woman, pressed her hand warmly, and broke into a series of pretty, winning phrases of welcome, which would certainly have sealed her fate in Prairie Avenue if she had not already been its least popular resident.

A receiving line was hastily formed, consisting of Mrs. Kennerley, her two foreign guests, and Aunt Lydia, who, though no French scholar, was valuable as moral support. It took a long time to present everyone, but the ordeal was not so bad, after all. In the first place, Madame Svenson, it developed, spoke English passably well. In the second place, she was not nearly so rude as she had seemed at first. Her initial gesture had been one of pure surprise: she soon became quite expansive, smiling often to reveal her large, very white teeth, and accepting the compliments of her Chicago admirers with naïve and child-like pleasure.

To be sure, Mrs. Mallard, who meant well, started off rather ill by declaring that she had "adored" last night's performance of *Faust*. "Ha!" said Madame Svenson. "Dot vos Nordica. You like? *I* don't!" Nor was she enthusiastic about *Carmen*, although she herself had sung Micaëla: "Minnie Hauk? She is vairy common!" But in general she appeared delighted with everything: "I like so moch America. I like so moch Chicago. *Ja,* I like all so moch!"

As soon as formal introductions were over the prima donna, asserting that she could stand no more (this, one hoped, was to be interpreted only literally), settled herself by the fire in a comfortable armchair. With what Mrs. Harper—who had evidently made up her mind to mount the bandwagon—called charming informality ("so *sans-gêne,* you know!"), she took off her bonnet, revealing an enormous quantity of untidy flaxen hair, and toasted her toes on the fender. Ned, watching fascinated from his corner, had thought at first she intended also to take off her shoes.

She drank several cups of very strong coffee and ate a great number of sandwiches and cakes. It was only after the fifth or sixth cup that her eyes began to glaze slightly. She stretched her arms wide, gave a prodigious yawn, and inquired of Giacetti, not at all in a whisper: *"Mais où-donc sont les messieurs? Est-ce que par hasard toutes ces bonnes dames sont des vieilles filles?"*

Every word of this question might not be understood, but its drift was obvious. Mrs. Kennerley hastened to assure her guest that Mr. Kennerley and some of his friends would be arriving any minute. But Madame Svenson did not seem entirely to believe her. She grew palpably bored, yawned many times more, leaned still farther back in her chair, and took little interest in what went on around her. She had eaten, she had drunk, as much as she cared for; she had said everything she had to say to Mrs. Kennerley's good women, and had listened patiently to everything they had to say to her. Now, if they would be kind enough to leave her alone till the men came in, she might be able to snatch a short nap. Although she did not express it, her manner made her meaning clear.

The ladies were less pleased than they had been. Mrs. Kennerley's sprightly chatter died away in a trickle of random remarks. Mrs. Harper said nothing more about charming informality, while her famous smile assumed the frosty glitter of an Alpine view. Even competent Aunt Lydia was reduced to sending a waiter for sherry. . . .

Slowly the group round the armchair began to disperse, while subterranean mutters of "Shocking bad manners!" and "Never saw anything ruder!" were unfortunately heard.

It was at this trying juncture that Mrs. Cobden appeared with a militant air. Plainly out to make trouble, she had constituted herself the spearhead of a minority party of malcontents. In spite of her ruthless self-consequence she did not quite dare assail Mrs. Kennerley or the guest of honour directly, but Mrs. Stack, as a kind of subsidiary hostess, could be called to account for the dissatisfaction of a part of the company.

"My dear Lydia," she said sourly, in a voice that was audible throughout the hall, "surely the comedy has lasted long enough! I should really like to know . . . I have been asked by a number of friends to ascertain . . . Is the woman going to sing, or isn't she? Because if not, we might as well go home!"

Aunt Lydia, Ned thought, was superb. She paled under the attack, but refused to yield an inch.

"My dear Emmeline," she replied, equally audibly, "you know perfectly well that Madame Svenson has *not* been asked to sing—nor will she be, under Corinne Kennerley's roof. If you are anxious to hear her, I suggest that you secure tickets at the Columbia Theater for *Trovatore* tomorrow afternoon. Meanwhile, may I ask Johnson to fetch your cloak?"

In the silence succeeding this report the door-bell rang, and Mr. Kennerley and Uncle Rock, first of their contingent, entered with the caution of African hunters exploring a dangerous bit of territory. Aunt Lydia smiled victoriously at the sight of reënforcements. Mrs. Kennerley ran to meet them, perhaps for the first time in years genuinely glad to see her husband. And Madame Svenson gave a loud laugh as she slapped Giacetti's shoulder: *"Ha! Mon ami—enfin des mâles de l'espèce!"*

The rest of the evening was, as far as Ned could judge, an unqualified success. True, Mrs. Cobden swept home in a temper, and it was believed that a few of the more timorous ladies followed her example. But those who had the courage to stay had a very good time.

Madame Svenson revived rapidly in the atmosphere of masculine homage and remained in high good humour. With the sixth sense of many Europeans, she appeared able at a glance to distinguish the importantly wealthy from the merely well-to-do; to the former she devoted herself, with simplicity and enthusiasm. Other shoulders than Giacetti's were not long in receiving a similar accolade; indeed, Ned was not sure that a knee or two. . . .

Most of the gentlemen seemed pleased. Madame Svenson was, of course, not in the least what they had expected; even Ned, who had never come closer to a prima donna before than a glimpse of Adelina Patti on the Promenade des Anglais, had supposed that Aunt Corinne's guest would be something of a siren. In the circumstances, however, with the room full of wives and daughters, it was surely better that she had turned out to be nothing of the sort. She neither looked like, nor patently was, a dangerous woman. Moreover, whatever slight uneasiness the ladies felt could be checked by the comforting reflection that Sigrid the great was the meteor of a moment: by this time next week she'd have safely left town.

At supper Madame Svenson ate twice as many oyster patties as anybody else, though she spurned the Kennerleys' vintage champagne for some steins of good Milwaukee beer. And when she found that Uncle Rock was an expert pianist she brought the party to a rapturous close by singing for nothing, in a voice as sweet and penetrating as a violin, both arias from *Aïda* and a few graceful Swedish folksongs that sounded as innocent as Mother Goose.

It was almost eleven when she took her departure, hearty and beaming to the last, distributing invitations broadcast to visit her and her husband next summer on their farm near Stockholm.

The Stacks were the last to leave. Aunt Corinne and Aunt Lydia had naturally a great deal to discuss. Mr. Kennerley and Uncle Hiram, incredibly, began to talk about business. The children, by this time growing sleepy, still were able to enjoy snatching a few final dainties from the devastated board under the noses of Johnson and Job, who had started to put the house to rights.

When at length Aunt Lydia called for her veil and her cloak Mr. Kennerley took her hand and thanked her profusely. "I'm sure I don't know how we'd have got through this ordeal without you, my lady. There are no words to express my gratitude. Ah, if only Corinne would see fit to expend such efforts on her neighbours instead of exploiting the town for that crude Swedish washerwoman . . . !"

Mrs. Kennerley looked as if she would like to annihilate her husband. For a moment Ned feared she might be going to slap his face; then, tired to death by the strain of the day, she began crying instead—not loudly or hysterically—but with the hopeless, concentrated woe of a desolate child. The tears poured down her cheeks; she made no effort to stop or to wipe them away.

Mr. Kennerley stood biting his lips with an expression of sorely tried patience; he said nothing. Uncle Hiram appeared cruelly embarrassed. The young people huddled together, not knowing where to look or what to do.

Finally Aunt Lydia roused herself. "Take the children home, Hiram, without waiting for me. You can send Tim back, if you will; I'll be ready to leave in just a few minutes. There, there, my darling . . . I know . . . *I know* . . ."

Placing her arm round the little trembling figure in bright

orange satin, she half led, half carried her friend upstairs. One could only applaud her skill, her resourcefulness, her instant response to the other's need. Yet somehow Ned had never so nearly disliked his Aunt Lydia.

Chapter 8

THE next day, which was a Saturday, Aunt Corinne and Aunt Lydia went to hear *Il Trovatore*. Dressed in full fig, they drove off after lunch in the Kennerleys' carriage, Aunt Lydia at the last a little remorseful, for her husband had come home early from his office, as he sometimes did on Saturday afternoons. Uncle Hiram, however, insisted on being left; he meant to take a nap; later on, if the ladies were gone too long, he could always find a game of poker at the club.

Ned, also, was deprived of his usual companionship: Miss Watson, the seamstress, had just arrived for one of her periodical sojourns and Almira's services as a model would be required for several hours. Feeling slightly at loose ends, he went out into the garden, in spite of the tireless east wind, to watch Tim spading up the annual bed.

Tim was one of his best friends; they'd taken to each other at once; many a pleasant hour had Ned passed in the stable, while the old Irishman varnished a wall, polished the harness and rows of silver trophies won at the Exposition Building, or fed and watered and groomed Queen and Quentin, the plump pair of bays that were his chief pride. With time Ned himself had grown knowledgeable: he had learned at a glance to distinguish a brake from a drag, a *vis-à-vis* from a victoria, and was looking forward, when spring weather finally came (if it ever did!), to holding the reins of the stanhope some Sunday in Washington Park.

Tim's great charm was his solemn absorption in the task at hand. Now, as he turned the wet, greasy earth, carefully removing stones and twigs and bits of glass, he was deep in plans for floral marvels to come. Here would be larkspur—there, snapdragons—in the corner a fine patch of "marry-goldo," French and African, orange and yellow, both tall and dwarf varieties: Mrs. Stack always said they were the usefullest cutting flowers you could grow. "No, I'm not putting in my seeds directly—would I want them to freeze, Master Ned? But the almanac says we're due for a change. That's how spring comes in Chicago—over night 't'will be eighty— an' I want to be ready when the wind swings south."

Ned had discovered the pale green spears of Aunt Lydia's prize tulips pushing up along the path, and was well on the way to becoming an expert on bulbs and their habits, when his eye was caught by an unusual occurrence across the street. The door to the Cobdens' grey granite house flew open, Mrs. Cobden stalked through it, descended the steps, and then traversed the avenue, coming straight towards them. Intention quivered in the angle of her uncompromising jet-trimmed bonnet. She was so wholly concentrated on her errand that she looked neither to left nor to right, but marched straight up the steps to the Stacks' front door, with her head in the air, and rang the bell smartly.

This was odd: never, that Ned could remember, had she called before; in any case Aunt Lydia was out, and Mrs. Cobden ought to know it, for she spent most of her days reconnoitring the neighbourhood from her parlour window; she could hardly have failed to observe the ladies' departure half an hour earlier in Mrs. Kennerley's coupé. But Mary Kelly must have admitted her, for she did not appear again: therefore one could only conclude that Uncle Hiram was the object of her visit.

Ned felt uneasy, though he did not know precisely why. After a few minutes he excused himself to Tim, on the plea of fetching his scarf (the day was raw enough to warrant it), and slipped into the house.

As he had surmised, Uncle Hiram and Mrs. Cobden were in the parlour. The door of course was shut, but their voices were so loud and angry that one would have had to be deaf not to hear what they said.

"There's none so blind as those that won't see!" the old lady was shouting, not very originally. "You poor deluded man —you're the only one in town who's not on to Lydia's tricks. You remember what I told you when you married her: once a loose woman, always a loose woman: as well expect a leopard to change its spots! I tell you it's true, whether you want to believe me or not. I'd never have spoken if I hadn't known you ever since we came to Chicago. As your oldest friend here I thought it my duty—"

"Damn your duty, Emmeline!" Uncle Hiram shouted back, at the top of his voice. "You're an evil-minded, interfering old parrot, that's what you are! It's true you and Hezzy are the oldest friends I've got: that's why I didn't put you out myself ten minutes ago. But you'd better go home now—yes, and stay home, too, for the rest of your life, as far as I'm concerned. And keep your nose out of other people's affairs, if you know what's good for you!"

He flung the door open so suddenly that it nearly hit Ned in the face. The latter flattened himself against the wall behind it to avoid Mrs. Cobden's furious exit.

"You mark my words, Hiram Stack," she cried, turning at the top of the steps to shake her fist at her enemy, "you'll be sorry for this!" (In spite of his nervousness Ned was interested to observe that in emotional crises people really talked the way they did in plays.)

Uncle Hiram's answer was to slam the door shut.

Ned felt thoroughly frightened. Mrs. Cobden might well

have been too angry—and too myopic—to see him, but there was nothing wrong with his uncle's eyesight.

The big man heaved a heavy sigh. His face was still portentously red, but his temper appeared to have calmed down. Silently he beckoned his nephew into the parlour and closed the door to the hall once more.

"My boy, I'm truly sorry you came in just then. I suppose you heard—you couldn't help hearing what Mrs. Cobden and I were saying to each other."

"Not much," replied Ned, glad to be able to be frank. "Really, sir, I was passing only a moment before you came out. I'd no idea of listening . . . I hope you'll believe . . ."

Uncle Hiram's brow cleared; he began to wipe the sweat from it with a huge fine white cambric handkerchief.

"That's all right, then, Ned; of course I believe you. But I do ask this—that you forget the little you *did* hear—dismiss the whole business from your mind as though it hadn't happened."

"Why, yes, sir, I—"

"I want you to promise me, on your honour as a gentleman, that you will never mention it to anyone—not to your aunt, or your cousins—to no living soul. The world," said Uncle Hiram sadly, "is a pretty wicked place. There are plenty of people in it who have nothing better to do but go about spreading cruel, unclean lies about their so-called friends. I'm afraid the old lady who's just been here is one of 'em. Why, on my soul, I'd never have believed . . . but that's no matter now. You understand me, young fellow?"

"Yes, sir."

"And you'll keep your promise?"

"Yes, sir, of course."

"Very well; that's all. I'll not need to refer to this again. Thank you, my boy."

He offered his hand very gravely, and seemed so terribly unhappy that Ned's heart smote him. Something about Uncle

125

Hiram's eyes reminded him of the look in Mrs. Kennerley's
when her husband was scolding her; he had never understood before that men could feel as women did, though denied
the boon of tears.

Tim's almanac proved trustworthy, a day or two later, when
Ned woke to find the sun out, the grass vividly green, and
robins singing in the garden. Spring indeed had come with a
rush. Fanned by a wonderful breeze from the south, Aunt
Lydia's tulips opened their coloured cups to the light. The
buds on the trees, so long imprisoned, burst furiously into leaf,
so that the whole avenue seemed lined with green lace plumes.

The air was warm and languid. Everything felt different.
And Ned soon found that life was different, too. Organ-
grinders played *Le Parlate d'Amor* and *The Wearin' o' the
Green*. The balloon man's whistle was heard almost every
afternoon as he trailed his gay cargo round the prosperous
blocks where business was best. Boys rolled marbles on the
sidewalks, or organized baseball nines in the vacant lots they
had skated over in winter. Ned, who knew he could never
manage to hit a ball under his cousins' skeptical eyes, was only
too thankful that Doctor Mallard forbade him so lusty a sport.
To atone for his defection he strove to develop an interest in
the National League and Tom's and Porter's deity, "Mac,"
the pitcher of the Chicago White Stockings.

Over on the lake front Joe and Jamie Mallard flew their
big red kite. They also offered their friends rides on the broad
brown back of Daisy, the family Alderney, who had ample
grounds to graze on at home and therefore was not driven
out to pasture with the neighbourhood cows in the fields near
the city limits. But this pastime palled when it became known
that the Kennerleys' father had given them a pair of shaggy
Shetland ponies: Sonny and Celia developed a mushroom
popularity at their respective schools.

At home in the evenings, instead of shutting themselves in

their houses and drawing the curtains tight, people sat on their porches, or, lacking them, spread rugs and cushions on the tall flights of front steps that appeared to be justified at last. After the lamplighter had made his rounds there was a good deal of informal calling, particularly among the young people slightly older than Ned and Almira; sometimes the dusk seemed full of laughing voices, the soft metallic buzz of guitars and mandolins.

As soon as the danger of frost was over Aunt Lydia had Tim fill the window boxes at 1817 with petunias and mignonette, and put up smart green-and-white striped awnings to shield the house from the afternoon glare. Her habits, too, changed with the weather: now she no longer waited for Uncle Hiram by the fire, but took up her post every day about half past five in the front parlour window. Flawlessly dressed, every shining strand of hair scrupulously in place, she sat quite still, surveying the length of the street with placid and ruminative interest. There was nothing of Mrs. Cobden's harpy severity in her glance, but Ned had a feeling that little escaped it and that, although she seldom commented upon what she saw, she was deeply delighted by her surroundings.

Early in May a wave of labour troubles swept the country. There were strikes everywhere, but nowhere so many as in Chicago. The Pullman factories shut down; some of the railroads, including Mr. Cobden's, were badly crippled for lack of help; riots took place in the lumber yards on the river, where the handlers were asking for shorter hours and higher pay as the price of remaining at work.

The disturbances came to a climax at a meeting in Haymarket Square: a bomb was thrown—no-one knew by whom— that killed a number of policemen. It was the first bomb that had ever exploded in America; Ned never forgot the excitement it caused. The newspapers were full of it; several prominent labour leaders were jailed on general principles; Uncle Hiram and Mr. Kennerley and their friends talked loudly of

Anarchists and foreign influence, and seemed both angered and terribly frightened by a mysterious element of the population they referred to constantly as "The People."

For days panic reigned in Prairie Avenue. Most of the women were afraid to leave their houses on any pretext. Social engagements were cancelled; cooks were sent to market instead of their mistresses, and children forbidden to stray beyond home territory. It was as long as a week before Ned and Almira were allowed to walk even as far west as Indiana Avenue.

In the midst of these agitations Uncle Hiram was called out of town on another trip, this time to look at some government lands for sale in the northern peninsula of Michigan. He was reluctant to go on account of his family, but Aunt Lydia insisted she was not afraid: Tom was almost seventeen now, and could handle a gun as well as his father. Tim also owned a pistol; he could sleep in the house if necessary. Aunt Lydia had from the first refused to read the newspapers; she was disposed to think the whole thing the invention of a few unscrupulous editors, pandering to the public's taste for gore. Besides, Uncle Hiram had not been feeling well lately. He had complained of dizziness, off and on, all spring; a change of air would be sure to do him good.

Accordingly, after many hesitations and much delay, he left, solicitous to the last; and he had hardly been got out of the house before Aunt Lydia was deep in plans for a picnic party in the country at Jackson Park.

It was only fair to say that the original project had not been hers. Aunt Corinne, the prospective hostess, was as valiant as her friend, though for quite different reasons: Mr. Kennerley had made more fuss than anyone about the Haymarket affair; he'd written open letters to the papers, headed a delegation of businessmen to Mayor Harrison, talked of going to Washington to demand that the President prosecute the labour leaders without delay, or even have them summarily shot.

(Why bother to try such obvious criminals?) In fact, he had appeared so apprehensive that his wife, out of sheer perversity, could do no less than proclaim her utter indifference to danger by the most extravagant possible means.

On the children's account the party was scheduled for a Saturday. It was to consist of Aunt Corinne and Aunt Lydia, Almira and Ned, the three young Kennerleys, and Roscoe's nurse, Nora. (Mademoiselle flatly refused to accompany them; as she had been in intermittent hysterics since the bomb fell, barricading her bedroom door every night and writing her will afresh every morning, she would certainly not be missed.) At the last moment Tom, who had had a "falling out" with Carrie Mallard and was therefore not in his usual form, was added to the list: it then became clear that the Stacks' rockaway would be needed as well as the Kennerleys', and perhaps a pony-cart as well; for Mrs. Kennerley's idea of a picnic was as complex as it was sumptuous. If she were not afraid of The People, she was, it seemed, frankly unwilling to meet Nature on anything like equal terms.

The servants were dispatched directly after breakfast to select a suitable site. When the picnickers arrived about noon they found a long folding-table, with chairs to match, set up in the shade of a big willow tree. The table was covered by a damask cloth, decked out with French china and Aunt Corinne's second-best silver; Johnson and Job, in their uniforms, were waiting to serve an elaborate cold lunch.

Tim and the Kennerleys' coachman, pistols in hand, were bidden to patrol the neighbouring woods, while Edna made coffee over a spirit-lamp and Nora, armed with a long-handled brush, made a preliminary tour of the banquet board to ascertain that no spiders or ants lurked unsuspected in the fine lace-edged napkins.

It was not, thought Ned, sipping cold bouillon from a fragile Sèvres cup, really a picnic at all—just a Kennerley party moved, at the cost of a good deal of trouble, outdoors and several miles south. Aunt Corinne was always saying how much she hated her luxurious surroundings. Now when, for once, she had a chance to escape from them . . . But perhaps that was what she imagined she had done, for she attacked the *crabe ravigotte* with a dauntless air and sampled the Château Yquem (which Johnson kept iced in a George II wine-cooler) as if it were some coarse peasant brew.

Aunt Lydia, always a loyal adjutant, seemed pleased with everything, criticized nothing; nevertheless Ned, knowing her now as well as he did, fancied she thought the whole business rather silly. Still lunch was very good; it was a beautiful day; and the spot Johnson had chosen was undeniably charming.

Jackson Park was mainly a wilderness, existing only on paper in the plans of the architects who were already looking forward to the future World's Fair. There were acres of rough heath, scrub woods, wild marshy meadows waiting to be drained; only here by the lagoon, where dragonflies flashed over lazy brown waters and leaves quivered faintly in the soft May breeze, there had been made a small green oasis of order and peace.

After lunch the men servants cleared the table and started washing up discreetly behind a convenient screen of syringas. Edna waved a huge feather fan above her mistress's head. Aunt Corinne, looking very pretty in frilly white organdie, with unwonted colour in her cheeks, smoked two cigarettes, to Ned's amazement; he had never seen a woman smoke before. Aunt Lydia settled herself on a cushion, her back against the giant willow, and took out her embroidery. (It was the same piece she had been working on all winter; her strong white hands moved so deliberately that Ned sometimes wondered whether they would ever finish it.) Celia produced sketching materials. Roscoe and Nora chased butterflies through the swampy meadow grass. Sonny found an old rowboat and offered to take Almira for a ride round the lagoon. Tom, making a pillow of his jacket, calmly went to sleep.

Ned was beginning to feel he might be forced to follow his example, when the whole party was roused by the sound of wheels on the other side of a little grove of oaks.

Tim did not give an alarm, as he had promised to do if danger were near; in a few moments a phaëton came into view in the lane that divided the grove from the butterfly field; Moonlight was drawing it, and Abner Kennerley held the reins. He was wearing his regular city clothes: frock coat, pale grey trousers, and the tall hat that was Prairie Avenue's badge of consequence: his appearance seemed to add the last touch of incongruity to Aunt Corinne's picnic.

Halting a few paces away, he jumped out, flung the reins to Job—who ran up with dripping hands from the water's edge as soon as he saw his master—and crossed the spongy turf in a dozen quick, nervous strides.

He began talking at once:

"Thank Heavens, I've found you! I could scarcely believe it when they told me at home where you'd gone. My dear Corinne—my dear friend—was this wise? I've not had an easy moment this last hour and a half. But . . . nothing's happened? You're all safe?"

"Quite safe, Abner," replied Aunt Corinne, with a queer little pucker of her mouth. "We've seen no-one to cause us the slightest alarm. And we've finished our lunch. I'm afraid you've had your trip for nothing."

Aunt Lydia looked up with her sleepy-cat smile.

"But now that you're here surely Johnson can find you something. We've had a veritable feast, thanks to Corinne's munificence. What do you say to cold crab and potato salad, and a slice of the best Stilton I've eaten in months? (Where do you find your cheese, my dear? Tebbetts can't do half so well for me.)"

Mr. Kennerley waved food away; he had lunched at the club. Removing his hat, he let himself gingerly down on a corner of one of the rugs; plainly outdoor pleasures were not to his taste.

A chill fell over the spirits of the party. Tom woke up; Celia stopped sketching; Almira and Sonny abandoned their boat and rejoined the others in silence. Only Roscoe and Nora, outside the circle, went on laughing and chasing butterflies across the sunlit field. Mr. Kennerley, Ned had noticed, often had this effect on people, though it was hard to tell why: he seldom rebuked the children as Uncle Hiram did; and today, once his fears had been assuaged, he seemed talkative and positively cheerful. He recounted at length an interview he had had recently at Springfield with the Governor: Oglesby quite agreed with him about the necessity for prompt action; the wicked men responsible for the Haymarket tragedy would be brought to justice within a few weeks; even The People, Mr. Kennerley thought, were coming to realize the difference between Democratic processes and a state of rank anarchy. Chicago, he hoped, would soon once more be a safe place for decent men and women. . . . "That reminds me, though, Corinne, of one of the reasons why I was so anxious to get hold of you—I've just had a telegram from the hotel in Hot Springs confirming your reservations. And I was able to get you and Roscoe rooms in the Arkansas Express tomorrow night. They told us at first at the station they had no space left, but I sent word to Cobden and naturally he found me at once what I wanted. Such tiresome red tape! I'd have the other children go with you, too, if it weren't for their schooling. As it is, I'll be happy to know that you and the little boy at least are out of harm's way."

Mrs. Kennerley sat up straight, at once all rigid defiance. "Oh, but I don't want to go! I won't—I won't! It's too absurd! Why should I?"

"Now, my dear, must we go through that argument again? You know you promised to do what I thought best till the troubles were over."

"Yes—but they *are* over! Everybody thinks so but you. Abner, you're as nervous as an old woman. There's no reason in the world—"

Mr. Kennerley frowned, and assumed the air of overdone patience that always exasperated his wife.

"I don't choose to repeat the whole story. If I tell you it seems best that you should go, believe me, I've sufficient grounds for thinking so. Besides, quite apart from the question of possible danger, it's time for you to take your cure. You remember how much good the waters did you last year; you came back quite made over. And Mallard is sure there's no better hydropathic in the country. This has been a long, hard winter . . ."

"But it's spring now! The weather's been perfect for days. Jack Mallard's an old woman, too; you can tell him I said so. You can't make me do it!"

Mr. Kennerley glanced at Aunt Lydia in a half-humorous appeal for succour.

"My dear lady, do you help me persuade her! If there's anyone's opinion she respects and will follow, it's yours."

Aunt Lydia laid her embroidery aside. She appeared to be considering deeply—as well she might, since it was her invariable policy never to disagree with a Kennerley.

"Hot Springs in May—how delightful it sounds! I only wish I could manage to go myself."

"Ah, if *you'd* come with me, I'd not mind half so much! Say you will, my dear—please say you will!"

Aunt Lydia shook her head smilingly.

"I can't leave the children, with Hiram out of town. And there's the Orphan Asylum board meeting on the fifteenth; I'll have to preside, if Dora Harper doesn't get back from New York. I'll write to you, though, darling, every week, and so must you write to me: the time will pass more quickly than you think."

Mrs. Kennerley wrung her hands, and then picked up her little lace handkerchief and began tearing it to pieces.

"You're against me, too! What shall I do?"

Her air of melodramatic despair seemed excessive for the situation. Aunt Lydia doubtless thought so, but could not say so. She looked a trifle uneasy: one could never be sure what Aunt Corinne might do; a thunderstorm appeared imminent.

Sonny, who had crept close to his mother at the beginning of the scene and sat fingering her dress—it was hard to tell whether seeking protection or offering it—startled them all by bursting into tears.

"Mamma, I don't want you to go!"

Ned felt horribly sorry for his friend. He could not imagine what the matter was, but he thought—and knew that Sonny thought, too—there could be no worse disgrace for a boy than crying in public. Surely only the direst distress had forced him to it.

Mr. Kennerley gave an exclamation, half of disgust, half of dismay. Aunt Lydia for once had nothing to say. It was Celia who created a diversion by overturning her box of sketching materials. She had not spoken since her father's arrival, but now as she fell to reassembling her clips and brushes and pencils and paints she suddenly began to chatter. . . . Of course they'd miss their mother terribly—of course they'd *all* write every week. Now as she and Sonny were to be left alone to-morrow, would she be permitted to ask Almira and Ned to spend the night? They'd talked of doing it all spring; perhaps Papa might let them have the Mallards for supper, too, if Joe would bring his stereopticon; that, too, was something they'd long planned to do.

She looked so bewitching, flushed and smiling as she propounded her scheme, that Mr. Kennerley, whose favourite she was, declared that she might have the whole dancing-class and welcome. He was sorry only that there was not time to prepare a real party. Also, for just a few days more, he preferred not to have the children go down town. What would Celia say, though, to a box next week at Hooley's to see Mr. Pinero's new play, *The Magistrate?*

Celia clapped her hands. Sonny and Aunt Corinne both seemed to have regained control of their nerves; Aunt Lydia resumed her embroidery; the crisis was past. But during the rest of the afternoon conversation stayed largely in the keeping of Abner Kennerley and his daughter.

On the following night, too, Celia ran things to suit herself. She was at her best as a hostess: no-one could have guessed, from the radiant security with which she received her young friends, that she had got back from the railway station just in time to change her dress for supper. Almira whispered that Aunt Corinne had been "awful"; Ned could well believe it. But Celia remained captivatingly gay. In fact, she went to such lengths to entertain the company that it was only after everyone had gone that Ned remembered Sonny had looked very pale and had hardly opened his mouth all evening.

Spending the night at the Kennerleys' was, naturally, a great adventure. In Ned's infatuated eyes everything in his beloved's house seemed uniquely precious. Before retiring he made a tour of his room, marvelling at the height of the ceiling, the thick softness of the bottle-green velvet carpet, the toilet set of *repoussé* silver, the rows upon rows of monogrammed towels, embroidered and scalloped and scented with lavender. It seemed scarcely bearable to turn out the light; when at last he did so, beams from the gas-lamps in the street, filtering through the elm trees on the lawn, made chequered patterns on the wall.

Ned lay awake for some time in his great four-poster bed, thinking over everything that had happened at Celia's party. His heart was bursting with love, and with sadness because there was no way for him to show it. . . .

That was his last thought before sleeping: when he opened his eyes, very early in the morning, to hear a robin singing in the greyness of the garden, he knew suddenly what he wanted to do. He had to give Celia a token—it hardly mattered what, nor how she chose to accept his pledge of devotion. But of course he meant to give her the nicest thing he had.

After making a mental inventory of his meagre store of possessions, it seemed plain that the only suitable object was his Swiss clock with the carved ivory Lion of Lucerne. It was little and fine and delicately wrought, as everything Celia touched ought to be; the pang it would cost him to part with it was nothing compared to the pleasure of offering this concrete proof of his feelings.

The longer he pondered his plan, while the robin went on singing and the ghostly light outside grew gradually stronger, the better it seemed to be. The only trouble was, he was anxious to carry it out *now*—not next day, nor even as late as that afternoon after school. Presently it occurred to him that there was really no reason why he should not get up and dress and run home directly. It would be easy enough to get in the back door at his uncle's, for the Marys were always about soon after five: all he'd have to do was think of some excuse. If he could appear at the breakfast-table with his treasure, surely Celia would realize that he was different from the rest, infinitely more worthy of her trust and affection. . . .

It took Ned some time to screw his courage to the point of action. When at last he stood shivering with excitement on the Kennerleys' doorstep a bright orange streak showed in the sky above the lake. As he hurried down the sidewalk the street-lamps paled in the rising glory; even the lantern on the milkman's cart looked wan and ineffectual.

In front of the tall yellow house he halted once more to catch his breath, and to wait till his rapid heartbeats calmed down a little; he felt bound on an errand of thrilling importance. The noise of a latch being lifted made him start with fright: a man was letting himself out the side-door that led to Aunt Lydia's room. For an instant of terror it appeared inevitable that they should meet. However, the man, though he did not see Ned, had noticed the milk-cart, which by this time was almost between the Stacks' and the Cobdens'. He crossed the garden quietly in the opposite direction and slipped into the narrow alley that divided Uncle Hiram's grounds from those of the corresponding house in Calumet Avenue. He was muffled to the ears in a dark overcoat and wore a broad-brimmed hat pulled over his eyes, but Ned saw at once that it was Mr. Kennerley.

Chapter 9

DURING the next few days Mr. Kennerley came to call every evening; no other visitors were admitted. His arrivals were obvious, but no-one heard him leave except Ned; and *he* would not have done so if his garden window, two storeys higher than Aunt Lydia's, had not been directly above it.

Ned slept badly each of these nights. Like most children of his age, his ideas about sex were vague and rudimentary, but he felt that something was terribly wrong; that Uncle Hiram would be fearfully angry if he knew; that Mr. Kennerley had no business to be where he was—his stealthy withdrawals at dawn were proof of that.

Then, one night, there came a change. Ned did not know till morning what had happened. From twelve o'clock on, the house seemed full of a curious confusion; it was exactly as if someone had been suddenly taken very ill. Lights were turned on and off, doors opened and shut; there was an intermittent murmur of voices; once Ned heard a cry—he could not tell whose, nor even whether it were the voice of a man or a woman.

At the breakfast-table Uncle Hiram was sitting in his regular seat. He explained to the children that he had been able to get through his business in Michigan sooner than he expected. At the last moment he'd caught a fast train to Chicago; there hadn't been time to send a telegram. What he made no attempt to explain was his physical appearance: even with his back to the bright May morning light, the alteration was shocking. His face was ashy pale, swollen with grief, covered with numberless wrinkles that Ned had never noticed before. It seemed incredible that the boys and Almira saw nothing amiss.

In spite of looking ill enough to be in bed Uncle Hiram had ordered his carriage as usual. In the hall Ned handed him his hat; his uncle took it as if he did not quite know what to do with it, stumbled going down the steps, and, for the first time in the six months Ned had lived with the Stacks, failed to look back and wave his hand as he drove away.

Ned could settle to nothing. He was sadly inattentive at his lessons; when he pleaded a headache to Mr. Leslie he was telling the truth, although not all of it. He had no appetite for lunch. Even the letter he had received that morning from his mother failed to give him the pleasure it ought to have done. (Mamma wrote from the Bristol, in Paris, to announce their sailing next week. Papa had had a great run of luck; the Ramsays' affairs had apparently never been more prosperous; Mamma talked of taking a cottage for the summer in Newport.)

In the afternoon he refused to join his cousins in an expedition to the West Side Dime Museum to see "Jo-Jo, the Dog-faced Boy," though that was something they'd planned for weeks. All he seemed capable of doing was to wander from room to room, staring out the windows, trying to swallow the lump in his throat, and wondering miserably whether he were going to be sick to his stomach.

Aunt Lydia, naturally, had not sent for him, nor did she appear at lunch; her room remained ominously quiet the whole day. Ned had a frightening glimpse in the upstairs hall of Janet: if Uncle Hiram's face had paled and swelled with grief, hers had darkened and shrivelled till it was more than ever like a nut—shame, despair, and pure terror were written there for anyone to read.

At half past five the door to the green-and-gold room finally opened and Aunt Lydia came out. She was wearing a beautiful, trailing white lace dress that was new to Ned, and looked, unbelievably, much as she always did. Her mental distress was indicated only by her movements, which were more deliberate than ever; it seemed to require a real effort of will for her to assume her traditional post in the parlour window, and she settled the folds of her gown with a kind of automaton stiffness.

Ned felt he could not stay in the house any longer, much less in the same room with his aunt. He ran out into the garden to wait for Almira, but wherever he went, and even though he could not see it, he went on being conscious of the still, white figure like a statue surveying Prairie Avenue. . . .

Shortly after six a hansom drove up to the door and Uncle Rock got out. He did not seem to see Ned, but hurried up the steps, looking painfully upset. He did not even ring, but Mary Kelly, who must have been just inside the door, let him in. A moment later Aunt Lydia got up—once more, it appeared, in spite of herself—and left the chair in the window.

Ned stayed outside as long as he could stand the suspense. In the hall he all but collided with Mary Kelly, who was crying with her handkerchief to her eyes. When she saw him she exclaimed: "Oh, Master Ned, yer uncle . . . !" and then stuffed the handkerchief into her mouth to muffle her sobs as she hastened away.

While Ned stood there, not knowing what to do, the door to the parlour swung open—just as it had done on the night of his arrival—and Aunt Lydia and Uncle Rock came through it. Again as on that night, Aunt Lydia stooped to take him in her arms: Ned felt her trembling convulsively, and her deep, warm voice broke on a note of anguish: "My dear little boy, you'll have to help me tell the others. . . ."

Before he could answer another cab drew up in front of the house. Doctor Mallard alighted from it and turned to motion the driver down from the box. Ned seemed to know by instinct what they were going to do.

"My dear," said Uncle Rock huskily, "won't you please . . . ? I can't bear this for you."

But Aunt Lydia stood up very straight; her voice sounded strong and quite under control.

"I'm all right. Take Ned to the schoolroom; I don't want him to see . . . And tell him, Rock, what's happened. There's no sense in making a mystery."

As the doctor and his helper bore their burden slowly up the steps a burst of wild wailing rose from the kitchen—the Marys' voices lifted in passionate lament, keening as only the Irish can keen, their sorrow half hysterical joy over the very completeness of disaster.

Upstairs in the schoolroom Uncle Rock explained, in a queer, expressionless voice, that it had been an accident. Uncle Hiram had fallen somehow from the platform at Sixteenth Street on the railway tracks. No-one had seen him fall; no-one even knew how he had got there. He had left his office over an hour ago, but Tim had been driving his horses round and round the Montauk Block without finding a trace of his master. Trains were passing constantly; it seemed a miracle none had crushed him, for he had lain there some time—he might have been lying there yet, if the Mallard boys had not happened by. They acted promptly and efficiently, but it was already too late: Uncle Hiram had broken his neck.

Mixed as Ned's feelings were about Aunt Lydia, he could only admire the extraordinary dignity and self-discipline she displayed in the first bewildering hours of her widowhood. She did not go to pieces, as Uncle Rock had doubtless expected; she would not even let him stay, insisting gently that it was not in the least necessary—if he'd send word to the papers, and see to it that no reporters were admitted to the house, that was all she'd ask him to do.

When her children came home she was waiting with Ned in the parlour to receive them. Her voice hardly faltered: tranquilly she soothed Almira's noisy sobbing and told Tom and Porter, who seemed too stunned to say much, that she counted on them to take their father's place.

It was a warm, still evening. Through the wide open windows was wafted the spicy scent of the mignonette and petunias in the boxes outside. Ned felt it would stay with him as long as he lived. Nor would he forget the fathomless look in the chestnut-brown eyes as Aunt Lydia said, again and again: "Remember, darlings, it was an accident. Dear Papa had been having these dizzy spells all spring. Doctor Mallard was very much worried about him. So you must not think for a moment . . ."

For Ned alone knew that that look was partly relief.

Book II : 1895-1896

"This is the rejoicing city that dwelt carelessly, that said in her heart, I am, and there is none beside me."

(ZEPHANIAH 2:15)

Chapter 1

I N THE end Ned found that by shuffling his appointments and hurrying a little he could just manage to leave for the West on Monday instead of Tuesday. There had not been so much to do in New York as he'd feared when he first came home from Europe: in less than a month he'd been able to sub-let the flat in East Thirty-Sixth Street and sell such of his parents' belongings as he felt he could part with without a pang. Still the ultimate hours were a rush: when he boarded the Chicago Express, late one crisp October afternoon—having at the last moment decided not to telegraph his change of plan to Aunt Lydia—it was with the hope that traces of flurry were not too obvious in his carefully composed man-of-the-world appearance.

Methodically he settled himself and his luggage in his section—there wasn't a great deal of room, nothing like a continental *wagon-lit,* but it would be all right if no-one came to claim the upper berth—; leaned forward to straighten his tie and smooth his hair with the aid of the inadequate strip of mirror between the windows, produced a yellow paper-bound volume of Verlaine, and then gave himself up, for most of the next twenty-four hours, to the voluptuous pleasures of introspection.

He thought about himself and his own affairs concentratedly and uninterruptedly, as only a young man of twenty-two can. . . . How much had happened since the last time he'd been in Chicago! Could it really be only ten years? It seemed a hundred! (The pretty girl and her mother in the section opposite had noticed the Verlaine already—or was it the mourning band on his sleeve?—and were whispering to each other. Ned trusted they'd spied his English bowler and Malacca stick as well. And why hadn't he worn the new blue serge instead of his oldest tweed?) . . . Until very recently Ned had seen none of his mother's relatives since the spring of Uncle Hiram's tragic death, when Papa and Mamma had sped back from Paris to snatch their darling from what had suddenly become, in their eyes, the mephitic atmosphere of Prairie Avenue.

That had been a strained and unhappy time for everyone. Ned remembered well the tension underlying the family interviews. Though nothing was said, much was implied. Aunt Lydia and (most unfairly) her brood had been transformed over night into untouchables. The Ramsays could not scuttle away fast enough to suit themselves. In fact, they had stayed in town only until the smoke had cleared from the domestic ruins sufficiently for it to be known that Mamma had been left a small annuity, the income from which would some day be Ned's. There was, also, a sum of cash that was Ned's outright, on condition that it be used for his education. With emotion Ned learned that this codicil to his uncle's will had been written and signed the day of the latter's suicide. (Now the ladies across the aisle were taking inventory of the foreign labels on his luggage. Ned was modestly proud of their number and variety. Not many fellows of his age, he felt sure, had travelled so widely.)

Thus materially bolstered, the Ramsays discovered the next decade to be the dullest, if on the whole the most comfortable, they had known. Although there were no longer intoxicating ups, there were compensatingly no downs at all. Many times bitten, Papa had at length grown shy of speculation. Not that he'd ever been willing to settle to a regular job . . . but at least they had now a regular income, and a permanent home on Murray Hill. Thence Ned was sent to school and eventually to Harvard, where his career had been quietly creditable: the *magna cum laude* on his diploma, dated last June, was proof of his scholar's abilities, while, socially, he had contrived to remain decently inconspicuous, yet bound on friendly terms to the soundest elements amongst his more distinguished classmates. "Harvard, after all, is a gentleman's college," Mamma had reiterated tirelessly when Papa complained, as he frequently did, that Ned's bills were alarming—though it was true that they were mostly for books and symphony tickets instead of the conventional cards and champagne—and that he himself had been just as well, and far more cheaply, educated at Hamilton near Utica. (Both young Stacks had gone to Yale.)

Mamma had lived to see her son graduate; a week later, without warning, she had died of a stroke, and the Ramsays' wanderings had begun all over again.

After his wife's death Papa appeared to lose interest in everything. His character deteriorated rapidly and seriously: he became peevish, intractable, not to be diverted by any ordinary means. Ned soon realized, as they exchanged England for France, and France for the Italian Lakes, that he and his father had less in common than he had always happily supposed. Without Mamma's warm, active presence to weld them together they often found little to say to each other. The boy's grief and bewilderment could not make him forget that he was, if nothing else, at any rate financially necessary to Papa. But unlimited life *à deux,* in the shifting series of dreary, denationalized *pensions* that were the best they could afford, was a formidable prospect.

It had therefore been frankly a relief to the younger Ramsay when strolling aimlessly after dinner, one languid August evening, along the chestnut-bordered waterfront at Lucerne, they had run full-tilt into the Stacks . . . Aunt Lydia and Almira, Porter, and a young woman with masses of raven hair and rolling violet eyes who seemed quite one of the family.

At the start, of course, a moment of painful embarrassment had to be lived through. Perhaps, if Ned's mother had been there, they might never have got over that, for Mamma's resentment had naturally burned far more fiercely than her husband's. The difficulty was bridged by Aunt Lydia's superb insouciance, her cheerful faculty—which, indeed, was shared by her children—of living completely and unimaginatively in the present. There were screams of recognition and welcome. Aunt Lydia, almost exactly the same—a trifle stouter, maybe, and with braids a trifle redder—gave her nephew a hug and a kiss. Ned, rather shyly, also kissed Almira, who looked, he decided, though she must be nearly twenty-one, like a little girl whose hair has been piled up on top of her head for a joke. (There was much too much of it still, which made it perplexing to achieve the flat, tight effect now universally the fashion.) Porter, grown huge and too hearty, grasped his cousin's hand so hard that it hurt: the dark young woman with violet eyes was presented as his *fiancée,* Miss Fanny King, of Washington. (No, Tom wasn't with them; he was at home in Chicago looking after the business, and Carrie, his wife, was there looking after him—Ned hadn't forgotten Carrie Mallard, surely?—and the children: Aunt Lydia was now a grandmother twice over!)

After a preliminary babble of greetings the party adjourned to a garden restaurant on the lake. There, over ices and raspberry syrup, it developed that Aunt Lydia and her young people had just reached Switzerland on their way from Milan to Paris and expected to spend a fortnight at the Schweizerhof. The Ramsays, too, were recent arrivals, having been driven north by the heat at Bellaggio; they had taken rooms in a house some distance back from the water, which, Papa maintained gallantly, had a beautiful view and was quieter than "those big international hotels." Aunt Lydia agreed, looking thoughtful; she was, Ned knew, recalling, in order to budget it mentally, the exact figure of Uncle Hiram's legacy. Meanwhile the young people chatted pleasantly, comparing their foreign experiences, while a full moon rose nobly over the Alps and silvered the waters at their feet.

It was late when the two groups finally separated, their plans already laid for an excursion on the morrow. In a day or two it had become quite a matter of course for Ned and his father to stroll down the hill from the Pension Beausite after breakfast to see what the Stacks had in mind to propose—or, rather, as Aunt Lydia remarked grimly, to inquire what new mess of train, boat, or diligence tickets the porter at the Schweizerhof had determined to sell them.

Aunt Lydia, it was not surprising to learn, thought Europe overrated. She had never been abroad before; it was not likely that she would come again. This summer she'd felt it her duty to make the grand tour for Porter's and Almira's sakes, but she confessed to Ned, on their first outing together, that she had been horribly bored in Italy . . . the heat, the dirt, the flies, the beggars . . . "and all those miles and miles of galleries, my dear: Fanny *would* stop in front of everything mentioned in Murray!" She was living at present in anticipation of a brisk shopping bout in Paris before sailing home with her loot to dazzle Prairie Avenue. In the meantime, though willing to admit that Switzerland was an immense improvement on what she had hitherto endured—the beds seemed clean, the people honest, and the food at least not liable to poison you— she could discern nothing in the scenery so vastly superior to the Adirondacks or the White Mountains as to compensate for the hardships that had to be suffered in order to see it.

With stoic indifference and a perfectly blank pair of eyes she permitted herself to be conveyed to various celebrated points of view . . . "Very nice, my dears; very pretty indeed," said Aunt Lydia kindly, on top of the Rigi. "And now where, children, did that wretched man tell us we were supposed to take our tea?"

Such enthusiasm as she did display was saved for the linens and laces in the booths along the quay. Napkins and table-cloths, doilies and runners, were bought by the dozen; a handsome store of handkerchiefs laid by. "They'll do for souvenirs for our friends at home; and if later in Paris I find things I like better, I can always, you know, give these to the servants!"

Aunt Lydia purchased a watch apiece for her children. She had also brought with her from Chicago a considerable assortment of alarm-clocks and other timepieces, all of which were said to be out of order: Mrs. Harper, it seemed, had given her the address of a little man behind the cathedral who was excellent at repair work, and much cheaper than anyone at home.

On such errands it was her custom to lean heavily on Ned's advice, and not only for his proficiency in German: she had not lost the flattering trick of consulting his taste that had first won his heart so many years ago.

Without actually saying so, Aunt Lydia made her nephew feel that she was much pleased by the way he'd turned out: though he still buried his nose far too often in books, he had, she insinuated, grown into an amiable and delightful young man.

Ned scarcely knew what he thought of Aunt Lydia. But he could not deny that her coming had saved his summer. And later when, this time by design, their paths crossed once more, it seemed like coming home to find the Stacks snugly ensconced in a luxurious suite at the Meurice in Paris.

In these final weeks of their sojourn on the continent the ladies' buying had reached a pitch of frenzy. Even Miss King, who had studied art quite seriously at home and meant to copy the Mona Lisa some day when she had time, was caught up in the whirl as she was made to realize the awful importance of choosing a trousseau. Ned was now in daily demand. He escorted Aunt Lydia and her charges to Worth's salon, and to sundry speciality shops where his French was as useful as his German had been in Lucerne. Aunt Lydia got everything she wanted, and she wanted a very great deal; but she had a kind of peasant shrewdness and was willing to bargain for hours rather than pay a penny more than she thought an article was worth.

Ned also accompanied his aunt to the studio of Monsieur Carolus-Duran, who was painting her portrait in full dress—low-necked white satin with all her pearls. Dora Harper, she said, had been done last year by Sargent; but Aunt Lydia would have scorned to imitate her neighbour; besides, might not a Frenchman be even smarter?

In the evenings, when they could neither shop nor see sights, Ned took pleasure in introducing his relatives to the best restaurants and to such plays as he deemed simple enough to be only partly unintelligible to Americans, and proper enough for what was intelligible not to shock them. Here, again, he was able to do what no-one else could: Porter didn't know the difference between plain *ragoût* and *tournedos Rossini,* and would have been quite as likely to expose his womenfolk to the doubtful attractions of some unspeakable Boulevard farce as to the chillier charms of a *matinée classique* at the Comédie Française.

On these expeditions Papa sometimes joined them; oftener not. He had seemed from the first—perhaps out of loyalty to his wife's memory—slightly ill-at-ease in Aunt Lydia's company. Moreover, in Paris he was almost on home territory: he had his *coiffeur* who shaved him daily; his favourite newspapers; the English library; regular whist at his club.

Ned could not tell what his father's opinion was concerning the sudden *rapprochement,* for somehow they had both shrunk from discussing it. For himself, once he had taken the plunge, he was unfeignedly glad—there were no Ramsay relatives, the Stacks were all he had—and never gladder than when, about a month after their return to Paris, Papa came down with double pneumonia.

Aunt Lydia then repaid handsomely the many trifling services of the summer. It was true, she was still as unserviceable in the sickroom as in the days of Ned's childhood. Illness depressed and death appalled her to the point where she was willing to do anything at all to keep them at bay. It was Aunt Lydia who insisted on having Papa removed at once from his *pension* in the rue Washington to the most expensive room in the best hospital in the city; she who paid for doctors and nurses and all possible luxuries for the invalid. The supreme proof of her attachment came when she cancelled her plans for sailing as soon as the specialist in charge pronounced the case a grave one.

As long as there was hope Aunt Lydia remained implacably cheerful. When it was gone it was her fortitude, the lacquered self-possession with which she went on being her tranquil, worldly, commonsense self, that pulled Ned through his second bereavement, kept him from going to pieces emotionally, and helped him more than anything else to face the ordeals ahead. She insisted on his joining them on the homeward voyage, which was an immense comfort in the melancholy task of bringing his father's body back to rest by his mother's. Later, when she said good-bye to him in New York, it was with the promise of a speedy reunion. "I'll not forget you, my dear. If something turns up to your advantage in Chicago, I'll let you know directly. It would be the best thing in the world for you to get clean away from here for the winter. Besides, there's nothing to keep you now. I'll write . . . I'll write. . . ."

Aunt Lydia was better than her word. She had been home hardly ten days when Ned received a telegram saying that the post of assistant music critic on the *Chronicle* was open to him.

"Salary twenty-five dollars a week to start—editor Asa Shipley great friend of mine—of course shall expect you to live with us," read the message. Love from all, and Aunt Lydia was devotedly his.

Such an offer he could not refuse. Though Meredith and Henry James had succeeded Dickens as models to be emulated, Ned was still as sure at twenty-two as he had been at twelve that he meant to be a writer. He had a boxful of manuscripts none of which he'd shown even to intimate friends. As with most young authors, the problem of the first commercial step had seemed insoluble. Now, thanks to Aunt Lydia . . .

At this point in his reflections Ned looked up to see that they were already a long way up the Hudson, it was growing quite dark, and not only his immediate neighbours but half the rest of the population of the car besides had departed. With a sigh he decided to follow their example, postponing the rest of his meditation till after dinner.

Chicago, the next afternoon, struck him as noisier and dirtier than ever. Of course, it had grown a great deal: as he entered his cab at the Twelfth Street Station, after handing his trunk check to the Parmelee man, a mass of new buildings on the horizon caught his eye. Some of these were impressive enough, but it was samenesses rather than differences he noticed most: the faint fresh-water dampness from the lake, the haze hanging over the city that was due far more to smoke than Indian Summer, the frantic tempo of traffic on Michigan Avenue, the scurrying pedestrians who risked their lives at every corner—nothing else was quite like it, and nothing else, Ned felt (though he did not know why), was quite so good.

The way grew more familiar the farther they drove. Here was the row of queer little shops in Sixteenth Street it had always seemed rather sporting to visit; the corner of Indiana where they used to keep their trysts with the balloon man on Sunday mornings after church; that rough bit of sidewalk just before the home stretch where Almira had once fallen while chasing a hoop and skinned her knee. . . . Then Prairie Avenue at last, and Prairie Avenue just as he remembered it, a calm and stately oasis after the clamour and confusion of the boulevard. The two lines of brown-leaved elms were taller now—in some places they almost met overhead—and the houses, the funny, ugly, somehow lovable mansions of Chicago's merchant princes, were undoubtedly grimier. Yet all was so nearly as it had been that Ned would hardly have been surprised to see a plump, pigtailed Almira march down the street swinging her satchel of school-books, or Joe and Jamie Mallard, in Indian warpaint and feathers, emerge whooping from behind the Harpers' lilac bushes as they prepared to scalp the long-suffering Maud.

It was like turning back the pages of his life to the winter he afterwards grew to think of as the dividing line between childhood and adolescence. So much, both good and evil, had happened to him then—much more than he'd been able to realize at the time—that he was almost fearful of disturbing his memories. That was why he had wanted to steal upon his past and recapture it at one blow. It was not until the cab was nearly at the door that it occurred to him perhaps his unexpected arrival might upset the family. But it was too late to worry or wonder. . . .

The tall yellow house was also just as he remembered it. The summer awnings had been taken down, but owing to the warm weather the flower-boxes were gay with petunias, a little straggly at the end of the season. Though the lawn was still green, the leaves had fallen from both trees—his aunt's prized horse-chestnut and a humbler but healthier cottonwood. These had been raked together in a neat pile, and the boy who must have done the raking—a half-grown, shock-headed youth in overalls—was busy now spading up the tulip borders. (Why wasn't it Tim? But Ned recalled that Almira had told him Tim had died two years ago.)

In the front drawing-room window sat Aunt Lydia, as Ned

had seen her so many times. This time the window was open to permit her to survey and direct the labours of the shock-headed boy. "Not quite so deep, Denny," she was saying, in her low, lazy voice, as Ned's cab drew up at the door. "If it's all the same to you, I don't want my bulbs to flower at Christmas."

Then she saw her nephew and rose with a smile and a rustle of mauve silk. "Why, child, what a pleasant surprise!" But she did not look surprised; Ned knew she made a point of not being.

The tall figure disappeared to reappear a moment later on the front steps. Aunt Lydia kissed her visitor warmly and seemed charmed by his explanation (which he'd hit upon suddenly in the brief respite afforded him) that he'd been so eager to see her he felt unable to wait an unnecessary twenty-four hours. "I only hope it hasn't put you out, my coming earlier."

"Not in the least, my dear; your room is quite ready for you. I thought perhaps you'd like the same one you had before. T'won't matter to a soul but Mary Murphy; we'd planned a fatted calf for tomorrow, with all the family assembled. I've an Englishman now in the stables, and he won't do a thing but drive the horses—but Denny will help you with your bags."

Mary Kelly, as rosy and smiling as of yore, though there were streaks of silver in her pretty black hair, had come to the door. . . . For the next few hours Ned felt he'd managed to get into a waking dream. It was strange yet soothing to find life at 1817 going on precisely as usual. The room with the birds on the wall and the Viennese porcelains looked as if he'd left it only yesterday. Doubtless the scarlet silk hangings had been renewed—no goods lasted long in a soft-coal city— but they were indistinguishable from their predecessors. Mary Kelly accompanied him upstairs—as if he hadn't known the way! Ned almost waited for her to draw the curtains, as she'd done on that first November night, and turn up the gas before lighting the fire under the black marble mantelpiece. But what nonsense! The sun hadn't set; it was too warm for a fire; besides, the old gas-jets had been replaced by modern electric globes.

Downstairs there had been a few alterations. The gold from Aunt Lydia's room seemed to have spread into the parlour, which now had quite an airy French appearance in keeping with the Carolus-Duran installed in state above the fireplace. When the newly electrified crystal chandelier and side-brackets had been switched on, as they were before dinner, the effect was positively dazzling.

In the dining-room, too, electricity made a cheerful, perhaps even a too cheerful, difference. The drop-light over the table, though masked by silk, shed such a fiercely relentless glare on the ferns beneath that they appeared to be withering under one's eyes.

Ned dined alone with his aunt and Almira, the former regretting that there had not been time to bid the boys and their wives (for Porter was now married, too) to a feast worthy of the name. Mary Murphy, however, had dauntlessly, on no notice at all, prepared a series of courses such as Ned had not coped with since his last meal at the Stacks'.

Almira had come in rather late, just in time to dress for dinner. She seemed glad to see her cousin, but tired and a little subdued, which was accounted for by the fact that she'd spent the whole afternoon teaching a kindergarten class at Hull House.

"I don't know what girls are coming to," said Aunt Lydia, with the air of a bewildered duchess. "When I was young it was considered quite enough to sew once a week for the poor. I'm sure the Sisters of Bethany still meet regularly at Grace Church just as they always did, but nowadays everyone wants to go slumming. I won't say a word against Miss Addams— of course, she's a wonderful woman and all that—but it frightens me to death to have Almira wandering about alone in that awful Halsted Street neighbourhood. Goodness knows what might happen—I never draw an easy breath till she's safe at home again!"

"Oh, Mamma," said Almira gently, "all my friends do settlement work. And you know I never go alone: Florence and Maudie and I take turns driving the girls over to the West Side. There isn't the slightest danger."

"Then this bicycling craze," continued Aunt Lydia, who was not easily checked; "and those horrid short skirts you wear! All I can say is, if that's the New Woman, I'm thankful I'm past forty-five and don't have to be one."

"I thought everybody cycled," Ned ventured to say.

"Everybody does!" cried Almira. "I'd be absolutely out of things if I didn't. I saw Mrs. Trask on a wheel yesterday; she's years older than Mamma; and Florence told me her mother's had one sent out from Field's—she practises in the laundry yard, where no-one can see her but the servants."

"Then Dora Harper's an even bigger fool than I took her for," rejoined Aunt Lydia. "After that, don't be surprised at anything—you may even see Mary Murphy and me some morning riding tandem to market!"

She laughed; the little crisis was over. However, the mild bickering between the ladies, which persisted throughout dinner, struck Ned as even more of a novelty than electric burners. It was more flattering, perhaps, than the oblivious kindness with which Aunt Lydia had been wont to treat her daughter, but one could not help feeling that these trivial complaints were the symptoms of some deeper disunion.

After dinner, as it was such an unseasonably warm evening, the family took rugs and cushions and made themselves comfortable on the front steps—or, rather, Ned and Almira did, while Aunt Lydia settled herself in a folding chair on the threshold above them. A wind had come up from the Southwest that fluttered the leaves still clinging to the elms and brought them down in crisp, rustling showers. (Not here ever the slow, soundless drift that made an elegy of European autumn.) It also carried an unmistakable whiff from the tanneries and rendering factories out in the Stock Yards district. Almira wrinkled her nose with distaste: "What a horrid smell, Mamma! Perhaps we'd better go in." But Aunt Lydia smiled. "I like it—it means Chicago to me!"

Tom and Carrie Stack, who had been summoned by telephone (another innovation), strolled round the corner from their house in Calumet Avenue to greet the newcomer. Porter and Fanny were dining out; besides, explained Aunt Lydia, they lived away up on the other side of the river, having taken an apartment in the Perugia, one of those new-fangled flat buildings at the farther end of Pine Street. "Can't think why they did it—it don't seem civilized to live all on one floor— and they might as well be in Timbuctoo for aught I see of them. But Fanny was set on it; she's made up her mind the North Side is smart; and of course Porter thinks whatever *she* wants must be perfect."

Tom and his wife looked just the same: the former a darker and slightly less bumptious edition of his brother; Carrie still freckled and friendly, very much the young matron absorbed by domestic cares. Presently Uncle Rock, who had been dining at the Calumet Club, also joined the party; he had aged a good deal, having gone quite grey and stoop-shouldered. But his smile was as gentle as ever and, like everyone else, he was delighted to see Ned once more in Chicago. "I hear you're setting up as an authority on music, young fellow. Bless me! I'll never dare perform for you again." . . . At which Ned laughed and blushed, and declared that, on the contrary, he was going to need all the help he could get in order to hide his abysmal ignorance.

For a time after Uncle Rock's arrival Tom attempted to introduce a few topics of general interest, such as Governor Altgeld's chances for reëlection and the recent troubles in

Cuba. His mother, however, brushed them brightly and firmly away. Of course Altgeld was no good—he was a Democrat, wasn't he? As for the Cuban revolution, it was a sad business; Aunt Lydia had come to the conclusion not to read any more about it. As long as there was nothing one could do to help, what was the sense in harrowing one's feelings unnecessarily? For her part, she thought it much more interesting to discuss the odd behaviour of Emmeline Cobden, whose old husband had just died, leaving her five million dollars, the balance of his fortune to be used to found a library for scientific research. "They say she's so mad she won't even wear black, and she's thrown out every book on the premises!"

There was also a disquieting rumour that the Harpers had sold their Romanesque palace to Levi Zinderstein, the clothing-store magnate, and were having plans drawn for something even more awesomely mediaeval near Lincoln Park. "What can they be thinking of, to move right out into the wilderness at their time of life? But I had it from Janet, who had it from the milkman, who's keeping company with Dora Harper's Nellie; and people like that are always sure to know. They say they're moving before Christmas and going to the Virginia Hotel till their new place is ready. I wish you'd find out from Florence if it's really true, Almira. I suppose they're trying to keep it dark as long as they can because they're ashamed of themselves, and well they may be."

"Oh, I don't think Mr. Harper would sell to a Jew, Mamma," said Tom. "He's got too much respect for his neighbours for that."

"We've never had anyone living here before that everyone didn't know all about," said Carrie doubtfully. "Mother Stack, will you call on Mrs. Zinderstein?"

"Certainly not, my dear; life's much too short to waste breaking in new people. But I shouldn't mind meeting her husband, in a semi-business way, of course. You might bring him to see me some evening, Rock. I'm told he's a positive genius at investments, and my bank balance is sadly depleted after a summer in Europe. I don't know why you and Tom wanted me to put so much into those Venezuela oil stocks: there's liable to be war there, too, and then they'll not be worth the paper they're printed on. That's nothing to talk of, though, on Ned's first night home. Tell me, has anybody seen the Littlefields' new coach-and-four? I hear Ezra paid a thousand apiece for the horses and they've all got short tails as they do in the East. If that's so, I don't know how I'll manage Simms; he's been badgering me for weeks to let him crop Queen and Quentin."

Up and down the avenue from house to house the talk moved casually, till almost every family Ned remembered had been mentioned. There was but a single significant omission, and that one Ned supposed would have taken precedence of all others. It was true a Kennerley had been alluded to when Uncle Rock saluted Almira with a playful "Fancy my finding *you* at home, miss! Is your young man still off with his ponies at Lexington?"

Almira replied demurely: "The trotting closes there this week, but Sonny is going to Louisville before he comes home."

It was too dark to tell from her face how she felt, but Aunt Lydia tossed her head and snapped, quite fiercely for her: "Lazy jackanapes! How his father can let him . . . at his age!"

Carrie hastily inquired whether her mother-in-law were going to bid for a box at this winter's charity ball, and the slight tenseness passed.

Ned felt delicate about reverting to the subject; but later in the evening he drew Carrie aside to propose a tour of the garden, and asked in a low tone whether there were anything wrong with the Kennerleys.

"Wrong?" said Carrie, in her loud, clear voice. "No; why should there be? They're richer than ever. I suppose, of course, you heard that Mrs. Kennerley died?"

Ned nodded; and Carrie went on: "Let me see, it must have been a year ago last spring. She was on a visit to some of her relatives in Charleston. Celia was with her, too. Quite sudden it was at the end, though Father said afterwards he wasn't a bit surprised. Did *you* know, Ned—but I'm sure you couldn't have known; none of us young people here had the slightest idea—that she'd been a drunkard for years? It must have been a relief to Mr. Kennerley when she went. If only he hadn't . . . almost right afterwards . . ."

Carrie paused uncomfortably. But Ned wanted to pursue his line and he did pursue it. "Yes; 'if only,' you say? What's the matter, Carrie? Has there been some trouble between the Kennerleys and the Stacks?"

"Trouble?" said Carrie, with her trick, which the Mallards all had, of repeating the key word of her interlocutor's sentence. "I should just think there had been—about as bad as it could possibly be! It must have hurt Mother Stack dreadfully; I don't know who else ever bothered to be so kind to that poor flighty creature. And even after her death the old ties were kept up for a while. Hardly a night went by that Mr. Kennerley failed to call. . . . I know there was a lot of talk— there always is when a man has so much money—but I never paid any attention to it. Anybody could see it was just a beautiful, disinterested friendship. Oh, I don't say it mightn't have ripened into something warmer . . . and I'm sure I can't think of anything more suitable . . . after all those years of intimacy! But then . . ."

Mrs. Tom halted at the end of the path farthest from the house and threw a glance over her shoulder to make sure the party on the steps was out of earshot.

"Yes," said Ned; "and then?"

"Have you ever heard of the Framinghams?" (Even Carrie, the unsubtle and unsuspicious, felt it proper to let her voice sink to a whisper here.) "But you *can't* have—how silly of me! It seems so natural to have you back that I keep forgetting you've only just arrived. . . . Well, my dear, they're new importations and all the rage just now. They're very smart; they're from the East"—Carrie spoke as if she were simply stating the same fact in two ways—"New York and Newport —that kind of thing. Albert Framingham—the men call him Bertie—is a broker; he came here just a year ago to open a Chicago office for his firm. I don't think they've got much money; they've rented that little old wooden cottage just south of the Bunners—you know the one I mean? It's nothing to look at, but Mrs. Framingham is clever at decorating; she's fixed it up to look quite elegant. They had letters to people out here, of course, and they hadn't been settled a month before they seemed to know everybody. *She's* not at all pretty, but she dresses very well—on what, I can't imagine—and she has what Mamma calls the social gift; goes everywhere and entertains at home at least three times a week. . . . No, I've not been to her house; she hasn't any use for Tom and me; she likes people to be very rich, or very prominent, or both. . . . Well, Ned, you'll hardly believe it, but the moment she met Mr. Kennerley and found out he was a widower she went after him tooth and nail and never rested till she got him. He's tied to her apronstrings now like a lovesick schoolboy—hardly dares call his name his own. Mrs. F. has refurnished his house, hired a whole lot of new servants, and receives at his parties just as if she had a right to—think how bold and horrid! The worst of it is, Mr. F. doesn't seem to mind what they do as long as he can sell Mr. K. enough stocks and bonds to make out. Tom says I don't understand, that's just the New York way—thank God I *don't,* is what I tell him! It must be very hard on Mother Stack. She never sees the Kennerleys any more. And it's hard on poor Almira, too. Sonny is in love with her, you know—he always was, even when they were nothing but children. I guess you remember that, Ned. It's made a regular rift between the families. And now that Celia's coming out—they couldn't have a ball last year because she was in mourning—Isabel Framingham's taken hold and is running the whole thing as if she really were her mother."

"And what," asked Ned, "does Celia say to that?"

"Oh," said Carrie impatiently, "you never can tell what Celia thinks about anything, can you? She's a cold little piece —I doubt if she cared much for her own mamma. And I guess she's smart enough to realize that Mrs. Framingham has perfect taste: as long as they're together morning, noon, and night she might as well get the benefit of it. But then I can't make Celia out, and that's a fact."

"What is she like now?" Ned tried to sound coolly offhand.

"What is she like? Oh, prettier, if anything. I must say, she's turned out a regular beauty. Half the boys on Prairie and Calumet are in love with her, including our poor Jamie. Why, sometimes he don't eat or sleep . . . but she'll have none of 'em. I guess she thinks there's no-one good enough for Papa's darling. Horrid, spoilt minx! There! I never could be fair to Celia Kennerley, I dislike her so. There's something else about her, too . . ."

Carrie broke off as they approached the steps once more.

"What else?" persisted Ned.

But Carrie only shook her head, firmly virtuous to the last.

"No," she said; "I won't say any more, or you'll call me a cat. Wait and see for yourself what you think of her. Come, we'd better join the others; I don't want Tom to think I'm trying to flirt with you; besides it's almost time for Janet to be fetching out the tea."

Chapter 2

THAT night Ned lay long awake, thinking over what Carrie had told him. He supposed he ought to be pleased that Aunt Lydia at last had got what Mamma would have called her "come-uppance." If his parents were still alive, they would, he knew, have grimly rejoiced that their erring sister had been punished in the very way her pride must find hardest to bear. Yet he could not help feeling a perverse twinge of sympathy for the sinner.

At the same time one had to admit she made no bid for it; neither did she act as if she herself had done anything to be sorry for. Her position seemed even more secure than during her husband's life. Then she'd had his name to protect her, and his fortune to buttress it; but now the money was hers, every penny. Uncle Hiram had made one of those old-fashioned American wills, so irritating to ultimate heirs, in which everything was left unconditionally to the wife. (It was, of course, assumed that the children would be handsomely provided for; that, however, was entrusted entirely to their mother's discretion.) People had talked, Carrie said. . . . Yes, but after all nobody could say for sure what Lydia Stack's relations were with Abner Kennerley. Even Papa and Mamma, full of gloomy suspicions, had been completely in the dark. Even Uncle Rock, her best friend, tortured by jealousy and faithful in spite of himself, had not had any more precise information than the three guileless young Stacks. Only two people in the world really knew . . . and, of those two, one was dead and the other would sooner have died than reveal his unsavoury secret. The upshot of Ned's cogitations was a resolve, as staunch as it was indefensible, to stand by Aunt Lydia, come what might; this was coupled with a lively curiosity concerning her rival.

Next morning, armed with explicit directions—for "Downtown" Chicago was more or less a mystery to him—he took a State Street cable-car to Randolph and then walked west towards the river. The neighbourhood was sooty and squalid, a congeries of theatres and bars, cheap shops and shoeshine parlours, but filled, like the rest of the city, with a vigorous, individual life. Most of the people looked swarthily foreign—how rare the Anglo-Saxon type was growing! They pushed and jostled, swore and spat. Ned was thankful he knew how to find the number he sought without asking advice.

The *Chronicle's* editorial offices were housed on the third floor of a dark, depressing building near City Hall. The Negro who tended the lift lounged unconcernedly at his post; the lift was old and rattled as it ran. Ned began to be nervous; he yawned several times; there was a lump in his throat he could not swallow.

The office itself seemed peaceful, almost deserted. A boy with carrot hair and freckles, who looked rather like a Mick version of one of the Mallards, was seated at a desk in the hall by the door, teetering back and forth in his chair and snapping a rubber band to relieve his solitary tedium.

To Ned's surprise Mr. Shipley was ready to see him at once. The latter's sanctum gave on a sunless inner court peopled by pigeons; it was small but neat; there was none of the confusion Ned imagined inseparable from newspaper offices. No-one was in the room but a stenographer—also small and neat—who left when Ned entered, and Mr. Shipley himself.

As soon as Ned saw him he realized he had seen him before: this was one of the men who used to call on his aunt—not frequently; but there was no mistaking the tall, round-shouldered frame, coarse iron-grey hair, gimlet eyes, and long upper lip of Asa Shipley.

The editor rose and offered Ned his hand. He also smiled, which cancelled the intimidating effect of the heavy furrows on his brow by bringing into play a whole network of laughter lines round his strongly marked mouth.

"Your aunt has talked to me a great deal about you," said Mr. Shipley, who spoke with an up-country Massachusetts twang. "She seems to think you're qualified to act as our assistant music critic. What do you say about that—hey?"

Ned felt instinctively this was no time to be too modest; one's best foot might be just good enough for Asa Shipley. He mentioned his qualifications briefly: he was a fair pianist, had studied theory and music history extensively at Harvard, heard concerts and opera in America and Europe since early childhood.

"You're really fond of music, then?"

Ned opened his eyes. "Very, sir. I'd have chosen it as my profession if I hadn't cared more to write instead."

"Good. The reason I ask is that many a man takes the first job offered him without realizing he may soon grow to hate what he's temperamentally unsuited to. The best start in newspaper work is genuine enthusiasm for what you're doing. I don't know but what too much technical knowledge is a handicap. Frank Twitchell, our first-string critic, can't tell A from B on the keyboard, but he's got natural taste, is a smart journalist, and knows what the public like to read. That's the way to go at it: say what you think and don't be afraid to show what you know, but remember whom you're writing for, and that you're not required to turn in a doctor's thesis on the classical symphony every time Thomas schedules Beethoven on the programme. Go straight to the point—see what I mean?"

"Yes, sir; I do." Ned had finally managed to swallow the lump. "I'll do my best, I promise you, if you're willing to try me."

Mr. Shipley smiled again. He was evidently a man of few words, and gave his caller the chance to say fewer still.

"You can start in at once. Your salary, as I told your aunt, will be twenty-five a week. That's a good deal of cash for a young chap without experience. I'm gambling on her hunch that you're just what we've been looking for. I've known Mrs. Stack for years and have the highest regard for her judgement —in such a case it hardly seems sufficient to call it intuition. Your hours—well, they'll be what you make them. Twitchell covers drama, too; he'll need you to pinch-hit when the opera's on, and so forth. There's plenty of leg-work you can save him besides; he's too valuable a man to waste time on routine interviews. Make yourself useful to him any way you can; you may learn a lot from Frank, if he cares to teach you. I'll turn you over to him now. Come this way, boy."

Franklin Twitchell was found at his desk, in an alcove adjoining the local room. The desk was complicatedly untidy; so was Mr. Twitchell, who was a stubby, nervous, round-faced man of about forty, very nearly bald, but with a compensating pair of magnificent bright yellow handle-bar moustaches. (Ned learned later that these were not waxed, though their owner groomed them so constantly—careless as he was in all other respects—that they appeared so.) A total contrast to his dignified employer, he plainly shared his dislike for formalities.

"How d'y' do? How d'y' do? You're Ramsay, are you? I've heard about you from the chief. Damned good thing you've come. I'm near crazy this week—four first nights in a row, and the orchestra starting their season at the Auditorium. Know anything about music?"

"Not too much," replied Ned frankly, divining at once that best feet were liable merely to trip and annoy Mr. Twitchell.

"That's all right. Not a soul in this town will ever know the difference. Like it, though, I guess?"

"Oh, yes."

"Well, *that* won't last. Wait till you've been in the game as long as I have. Lord! To think I actually used to pay money to hear a string quartet! . . . This is your desk, next to mine. Use a typewriter? . . . That'll help. We ought to have a room of our own, but you'll have to make out the best way you can, same as I do. Sometimes the racket's enough to split your eardrums."

Ned observed that it seemed quiet enough now, but Mr. Twitchell snorted. "Wait till it gets near deadline, round eleven at night. That's just when we poor devils have to do our work, too. Another thing: as we go to press so early, don't flatter yourself you'll ever hear the last act of an opera under any circumstances. They say the end of *Traviata's* mighty fetching, but I couldn't tell you about that. *First* acts, now . . . I suppose I've heard the opening of that same *Traviata* thirty or forty times in the last ten years. My God, man, do you realize the whole damned thing's in waltz time? Da *dum,* da *dum,* da *dum,* da da da *dum,* da *dum* da, da *dum* da, da *dum* . . . Hell, what's the difference? You starting right in? Let's see, then: you'd better take Melba on Sunday (I've an Actor's benefit) and Bloomfield-Zeisler at Steinway Hall on Wednesday. (That's easy; nobody cares a rap about pianists anyway, unless they're Paderewski.) Give 'em each five hundred words; it's twice what they're worth. And as long as I've four opening nights, you might as well do Thomas on Friday afternoon as well. He's good for a thousand if they'll give you the space; better keep it under eight hundred, if you can; say, seven-fifty. Happen to know whether he's playing anything special?"

Ned answered that the concert was opening with a Bach Suite, to be followed, he thought, by the Haffner Symphony.

Frank Twitchell made a face. "Never heard of him. Seems to me they said it would be Mozart."

Ned opened his mouth to explain, but then closed it again: there was no point in getting on the wrong side of one's boss on the very first day.

As a matter of fact, before they parted, he felt he was on

his way at least towards the right one. Frank Twitchell was a friendly little man; he ended by asking his new assistant to step across the street for a drink, which they had in a sombre room that smelled of beer and cabbage and reminded Ned of some of the humbler restaurants he'd known in Munich.

Over their steins of Pilsener Mr. Twitchell confided that he had been born on a farm near Cedar Rapids, and that when he was eighteen and just out of school his one ambition had been to get to Chicago. "I thought it was the Great White City sure enough, but I've had over twenty years of it now and Lord! How tired I am! I'd give my soul to light out for the East. This is a hick town like every other town in the Middle West—it's bigger than most, that's all, and dirtier by a good deal. New York's the only place for men in our line: don't you forget it and get stuck here before you know what you're doing. You ain't married yet, are you? . . . Thought not. Well, don't marry for a while, if you can help it. That was the mistake I made, though Sal's a wonder and we get along fine together. But what can you do with a wife and three kids? They've got to eat, damn it! I can't afford to take chances, and old Shipley knows it. He keeps my nose to the grindstone because I've let him see how much that forty-dollar cheque each week means to the Twitchells. Oh, sure, the job is mine for life, but I'll never be able to better myself. Times when I think of the plans I used to make . . ."

After taking leave of Mr. Twitchell Ned cut across town to the boulevard and turned south. It was a dark day with a cold wind off the lake, but Ned was too happy to care about the weather. He had a job—his first job! What could be more thrilling? Now that the strain was over he admitted to himself he'd thought all along something would go wrong. Even though Aunt Lydia had promised that the matter was as good as settled, his natural pessimism forbade him to believe her.

In his present mood he was disposed to admire the many new buildings on Michigan Avenue. The Auditorium caught his eye by its air of rich solidity; he supposed he'd get to know it well this winter. Across the street loomed the Art Institute, dignified and severely classic; but Ned missed the glass Exposition Building and the old Armories whose sites it had usurped: why was his country so hasty about sweeping landmarks away? In Europe they clung to the ancient good and modernized by degrees; one could return to Paris and London year after year to find their faces substantially the same. But change was the very essence of American cities: six months' absence from Chicago, and the whole horizon might have altered. (Was that very tall tower in the distance the famous Masonic Temple?)

His next business was to find a place to lunch. Due deliberation led him to the Richelieu, which he remembered his father had once told him was the only house in the Middle West that "did you really well." He ordered the most expensive meal on the menu, hesitating between a Chablis and a Pouilly *fuissé* just long enough to show the waiter he knew his way round a wine list.

Then he went home to tell the good news to Aunt Lydia.

Five o'clock found him dressing for his third and, oddly, most momentous interview of the day. It took a long time to choose his shirt and tie; he knotted the latter a dozen times, still dissatisfied with the result. As he brushed his smooth brown hair diligently, and removed an almost invisible speck of lint from one blue serge shoulder, he thought what a fool he was. Women never minded how a man looked; moreover, the things in his appearance he most disliked—his narrow chest, pointed nose, and slightly sallow complexion—there was no remedying.

How strange it seemed, at the Kennerleys', for the bell to be answered by a stiff English butler instead of black, smiling Johnson! Stranger still to realize that, wander upstairs and down as one might, never more would one come upon little Mrs. Kennerley, flitting like a lost bird among her hoard of possessions. . . . As Ned followed his supercilious guide through the entrance hall he saw that the great Moorish lantern was gone—a good thing, too: it had always looked like a malevolent eye, defying you to enjoy yourself under those baleful beams. A crystal chandelier, grandiose enough for Versailles, had succeeded it. The whole scheme of decoration, in fact, was determinedly French. If Aunt Lydia's house had gone rather shiny and gay, Mr. Kennerley's appeared to have suffered a Midas touch—there was gold everywhere. . . .

The drawing-room proved the climax to this parade of Rococo run riot—a wilderness of tortured gilt furniture, arch marble Cupids, Aubusson carpets, and frivolous silk brocades. Even a dozen lighted lamps and a cheerful fire in the grate could not relate such a splendid apartment to life; profusion had overreached itself; here was the brittle impersonality of a stage-set or of something seen in a museum.

A moment later all was forgotten as Celia rose from a spindle-legged couch *à la Pompadour* to receive her visitor.

Ned stumbled on the threshold—something he'd vowed he'd never do—and held out his hand, saying he hardly knew what.

"How do you do?" said Celia, in the cool, silvery voice he remembered so well. "I'm glad to see you, Ned. I've ordered tea; sit down—no, here beside me; I want to look at you."

Ned obeyed in a trance. The couch was stiff and uncomfortable; it creaked and one couldn't lean back. The young people stared at each other for a minute in silence; then Celia, with a little laugh, looked away.

"You haven't changed," she said. "I mean, not in the things that matter. Of course, you're a man now, but I can see you're still the same Ned Ramsay you used to be."

Ned did not know whether this were meant as a compliment or not.

"You're just the same, too," he told her. "Only a hundred times prettier, Celia."

"Am I?" said Celia, without coquettishness. "I wonder . . . I'm pleased you think so anyway."

But was she the same indeed? Ned, taking shy inventory of the friend of long ago, came to the conclusion that his first impression had been wrong. Of course, she was taller: small as a child, she had grown into a Lily Maid of slender, willowy grace. In general, however, her charms had been heightened, not altered in quality. The rose-leaf skin and delicate features were much as they had been, the golden gleaming of her hair undarkened; the great blue eyes still gazed straight ahead with unabashed assurance. Her manner was perhaps a shade less imperious than in the past; she was no longer preoccupied with convincing other people of her vast importance. But what worried Ned chiefly was that there seemed to be a veil of ice, impalpable, estranging, drawn between her and the world: she saw you, and she didn't; she heard you, but it really didn't count—and this it was that made him fear he'd lost his old playmate for good.

He and Celia, he found, had not very much to say. They were scrupulously polite: each asked how the other did, expressed proper sympathy for respective family bereavements, inquired decorously as to future plans. Celia showed a certain languid interest in Ned's job on the *Chronicle*. "Does that mean you can go to everything you want without paying for it?"

"Not quite," Ned replied, smiling. "I'll have to be content with Twitchell's leavings—naturally he's got first choice."

"Papa has a box at the Auditorium. I go to the concerts sometimes on Saturday nights. Will you go with me?"

"I'd like to very much, whenever I can. But of course I'll have to be there Fridays, too, when I've a review to write. And I imagine you'll have plenty of more exciting things to do this winter. You're coming out, aren't you?"

"Oh, yes," said Celia; "I suppose I am. It's a bore, isn't it?

What is there to come out for, when you know everybody already?"

"Why do you do it if you'd rather not?"

"Oh, well, Papa would be so awfully disappointed. And what would I do if I didn't? There's nothing *to* do in Chicago. I'd like to go abroad; maybe I shall in the spring."

"Europe's very interesting. But I think Chicago's interesting, too. I like it here, you know."

"Do you? I can't see why. Of all deadly holes . . . ! But then you're a writer, and writers can find something to amuse them wherever they are—even in a mausoleum like this!"

Celia cast a scornful glance at the gilded wilderness and shuddered, not altogether theatrically.

"Do you live here all alone with your father since your mother died?" asked Ned, as it occurred to him that loneliness might well be Celia's main trouble.

"Yes; most of the time. Roscoe's at Groton now. One of Papa's friends persuaded Papa to send him to boarding-school, and I'm sure I don't miss him. Sonny's here off and on, of course. He's supposed to be learning the business, but I must say I don't know *when*. Last summer he went salmon-fishing in Canada, and then shooting in Scotland; now he's down in Kentucky with his stable of trotters. A hard life, isn't it?"

Ned said he thought he would find such a programme more arduous than writing reviews for the *Chronicle*. "I'm not much of a sportsman, you know." He was fairly well able to guess who "one of Papa's friends" might be; evidently Celia did not care to introduce the interloper's name until she had to. However, when the butler brought the tea-tray he announced that Mrs. Framingham was at the door and would like a word with Miss Kennerley if it were convenient.

"Oh, I guess it is," said Celia, half stifling a yawn. "If I don't see her now, it'll have to be later. Do you mind, Ned?"

"Not at all." Ned was rising already. "I ought to be going anyhow."

"Oh, goodness, I didn't mean for *you* to leave! Please stay— if you don't, *she* will, for hours—and I'm dining at the Bunners'. Show her in, Grimshaw."

Ned's first reaction on beholding Mrs. Framingham was that he must have seen her before. Since, however, he was unable to place her as he had placed Mr. Shipley, it seemed clear that the lady must simply resemble a number of other people. She had, in fact, the great American face—or, rather, one of various well known American faces. This was the pointed edition—sharp-featured, thin-lipped, with vigilant eyes and a smile as metallic as it was punctual. Her salient trait was an almost aggressive elegance: she was a fashion-plate from the top of her exquisitely coiffed head, with its saucy bonnet contrived out of cherry-red ribbons and sheer audacity, to the toes of the grey suède slippers that matched her faille afternoon frock.

Pausing in the doorway, she put her head to one side, pursed her mouth roguishly, and exclaimed: "Dear Celia, forgive me —I thought you were alone!"

"That's all right, Aunt Isabel," said Celia, indisposed to respond to the other's archness. She presented Ned; Mrs. Framingham smiled again, though her eyes looked harder than ever, and said: "Oh, you're Almira Stack's cousin who's come to live with them."

Celia explained that Ned was going into newspaper work.

"Is he, my pet? How interesting," said Mrs. Framingham, looking profoundly uninterested.

"And he's a very old friend of mine," added Celia firmly. "I haven't seen him for ten years."

"Dear me, what a tremendous lot you must have to say to each other! I apologize for intruding on your flow of reminiscences. I'll not stay, I promise, more than a minute or two. Miss Dodd at Field's just sent out these samples, and I couldn't resist running across the street to show them to you. If your party's to be on the fifteenth, we've none too much time, you know. Perhaps Mr. Ramsay will pardon us. . . . This is No Man's territory, but if he's very good, we might let him take a peep. . . ."

"Don't mind me," said Ned, affecting to be wholly engrossed by the slice of layer-cake Grimshaw had handed him.

"Then, darling, here we are! . . . Now what do you think? To be sure, white's the classic choice for a débutante, and you'll look like an angel; but there's a pink *peau de soie* that would be simply entrancing with your colouring, and a blue *séduisant* I've quite fallen in love with myself. Do you see what I mean? . . . A plain round neck and gigot sleeves, of course. . . ."

Mrs. Framingham had opened her bag and flung her samples broadcast on the spindle-legged couch. There were a great many of these, which she shuffled about with bewildering rapidity till Ned could scarcely have told them apart. Celia sat still while her friend went on casting lengths of silk and satin across her chest; the latter kept up meanwhile a constant admiring twitter: "*Chiné's* always smart—and with your figure . . . But isn't that corn-coloured *duchesse* the most perfect match for your hair? Darling, I don't know . . . Your father wants you to have the best of everything, so I think we needn't hesitate in ordering at least half a dozen. Abner's so generous! The shops out here are marvelous. I don't mean to say they haven't everything we've got at home and more. Still, if there had been time . . . I've the most wonderful little woman in New York, quite hidden away in the West Thirties. She'll do anything for me, *anything!* The cleverest hands, and that French touch, don't you know. . . . In the spring, if I take you to London . . . But, darling, for your very own ball, which is it to be?"

Celia, who had remained motionless, as indifferent as one

of the Cupids above the mantelpiece, gave a delicate yawn—
and then smiled to take the sting away.

"I'll take the white *crêpe-de-chine,*" she said: no more.

"Perfect! Quite perfect! How clever you are! Just what I'd
have chosen for you myself. The white it shall be, then."

"And—ah—thank you very much for your trouble, Aunt
Isabel."

"Trouble, my dear? It's been the greatest pleasure. I'll telephone to Miss Dodd first thing in the morning—or, better
still, pop in to see her in person—and we'll get things *en train*
as soon as possible. I'll let you know without fail the earliest
date she can promise a fitting. Darling, as long as I'm here,
I believe I *will* take a cup of tea, after all. I've had an exhaust-
ing afternoon battling the crowds down town. . . . Quite
clear, you know. . . . That's right; no, nothing to eat; thank
you, dear."

Mrs. Framingham relaxed—as far as she ever did so—in a
bergère across the hearth from the couch where Celia and Ned
were sitting; struck a felicitous pose, and began to chat gaily
away. . . . She told them how much she loved Chicago.
Really, no-one could imagine . . . she herself had not guessed
. . . Her friends in the East had warned her she'd never be
able to stand it a month; they'd thought her quite mad when
she insisted on coming out with Bertie. Even now they
wouldn't believe her when she wrote she was perfectly contented and had no desire to go back. The skyline, you know,
so dramatic—and the lake, so beautiful—though Bertie found
the winds occasionally rather hard on his chest. But it was,
above all, the people, the dear, kind, genuine Chicago people
. . . How could she hope to express her gratitude for the wonderful hospitality, the unparalleled warmth, with which the
city had taken them to its bosom and made them feel at home?
New Yorkers were by no means so cordial. Boston was even
worse. (Mrs. Framingham, it appeared, was a native of Boston.) Nobody, however, had been so good as Celia's papa.

(Mrs. Framingham pronounced it *à l'anglaise* with the accent on the second syllable.) What *hadn't* he done? Loaned them a carriage, introduced them to his friends, got Bertie at once into the Chicago Club and the Saddle and Cycle . . . Why, he'd even found them their house, the quaint wooden cottage where they were so idyllically happy! . . .

Celia cut this rhapsody short by remarking prosaically that her father had owned it for ages—he'd taken the place in part settlement of a debt when his competitor Mr. Somers went into bankruptcy—and no doubt it was a relief to get it off his hands.

Ned had an instant flash of recollection: did Celia, too, remember the white-faced man stumbling out of her father's library, so many years ago?

Mrs. Framingham, to whom the name Somers conveyed nothing, switched the subject suddenly to the young people themselves. Ned was diverted by the dexterity with which she managed, without resorting to crude catechism, to extract a complete *dossier* of Celia's social activities during the last twenty-four hours: in a very few minutes she became mistress also of the facts concerning his parentage, family connections, and probable income. As nephew to her predecessor Ned guessed he must be suspect; still more so, perhaps, in the rôle of a possible suitor for Celia. In order to test his theory he prolonged his call deliberately, amused by Mrs. Framingham's determination to stay as long as he did. (Was it to forestall hypothetical advances to her charge, or merely that she wished to avoid providing conversational fodder for him and Celia?)

Celia, who had hardly opened her mouth since "Aunt Isabel's" arrival, at length glanced at her watch and excused herself: it was time to dress for her dinner-party. Ned took formal leave of his hostess; Mrs. Framingham gave a high little shriek, crying out that she herself should have been at home long ago. Bertie would never forgive her—he always expected her to be in her own drawing-room, with the shades drawn and the fire lighted, on the stroke of half past five.

"If I disappointed him, he'd stop at the club till all hours drinking brandy and soda; you know, brokers' offices out here shut so shockingly early. . . . Good-bye, angel; rely on me for the frock. I'll see you tomorrow, no doubt. Are you going to the Fortnightly? Dear Mrs. Mallard is reading her paper on Ruskin. They say she's been getting it up for a year and I think we really ought . . . *Sesame and Lilies!* It seems to me I doted on it when I was a schoolgirl. . . . Oh, my dear, though, I almost forgot—are you free on Sunday week? I'm giving a tiny supper for Paul Pisarcyk—you know, the Polish violinist. It's not really a party—just half a dozen intimate friends who care for good music. He's playing that afternoon at the Auditorium, and after the concert he comes to me—he always does, when he can. Quite informal, my pet, and no young people: Paul so dislikes modern American youth. But you know I can do nothing without you. . . . You'll come? Splendid! Your papa's already accepted, and of course I want Sonny, too, if he should surprise us by getting back from Louisville. . . . Good-bye, Mr. Ramsay; I hope you'll come to tea some afternoon. Let me see, we go different ways, don't we? *A rivederci,* then . . ."

Ned laughed to himself all the way home at the pointed manner in which he had been excluded from the invitation. However, the following week, after his first initialled reviews had appeared in the *Chronicle,* he received a card reading:

Mr. and Mrs. Albert Framingham
request the pleasure of your company at supper on Sun-
day, October 27, at 7.30 o'clock
Music   *R.S.V.P.*
                                              2120 Prairie Avenue

Chapter 3

Nᴇᴅ's first few days at the *Chronicle* were not so hard as he had feared. In the beginning, of course, he was too conscientious: made copious notes on the margin of his programme, consulted his watch with nervous persistence, fairly scuttled across town to the office on the stroke of ten-fifteen.

At that hour the local room was all buzz and apparent turmoil, knee-deep in papers, restless with typewriters and telephone bells, which basic disturbances were punctuated by recurring cries of "Boy!" from reporters who'd finished their "leads." (These were but sluggishly answered, Ned noticed, copy-boys being constitutionally exempt from the frenzy prevailing as deadline drew near.) The hub of excitement was the big central desk where, tousled and harried, Fitzroy, the night city editor, presided over his frantic kingdom.

To start with, Ned was sure he could not settle his mind to write. But nobody paid any attention to him; the mounting confusion was none of his concern; all he needed to do was to make a quick mental sketch of what he wanted to say —words followed as always with blessed ease.

In twenty minutes he succeeded in turning out five hundred of them about Madame Melba, allowing himself a few mild satirical gibes at the old-fashioned prima donna "concert party," with its complaisant contralto; the tenor and baritone, faintly *décontenancés* (no, he must say that in English) as they ploughed through the quartet from *Rigoletto;* the tireless flutist, so handy for cadenzas. . . . Timidly he submitted the sheets to Frank Twitchell, who had come in quite a little later, but had already "knocked off," as he expressed it, more than half of his piece on Irving and Terry.

Mr. Twitchell halted his own composition long enough to race through his junior's maiden effort and cross out an adjective or two ("A little too fancy, my boy, for our pap-fed public!"); then he nodded. "It'll do," he said briefly; and Ned had never felt happier.

Thomas and Bloomfield-Zeisler were, naturally, a good deal less trouble, since they deserved the serious consideration one wanted to give them. Mr. Twitchell made no comments, either favourable or unfavourable; but when both articles were published substantially as written, with a modest "E.R." at the foot of each column, Ned felt launched on his professional career. This feeling was strengthened at the end of the week by the receipt of his salary: he handled the limp notes almost reverently, unable to believe his services could be worth so much money.

The days were less interesting, largely spent collecting items for the "Sunday spread" from the dingy, indomitable tribe of theatrical press agents, and sorting them out for his chief's approval. On the whole, however, Ned was content with the way things were going.

During the initiation period he had little time at home. But it *was* home: there, too, it appeared, he fitted in well and his society was a positive benefit to his aunt and cousin. More than once his presence alone had served to appease the small differences that rose too frequently between them. These were not actual quarrels—both Aunt Lydia and Almira were too good-tempered to quarrel—still something was amiss where all had been harmony.

Such an occasion presented itself on the day Ned's invitation to the Framinghams' party arrived. The same post had also brought a card for Almira: the question at dinner was, what to do about it. Almira herself was not enthusiastic: "They've never included me in anything before. I don't see why they begin now. Besides, Mamma, *you're* not going."

"I've not been asked," said Aunt Lydia equably.

"Well, I think Mrs. Framingham *ought*—"

"Why should she? I haven't called on her yet."

Ned suspected the little pause that followed meant: "No—
nor do I intend to." But his aunt's voice was still firmly cheerful as she added: "There's no reason on earth why you
shouldn't go if you want to. In fact, I think you'd better. I'd
really like to know what goes on at those precious Sunday
nights. Mary Bunner told me she hardly slept a wink the time
Calvé and Sothern were there; the piano kept up till two in
the morning, and her Delia heard from Mrs. Framingham's
cook that after that the whole party went down to the kitchen
and scrambled eggs—it took half the next day to clean up
the mess. But as long as Ned can look out for you . . ."

Ned pointed out that he expected to decline on the plea
of being in mourning, and Aunt Lydia's face fell a trifle.

"That's true, my dear, of course; I forgot. What a pity for
you! And for me, too: Almira never notices anything; she
might as well not be there, for all the good it'll do. Wear your
green *mousseline de soie*, baby, and I'll let you have my emerald bangle to go with it. I meant to give it to you at Christmas anyhow."

Almira replied that Mamma was too sweet to lend her the
bangle . . . "but truly, *truly*, I don't want to go! I'd much
rather not. I can't see why Mrs. Framingham—"

"You know very well why you've been invited," said her
mother crisply. "And why you've got to go. If you don't, that
woman'll think I kept you away on purpose. Now don't be
silly, child; there's no use in discussing it. A little more apple
pudding, Mary."

During the rest of the meal the pros and cons were debated
with spirit. The issue was still uncertain when Ned was called
from the table by the telephone: Mr. Twitchell, it developed,
wanted an interview with Paul Pisarcyk, who as a compatriot
of the all-conquering Paderewski should be of interest to read-

ers of the *Chronicle*. The violinist was scheduled to arrive in Chicago the day of his concert and refused to see the press before playing; he was also departing thence that same night for Detroit. Could Ned, therefore, undertake to tackle him in his dressing-room, as Twitchell himself would be busy writing reviews?

Ned explained the situation as he saw it, and Frank Twitchell chuckled with glee. "Jiminy! I'd clean forgotten you were one of those society dudes. That makes the whole business as easy as pie. Grab hold of your man in the lady's parlour —he'll be a damn sight readier to talk after he's had a few drinks of champagne."

So, since Aunt Lydia saw no impropriety in combining pleasure with duty, Ned penned an acceptance instead of regrets. Almira, too, was "most happy" as long as she hadn't to go alone; and on Sunday evening the cousins, arrayed in their best, set forth on foot (the Framinghams lived too near for it to be worth while ordering Simms and the brougham).

They did not talk much on the way. Almira, who wore a lace scarf over her hair, seemed deeply engaged by the effort of holding it straight and at the same time keeping her long skirts off the pavement. Never a chatterer, she was even quieter now than she had been as a little girl. Perhaps she was not very happy any more—that one could understand—but even her griefs were placid.

"I'll be glad to see Celia again," said Ned, just to make conversation. "I haven't seen her since the first day I was here; my evenings have been pretty busy, you know. I wonder if Sonny's got home and will be there, too."

Almira stopped at the Framinghams' gate and flung her cousin what from any other woman must have been called an inscrutable look. (Was the mantilla to blame?) Then she lowered her eyes with a blush.

"He's home—he'll be there," she said.

The Framinghams' cottage stood some distance back from

the street behind a tangle of smoke-blackened shrubbery. Gothic and angular, its high peaked roof and quaint scrolled *façade* were no longer in fashion—or, it might be, could not compensate for sundry inner deficiencies—for the place had stood tenantless and forsaken a number of years. Now, smartened by shiny chocolate-brown paint, with lights streaming hospitably from every window, it presented a far more cheerful appearance.

Within, the effect was unexpectedly sumptuous. Mrs. Framingham, Ned observed, might coax her friends to embark on uncharted seas of Louis XV, but she herself had been wise enough not to discard her ancestral Chippendale and Sheraton, which filled without crowding the two little communicating parlours.

Both rooms were busy when Ned and Almira made their entrance. Plainly the guest of honour had just walked in: a blond mop-haired young man, with the mask of a quizzical lion cub, he had taken his stand near the door to the hall to receive the congratulations of his admirers. His accompanist, also young, also blond, also mop-haired (though, appropriately, to a more limited degree), stood one modest pace to the rear, keeping a wary eye on his employer as he accepted his own meed of praise.

"Paul, this is Mr. Ramsay—*Ramsay, the critic,*" said Mrs. Framingham magnificently, adding in a rapid, absorbed, hostess's voice: "Wah-wah-wah, Mr. Ramsay." (It was pleasant to note she was human enough to have forgotten the accompanist's name.)

She then turned as duty bade her to Almira, but Monsieur Pisarcyk did not wait for any more introductions. His face lighted up as he seized Ned by the elbow: "Ah, sir, you are ze gentleman from ze newspaper of whom I have heard! *Allons donc,* let us sit down together while I explain you a little how I make my career."

This was an unlooked for stroke of luck. In the pursuit of

his errand Ned had foreseen some opposition, if not from
Pisarcyk himself, at any rate from the Framinghams. On the
contrary here he found himself, not three minutes after his
arrival, actually being encouraged to take his place on the
long settee in the window next the principal celebrity of the
evening. From that vantage point, since nothing was expected
of him save to smile agreeably as he made a few mental notes
on his companion's voluble reminiscences, he was able to enjoy
a sweeping survey of the general scene.

At a glance one saw that the Kennerleys had not yet appeared. The Harpers were there, and the Littlefields, stage
properties of time-honoured local significance. (How odd their
air of pre-arranged informality, the resolution with which
these stately elderly folk embraced what they obviously felt
to be their hosts' *vie de Bohème!* Not thus had they viewed
poor Aunt Corinne's similar attempts in the days of long ago:
but it was smart now to be Bohemian!) There were also
several younger couples from the North Side—did Mrs.
Framingham agree with Fanny Stack that it was the coming
part of town?—and a man and a woman whom Ned had not
met. The first was Dan Maxwell, a brash, bullet-headed young
fellow from the West (Elgin? Aurora? or some remote Da-
kota?), whom Uncle Rock had spoken of recently as the
cleverest lawyer in the city. The second, a dark, brooding
creature in a tea-gown of rust-brown cut-velvet, had features
a touch too pronounced for private life; it was hardly surprising to learn that she was Mrs. Terence Bannister ("Mrs.
Terry" for short), a well known Irish actress who was presenting a season of Ibsen at Hooley's.

Bertie Framingham moved easily amongst his motley assortment of guests, bearing a tray with decanters and glasses
(just as if he were the butler!). He was a tall, athletic-looking
man, with the high colour and fixed stare of a tailor's wax
dummy; Ned ticketed him instantly as the kind of well-born,
well-bred New Yorker who was that and nothing else. Al-

lowances had to be made for a broker's professional joviality; he clapped old Mr. Littlefield on the back with a loud, unamused laugh that stopped just short of a bray, and insisted on pouring Holland Harper some sherry in spite of the latter's protest that he never drank before dinner. ("You must try this, sir; I'll not take no for an answer; it was sent me by my cousin at the Embassy in London from the Prince of Wales's private stock.")

Mrs. Bertie, meanwhile, was just as actively engaged soothing and stimulating the company by turns, welding the discrepant elements together with the skill of long practice. She had a word for everybody, and that the most tactful one possible. There was no sense of preoccupation on her part, nor of anything save the most complete satisfaction with her party just as it was. Nevertheless, a slight heightening of colour, an extra edge of excitement in her rather shrill voice, told Ned, even before they entered the room, that the Kennerleys had come at last.

Two opinions might exist concerning their characters and deportment, but no-one could deny that the family was still the handsomest as well as the richest in town. Kennerley, Senior, at sixty was much what he had been at fifty: his hair was now pure white and his face more deeply lined, but the ice-blue eyes had not lost their keenness nor his carriage its superb self-assurance. Kennerley, Junior, was even better looking; to his father's fine figure and regular features he added the vivid colouring of his mother and a restless charm peculiarly his own. As for Celia, she had only to pause on the threshold like a beautiful statue for the atmosphere of the room to be altered. Everybody stared, the women with envy, as they twitched uneasily at their own laces and ribbons; the men in admiration. Even Monsieur Pisarcyk, enmeshed in rapturous self-analysis, stopped short in the middle of a *"Voyez-vous, mon cher, pour moi il n'y a que la musique classique qui . . ."*

to appraise with European frankness the Botticelli angel in clouds of floating blue.

None of the Kennerleys offered an excuse for their tardiness, and their hosts did not appear to expect it. Mrs. Framingham made the necessary introductions. Mr. Kennerley and his children were charmed. Messrs. Harper and Littlefield welcomed their crony demonstratively, obviously feeling him to be a sort of moral reënforcement. The less musical ladies also looked relieved. Mrs. Terry, too, who had been sulking in silence a little apart, began to show signs of returning animation. Here, perhaps, at last was a millionaire who . . .

Ned seized his chance to slip away from the violinist, intending to speak to Celia, but found himself forestalled by young Maxwell. The shift in the crowd brought him instead next to Celia's brother, who grasped his hand with enthusiasm.

"Ned! What fun! When on earth did you get here?"

Sonny smiled his brilliant, nervous smile and mopped his forehead, which was perpetually a trifle moist. Ned reflected, as they exchanged greetings and scraps of information, that nobody could be *that* glad to see anyone. But how resist such eagerness to please? Before they separated the young men had made an engagement to lunch together the following day.

Mrs. Framingham's supper arrangements seemed as novel as everything else about her party. The basement dining-room was set with small candle-lit tables; there were no place-cards; people were supposed to sit where they liked. Even the menu was unhackneyed: the long buffet offered veal *en casserole* and bowls of steaming spaghetti as its most substantial dishes; the plain green salad was spiced with garlic (Mr. Framingham announced he'd made the dressing himself); while a gnarled and weazened old man, whom his mistress addressed in Italian as Giuseppe, passed Chianti in straw-covered bottles instead of Prairie Avenue's conventional claret or champagne.

Ned was determined to sit beside Celia, and he succeeded,

though powerless to detach her from Dan Maxwell, who pulled out her chair with a flourish and insisted on waiting upon her with overdone attentiveness. The fourth seat fell, at Mrs. Framingham's behest, to Mrs. Harper: Ned all but gaped till he remembered one of that lady's most persistent poses was perennial youth. He duly fetched her supper and began a lifeless game of questions-and-answers while waiting for the golden head to turn in his direction.

In the meantime, as their table adjoined their hostess's, it was possible to observe the varied techniques of Aunt Lydia's successor.

To begin with, Mrs. Framingham concentrated all her forces on a fidgety French dialogue with Monsieur Pisarcyk, leaving Mr. Kennerley to the resourceless Mrs. Terry, who cupped her chin on her sculptured hands, leaning far forward, her face a frozen picture of boredom as she obviously tried not to listen to her companion's exposition of the wholesale grocery trade. (Why had one ever imagined that actresses were clever off the stage?) When at length a change of partners seemed inevitable, doughty Isabel attacked her landlord with sprightly impertinence. Would he (she demanded) ever have recognized his hideous old house in its becoming new dress? Of course, there'd been limits to what she could do, some horrors she'd been unable to get rid of: she called the company to witness—had they *seen* that purple stained-glass window on the stairs? On the whole, however, she flattered herself she'd done an excellent job. Did not Abner agree with her? And wouldn't he give her a further chance to show her powers in furbishing up the restaurant in the Kennerley Block? If he were willing to trust her, she knew precisely how to set about it. Really, in these days of enlightened taste, such tawdry gimcracks were unforgivable. . . . Ned, who was sure that Mr. Kennerley considered his Moorish and Pompeian parlours the height of fashion, rather looked for an explosion: none came.

But Mrs. Framingham had not done with her teasing: she

criticized her neighbour's new watch-chain, the flower in his buttonhole; decried his parsimony in refusing an authentic El Greco she'd unearthed for his picture collection; gaily insisted *she'd* have to order the supper for Celia's ball, as otherwise he'd take the easy way and just have it all "sent up from Kennerley's."

Mr. Kennerley parried these thrusts with uncharacteristic good humour. Clearly he did not take them seriously; clearly, too, he found Isabel Framingham a diverting little creature. Even the blandest diet might pall eventually; perhaps *sauce piquante* was agreeable after years of Aunt Lydia's soothing syrup.

Presently the conversation jumped to affairs in Vermont. Mrs. Framingham now wanted advice: she was thinking of buying The Hall, her father's old summer place in the hamlet where, it appeared, Abner Kennerley had been born. (This was news: did that fact alone make her a pearl of great price to the Green Mountain farmer boy who'd made a fortune out west?)

Ned found his eavesdropping so entertaining that he paid scant heed to Mrs. Harper, who had settled down to a circumstantial account of the sins of her last cook but one. Dan Maxwell, annoyingly, refused to relinquish Celia; it was some comfort to see that she failed altogether to respond to his advances, leaning back in her chair and nibbling a bit of bread with a look of secret withdrawal—she was *there* less than ever, tonight! . . . Just the same it came as a shock when Mrs. Framingham rose to assemble her ladies, and Ned realized that supper was over.

Left to their port and cigars, the male part of the company fell naturally into two groups: the young Poles attached themselves to Ned and Sonny (who also spoke French); the rest congregated round their host. Ned was not so much engrossed in musical chit-chat as to fail to catch echoes of the elder men's conversation, in which, to begin with, Holland Harper pro-

vided the focal point. The news of the sale of his house to
Levi Zinderstein was now out: he was warmly congratulated
by his future North Side neighbours on the impending move,
which was as vigorously deplored by those on the South. It
was astonishing to see how hard Mr. Kennerley and Mr. Littlefield took what they regarded as an act of real treachery:
would this have been so if they had not been uncomfortably
conscious of a trend?

Mr. Harper defended himself through a number of varia-
tions on the theme of "You fellows will all be seeing the light
and coming up our way pretty soon." But he found a new
subject as soon as he could in Hezzy Cobden's will. Most of
those present approved of the library project; one gathered
that each of them had already in view some private benefac-
tion, by which he hoped to be remembered in the home of
his choice (not his birth). Museums and hospitals, schools
and settlement houses, the Orchestra, the University: there
seemed little doubt in anybody's mind that every one of these
was, or shortly would be, the greatest thing of its kind in
America. There seemed even less that Chicago was destined to
be the first city of the New World. It was the best possible
place to live in now—the heart of the country geographically,
commercially, spiritually even, since its coming of age with
the Fair of '93.

The enthusiasm waxed contagious; it was far more outspoken than Ned remembered it ten years ago. And why not?
Who had a better right to speak thus than the men who'd
made Chicago, out of their faith and strength and industry
and perseverance? It mattered not that their goals had been
primarily personal: the net result bulked larger than individual ambitions. . . . Poor old Hezzy, though! They'd miss
him. He was the first to leave the ranks of the original pioneers
(if one excepted Uncle Hiram, whose exit had been tragically
premature). The round table at the club would not be the same
again, declared Mr. Littlefield, shaking his noble white head

sorrowfully. Had they noticed, by the way, that there'd been a bequest to the attending physician of a cool ten thousand? That was a stroke of luck for old Jack Mallard. No-one envied him the windfall—what need had Prairie Avenue's princes of legacies? All the same a slight uneasiness made itself felt, a dawning suspicion that, if his luck kept on, old Jack might end up well nigh as rich as any of the lot. (And who would be next on the list to contribute his share?)

When Mr. Framingham led his troop upstairs to join the ladies it was to find the front parlour (no, drawing-room was now the proper word, wasn't it?) rearranged with chairs in rows. Nobody was naïve enough to suppose, as they would have done in the eighties, that Monsieur Pisarcyk was expected to supply the entertainment: even as Ned took his place by Celia—having opportunely spied her in a corner, whence it would be possible to exclude the enterprising Maxwell—the doorbell rang, four men with fiddle-cases were admitted to the hall, and Mrs. Framingham rose in a flutter to announce the Kneisel Quartet.

Ned had never liked her so well as during the music. She really listened to Beethoven and Brahms, hunched up in her chair, careless for the time being of her appearance and the behaviour of her guests. No-one else—save, it was to be presumed, the pair of professionals—could have cared as she did. Ned's thoughts wandered more than he meant them to. During the glories of the slow movement of *Razoumowsky Number Two* he found himself glancing speculatively at Mrs. Terry, rapt in a picturesque, and hardly spontaneous, trance; then at Celia's cold, pure profile (where were her thoughts? No penny could possibly have produced them!); finally across the room at Sonny, who sat on the couch next Almira. (He had taken a bit of her green muslin dress and was fingering it idly; the look in his eyes gave his secret away.)

This glimpse of young lovers remained the most vivid impression of the evening, though there were others: the party grew livelier the longer it lasted. The formal programme was followed by "stunts": Pisarcyk could not resist seizing his violin and playing part of a Mozart sonata as well as a selection of national melodies, mazurkas and czardas (or was the czardas Hungarian?). The pianist, also properly patriotic, contributed a group of Chopin. Mrs. Terry, genial at last after three Scotch-and-sodas, told stories in dialect and recited Yeats and Tom Moore in a murky mezzo soprano.

Ned's deferred conversation with Celia was perhaps his chief disappointment. Sandwiched in unsatisfying installments between bits of the music, it turned with tiresome insistence on her desire to have him attend her coming-out ball: she either could not or would not understand his reason for refusal. "I don't see why you can't come—you're *here,* aren't you?"

"Yes, but I told you already, I had no choice. Twitchell asked me to do it."

"Well, all I can say is, for somebody who accepted against his will you seem to me to be having a wonderful time."

"That's hardly the issue," Ned pointed out patiently. "As long as I promised my boss to get the interview I had to do it the best way I could. And since I've accepted the Framinghams' hospitality, it wouldn't be fair to sit by myself and make faces, would it?"

"If you can go to Aunt Isabel, whom you've scarcely met, you can certainly come to me, one of your oldest friends. *Please,* Ned; it won't be half so much fun without you."

"How can I, Celia, dear?" Ned was flushed with distress. "You know I'm in mourning—people in mourning don't go to balls."

"They don't go to supper-parties either. It's horrid of you. If you were really as fond of me as you say you are, you'd not be so obstinate."

"Obstinate? You're the one who's that! If it were anything else in the world—"

"Ah, but this is the one thing I want!"

"That's unreasonable."

"Very well, then, I'm unreasonable."

"But that's no excuse for my being so, too."

So it went, *da capo;* at the end neither had yielded and nothing was settled.

Very late indeed did the gathering break up, and then only because Pisarcyk's accompanist—whose name till the last no-one contrived to catch—glanced at a clock and discovered that their train to Detroit left in a scant half-hour.

Ned and Almira walked home even more silently than they had come. He was depressed; so was she, although she had looked so rosy and happy while Sonny was sitting beside her. Inside the front door she kissed her cousin good-night—an unusual thing for her to do—Ned saw that her eyes were full of tears.

He had intended following her upstairs directly, but a light shining through the half open parlour door arrested his attention. Could Mary Kelly have forgotten . . . ?

Aunt Lydia rose from her seat by the smouldering embers as he entered. She was fully dressed and in spite of the hour perfectly wide awake.

"Now tell me, my dear," she said, in a bright, interested voice, "unless you're too tired—I want to hear all about the party!"

Chapter 4

NED had not lived in Chicago a week before discovering that 1817 Prairie Avenue was much quieter than it used to be. It had long lacked a master; Tom and Porter, who'd once filled the place with their cheerful clatter, were now also gone. And Almira was out a good deal

of the time. Although two years had passed since she had made
her début, she was still counted in everything: her nights were
spent dancing, and her days strolling, shopping, or "slumming"
(as her mother would refer to her charitable enterprises) with
the group of girls with whom she'd grown up.

She seldom saw these friends at home. Where, indeed, could
she have received them? The library was too small and inconvenient; the old schoolroom upstairs, unbecomingly shabby.
The drawing-room remained Aunt Lydia's, and only Aunt
Lydia's, as firmly now as in the years of her children's adolescence. No-one would have dared intrude on her there, nor
even to enter the room when it was known that she was in the
house, except by invitation. It seemed, as always, an indivisible
unit with the green-and-gold chamber beyond, the whole con-
stituting the private domain of Mrs. Hiram Stack.

During Ned's first fortnight his work at the paper kept him
fairly constantly busy in the evenings. However, the night
after the Framinghams' party, his aunt led the way to her
sanctum. They had dined *tête-à-tête;* Almira was playing
whist at the Mallards'; and when Ned would have excused
himself to go upstairs to read, Aunt Lydia bade him stay.
"That is, my dear, unless you've something better to do. I'm
afraid this mourning time must seem very dull; it's hard on
young people, I know."

"But won't I . . . ?" began Ned, embarrassed. "I mean,
don't you . . . ?"

Aunt Lydia smiled benignly.

"There's nobody coming but Rock Terriss," she said; "and if
you don't mind him, I'm sure he'll have no objection to you.
He's always been fond of you, Ned."

Ned could not deny it. He, too, was fond of Uncle Rock:
as things worked out they made a cosy trio by the fire, in the
pleasant rose-shaded room with its thick, warm curtains drawn
against the November night. The men did most of the talking:
Aunt Lydia sat and sewed, turning her comely, good-

humoured face first towards one, then towards the other. She had read neither "Little Rivers" nor Mr. Crawford's latest novel, thought the Ibsen season a bore, and had only elementary ideas about the Bach style of Theodore Thomas; but the words she dropped here and there were usually apt and invariably agreeable. Uncle Rock played the piano later —years of intensive concert-going had not lessened Ned's admiration for his old friend's sincere, unspectacular musicianship—and the evening ended with Janet's bringing tea and cakes, as she'd been doing for a quarter of a century. (Janet was now complicatedly wrinkled and as cross as a witch, but the cakes were still delicious. It was interesting to see that she brought a decanter of whiskey as well.)

After this, whenever he was free—unless Aunt Lydia herself were dining out (which happened more often than during her husband's lifetime)—Ned found that she expected his company. Uncle Rock came at least three times a week, though he was by no means the only one. Asa Shipley called almost as often; old Mr. Littlefield dropped in, too; there were others. One night Ned was rather taken aback as a dark, Oriental looking personage with handsome heavy-lidded eyes and drooping moustaches made his entrance, half doubtfully, half self-assured. Aunt Lydia introduced him as their prospective neighbour, Levi Zinderstein. (Where and how had she managed to meet him?)

The sole rule seemed to be that she saw just one gentleman at a time. With all her manner was the same: she accepted their homage as a matter of course; deferred to their judgement because they were men (and men ought to know best); seldom dissented and on no account contradicted, however disparate her visitors' views from her own. Mr. Shipley, for instance, as a Democrat, a Free-trader, a Bimetallist, with an unconventional interest in labour problems, represented everything that was anathema to the Stacks and their circle.

Aunt Lydia cared little for culture or politics; her social

curiosity was likewise strictly limited. Chicago was the one place that counted, and even there her thoughts scarcely strayed beyond her home quarter: Hyde Park and Kenwood were much too far away; what happened on the North Side was so remotely cogent that it might also be said not to have happened at all.

On the other hand, she had an extraordinary zest for business. Tom and Porter held titular posts at Stack and Company, but Aunt Lydia, as vice-chairman of the board, attended all directors' meetings and had a strong voice in matters of policy: no detail of management was too small to attract her attention. She also took a most unfeminine interest in the stock market; was forever scanning the financial pages of the newspapers, arranging and rearranging her list of investments, asking her brokers' and bankers' advice (which she followed only after resorting to an elaborate system of checking and making quite sure it was the best thing she could possibly do).

Here was one subject on which she occasionally waxed eloquent: again and again she strove to impress on her nephew the sovereign importance of money. "If you've got enough of it, nothing on earth can touch you—and you must learn to look out for your own, my dear. Trust no one; be sure *you're* sure what you're doing. I know you're an artist, not a business-man, but that's all the more reason to be careful. You mustn't end up as your poor father did."

Save when the caller was Uncle Rock, Ned made a practice of rising and saying good-night soon after Janet's arrival. Aunt Lydia showed no anxiety to be rid of him, but neither did she urge him to stay; and it was obvious that most of her interviews lasted till very much later. No matter what time he went to bed, the lights were still burning downstairs, and a drone of voices was still to be heard behind the drawing-room doors.

Try as he might, Ned could not help speculating as to the exact nature of his aunt's relations with her friends. She looked and acted propriety itself; she seemed too sensible, too practical, for a *grande amoureuse;* one could not imagine her in an attitude even faintly approaching the lascivious. Yet there was something odd about her predilection for men, and Ned had not forgotten what he alone knew of her liaison with Abner Kennerley.

She had no female intimates; Mrs. Kennerley had never been replaced. In spite of this Aunt Lydia's position was vastly improved. She appeared to have lived down the scandals and lurking suspicions that had threatened her youth. Perhaps this proved her contention that money alone mattered; certainly she was now so rich that it would have been difficult to snub her. In fact, she seemed to have everything she wanted except one thing—and how could one be sure she still wanted that?

Ned's resolution to observe mourning for the conventional six months was put to the test, a few days later, when the Kennerleys' invitations came: there was to be a tea in the afternoon, followed by a dinner for Celia's young friends and a dance for all ages, later in the evening. Almira loudly bewailed her cousin's bad luck; Aunt Lydia, too, expressed regrets, while admitting she could but applaud his niceness of feeling.

Ned accepted their sympathy without saying much in return. It occurred to him that, as long as he had to play it, he might as well make the most of his *beau rôle.* There seemed no point in confessing that, in a way, he was relieved: he still had not learned to dance very well and was reluctant to let Celia know it. Moreover, the two occasions on which he had seen her had been enough to show him how the land lay, emotionally. His feeling for Celia had nothing in common with the mildly agreeable attraction he'd felt towards various girls he'd flirted with in his college days. There were some things about her he didn't like, much in her life he frankly deplored; yet he felt bound by a tie as deep as it was indefinable.

Accordingly, after long deliberation, he sent her a bouquet of orchids with a note, and would have been willing, though not precisely content, to let the question rest there, if at the last moment Aunt Lydia had not changed her mind. Dancing all night, she declared, was one thing; tea and sandwiches in the house of an old friend, quite another. It was a symbolical performance, signalizing a young girl's assumption of her adult place in the world. Aunt Lydia herself was going: at such times of tribal rejoicing personal feuds were put aside; what mattered was to uphold neighbourhood solidarity. Besides, Ned had known Celia for years; it would not do to risk hurting her feelings.

"After all, the child has no mother," said Aunt Lydia, in a voice of steel.

Ned, who cared for teas as little as the average young man, sighed as he agreed with her.

Celia's coming-out party was much like other coming-out parties in Prairie Avenue; its grandeur implied a superlative degree rather than difference in kind. The traditional red carpet was laid to the street; the traditional striped awning protected it. Inside, there were flowers and music and many bright lights; the warm air was heavy with the scent of too many roses. Voices rose to a roar as Ned and his ladies entered; it took them a good twenty minutes to fight their way to the end of the picture gallery, where Abner Kennerley and his daughter were receiving their friends. (Here some old landmarks were missing: "A Sunset in Holland" and "Sheridan's Ride" had given place to Millet and Corot—Aunt Isabel evidently favoured the Barbizon school.)

Mr. Kennerley, at his best as a host, looked courtly and distinguished; his cheeks were slightly flushed and he inclined his head more amiably than usual as he accepted the congratulations of his long list of acquaintances. He greeted Aunt Lydia as if nothing had changed between them: Aunt Lydia gave him her perennial smile and leaned forward to kiss Celia, who looked like a rose herself (that, too, was traditional) in her filmy pink frock. Mrs. Framingham, radiant in peach velvet and pearls, stood just beyond them: not officially in the receiving line, yet not quite detached from it either. She managed a flustered, effusive "How do you do, Mrs. Stack? I'm delighted—"

That, however, was as far as she got. Aunt Lydia raked her rival from head to foot with a look both searching and comprehensive; then she bowed, very slowly and grandly, and moved on without saying a word. Nothing could have been more correct; nothing more flatly insulting. Mrs. Framingham seemed for once at a loss. She opened and shut her mouth several times like a fish; finally pounced with a scream on Almira, next in line, and pretended to be extravagantly glad to see her.

This ruse availed her as little as such paltry tactics generally do, for Sonny, who had refused to stand up with his father and sister and had been drifting about smiling at everybody without really seeing them, promptly carried off his girl for a glass of champagne.

Ned glanced round to see if his aunt needed succour, and found her enthroned in a corner, with old Mr. Littlefield and young Mr. Maxwell in devoted attendance. (Trust Aunt Lydia never to be odd woman out!) He was therefore free to do as he wished: what could that be? Like most shy young men in company, he was consumed by a fear that nobody would speak to him (only surpassed by a still fiercer panic lest somebody *should!*). There seemed little hope this early of a word with Celia; the one alternative appeared to be food.

Cleaving a skilful passage to the buffet through the hordes of dreadful old ladies who infested teas (and whom one had long supposed to be dead), he came upon a plump young lady in a plumed bonnet wedged next to the table itself: thus unassailably placed, she was disposing of a plateful of *petits fours* interspersed with lobster salad sandwiches with as hungry a celerity as if her life depended on it. Florence Harper had grown so much stouter that at first Ned did not know who it was. The pair saluted each other with modified warmth; they had never really been friends.

Florence, divining the purpose with which he'd approached, recommended the chocolate *éclairs*. "Don't waste your time on the cream-puffs, though; they've nothing but custard inside." Then, in an effort towards sociability, she volunteered that she had read several of his criticisms in the *Chronicle*. "You *are* 'E.R.,' aren't you? I thought they were quite good, and Mamma says you're very clever. I suppose I'll see you at the dance tonight?"

Ned explained why she wouldn't, and Florence shook her feathered head commiseratingly. "Why, that's a shame! It'll be a regularly elegant party—you know how the Kennerleys do everything. They're spending thousands on the decorations alone; Mamma says it isn't suitable for a young girl just out of mourning herself. The Bings and the Astleys up on Pine Street —you know we've got lots of friends on the North Side now: have you heard we're moving soon?—well, they told her they don't think it's at all the thing—they blame it mostly on that Mrs. Framingham, I guess—and Gussie Bing's not even being allowed to go. She's cried her eyes out all week, poor dear! It's too bad for you, Ned. I know you were always fond of Celia. Of course, you'd not have had much chance with her tonight, anyway. A girl's always popular at her own party."

"Celia's popular at anybody's party," said Ned firmly. "At least that's what I understand. According to Carrie Stack, half the boys in town are in love with her."

"*Carrie Stack!*" said Florence, with a sniff. "I'd not pay much attention to what *she* says about anything. She's just jealous on Jamie's account, because he really *is* wild about Celia. Poor fool! It doesn't do him a bit of good, and it never will. I could've told him so, ages ago. Celia doesn't mean to marry anyone in Chicago—you can depend upon that."

"Then whom, do you think?" said Ned. "I mean, I imagine she'll marry someone sooner or later; most girls do, don't they?"

There was one for Florence, who was twenty-three past. That she made the personal application was plain to see from the sudden flush on her long pale face, the spiteful spark in the olive-green eyes behind their disfiguring glasses.

"Oh, some old duke or other!" she snapped. "You can bet she'll try for a title if she can. Why else do you suppose she's coaxing her father into taking her abroad in the spring? And that Framingham cat's going along—she knows whole carloads of dukes, I expect! Oh, I don't say they won't bring it off: Celia's pretty enough for anything, and then there's all her money, too. But if I were a man, duke or not, I'd think twice before proposing to Celia Kennerley."

Ned considered this before replying, quite simply: "Why?"

Florence bridled and coloured furiously.

"Oh, *because*—she's terribly spoilt, for one thing. Terribly headstrong, too. I don't need to tell *you* that. And then look at her mother! I mean, after all . . ."

"What about her mother? I was very fond of Aunt Corinne," said Ned, who was anxious to get to the bottom of Florence's irritating air of mystery. (Come to think of it, Carrie had been mysterious, too.)

"Well, so was I. But she *was* peculiar. You can't deny it. And everyone knows now she drank like a fish. I can't imagine why we never guessed when we were children. They used to call it 'sick spells.' Sick fiddlesticks!"

"But that doesn't mean that Celia—"

"Naturally not. I never said it did. All I say is, she's awfully spoilt and awfully, awfully nervous, and she does take some sort of tonic for her nerves—it's the only thing that seems to keep her going sometimes. I'm sure I haven't the least idea what's in it; I never asked, and I never will," said Florence virtuously. "And I'm sorry I spoke," she added, as Ned began to exclaim: "Of all the vicious nonsense!" "I wouldn't have, if I'd thought it would upset you so. There's Mamma beckoning; I've got to go. I guess it's time to dress for dinner."

And that was the whole of Ned's conversation with Florence Harper.

That night, after supper-on-a-tray, he had settled himself with "Middlemarch" by the drawing-room fire when Aunt Lydia and Almira rustled in, in a billow of silks and laces, on their way out to dinner. They both kissed him good-night and said, sincerely, what a shame it was and, insincerely, that they would much rather have stayed home with him.

Ned kissed them back and smiled quite cheerfully. It would have spoiled his secret to share it; the fact that nobody knew what he intended to do cast a veil of glamour over the whole proceeding.

At a quarter to twelve he shut up his book (it was easy to leave off anywhere in George Eliot—was that perhaps one of the comforts of Mid-Victorian literature?), donned his outdoor clothes, and walked into the street.

Prairie Avenue was crowded tonight; the whole block where the Kennerleys lived was lined with the carriages of guests from other parts of town. On their boxseats the coachmen sat huddled forlornly, bearing the long, cold hours of waiting as best they could. (What a contrast their dark, patient vigil to the great house blazing with lights, and the cheer and gaiety one knew were within!)

Ned stopped to speak to the doorman—who was Thomas, Mr. Kennerley's groom—and then cut across the lawn to the back of the conservatory, where Celia had told him the door would be unlatched. She had not forgotten. . . . He let himself in, feeling agreeably like a housebreaker devoid of sensations of guilt, and the next moment gasped at the difference in temperature: here, whatever the calendar said, it was June.

Hastily doffing his hat and coat, he gazed about him wonderingly. Coloured lights had been strung through the palms and flowering shrubs; under the high central dome, where Mrs. Kennerley's aviary had been, a little fountain tossed its silver spray above a round marble basin. The place seemed deserted: the distant sound of shuffling feet and the strains of the Druids' March from *Norma,* played in Johnny Hand's briskest manner, showed that the guests were going in to supper.

Celia had timed the tryst perfectly. Before Ned had been there long enough to grow nervous he saw her approaching along the rose walk, tall and fair in her gleaming white gown. She smiled when she saw him and waved her hand; it was not until she had come quite near that he noticed she was unusually excited—her face very pale, her eyes darkly glittering.

"Well, you came, after all!" she exclaimed, as soon as they were within speaking distance. "You know, I almost thought you wouldn't. You didn't sound awfully keen when I suggested it this afternoon. How do you like me?"

"You look beautiful," replied Ned. "I never saw anyone more so." (What else *could* one say? Yet he cursed his refractory tongue: why was it easy to be clever with everybody except Celia?)

"I think, myself, the dress turned out pretty well," said Celia, revolving complacently. "Aunt Isabel fussed so, it really ought to've. They all say it's a great success."

"And *you're* a great success, too, I suppose." Ned tried his best not to sound jealous. "Are you having a good time?"

"Oh," said Celia, "you know what it's like: the men have to dance with me tonight, whether they want to or not. *I* don't give a rap how they feel—they're nothing to me!"

This was not so comforting somehow as Celia might have meant it to be. Ned found himself blurting out, to his dismay: "You don't like Chicago—you don't care for the people here, do you? It's true, then, what Florence says—you're planning to leave as soon as you can and go abroad to marry a duke!"

Celia laughed on a high note of scorn.

"Is that what Florence says? And you believed her, of course?"

She danced about in a circle, so that her gauzy skirts took the air; then settled herself like a butterfly on the edge of the marble basin, looked up at Ned, and laughed again, a queer, breathless laugh that was not in the least like her own. "Come, sit here beside me—there! That's right. Poor Neddy! You're a nice boy; I shouldn't tease you."

"Yes, but *do you—*"

"Oh, yes, yes, *yes!*" cried Celia. "I do want to go—of course I do—to Europe or anywhere else. What does it matter, as long as it's a million miles from here? I'm not happy here, Ned. I never have been. This isn't my place. If only Papa . . ."

She leaned forward, her eyes enormous and pleading. Ned was suddenly reminded of Aunt Corinne. For a moment he felt closer to Celia than ever before; they seemed, unaccountably, on the brink of an understanding such as he had always hoped for between them. Then, unaccountably also, she laughed for the third time—that dry little laugh that had no merriment in it.

"But he will, you know—he always does what I want, sooner or later. Poor old Papa! And if I have trouble making my plans, Aunt Isabel has promised to help me, too. Then I'll travel and travel till I've seen the whole world, or as much of it as I care to. You're luckier than I, Ned; you've been to Europe over and over."

"Yes, but I always come back—and you won't. You don't want to, I guess, ever at all—is that it?"

"Oh, I'm not sure. I might some day, sooner than you think. How can I tell now? I might even decide to marry and settle down—who knows?"

"Marry *whom?*"

"Oh, I'm not sure," said Celia again. "Anybody handy . . . Dan Maxwell, perhaps. He asked me tonight."

"He *did?* Of all the cheek! And what did you tell him?"

"Can't you guess? When I haven't found out yet what I want for myself, how can I give it to anyone else? Oh, Ned, don't you see . . . ? You're my one friend, the only person I can really depend on. Never forget that, my dear. . . . I've got to be going in a minute, or Papa and Aunt Isabel will be sending out relays to look for me. I'm engaged for supper— mercy! I almost forgot. What will he think?"

"By 'he' you mean that bounder Maxwell, I presume," said Ned bitterly; and Celia's laughter broke out once more—by this time it had grown to be almost incessant.

"No, you're quite wrong—it's Jamie!" (But that was cold consolation, for wasn't Jamie Mallard in love with her, too?)

Ned had not the heart to try to keep her longer. The romantic tryst was a failure. His mind was struggling now with a new problem, a new fear: what Carrie had hinted at, and Florence as good as stated openly, was, it seemed certain, dreadfully true.

He could find no words to thank Celia when she plucked a camellia and fastened it to his lapel. The great eyes came nearer than ever, but that meant nothing now that he saw they were drained of expression. Even the fleeting kiss she pressed on his forehead gave him little of the expected pleasure. He said good-night and made his exit through the door by which he'd come, never daring to look back, for he did not want to see what he was afraid he must: not for nothing had Celia planned to meet him in the conservatory; he knew as well as she did what she had hidden under the flat, glossy leaves of the camellia tree.

Chapter 5

THE next evening, after Ned had finished his review of Godowsky, he was asked to supper at Henrici's by his chief, who had polished off Lillian Russell in a scant thirty minutes and was anxious to air *viva voce* his scathing opinions on comic opera stars and their tawdry vehicles.

It was very late when he got home; all the houses along the avenue looked dark and withdrawn. Before going upstairs Ned stepped into the drawing-room to reclaim "Middlemarch," which he had left there the previous night. A faint light showed under the folding doors that led to Aunt Lydia's room. This was not surprising: its owner had not slept upstairs since her husband's death. But there were voices, too . . . his aunt's, and a man's, which after a moment he identified as Abner Kennerley's.

Ned knew he ought not to listen, but there seemed to be times in everybody's lives when the strictest code of ethics had to be suspended temporarily: how could he *not* try to unravel the mystery that had plagued him for years? As a matter of fact, he was not able to make out much of the conversation. Both voices were pitched low—naturally, at this hour of the night. Besides, it was to be presumed that Aunt Lydia and her caller were seated by the fire, quite at the other end of the room. They were evidently having an argument. . . . "I beg you'll reconsider," said Mr. Kennerley, in his usual petulant way. "After all I have done, have you no feeling . . . ?"

The rest of the sentence was lost, but Aunt Lydia replied very distinctly: "You haven't done a thing you didn't want to do."

"That's as it may be, but surely you owe . . ."

There ensued a long masculine mumble, which Ned failed to understand. He had about decided not to listen any longer, when there was a noise of chairs being moved and Aunt Lydia's voice sounded much nearer—just on the other side of the panel, in fact.

"Very well, then," came the clear contralto tones; "have it your way. When *haven't* you had it? I'll do what you ask, Abner Kennerley, but mind you, it's the last thing I'll ever do for you. As far as I'm concerned, my dear, you can rot in hell for all eternity."

There was no more emotion in her voice than if she had been commenting on the weather, or bidding Janet fetch her a second cup of tea.

Another long mumble followed. Then Aunt Lydia spoke once more: "And leave the key upon the table. You'll not be needing it again."

That was all. Ned spent half the rest of the night striving, with only partial success, to put the pieces of the puzzle together.

The next day, which was his holiday, he lunched at home with his aunt and cousin. The former, who throughout the meal had appeared somewhat absent-minded and was certainly less talkative than usual, set her coffee-cup back on its saucer with a little click (having drained the contents quickly with something less than her customary enjoyment) and remarked: "Mary, tell Simms I want the brougham at half past three."

Almira looked up in astonishment: "Why, Mamma, I thought you'd planned to stay at home this afternoon! It's snowing so hard, and you said last night you meant to look over the minutes of the Antiquarians' meeting with me, and make up the list of patronesses for the Visiting Nurse bazaar."

"Did I, dear? I'm sorry; they'll keep till tomorrow, I fancy. Today," said Aunt Lydia purposefully, "I've other fish to fry!"

She disappeared directly after lunch. When she came back

an hour or so later, Ned and Almira were playing double patience in the library.

"Children, will I do?"

"Why, Mamma," cried the guileless Almira, "you look perfectly lovely! But you're wearing your sables—and isn't that the new dress from Redfern? Where on earth . . . ?"

She stopped, abashed; never before had she ventured to ask where her mother was going.

But for once, evidently, Aunt Lydia had no desire to keep her destination a secret. As she swept out into the hall and through the door Mary Kelly held open, she tossed her head and snapped her cardcase shut like a trap.

"I'm going to call," said Aunt Lydia, as nearly vicious as it was possible for her to be, "on Mrs. Framingham!"

That night at dinner neither Ned nor Almira, it went without saying, felt like broaching the subject; and Aunt Lydia, contrary to her custom, made no report of the day's occupations. Within the prescribed week Mrs. Framingham returned her neighbour's call; that much was certain, for her cards lay on the tray in the hall for all the world to see. But as far as one could tell amenities went no further.

As the cold, blowy autumn turned into a blowier, snowier winter Ned found himself too busy at the office to worry very much about his family's affairs. Not that his work was more interesting. . . . New plays did not open every week and, when not otherwise occupied, Frank Twitchell naturally took the pick of the concerts. Ned spent three nights at Steinway Hall to one at the Auditorium and grew progressively less patient with the endless series of inept beginners' recitals he was forced to sit through.

Happily, his relations with his chief remained cordial. They drank coffee or beer together several times a week and, just before Christmas, Twitchell asked his young friend to dine with him and his wife. The two men boarded an Illinois Central train that whisked them out to one of the newer suburban developments, a flat and weedy wilderness of half-paved roads and jerry-built houses: to judge, however, by the profusion of street-lamps running right out into the tenantless prairie, its sponsors felt convinced Catalpa Park was destined for a boom.

Sal Twitchell was a bright, bird-like little woman, all energy and enthusiasm; patently it took a superabundance of both qualities to keep the show going for five Twitchells (soon to be six, for a baby was expected at Easter), their dog, their cat, their pair of canaries, and, in season, their pocket-handkerchief lawn-and-garden combined. But that the effort was successful was demonstrated by the excellence of the hot meal punctually served; the children looked healthy and cheerful and had engaging good manners; Ned felt the shabby, crowded cottage to be a real home.

After dinner, while Mrs. Twitchell, disdaining help, washed up in the kitchen, Frank Twitchell and his guest had a long talk in front of the hissing gas fire. The former did his best to persuade Ned not to linger too long in Chicago. "I dare say it's pleasant, with the friends and the background you've got—but what will it lead to? Don't be fool enough to get stuck in hack journalism like me! I've had to do what I've done for my family's sake, but you're young and free—you've no excuse for not pulling out while there's time. One winter won't hurt you: you're getting lots of good experience and, better still, learning to have confidence in yourself. But there mustn't be another! New York's the place for you . . . or Europe."

Ned listened attentively, saying little in return. In his heart he was beginning to feel that very likely Twitchell was right. Chicago *was* pleasant: no-one else save his parents had given him the warm, spontaneous affection he received from the Stacks. But they were not artists, and neither were any of their friends. Art, on Prairie Avenue, seemed merely a symbol of material success: it was something you bought bound in a book, or framed on a square of canvas, or perhaps listened to, for an hour after dinner, from a comfortable box at the Auditorium. Of the young men Ned knew, not one shared his desire to write. All of them were, or were going to be, bankers and brokers, doctors and lawyers and merchants, like their fathers and grandfathers. Ned's nascent ambitions set him apart as something harmlessly freakish. The sense of loneliness that goes with the writing vocation sometimes swept over him in a flood. Was it pleasure or pain? He could not tell, and he was still too young to realize that to be misunderstood at home is perhaps the best stimulant a young author can have.

During the holidays concerts fell off. There were more parties than ever for the younger set, but Ned steadfastly refused them all. (It was hard to do this, though not so hard as his aunt and Almira supposed.) Christmas itself passed quietly: the only guests, besides Uncle Rock, were Tom and Porter and their wives, and of course the grandchildren. The John and Harvey Stacks were not included any more. Almira told Ned that her mother had stopped asking them as soon as Uncle Hiram died. There hadn't been any trouble; Aunt Lydia announced calmly that she just could not be bothered by people who lived so far away, and who probably didn't want to be bothered by you. There was a sumptuous tree, and the usual staggering amount to eat, but the day seemed tinged with dullness: two-year-old Hiram and three-year-old Jane were too immature still to interest their grandmother, though she lavished presents upon them and popped peppermint patties into their mouths, with business-like promptness, whenever they showed signs of dawning displeasure.

Aunt Lydia had lately appeared altogether a little remote. Ned dated the change from the night of the conversation in the green-and-gold room with Abner Kennerley. She made no complaint, went her way with much of the old assurance and serenity; still there was sometimes a vagueness in the brown ox-eyes, a hint that while she was saying one thing she might be thinking another.

Almira's spirits, too, had suffered a more obvious eclipse. She might dance every night until dawn and sleep half the morning away—Ned's breakfasts, these days, were solitary affairs—but she looked pale and distraite and her eyes often showed that she had been crying.

This was easily accounted for as soon as Ned had ascertained that Sonny did not telephone any more, nor call in the evenings to take her to parties. What had caused the lovers' quarrel, it seemed impossible to say. The one good result was a marked increase in amiability between mother and daughter: the fact that they had *both* broken with Kennerleys served to bind them together more closely than ever before.

Ned's friendship with Sonny remained unaltered. The latter several times asked him to lunch at his club and was as cordial and charming as only he knew how to be. The two young men, however, soon discovered they had little in common except their distaste for business. Sonny worked after a fashion because his father and everyone else expected it—there was no leisure class in Chicago—but his real passion was sport: his trotters and hunters, his tennis and golf, seemed to absorb half his time and all his interest.

It was some weeks before Ned found his way back to Celia. Shortly after her formal début Mrs. Framingham took her to New York, whence impressive reports of her social triumphs trickled back to appear, with embroideries, in the local press. The ladies returned just in time for the Christmas balls, which Ned had eschewed. Once or twice Celia asked him to dinner, but it happened invariably that his work interfered. Finally, one crisp, cold Sunday early in the New Year, they met at church, where Ned's absorption in the blonde vision before him kept him from savouring to the full the stately self-possession, the studied indifference, with which Aunt Lydia and Mr. Kennerley—*vis-à-vis* as they had been for over twenty years—played their parts in the tragi-comedy of their own devising.

When the service was over Ned approached Celia, who stood on the steps with her muff to her face, exclaiming at the cold, and asked if he might walk home with her. He would scarcely have dared to suggest it if her perennial duenna had been present: fortunately for him, the Framinghams were Presbyterians and worshipped at the Second Church on Michigan at Twentieth.

Celia seemed very glad to see him, and totally unresentful of what most girls would have felt to be unwarranted neglect. Before they parted she proffered an invitation to a theatre party on the following Saturday; Ned accepted, with the proviso that, if Twitchell needed him, he would have to sue for release. Celia said she understood perfectly—again quite unlike other girls (and unlike herself at the beginning of the winter).

All week long he was divided between a fear that something would turn up to force him to break the engagement, and an equally lively dread lest nothing should. As luck would have it, he was free, and the evening proved unexpectedly agreeable. At the last minute Mr. Kennerley was unable to go; Maud and Joe Mallard were there (luckily, not poor Jamie!) and the inevitable Framinghams. Marlowe and Taber were wonderful in "Romeo and Juliet;" Celia was at her exquisite best; even the presence of Aunt Isabel, alertly watchful under her nodding aigrettes in the back of the box, could not spoil one's pleasure. (Did she really imagine, though, that her pose of elaborate unconcern could deceive the young people into thinking she was not listening avidly to everything they said?)

After that, Ned made a point of seeing Celia as often as possible. He went walking or skating with her when the weather permitted; had tea by the fire in the Louis XV drawing-room when it didn't; each week without fail he ordered flowers from Samuelson's on Michigan Avenue, enduring agonies of indecision as to whether carnations or roses . . .

For the first time in his life he regretted his poverty. Ned had never felt poor before; he had had enough always for his own modest wants. But now what a joy it would have been to shower blossoms on his love—jewels and rare perfumes and everything else rich and delicately fine! (It mattered not that she had all she wanted already.) And how not be jealous of that braggart Dan Maxwell, who could afford to send her orchids every day, and took her sleighing to Washington Park on Sunday afternoons with his smart cutter and prancing black mare?

Celia never touched liquor in public. In this she resembled her mother, who had been wont to shut herself up, every once in so often, and drink herself by degrees into insensibility. What one had observed in the old days had been, it seemed likely now, merely the beginnings and ends of her debauches. Celia, of course, was much younger; her addiction was not yet by any means so strong. Ned grew to recognize the signs very clearly: she would invariably be pale, her glance wide and unfocussed. There was a nervous gaiety in her manner, a tendency to answer at random and laugh immoderately for no reason at all.

It did not occur to Ned to blame her for what was undoubtedly an unhappy inheritance. His early life had inured him to shocks: although grieved and alarmed, he was no more surprised than he had been at the revelation of Aunt Lydia's long record of moral turpitude. He did ask himself sometimes whether her young friends knew as much as he did. None of them had been so outspoken as Florence, but Celia's "nervousness" appeared as well established as Aunt Corinne's "sick spells;" the only difference was that the former had not so far prevented the victim from performing her social obligations.

How many older people shared the secret? It seemed impossible that her father and Aunt Isabel, to go no further, should not have suspicions at least. Yet Abner Kennerley was palpably satisfied with and boundlessly proud of his only daughter, and Mrs. Framingham's hovering solicitude had solely to do with matters of dress and deportment: was Celia's jacket of *frisé caniche* an exact duplicate of the new Duchess of Marlborough's? Had she duly paid her *visites de digestion?* Above all, would she promise to be careful not to dance more than twice at the Littlefields' german with any of her many devoted young men?

Ned, watching with eyes full of love and pity, felt absurdly responsible, though powerless to alter the irremediable.

Lent brought a temporary lull in festivities. Most of the débutantes went south; those who remained were supposed to solace themselves by redoubled application to good works. For diversion they joined their married friends in attending numerous series of lectures. Miss Stack and her sisters-in-law were of this culture-hungry company: Mrs. Porter was rumoured to be intellectual, and naturally Carrie and Almira had no mind to lag behind.

Celia laughed such drab occupations to scorn: she had no taste for settlement work and airily refused to sit through "The Conundrum of the Time" or "The Cheer We Find in Thoreau." And just then it fell out that Dan Maxwell was sent to California by his firm to handle a ticklish and long drawn-out lawsuit. Her increased hours of leisure were therefore mostly Ned's: even the delirious week when Grau's Metropolitan Opera arrived did not spoil things, for Frank Twitchell, providentially, was laid up with influenza—which meant that Ned could regally offer his beloved one of the best seats in the house for the whole season.

What dimmed one's pleasure a little was that it was clear things could not go on very long as they were. It was hard to rejoice wholeheartedly over Celia's having stayed at home when she was preparing to leave quite soon on a much longer journey. For the Kennerleys' European plans were rapidly taking shape: they were sailing for England early in May. A house in Grosvenor Square had been hired in advance; a suitable corps of servants engaged. Mrs. Framingham had written already to various London friends, invoked the aid of "our cousin Reggie Trafford at the Embassy," set all kinds of discreetly intricate machinery in motion. . . . Celia was to be presented at one of the first drawing-rooms of the season and was assured, with her mentor, of the entry to the royal enclosure at Ascot. There was talk of taking a yacht to Cowes . . . that is, if it did not seem pleasanter, later on, to run over to Paris instead . . . or even as far as Moscow for the Imperial coronation ceremonies.

As Celia sketched her summer schedule Ned, trying not to be jealous, found himself muttering: "Florence was right, after all—I might have guessed it!"

Celia laughed unsympathetically.

"That's all you know! Why would I tie myself up to a man, when I've been scheming for months to get away from everybody and everything and be as free as air? Liberty, that's what I want—I'd like to see some silly duke try to talk me out of it, I can tell you!"

Ned would not argue the point, but his views were unchanged. If Celia were too single-mindedly bent on achieving her immediate goal to be aware of others more august and substantial looming beyond it, Isabel Framingham was perfectly frank about her ambitions. She dropped broad hints concerning divers acquaintances of young Trafford's: there was the Marquess of Witheredge—dear Ronny, a delightful boy! —and Lord Guisborough, who was only a baron (but the title was one of the oldest in the kingdom—besides, his mother was Jenny Vanderlyn from New York—one knew what the Vanderlyns stood for). Of course, it was far too soon to say. . . . Celia must see the world and feel constrained in nothing. Still there it was—Europe was a larger field. What, pray, was the alternative? A season or two of dining and dancing with the young set in Chicago—and then what? One fancied dear

Celia destined to better things. The Middle West, charming as it was, lacked perhaps the fixed inherited standards that were such a comfort at home. "Why," ended Mrs. Bertie trenchantly, glancing sharply round her to make sure the subject of conversation was not within hearing, "if we didn't take steps to prevent it, who knows but what the child might end by throwing herself away on some impossible person? A Dan Maxwell—a Jamie Mallard . . . !"

"Or a Ned Ramsay," Ned finished the sentence sardonically to himself, before nodding grave agreement that naturally such a catastrophe was at all costs to be avoided.

It was Mrs. Framingham's idea, also, that her friends should depart from the local scene in a final blaze of glory, a glittering apotheosis suggestive of Elijah's chariot that would symbolize their translation to a higher sphere. For this purpose the week after Easter was chosen; after some debate it was decided to give a fancy-dress ball. When first propounded the scheme sounded reasonable: young people loved dressing up; one of the most successful entertainments of the winter had been the Harpers' *bal poudré* at Christmas. Prairie Avenue visualized a pretty, colourful assembly of débutantes and their beaux, with a row of admiring parents to play propriety on the side lines. But when the invitations came out it was discovered that everybody had been asked; stranger still, that all, young and old alike, were expected to come in costume.

The idea was revolutionary. The ladies meeting on their way to market were in a flutter. As Mrs. Bunner said to Mrs. Mallard, it hardly seemed decent. . . . And yet, as the Framinghams elucidated their theory, it really made sense. Since nobody's dancing days were over any more and the era of the chaperon, if not quite dead, was certainly dying, why should not fathers and mothers—yes, and grandfathers and grandmothers, too—take part in the fun instead of blighting the picture? Such frolics were the rage in New York: Mrs. Bertie had attended several in Newport and Tuxedo as well: was it not high time for Chicago to join the procession? (And who more appropriate to lead it than Chicago's First Family?)

The argument appeared unassailable. Middle West society had always looked east for its inspiration—naturally enough: hadn't its leaders all come from there? What Fifth Avenue tried one season was generally reproduced by Prairie the next. Here for once, thanks to such accomplished liaison officers as the Framinghams, the time lag might be reduced and the new kind of party acclimatized before it had grown stale in its place of origin.

Besides, it was disseminated by degrees that the utmost latitude would be permitted in the selection of costumes. No-one need go to elaborate extremes; in fact, those who preferred a minimum of effort might pass muster simply by achieving a characteristic "head." Middle-aged men were encouraged to cast themselves as ambassadors, in conventional evening clothes plus a ribbon or two to simulate orders. Mrs. Harper opened vistas for dubious matrons by letting it be known she intended to go as Titania in her best new dinner gown, with wings and a wand and a slightly higher than usual diamond tiara.

The more people thought about it, the keener enthusiasm grew. Mr. Littlefield, said his wife, would at last have a chance to demonstrate his striking likeness to the "Iron Duke;" Mrs. Mallard and her sister, Mrs. Trask, had, it developed, for years been suppressing a desire to appear as the Brontës (which two, it was not quite clear). And the younger set, of course, or at any rate its feminine half, talked of nothing else for weeks. Museums and libraries were ransacked for ideas, department store counters for materials: Fanny Stack and Almira, who had come back from Europe the proud possessors of Breton peasant costumes, complete with *coiffes* and silver jewelry, did their best not to be complacent.

Only Aunt Lydia held aloof from the prevailing excitement. She had been asked to the party, of course: it would have seemed queer to Celia not to include her mother's best friend, and Mr. Kennerley, one surmised, had no intention of proclaiming their rupture to the public. In the circumstances Ned had rather expected his aunt to send her regrets by return post. This she had not done; nobody knew whether she meant to go or not; her heavy silence on the subject precluded questions as well as the kind of informal discussion that otherwise would have seemed natural to her young people.

On the other hand Ned, as Celia's chief intimate, had a part in the conferences that took place almost daily round the Kennerleys' tea-table, and in which his interest was no longer academic now that his six months of mourning were over. He was present on the fateful afternoon when Bertie Framingham was coaxed into promising he'd be the "Laughing Cavalier." He was also at hand, next day, to cushion the shock of Mr. Kennerley's curt decree that he had no intention of being anything at all. ("Absolutely not! My dear Isabel, how could you have ever supposed . . . ?")

This blow was almost immediately followed by another more serious: Sonny, who had wandered in late from the office and stood with his legs apart in front of the fire, announced blithely through a mouthful of muffin that *he* was going as a pirate.

Mrs. Framingham uttered an attenuated shriek of dismay.

"Oh, but darling, you *can't!* I've quite set my heart on Celia's being Juliet, and there's obviously nobody else to play Romeo."

"Romeo, shucks!" said Sonny, with a broad and cheerful grin. "What's the matter with some of the chaps who hang around the house all day like love-sick cats?—Dan Maxwell, for instance, or Jamie Mallard?"

There was another shriek.

"Don't be absurd! Mr. Maxwell would look like a beefeater in doublet and hose, and as for Jamie's red hair and freckles— *je vous demande!"*

Sonny, however, refused to yield to persuasion, and Mrs.

Framingham, at length acknowledging defeat, swept the room in a despairing half-circle till her glance rested on Ned, slim and composed in his corner.

"Mr. Ramsay, would you mind standing up a moment? Celia, dear, you, too?—there's an angel! You're well matched in height. . . . A touch of over-slenderness won't hurt; it gives, in fact, a kind of plastic quality. . . ."

Mrs. Framingham raised a meditative forefinger to her lips and narrowed her flint-grey eyes in rapt appraisal.

"I never, never thought . . . Too blond, of course, by far; but then, darling Celia's no brunette either. Honestly, I believe we've hit it. Dear Mr. Ramsay, *you* shall be Romeo!"

Romeo, accordingly, Ned was. Once the first shock of amazement was over he found he really did not mind very much. Lingering doubts of his suitability for the assignment were silenced by the reflection that, if he did not accept it, someone else would—and he could not bear to let any other man pose as Celia's lover, even at a fancy-dress ball.

Celia took the whole thing as a matter of course. She was apparently unaware both of the romantic implications of the rôles and of the underlying parallel offered by their respective families: were not the Kennerleys and the Stacks rapidly becoming Prairie Avenue counterparts of the Capulets and the Montagues? Ned wondered whether Mrs. Framingham had created the situation with deliberate malice, or if—this was even a bitterer pill to swallow—she had chosen him merely because, of all Celia's suitors, he was the least likely to menace her plans.

Preparations for the party proceeded thenceforth without a hitch. Mrs. Framingham, whose varied attainments included a pretty talent for water-colours, sketched the costume designs: with her usual flair for the unusual she had unearthed, on the remoter reaches of North Clark Street, another of her wonderful little women; Ned had occasionally, on his free afternoons, to accompany the ladies to Mrs. Voigt's for a fitting.

The last of these expeditions was set for Good Friday, just a week before the ball. The weather was shocking: borne on a cruel east wind, one of Chicago's freezing spring rains was sweeping the city. The lake was dotted with angry whitecaps and brown with churned up sand and mud. Ned had lunched at home with his aunt, who for once had nothing to do. She seemed depressed: after ascertaining his plans for the afternoon she established herself at her favourite post in the front window, although on a day such as this the prospect was dreary indeed. Ned turned to wave good-bye over his shoulder as he hurried down the street; his last impression was of Aunt Lydia's eyes, fixed indolently upon nothing at all, above her punctual parting smile.

At the Kennerleys' Grimshaw told him Miss Celia had gone out to lunch; she had said she might be a few minutes late; would Mr. Ramsay wait in the drawing-room, where a fire had been laid?

Even a fire could not reconcile Ned to the metallic splendours of this soul-chilling apartment. It was bad enough when there were people in it; alone, he felt he could not bear the marble Cupids' simpering smiles and sought refuge across the hall in the library, the one corner that was still as it had been in his childhood. Mrs. Framingham, one gathered, had not yet got round to the books; literary pursuits as such appealed to her as little as they did to her patrons.

The contents of the handsome walnut shelves were the stereotyped millionaire's miscellany. One had never been sure whether there were three or four Shakespeares, but Aunt Corinne's tastes had also run divertingly to French court memoirs: Ned was deep in the exploits of Cardinal de Retz when the sound of the front door's being opened caused him to raise his head. He heard Celia's voice in the hall, then Grimshaw's; then there was silence. He supposed she had gone to her room, and returned philosophically to his book. But a moment later Celia appeared.

The library was dark and Ned, in the far corner behind a tall silk-embroidered Chinese screen, was not immediately visible. He meant to call out at once, but something in Celia's face stopped him. Her eyes were dilated, her lips twitched uncontrollably; in spite of her fur-trimmed cloak she was shivering a little. As if drawn by invisible cords she swiftly approached the shelf at the opposite end of the room from where Ned was sitting, reached up her hand, and removed a fat morocco-bound volume of Macaulay. Even before she made the gesture Ned guessed what she was going to do; his exclamation was only partly involuntary; somehow he could not bear to spy on his love.

Celia started violently and turned as white as chalk. Nevertheless she did not drop the book she was holding, but replaced it as if nothing had happened; her voice showed only a trace of tenseness. "Neddy, is that you? How you startled me! The carriage is waiting. Aunt Isabel has just telephoned; we're to meet her at Mrs. Voigt's in three quarters of an hour."

An hour later they confronted each other in the costumer's dingy small waiting-room—Celia radiant in her princess gown of shimmering flesh-coloured brocade shot with gold (far lovelier than Julia Marlowe!); Ned in black velvet and rhinestones and a feathered hat, with a sheathed sword dangling proudly at his side. (He had baulked only at wearing a wig and the ladies, after a brief but poignant struggle, had graciously yielded.)

Mrs. Framingham revolved round the couple, clasping her hands ecstatically: they were perfect, quite perfect! Celia was simply a vision, no less. One could not imagine anything more divine; it would be sacrilege—painting the lily, surely—to risk a single additional touch. As for Mr. Ramsay, no-one would have believed . . . a creature of romance, my dear! Did Mrs.

Voigt think his belt was slightly too loose? And possibly the cape might be shortened a trifle—oh, but a hairsbreadth only! "'The little less—and ah, what worlds away!'"

This beatific monologue continued for some time unchecked, while Mrs. Voigt, a sallow, square-featured woman with a jaded eye and a mouth perpetually stuffed with pins (why were ladies of her profession so drably out of keeping with their tinselled and glamorous wares?), muttered assenting or dissenting phrases—they were never whole sentences—in response to Mrs. Framingham's flow of suggestions and inquiries.

Ned, faced by the mirror, was forced to admit he looked far better than he could reasonably have supposed, although he felt strangely discomfited, as men often do, at being deprived of his proper manly length of trouser-leg. As for Celia, she must have known she was beautiful, but she always seemed to take her looks for granted and was heedless of their effect on other people. After a brief glance in the glass she stood in an attitude of barely restrained impatience, finally broke in on her chaperon's artful eloquence with an abrupt "All right, then, Aunt Isabel. If we've nothing further to do, let's run along, shall we? Or are you going to try on *your* costume? By the way, I've never seen it, have I?"

"No, dear," replied Mrs. Framingham; "nor do I intend you shall, till the great night arrives. That's a secret between Mrs. Voigt and me; I've had it sent home already. All I can say is, I hope you'll like it as well as we do."

Ned, who was ready to leave long before the others, filled in the time by smoking a cigarette and inspecting, for lack of anything better, Mrs. Voigt's portfolios of costume designs. Which one, he wondered, had Mrs. Framingham chosen? It must be something magnificent: for days she had been torn between Tiepolo's "Armida" and Gainsborough's "Mrs. Siddons," though when the subject last came up she'd begun to waver in favour of the seventeenth century . . . Rubens, perhaps, or a duchess of Van Dyck's. . . . Suddenly a water-colour sketch pinned to the last page of one of the portfolios caught his eye— Aunt Isabel's work; she had even initialled it. Plainly the seventeenth century had won the day: the gown was inspired by Philippe de Champaigne's "Marie de Médicis" in the Louvre— rich green-blue velvet all sewn with pearls and gold fleurs-de-lys, with a long train and a magisterial ruff. Ned unpinned the sketch and considered it thoughtfully; then, just before the ladies returned, folded it neatly and slipped it inside his breast pocket.

Chapter 6

PRAIRIE Avenue had never beheld such a rout as the Kennerley's farewell ball; it was talked of for years afterwards, looming perhaps even larger in retrospect, as it became increasingly clear that nothing like it would ever be seen again.

When Ned and Almira arrived they were excited to find a calcium light playing on the big brown house, and a crowd already gathered in the street to watch people alighting from their carriages. There was novelty even in the mode of entrance: a small lift, which had been built into the walls of the vestibule, conveyed the guests to the dressing-rooms on the floor above, so that they made their first appearance streaming down the grand staircase, a colourful throng. The hall had been transformed into an Italian pleasure garden, where, in a bower of greenery, Mr. Kennerley and his children received their friends. Grimshaw, at the foot of the steps, was calling out names . . . though that was hardly necessary: "everybody" had been asked, but, as Celia had disarmingly explained, of course nobody else.

The cousins fell into the procession behind the Framinghams. "The Laughing Cavalier," Ned decided, rather belied his name; he looked uncomfortable in his great plumed hat and jerkin and appeared preoccupied by his efforts not to trip over his wife's long velvet train. Mrs. Framingham, on the other hand, was positively twittering with self-satisfaction. She cast exultant glances about her, as if sure that none of the other ladies could rival her gleaming magnificence. Indeed, her dress was almost too handsome; it somewhat dwarfed its possessor, whose fashionably slender, not to say meagre, proportions were not robust enough to support such a royal weight of gold and precious stones.

She was welcomed with acclamations by her hosts, and after a show of squealing reluctance was persuaded by them to take her place in the receiving line. . . . After all, as Mr. Kennerley affably put it, this was her party as much as his. . . . Ned followed Almira into the ballroom, which Mrs. Framingham, whose tastes ran to a Medicean sumptuousness as long as someone else supplied the Medicean purse, had hung with cloth-of-gold. She had also insisted on replacing with candles the bulbs in the chandeliers, so that the scene was suffused with a magical and immensely becoming radiance. A number of couples had already started to waltz; Almira was at once approached by Joe Mallard; but after relinquishing his cousin Ned returned to the entrance hall. Celia had promised that afternoon to dance with him as soon as she was able; it did not, however, appear likely that she would be free for some time. Meanwhile he had far rather wait for her than seek another partner. (If there were a second quite as compelling reason for his action, he kept it prudently concealed.)

The crowd on the staircase was denser than ever. Among familiar figures in unfamiliar guise Ned spotted Mrs. Mallard and her sister in pokebonnets and corkscrew curls, with Doctor Mallard, a bearded Forty-Niner, wearing a red flannel shirt and topboots. There, too, was Mrs. Harper with her wand and tiara, fit to lead the grand march at the Charity Ball . . . and Uncle Rock, who had said all along he didn't mean to come. (Why had one never guessed before that a white wig and grease-paint would make him a perfect Abbé Liszt?)

After Uncle Rock and the Harpers there was a vacant space, as if whoever followed was waiting on purpose to make sure of commanding general attention. Ned held his breath, for he alone knew—or thought he knew—what was going to happen next.

Aunt Lydia suddenly appeared at the head of the long curved flight of steps. She stood where she was for a moment, majestic and glittering; then superbly swept down alone. There was no need for Grimshaw to announce (as he did): "Mrs. Hiram Stack." Neither was it necessary for him to add (as he didn't): "Mrs. Hiram Stack as Mrs. Albert Framingham as Philippe de Champaigne's 'Marie de Médicis.'" From the prongs of her pearl-and-sapphire-studded crown to the tips of her jewelled slippers the duplication was crushingly exact, with this difference—that Aunt Lydia had been endowed by nature with the physique and the presence that suited the part. She was not a woman pretending to be a seventeenth-century queen—she *was* a seventeenth century queen, in all her pomp, her hierarchical dignity, her naïve assumption that royalty was self-evident, eternally important. Mrs. Framingham's miscalculation made the other's triumph the more complete. It was as if the old portrait had really come to life to preside over the revels and accept the homage of her faithful subjects.

If everyone present had sunk to the floor, it would have seemed perfectly appropriate. As it was, they gasped instead and made way for the new arrival. Ned could not remember afterwards whether anybody had spoken; he supposed the conventional greetings must somehow have got themselves said. One terrible moment the two Maries were bowing to each other; the next, Aunt Lydia had laid her hand on Uncle Rock's arm and sailed off to the ballroom, leaving the field this time to the vanquished.

Before supper was over Romeo and Juliet, who were not very hungry, left the dining-room and wandered back through the deserted halls into the conservatory. Once they had shut the door behind them they were alone in their private forest with its good smell of wet earth and growing things; there were no sounds but the rustle of Celia's silken draperies on the gravel and the silver splash of the little fountain. Slowly they strolled along the rose path. . . .

"Those," said Celia instructively, "are Papa's new African curly palms. Aren't they hideous?"

Ned's reply was inarticulate.

"And there, just beyond, are the Australian elkhorn ferns he bought at the Horticultural Show. He's so proud of them, but I can't see that they're any finer than ordinary ferns, can you?"

"Celia," said Ned, "I must say I should think, at a time like this, you might find something better to talk about than your father's botanical specimens."

"Why, certainly," said Celia. "We'll talk about anything you like."

She seated herself on the rim of the marble basin, looked up at her partner, and smiled amiably. "*You* choose; it's all one to me."

That, of course, was just the trouble. Celia had been her best, her happiest self the whole evening, nearer, it seemed, than ever before; but Ned could take no comfort in her nearness, since he saw that her appointed orbit must soon bear her far away again.

Without meaning to he burst out: "What does it matter what I say? It's all over. I love you, and you know it—you're going away, and you're never coming back!"

Celia bent over the fountain, so that her long yellow hair, unbound, fell over her face till it all but touched the water; when

she turned to him once more her eyes were as clear and un-
troubled as ever.

"Never's a hard word. I don't want to make plans now or
promises—how can I? But I expect I'll come home sooner or
later. Chicago *is* my home, after all, whether I like it or not.
And when I do come I hope I'll find you waiting for me. In
the meantime I'll write as often as ever I can; you must write
to me, too. We'll keep in touch that way. . . ."

"Writing! What good's a letter, when it's *you* I want?"

Ned had always known that some day he would propose to
Celia. How many times he'd planned it in his childish dreams!
Reality, however, came as a shock. True, there was nothing
amiss with the setting; the costumes they wore were far more
picturesquely appropriate than the stiff trappings of the
eighties his boyhood fantasies had clothed them in. But somehow he had seen himself sternly passionate, pleading his suit
with a whirlwind intensity no woman could resist. . . . Instead of which he heard his voice (*was* that his voice?) whin-
ing and toneless as a sulky schoolboy's, muttering: "How can
I keep you? What have I to offer you?"

It was, annoyingly, Celia who was poised and mature. For
a blissful moment she gave him both her hands; her blue gaze
remained steadily his as she answered, very gently: "You've
got yourself, haven't you? Neddy, it's almost enough . . . but
no, it's better like this. Understand me—but don't try to love
me!"

Ned attempted to tell her he understood and loved her, too.
He attempted also, with faltering fervour, to make her see
how he had felt about her from the first. Not that he'd cherished romantic illusions. . . . Simply he had known himself
unfree, dedicated—hers to take and use as she would.

Celia replied, still gently, that she knew how it was—yes,
she'd always known. Her eyes shone bright with most becoming tears; her tranquil sympathy seemed the measure of Ned's
hopelessness. He saw now, with despairing clarity, that it was

easy for her to be kind because she did not care—never had cared, most likely never would. (Was it any solace to be sure, as he was, that no other man mattered more than he?)

The kiss she gave him cost her nothing; it might have been a farewell handshake. When at last she deemed it time for them to go—"The music's begun and I'm dancing the german with Jamie!"—she tucked her arm in his confidingly. Ned longed to say something wildly extravagant, but was checked by her candid commonsense. . . . "But you *will* write, my dear? Promise you will! I shouldn't be surprised if we met much sooner than we think. If not in Chicago, maybe in Europe! Why mightn't you go abroad, too?"

At the conservatory door Ned said good-bye; he could not face the crowd just yet. Celia said she saw his point—what *didn't* she see tonight? So much sweet reasonableness was maddening! They parted the best of friends. Then Celia, kissing her hand, floated away in her princess gown, and Ned turned back into the rose walk once more.

In the ballroom Johnny Hand and his musicians were playing one of the songs of the season: how Ned hated the cheerful tune and still more its foolish words! . . .

> "Oh! Jane, she doesn't look the same,
> When she left the village she was shy.
> But alas and alack!
> For she's come back
> With a very different twinkle in her eye. . . ."

It was absurdly unsuited to an elegiac mood. Striding gloomily along, Ned refused to listen to the small insistent voice that whispered: "What would you have done if she'd accepted you?" If only he could have kept the whole place to himself! All evening, unfortunately, other couples had found it a convenient refuge for flirtation. And now that supper was over . . . "I beg your pardon!"

Ned was on the point of beating a tactful retreat, but the young man dressed as a pirate, who sheltered by Mr. Kennerley's curly palms was warmly embracing a young woman in Breton peasant costume, raised his hand in protest.

"Hi there, old chap!" said Sonny, smiling sheepishly—though by no means so sheepishly as one would have supposed circumstances demanded. "Don't go—we need you!"

In spite of his melancholy Ned could not help smiling a little.

"I should have thought this was one time . . ."

Almira released herself and slid to the other end of the garden bench under the palms. She straightened her cap of lace and began putting her hair to rights. Her face was crimson, her round grey-blue eyes big and troubled; she looked like a little girl caught doing something naughty.

"Sonny, you shouldn't . . . Oh, Ned, I don't know what to say!"

"You don't have to say anything, Mira," said Sonny easily. "Ned knows how things are between us. I guess he's always known. And I can't think of anyone I'd rather have be the first to congratulate us. We're engaged, old boy; we have been for at least five minutes."

"Good enough," said Ned; and he meant it. "But to tell the truth I thought you were engaged all winter."

"It's not my fault we haven't been. Your cousin's an obstinate woman, Ramsay. I doubt if I'd got the best of her scruples now but for a little soft music and a glass of champagne."

"Sonny, how *can* you?" cried Almira. "Ned, don't believe a word he says. We're not engaged—we can't be, ever—there's just no sense in it. Help me make him see what I mean."

"Why, of all the blamed nonsense . . . !" Sonny began hotly; then stopped as he saw Almira's imploring look.

Ned faced them both, his hands clasped behind his back—Romeo had no trouser pockets!—glancing from one flushed, desperately earnest face to the other.

"I must say," he felt his way with care, "I agree with Sonny.

You've been friends all your lives. Surely you know each other now as well as two people can, put your feelings to every possible test . . ."

"That's what I tell Mira," Sonny broke in excitedly. "I've loved her ever since I've known her, and I've known her ever since I can remember. There never was a time when she wasn't the only one for me, and I the only one for her—or pretty nearly. So what on earth are we waiting for? There now, Mira —deny it if you can!"

"I don't deny it," said Almira. "You know I care for you; I always have. But what's the use in hoping when our families hate each other?"

"We're not marrying our families."

"No—but they could make things so awful we'd wish ourselves dead. Oh, Sonny, dear, please, *please* be reasonable! *I've tried to be, this winter.* . . ."

"And a devil of a lot of good it's done—making us both miserable for nothing! Oh, I let you have your way for a while, just to show you how stupid you were. Haven't called, or telephoned, or written you a line. . . . Didn't even send you a Christmas present, because you said you'd rather I wouldn't. What's it all amounted to? You've been wretched, and so have I, and we both feel exactly the same as we did before. Hanged if I'll stand it another day! I don't give a damn what my father says—or as far as that goes, your mother either!"

"Then you think," said Ned, "they'd be opposed . . . Have you talked to Aunt Lydia?"

Almira dropped her eyes.

"I don't need to. I'd rather die than mention it. I know how she'd feel without asking. She—hates Mr. Kennerley!"

Ned turned to Sonny.

"What did your father say when you told him?"

Sonny shrugged his shoulders.

"Damned near took my head off. Oh, in a gentlemanly way, of course. I've never seen him lose his temper, have you?

227

Lord, if only he *would!* . . . He said he had no wish to influence me; naturally, I'm free to marry whom I choose. But if I take Mira, I'll have to get along without his blessing. That means getting kicked out of the house, losing my job, being disinherited . . ."

"Can he do that?"

"Don't see what's to stop him. The money's his, every bright silver dollar. He made it; I guess he feels he has a right to dispose of it as he likes."

"Didn't Aunt Corinne leave you anything?"

Sonny shook his curly black head.

"She hadn't much to leave. Most of what she had was an annuity that stopped when she died. And the rest went to her people. It often seems to me," said Sonny feelingly, "that Mamma was related to half South Carolina!"

"What have you got of your own?"

Sonny shook his head again.

"Not even the two traditional red cents."

"I thought you were rich."

"Everybody does! Everybody always thinks a rich man's sons must have money. Maybe they have, in some families; all I know is how it is in mine. Papa gives me an allowance, and anything else within reason . . . Oh, laugh if you like! Perhaps a racing stable *isn't* reasonable—but you know as well as I do he's all for show. But whatever I get depends on his pleasure; he could stop the whole business tomorrow—and then where'd I be? It's unfair, it's rotten, it's any nasty word you like—but that's how things are with the Kennerleys. Pretty picture, isn't it?"

The silence that fell was filled by the fountain's soothing tinkle and the distant strains of *Oh! Jane, she doesn't look the same.* There was also—was there not?—the sound of a quick, impatient step on the gravel. . . .

"I've been looking for you, boy. The german's about to

begin; it's time you found your partner. You, too, Ned, I dare say . . ."

Almira and Sonny had sprung to their feet as if they'd been surprised in an act of immeasurable guilt. None of the trio could speak directly; Abner Kennerley's voice had produced its usual chilling effect. Then Ned managed to murmur (he hoped not faintly) that he hadn't a partner yet; Sonny added, perspiring profusely, that he'd found his already.

"Really?" said Mr. Kennerley, ignoring Almira. "I fancied Florence was expecting . . . but doubtless I was mistaken. In any case I think you had better return to the ballroom at once. This is your party as well as Celia's; your duty now is to *all* your guests. I'll see you, then, presently."

With a curt nod he moved off again and was soon lost to sight in the tangle of shrubbery. Almira burst into tears.

"You see—you see how right I am! There's just one thing to do, and that's for us to try to forget each other. Oh, I'd never forgive myself . . . I'd sooner die . . ."

"Nonsense!" said Sonny fiercely. "Stop it! Here, stop, I say!"

Almost forcing her down upon the bench once more, he began hugging her as hard as he could.

"Listen, darling, whatever happens, we belong to each other —get that through your silly head! I love you and I won't give you up. I've got to have you—*got to*—see? Anything else is too bad to be true. Now, Mira . . ."

Almira, once having started to cry, found it impossible to stop.

"Oh, I can't—I don't know—I've tried so hard! What ought we to do? What *can* we do? Ned, you must help us. You will, won't you, dear Ned?"

After a moment's indecision Ned sat down on the other side of his cousin and patted her shoulder; then he took her hand and patted that, too. He hardly knew what to say. All he was sure of was that Sonny's angry sincerity—still more, perhaps,

Almira's woe, as simple and intense as a child's—had shown him the difference between real love and the half imaginary, more than half self-induced quality of his feeling for Celia. Here beyond a doubt were the true Romeo and Juliet. As this thought flashed over him so did another—and for once, with Ned, thought and speech were very nearly simultaneous. (How easy it was to find the answer to other people's problems!)

"Why," he said, surprised himself at the simplicity of the solution, "there's nothing to it: all you've got to do is elope!"

Chapter 7

THE week after the ball Celia and her chaperon left on the first lap of the long trip to Europe. Mr. Kennerley was to join them later in New York, where Mrs. Framingham planned to refurbish their wardrobes for the splendid ordeal ahead. The ladies took their departure in a flurry of kisses and posies and farewell acclamations . . . not so much tributes to Miss Kennerley's personal popularity as to her pivotal position as Crown Princess of Prairie Avenue. With her removal for an indefinite period the whole social structure of youth on the South Side appeared to be tottering.

At the station Almira, Maud, even Florence, the tart and unsentimental, were dissolved in tears; their attendant young men were grimly dejected. Celia, enchanting in a pale grey travelling suit with a bunch of sweet violets pinned to her belt, distributed smiles and embraces and promised to write to everyone. Her last words with Ned were neither more nor less cordial than those she exchanged with others, but Ned did not care: their real good-bye had been spoken already. As he shook hands with Mrs. Framingham he fancied the latter's eye rested on him with something less than its usual indifference: there was an air of subdued triumph about her, as if up to the last she had feared he might bring her schemes to naught. (Ah, if only he'd shared her delusion, defeat would not seem so cheerlessly blank!)

After the train had puffed away from the Twelfth Street platform the young people strolled home along the boulevard in a disconsolate body. Ned found himself next to one of his principal rivals: grief had paled temporarily the ruddy Mallard complexion, so that its owner's freckles stood out startlingly clear.

"Well, that's that, I guess." Jamie heaved a dolorous sigh. "What kind of flowers did you send her, Ned?"

"Violets."

"I thought as much. I did, too. So now we'll never know whose . . ."

"Oh, she'll wear the others in New York," remarked Ned philosophically. What was the good in sharing one's secret fears and pains? He switched the subject suddenly to Ben Brush's chances of winning next week's Kentucky Derby.

With the coming of spring there were decisions to face. For one, concerts had fallen off so considerably that it was plain the *Chronicle* would not much longer require the services of an assistant music critic. Mr. Shipley sent for Ned to tell him so, but offered to keep him on the payroll as a member of the local staff, at a slight increase in salary, until autumn reopened the theatrical season.

It was gratifying to know he had proved his worth, even though it were in an unspectacular way. But Ned had discovered that he had no real leaning towards a journalistic career. He felt he had got already what he wanted out of his winter's work—experience in dealing with people and, still more valuable, a belief in his professional future. To linger on might be pleasant, but hardly consonant with serious literary ambitions. The better he got to know his colleagues—who were a

231

friendly, approachable lot, much given to gossip over a convivial coffee or beer in the intervals between assignments—the more surely he saw that their life was not for him. All of them, too, had once wanted to write; most still planned to do a book some day; but these projects were generally indefinitely postponed owing to the immediate pressure of their jobs. And the longer they steeped themselves in the cheerful, bustling atmosphere of Newspaper Row the harder they'd find it to concentrate on purely creative goals: their books, when they finally got down to writing them, one could not help feeling were likely to be factually interesting, but little more.

This conviction Ned admitted shyly to Asa Shipley, as well as his cherished desire—which had been part of him for so long that it seemed to have grown with his growth and nourished itself on his inmost thoughts and emotions—to try his hand at a novel.

Rather surprisingly, Mr. Shipley understood.

"You'd better get the writing fever out of your system, boy. Maybe you've got what it takes to write fiction—maybe not— but this much I know: you'll never be content till you've made a stab at it. Good luck to you, and don't forget you've a job waiting for you if you want it again."

Ned parted from his employer with expressions of mutual esteem, and from kindly Frank Twitchell with real regret. Then he retired to the tall yellow house to cope with the daunting problem of breaking the news to his aunt.

Still more surprisingly, this proved to be even easier than the conversation with Mr. Shipley.

It was difficult to say whether she really approved of his plan, or whether her amenability were not simply part of a lifelong policy of letting her family go their own way as long as they let her go hers. She raised no objection even when Ned told her he thought it would be best for him to leave Chicago for a while. Not that he was tired of it: it was only that the Stacks made him too comfortable, too contented; one felt a

certain austerity more appropriate to the task of creation. . . .
California, perhaps? Or, if that were too lush, some seques-
tered New England village. There was no financial reason—
was there?—why he should not go. His income, small as it
was, sufficed for his needs; there was the money he'd saved
from his salary, besides. . . .

Aunt Lydia said at once that of course Ned must do what
he liked. He would be welcome to return; his room was there
whenever he wanted it. "I hope you know how happy I've
been to have you with us this winter. I want you to feel you've
a home here always as long as I live. I'll miss you very much,
my dear."

Ned replied that he would miss her very much, too. And
the greatest surprise of all was to realize that this was deeply
true.

In fact, it was only the strength of his affection for Aunt
Lydia, and a persistent reluctance to displease her, that caused
the scruples he felt about abetting the plans of the lovers, in
which he soon found himself heavily involved.

Events moved with exceeding swiftness once Mr. Kennerley
had left for Europe. As soon as he was gone the whole atmosphere of the big brown house seemed changed. Spring had
come over night both indoors and out: in the gilded drawing-
room, where Ned had kept his winter trysts with Celia, he sat
now every afternoon with Celia's brother, while robins sang
in the garden, the scent of lilacs blew through the open windows on a languid breeze, and Almira, inexpert with nervousness beneath the clambering Cupids' marble stares, made tea
for the two young men.

At first it seemed hard to grasp the urgency of Sonny's feelings. Almira's one could comprehend more readily: she was
twenty-one past, quite old enough to get married, and, unde-
manding as she was, could certainly be under no illusions as
to the degree of her importance at home. Sonny was handsome
and charming and utterly devoted—her first suitor, it was

233

true—but how could she hope for a better one? On the other hand, though he was extremely fond of his cousin, Ned had to admit there were many prettier and livelier girls in Chicago than Almira Stack. Gradually, however, he began to perceive that it was her very lack of sparkle, the steadiness of the light that neither waxed nor waned and, one guessed somehow, would never go out, that formed the basis of her appeal. It was a remedy against the taint in the Kennerley blood, a refuge against the unknown future. For there was no doubt of it: Sonny clung to Almira as to his sanity; it was his desperate need that finally forced his more placid and timorous love to a drastic decision.

Ned had felt from the beginning that his original inspiration was the only possible course to pursue. What else, after all, could they do? It was no use discussing the families' feud: there it *was,* sinister, undeniable, darkly resisting the subtlest efforts towards appeasement. If it was hopeless to seek their parents' consent, then the sooner the young people acted without it, the better.

The moment was favourable, such an one as might not come again for months. Sonny had better apply for the marriage license out of town; there'd be no trouble in getting it, as both parties concerned were legally of age. Then, some afternoon, he and Almira could take the train to Waukegan, seat of Lake County, and after the ceremony continue across the Wisconsin state line to the Kennerleys' summer place at Lake Geneva. The house had been shut since Mrs. Kennerley's death; there was only a caretaker in charge, and Sonny declared he'd have no trouble in squaring old Whittaker.

Meanwhile Ned engaged to keep Aunt Lydia in ignorance till as late in the day as he could, and to reveal the elopement when concealment was no longer possible. If her reaction were not too explosive, the bride and groom would rush back to town to sue for forgiveness. If, on the contrary, she proved adamant, they could stay where they were indefinitely. Sonny, of course, might choose his own time to write to his father. It would, happily, be some days before Mr. Kennerley heard what had happened; many days more before an answer was to be expected. Sonny had a simple faith in the power of absence and time to cool the first fierce resentments; Ned, less sanguine, still felt there was everything to be said for presenting an accomplished deed.

All that was necessary now was for Almira to summon the courage to take the first, and perhaps the only, decisive step of her life.

Ned appreciated better than Sonny, who often grew impatient with her recurring doubts, how hard this was for her to do. She was docile by nature and, moreover, had lived so long under a benevolent despotism that the thought of revolt appalled her. But finally, after a week of her *fiancé's* wild pleadings, varied by a calmer cousinly insistence that, if she weren't brave now, she might never have a chance to be so again, she flung up her hands and cried: "Yes, then—*yes!* I'll do it! Only, please, get everything fixed as quick as you can. For if you don't, I'll start thinking . . ."

On the night before the elopement Ned lay wakeful for hours, counting the trains that rushed by in tumultuous succession. (How strong the smoke smelled, and how the glass in the windows and bookcases rattled! Surely, surely there were more of them than there had ever been before.) A prey to last-minute misgivings, he strove in vain to quiet his nerves by listing methodically the various steps he'd have to perform in keeping his part of the bargain. They'd hit upon a Thursday, as Aunt Lydia would be safely out of the way at a Fortnightly meeting. In the evening the family were invited to dine on the North Side with Porter and Fanny. It would be easy to trump up some excuse for Almira's non-appearance. . . . Only that afternoon it had been decided to take one of the maids into their confidence to help with the packing. Almira had said at once that Mary Kelly was no good—she was too simple not to let the cat out of the bag. And Janet was no better than Mamma's secret agent. That was another reason for choosing Thursday: there'd be no-one home but "Murph." . . .

In spite of their fears everything passed off according to schedule. Half an hour before lunch Aunt Lydia, dressed in her best and serenely unsuspicious to the last, drove off in the victoria. Half an hour after the meal—which neither of the young people made much pretence at eating—Ned ran out to look for a cab on the avenue. (It had been agreed with Sonny that it would be safer for the runaways to meet at the station.) By the time he had got back to the house with his hansom Almira, hatted and cloaked, stood in the hall, while Mary Murphy, breathing heavily with emotion, was coming downstairs with a bag in each hand.

There was time for only the briefest farewell. Ned kissed his cousin warmly, very conscious of her nearness and of the big eyes blinking back the tears. Mary Murphy flung her apron over her head and burst into loud sobs; then emerged from eclipse with an empurpled countenance to exclaim: "God bless yez, Miss Almira, dear. Sure, haven't I always prayed yez and yer young man would come to yer senses before t'was too late? Don't worry; t'will all be all right, with the Lord's help—and Master Ned's, of course. I've packed the pink muslin as well as the blue chambray, an' if yez haven't enough gloves an' handkerchiefs, don't forget to let me know. . . ."

Ned was waiting in the window when his aunt came home about six o'clock to explain that Almira had gone to bed with a sudden neuralgic headache and would have her supper on a tray; she was trying now to get some sleep and begged her mother not to worry; they'd already telephoned to Fanny. Aunt Lydia received this information with her usual equanimity. She expressed regret but no concern and retired to dress; Ned felt that the situation was saved until morning at least.

The Porter Stacks' dinner was given in honour of Mrs. Porter's sister, who had just arrived from Washington for a visit. Ned was placed next her at table, but his thoughts kept straying and afterwards he was not even able to recall what Miss Betty King had looked like, retaining only a vague impression of hazel eyes and a dragging semi-southern voice.

After dinner the party adjourned to Fischer's Garden, north of the park. It was a very fine evening, mild enough to sit out without wraps; a gentle breeze from the lake just stirred the feathery foliage of the elms overhead. Porter ordered beer for the men and ices for the ladies; then the company settled down to enjoy the good German band in the *Dichter und Bauer* overture and a selection of lively Strauss waltzes.

Aunt Lydia's ideas of a chaperon's duties were, as one might have expected, fairly relaxed. She sat, with a lace shawl draped on her copper-coloured braids, well back in her chair, nodding her head in time to the music and chatting in an undertone with Uncle Rock; her young charges were free to stroll as they liked among the flowerbeds in the warm May moonlight.

It was past eleven before she ordered the carriage; when they had driven as far as Twelfth Street she suddenly called to Simms to stop, and said she wanted to walk the rest of the way home. Ned and Uncle Rock got out to walk with her. It had grown much cooler; the breeze had freshened so that the green taffeta folds of Aunt Lydia's evening cloak billowed like a sail; the ends of her scarf blew straight out behind. But she laughed and said she did not care.

Ned had never seen her in such spirits. Her stately tread had quickened; she seemed under the sway of some happy and barely suppressed excitement. And she talked more than he had heard her do in weeks. . . . A high wind like this, said Aunt Lydia, lifting her chin, always put her in mind of the Fire. . . . Only, of course, the gale that had blown then was one of those hot, dry Southwesters. "Will you ever forget that night, Rock? . . . We were living on Ontario Street, Ned, near the corner of Clark, in a brown-painted cottage with a big garden. It seems hard to realize it now, but in those days it was almost like the country. Uncle Hiram was out of town on one of his business trips and your family were in Europe for the summer; I was alone with the children—just the boys; Almira hadn't been born or thought of—except for my coloured girl Dulcie, who wasn't much more than a child herself. . . . Dear me, how long ago it seems! Porter was teething; I'd been up with him two or three nights in a row and was so worn out that I'd gone to bed early that Sunday. About one in the morning, I think it was, Dulcie pounded on the door, crying that the city was afire and I'd better make haste if we weren't to be burned in our beds. I got dressed somehow and rushed out on the lawn: the sky towards the river was an awful bright red, the air was choking thick with smoke, and brands and molten cinders kept flying about, starting new blazes wherever they lighted. Poor Dulcie was bawling that the Day of Judgement had come—and I must say it looked like it! Just then a man ran by in the street ringing a bell and shouting that the Water Works had gone. That meant the end, of course; nothing could be saved. Dulcie and I got the pony harnessed—I'm sure I don't know how, for I'd never done such a thing before in my life—and we hitched our cow to the back of the pony-cart. I'd have liked to take the chickens, too, but they were flying every which way, poor things! squawking as though the butcher were after 'em. Then I dressed the children and tried to put a few things in the carriage—some of the silver, and a picture or two I was fond of. The boys were too little to be frightened, but Tom kept crying he wanted his toys and his kitten. . . . I couldn't bother with playthings, but I did go back into the house the last thing and found poor Tiny hiding under the dining-room table. She scratched me pretty badly, but I managed to get her safe away. Oh, if only I'd had a man to help me!"

238

"Yes; where was I?" said Uncle Rock. "Very remiss it was of me, indeed, my dear Lydia!"

"I'm sure it was the only time you ever failed me," said Aunt Lydia, with a softened look. "And it was hardly your fault, Rock; you didn't know yet that I even existed! . . . Well, we got out into the street, and just as we did the barn roof fell in —there wasn't any time to lose. The place was a mess, all cluttered with carts and horses and people running to and fro carrying things. One man had an enormous mirror with a heavy gold frame, and another, a marble statue almost as big as he was: I guess they were too scared to remember what would burn and what wouldn't. But the queerest sight of all was old Mr. and Mrs. Buford, who lived on the corner, sitting on their front doorstep, each with a birdcage in hand, crying as if their hearts would break.

"Hopkins, the grocer, called out to me that the Gas Works were going, too—I'd better head for the lake. I didn't know where else to go; it seemed the only thing could stop that dreadful fire. It wasn't far—the shore line came a whole lot farther in than it does now, Ned—but it was hard driving through the terrible heat and smoke and confusion. The pony kept trying to rear—he was half mad with fright, naturally— and Dulcie did nothing but moan—she was no good at all.

"Down on the water's edge were hundreds of people, men and women and children, praying and cursing by turns. Some were so crazy with fear that they couldn't believe they were safe and ran right out into the water. They'd have been drowned, I suppose, if the lake had been rough; but with an offshore wind it was almost as calm as a millpond. We were a lot better off than most, for at least we had the cart to cling to. I made the children as comfortable as I could, and told Dulcie not to leave them, whatever happened. Then I walked a little way along the beach to see if I could find anyone I knew. The dawn was breaking by this time, but the light it made was nothing to that horrible glare behind us. . . . After a while I heard a woman crying as if she were in terrible pain. I stopped to look, and there, half hidden under a broken old willow tree, was a poor creature rolling and screaming. I could see with half an eye what the trouble was—she was having a baby right there on the sand. She seemed to be all by herself; nobody paid any more heed to her than if she'd been some kind of animal. I'd never been a midwife, but I'd had two children of my own and I had some idea what ought to be done. Just as I was wondering how best to begin I heard a man's voice at my elbow saying: 'If you can take her head, I'll get hold of her feet and we'll move her up on the bank out of harm's way. I've some brandy in a flask here, too. . . .'"

"You can imagine what I thought," Uncle Rock took up the tale. "There you were all in white, as you are now, but with your long hair streaming down over your shoulders. I'd never seen such hair; you looked like a sea nymph just risen from the waves, it seemed to me."

Aunt Lydia laughed.

"I was a lot more useful than a sea nymph would have been. We stayed with the woman till the baby came and we saw she was going to be all right. What a time we had! I forgot where I was or what had happened; I didn't even think about Tom and Porter till the danger was past. Then it struck me all of a heap: *I* had a family of my own. I was looking about in desperation when I saw poor, silly Dulcie running past me up the beach; she'd lost her head completely and left the babies by themselves to search for me. I gave a great cry; she saw me, and fell flat in the sand, laughing and crying and kissing my feet. We must have looked pretty funny."

"What happened then, Aunt Lydia?" asked Ned, as the story seemed to be over.

"Oh, that's really the end, my dear. We stayed on the shore for hours after that, for the fire went on raging all day. Uncle Rock stayed with us; he fetched the pony-cart, and we made ourselves as snug as we could by the willow tree, so we could

keep an eye on the mother and child. Uncle Rock even tried
. . . have you forgotten, Rock?"

"How could I forget?" said Uncle Rock, with a chuckle.
"That was the first and only time in my life I milked a cow!
I'm afraid it wasn't a great success."

"But oh, how glad I was to have you there! Truly, I don't
know what we'd have done without you. Towards evening,
Ned, the wind dropped—what a mercy that was!—and it began to rain a little. We knew then we were saved. And before
the second night came Uncle Hiram found us. He'd had a
fearful time getting back to the city and he was mighty near
out of his mind with worry. We drove out through the black
charred ruins to Evanston and spent the winter with the Harvey Stacks. In the spring your father and mother came home
and we all bought land on Prairie Avenue, and there we've
been ever since."

After a pause Ned said: "What became of the poor woman
and the baby? Did it live?"

"It lived that time all right," replied Aunt Lydia. "But it
never grew strong, and a year or so later it took pneumonia
and died. Poor little Lyddy! Janet would name her for me,
you know."

"Janet!" cried Ned. "Do you mean—"

"Why, hadn't you heard it before?" said Uncle Rock. "I
thought of course your aunt had brought you children up on
the story."

Aunt Lydia shrugged her shoulders and increased her already rapid pace. "It's all so long ago. What's the use in recalling what's over and done with? I don't often think of
those bad old times. I can't imagine what made me remember
tonight. . . ."

The rest of the way home she spoke hardly a word. Uncle
Rock, too, was silent; perhaps the conversation had started him
on a reminiscent train of thought. Ned himself had much to
ponder: how hard it was to associate his aunt and her old

friend with the perilous past of pioneer Chicago! It seemed as if they must always have lived the life they had now, spacious and leisured, sedately devoid of adventure.

At the corner of Indiana Uncle Rock bade his companions good-night, but it was not until she had reached her own front steps that Aunt Lydia woke from her trance. "Ned, my dear, will you lock up and leave a light in the hall for me? I'm going to run upstairs a minute to see how Almira is. Poor child, I'd quite forgotten . . ."

This brought Ned back to reality with a bump of alarm. He said at once—perhaps too hastily—he was sure his cousin must be asleep; but Aunt Lydia declared that, if that were so, she'd not dream of waking her. "I'll just peep through a crack of the door. . . ."

Ned was appalled. Here was a hazard neither he nor Almira had foreseen: such unwonted maternal solicitude seemed most unnatural. Could his aunt's suspicions have been somehow aroused? At all events, one could not forbid her access to the upper storeys of her own house; as she continued to insist it became plain that nothing but the truth would do.

On the doorstep, with the key in his pocket, Ned confronted her, outwardly calm but inwardly quaking.

"Aunt Lydia, there's something I've got to tell you. Almira's not here."

"What do you mean?"

"Not in her room—not in the house at all."

"Indeed! Where, then, may I ask . . . ?"

"She's at the Kennerleys'. Not in town . . . at the house in Lake Geneva."

"So! And when are we to expect her back?"

"She isn't coming back. At least, not for a while. She . . . she's married, Aunt Lydia. To Sonny. They went to Waukegan this afternoon. They asked me to say . . . to try to tell you . . ."

Ned's voice faltered and stopped before the dawning amazement in the chestnut-brown eyes. Aunt Lydia stood still for a moment. She had gathered the folds of her taffeta cloak around her; it shone vividly green in the flickering gaslight; the hand that held it in place rose and fell with the rising and falling of her bosom beneath it.

It was hard to tell how one had imagined she would take the news, but Ned was certainly not prepared for what happened now. His aunt raised her free hand to her throat, then suddenly burst out laughing at the top of her voice—she who seldom laughed, who had never, as long as he'd known her, shown any strong emotion . . . no, not even on the fearful night when they had brought her husband's body home. The contralto peals rang out almost frighteningly in the quiet street, unbridled, unmodulated, strangely lacking in mirth.

Ned begged her to stop, though she paid no attention to him. Finally, in desperation, he unlocked the door and half led, half pushed the tall figure through it. But even in the hall Aunt Lydia went on laughing.

Book III : 1904

Chapter 1

AFTERWARDS Ned realized what a near thing it had been: but for the Russo-Japanese war he would not have gone to America at all that spring, and would therefore have failed the Stacks at the time they most needed him. He had been spending the winter in Rome, where the unexpected news of the success of his latest novel caught up with him. For years a trip to the Orient had beckoned tantalizingly on the horizon; now, when at last ambitious plans were possible, unsettled international conditions proved an equally daunting obstacle. After debating various alternatives—all, miraculously, within an enlarged financial reach—he decided suddenly to sail for home.

He arrived in New York early in June to find "Queen Margot" in its third edition, with several more printings agreeable probabilities. How delightful it was to be done forever with the tentative stage of a writer's career! To be received with enthusiasm by his agent and publishers; to find the latter generally non-committal gentlemen passionately interested in his future projects, and as eager to offer new contracts as in the past they had seemed reluctant (often making Ned feel they were doing him an immense favour by taking on yet another unpromising literary property). Oh, they'd never said so straight out: there were always a number of excellent reasons for one's poor showing. . . . It was a bad season for first novels. . . . The market was dull. . . . Musical fiction had fallen off lately. These excuses were proffered with a glassy-eyed speciousness that did not deceive the wretched author for a minute: he knew his sponsors were quite simply convinced that, if he wrote better, his books would sell better, too.

Looking back on his struggles, Ned was thankful he'd gone on believing in his own talents in spite of the odds. At least he'd always been *printed;* success at thirty-one was sweeter than it would have been a decade earlier. Best of all, once having achieved the formula, he could repeat it indefinitely.

It had been stumbled upon by a happy accident. The modern transatlantic scene having failed to suit—Ned had been wont to present a more or less Jamesian hero against a background of the subtleties of continental Europe—and America providing no immediate inspiration—after all, his easy cosmopolitanism had kept him from more than half knowing it —he bethought himself finally of French history, which years of reading and travelling had made more familiar than his own. What if he chose some picturesque figure of the Renaissance and, sacrificing nothing of psychological truth or of a hard-won felicity of phrase, wrote about him, or her, as intimately and cosily as though it were—well, say Aunt Lydia Stack?

Since the result of the venture clearly showed that Ned had hit it at last, unlimited vistas were opened up: the sixteenth century swarmed with possible protagonists; and if, later, one tired of them, were there not even richer stores to be tapped in the seventeenth and eighteenth centuries as well? In short, the future looked radiant; there was not, that first week in June, 1904, on the whole of Manhattan Island a young man more thoroughly pleased with life and himself than Edward Ramsay.

It might have been pleasant to linger in town indefinitely enjoying the fruits of his labours, if the season had not been over and most of the people he knew preparing to scatter for the summer. Ned had numerous acquaintances, though few intimate friends: his background caused fellow writers to judge him a butterfly, whereas in social circles he could not but fear his profession made him appear a grub. But in any case New York was not home. After more than two years away from it he felt an imperious longing for the red-painted barns and flat, verdant cornfields of the Middle West. About Chicago his emotions were mixed: he could do neither with nor without it; it seemed as impossible to settle there as to abandon it permanently.

Ned had often discussed this with Frank Twitchell, now long established in the Promised Land as the well paid and influential music critic of the *New York Clarion*. Frank, of course, could not see the point: *he* was all for the larger field, the amenities of a mellower civilization. In fact, New York itself hardly satisfied him any more; lately he'd begun to hint wistfully at what he might have done in Paris or London. (Wasn't it odd, then, to note the nostalgia in his voice when the talk turned, as eventually it always did, to days gone by in the big smoky city with its restless vitality and scurrying people, blown as it were towards their goals by eternal gales from the lake or the prairie?)

To Ned, Chicago was as much more alive than New York as New York was than Europe. If it were impossible to do one's best work there, it was just as impossible to work anywhere else without returning at intervals to recharge one's batteries (the spiritual energy thus acquired to be used later as one willed). Moreover, each time he went back it was like touching home base, the one place in the world where he was primarily neither novelist nor agreeable bachelor-at-large, but accepted unquestioningly as Robert Ramsay's son and Hiram Stack's nephew. The closest ties he knew were with Aunt Lydia and her children: when he returned to his hotel one evening, about a fortnight after landing, to find a letter from the former in his mail-box, his doubts as to the future were resolved at once. His aunt wrote in her usual cheerful strain, urging him to come for a visit; she alluded to no troubles, made no complaints; but, knowing her now as well as anyone could, Ned read something between the lines that induced him to send her a telegram, pack his bags, and leave for the West the following day.

Simms was on the platform to greet him, and Aunt Lydia herself waited outside in the victoria behind a bay mare that could not really be Queen, but looked so much like her that it might as well have been. The meeting was warmly affectionate; his aunt excused herself for not getting out of the carriage; she'd been afraid to leave the basket of fruit they'd just fetched from Kennerley's. On the way home from the station she told him she was delighted he'd come, as she was a poor old woman and did not expect to live much longer. . . . That, of course, was absurd: she had grown a good deal stouter and her braids were certainly redder, but smiling and rosy in her lilac foulard, her lap piled high with peaches and pears and melons and grapes, she might, save for her high plumed hat, have posed for Demeter, the harvest goddess.

Ned told her this; she told him, in return, that *he* was looking very well, too. (Wasn't his hair, though, a little thin in front?) She remarked, also, that she had read "Queen Margot" and enjoyed it immensely; everybody she knew who'd read it had liked it. . . . "But, my dear, she really *was* . . . wasn't she? I mean, I'd no idea . . . And what, exactly, *is* a farthingale?" . . . Ned was to have his old room, naturally; she only hoped he'd be comfortable. It had been years, asserted Aunt Lydia, chuckling, since she'd seen the upper storeys of 1817. . . . The new chambermaid was a ninny.

(Janet, Ned knew, had died last winter after a long and terrible illness. Almira had written him not to mention it to her mother, who could not bear to speak of her loss.) As for butlers—necessary now that Mary Kelly had unfeelingly retired to live with a widowed sister—Swedes weren't smart and Englishmen drank. The present incumbent, French Dominique, *looked* all right, but Aunt Lydia suspected he did not know how to clean silver. . . . Uncle Rock was coming to dinner. She'd meant to have the children: Tom and Carrie were engaged, and Porter and Fanny lived in Winnetka the year round—had one ever heard of such foolishness? though they pretended they liked it. As for Sonny and Almira, they were in the country, too—temporarily only, thank Heaven! They'd just moved out for the summer to their big new place west of Lake Forest and were hoping Ned would come for the week-end. . . . How were they? Very well. Everyone, Aunt Lydia was glad to say, was well, including the grandchildren, all eight of them—Tom's two, Porter, Junior, and Almira's four little girls: Corinne and Lydia, and the twins, whom Ned had not yet seen.

Aunt Lydia patted Ned's hand while she spoke, as though to reassure him. Of course, if anything were seriously wrong, she would hardly have broached the subject before Simms . . . and how could there be anything seriously wrong? Still Ned was not satisfied. There were gaps and elisions in her conversation just as there had been in her letter; the great ox-eyes were not so serene as the calm, purring voice. Whatever was amiss, he'd find out sooner or later; there was no hurrying Aunt Lydia. Her way with unpleasantnesses was to approach them by degrees, like a hunter stalking big game, aware that the first shot must be decisive.

There was just time before dressing for dinner to run down to salute Mary Murphy, still presiding, half blind and hoary with antiquity, over her basement kitchen, assisted by a series of timorous Annies and Mollies, none of whom, according to their mistress, stayed long enough to settle in. Uncle Rock appeared punctually at seven. (Here was one person who had not changed; it seemed he had early grown as old as he ever would.) After dinner, when Ned proposed a move to the front steps, Aunt Lydia said that, warm as it was, it would be safer to remain inside; the smudge from the factory chimneys, and what had become an almost incessant rain of cinders from passing trains, made outdoors disagreeable.

So they sat in the drawing-room instead, with the windows ajar, which was surprisingly comfortable; it took several days for a heat wave to penetrate these solidly built, high-ceilinged old houses. Undeniably the place was a clutter: its owner had gone on buying for so many years, without breaking, or losing, or giving anything away, that one had to thread through a maze of superfluous chairs and tables and *bric-à-brac*. However, Monsieur Carolus-Duran's Aunt Lydia smiled from her gilt frame over the mantel at the equally benign real Aunt Lydia on the familiar pink sofa below. Presently the perennial embroidery hoops and what one had come to consider a "property" piece of work were reassuringly produced. Ned glanced with satisfaction at the rose-shaded lamps, sniffed the odour of mignonette and petunias in the window-boxes, and felt somehow that he had never been away.

It took some time, of course, to catch up on the gossip of the quarter. Aunt Lydia's bulletins had a documentary thoroughness; one of her most endearing qualities was an unquenchable curiosity about her neighbours' affairs, and a rather touching assumption that everybody else must be interested, too. (As a matter of fact, all being grist to the novelist's mill, Ned *was* interested.) . . . Old Mrs. Cobden, it appeared, had taken to drugs and collecting Old Masters (one of each master!). After some years of solitude she'd begun importing a succession of nieces from the family home in Ohio. Unfortunately her temper had grown so violent that none of the nieces could stand it—they were continually being sent back to Youngstown to be credited. . . . The Zindersteins fitted in better than one had feared. (Alas, though, they weren't any longer the only Jews on the avenue!) They gave to everything without demur and still seemed pleased if one asked them to dinner. . . . Dora Harper? Ah, there was a case! Since she'd lost her dreadful little old monkey-husband a few years ago she'd been unable to settle down, but drifted aimlessly round the world, from New York to Newport to London, wondering why her beauty and her money did not seem to assure her social success. "Dora was always a dull woman," said Aunt Lydia, with comfortable malice. "She don't realize that looks may attract, but it's brains that hold: makes me think of a mountain climber who's used up so much breath getting to the top she's too tuckered out to enjoy the view!" . . . Grace Littlefield's husband had died recently, and Mary Bunner's, too. "Seems as though there's hardly a man left on the block—they're beginning to call us, you know, the Prairie Avenue Widows!"

Ned had wondered about this before now: why had so many of the "strong old roosters" (to use a pungent phrase of Uncle Hiram's) vanished comparatively early from the scene of their triumphs? Was it because their lives had been too hard in youth? Or had they expired from pure boredom, since there was really nothing left for them to do?

Then he recalled the one among them who had not gone, whose wiry pliancy had outlasted the ruggeder qualities of the other original pioneers. (One had felt from the first he'd be durable goods.) Ned shrank from introducing Mr. Kennerley's name, but his aunt had apparently long outgrown her sensitiveness on the subject: as if guessing the trend of his thoughts, she started suddenly to talk about Abner and Isabel. . . . What a life they'd led! . . . Ned must have heard something of that: he'd not forgotten—had he?—that after they'd married Celia off to the Duc de Longuyon (the best they could have got in England was a rather new earl or a much too old marquess), Mrs. Framingham persuaded her friend to buy a colossal steam-yacht and tour the world in it *à trois*. They'd embarked on cruise after cruise, always with Bertie Framingham in tow; attended regattas at Kiel and Cowes; hobnobbed with a royal flush of crowned heads. . . . "I wish," remarked Aunt Lydia pensively, "I could've seen the black satin knee-breeches Abner wore to the Kaiser's levees—his legs were always like pipestems!" . . . The winters they spent exploring the Mediterranean and the Greek Archipelago. (Must have been hard on Isabel, who was a wretched sailor.) But Bertie *wouldn't* die! In the old days they'd always pretended he was incipiently tubercular. Unluckily he grew healthier and healthier instead—why not? With all that fresh air!—and in the end his wife got tired of waiting and simply divorced him. "You were abroad last year when it happened, Ned, but I dare say you saw the accounts in the papers. It made an awful scandal, especially as that harpy turned right round as soon as she had her decree in her pocket and married Abner: in California it was, just after Christmas. Of course the fuss'll blow over in time—in fact, it already has, more or less. With a fortune like that . . . Perhaps Chicago won't quite forgive them, but then, I doubt if they'll be much in Chicago any more. I hear Isabel thinks we're provincial. Maybe we are: I don't care!"

Aunt Lydia paused to laugh unresentfully. "All the same she'd better watch out for Abner; his business means more to him than any woman. . . . Oh, yes, they're here now—didn't you know?—arrived last week, bags and baggage, to open the house. It's their first official appearance since the wedding. And Celia's here, too. I can't imagine why—she's never bothered to look us up before—unless it's to lend the family her moral support. I don't suppose we're likely to snub our first duchess! But you'll be seeing the lot of 'em tomorrow at Almira's. . . . My dear, will you ring for Dominique? It's so close tonight, I think we'd better have gin slings instead of tea."

When Uncle Rock rose to go Ned offered to walk home with him. He'd wanted a breath of air, but by this time what breeze there was had dropped; the rows of elms stood motionless like trees on the stage; nothing moved save the swarms of sandflies clustered thickly about each gas-lamp. How quiet it was! Their footfalls on the worn limestone pavement were the only sounds between trains, except for the clip-clop of an infrequent horse-cab or the even less frequent whine of an electric coupé speeding past like an oversized mosquito.

By tacit consent the two men strolled down to Twenty-Second, then north again by the railroad and lake as far as the Fort Dearborn Massacre Monument before turning west to Indiana. It was the route Ned had taken countless times in his boyhood. He knew every step of the way; he'd covered it mentally over and over for years. Yet—wasn't it queer?—it always looked new after even the shortest absence, and he still was never quite sure of the order the houses came in.

Half way back along Calumet Avenue they paused before a tall grey granite castle that bore a comic resemblance to its model, the Hôtel de Gouin in Tours. The spacious grounds of the town residence of Mr. and Mrs. Abner Kennerley, Junior, adjoined at the rear the garden of Kennerley, Senior, mute reminder of the reconciliation that had followed the elopement within a twelvemonth—even sooner than Sonny and Almira had hoped. It was one of the handsomest houses in the street, and the newest one, too: since its erection, some six or seven years ago, no further additions had sprung up either on Calumet or Prairie. People, in fact, said Uncle Rock, in his gentle, melancholy voice, were beginning to move away. "How can you blame 'em, with this terrible dirt? Why, even the trees can't stand it; they're dying much faster than the city can replace them. . . . No, the houses aren't empty; they're dark because nearly everybody goes out of town for the summer now. And I guess they fetch pretty good prices still. But half of them belong to families you never heard of. Lord, Ned,

Zinderstein's an aristocrat compared to some of the fellows who are moving in! I'm afraid the old neighbourhood's falling to bits. If it holds up long enough to see *me* through, I'll be grateful. I suppose I'll stick while your aunt does—and one thing you can bet on: Lydia Stack will never desert Prairie Avenue!"

Ned agreed; it would be impossible to imagine her anywhere else.

When he got back to the house the lights were still lighted in the drawing-room, though his aunt was no longer there. She had retired to the bedroom, leaving the door ajar; Ned paused just outside it, intending merely to call out good-night.

Aunt Lydia rose all-a-swirl in her silk-and-lace dressing-gown and beckoned him in. Her long hair fell like a mantle over her shoulders: Ned was reminded suddenly of the morning interviews in the old days. How much had happened since then! How the world about them had changed, and they with it! Only the green-and-gold chamber looked as it had; only Aunt Lydia remained steadfastly, comfortingly the same. The litter of boxes and Bohemian glass on the toilet-table, the faint odour of *violet sec* that reached him as he crossed the threshold, were symbols of a past that here alone was still the living present.

Ned saw at a glance that the time had come to get down to business. His aunt bade him shut the door and be seated; she, too, resumed her place and began again to brush her hair, but the action was purely mechanical; the eyes in the looking glass were fixed unwaveringly on some immediate purpose. For a moment she did not speak; Ned, watching the rhythmic, deliberate motions, repeated to himself:

> *"Ihr gold'nes Geschmeide blitzet,*
> *Sie kämmt ihr goldenes Haar.*
> *Sie kämmt es mit goldenem Kamme . . ."*

"My dear," said Aunt Lydia finally, "I thought you were never coming back. I couldn't say this in front of Rock—

though he probably knows the whole story. Men are all alike; they never give one another away. I need your help, Ned—need it badly."

"Why, of course, anything I can do—"

"You can do a great deal, if I'm not mistaken."

"What's the matter, Aunt Lydia?"

"It's about Sonny and Almira."

Ned felt he had known all along it might be; his aunt's comparative silence on the subject that otherwise would have been first on the list meant more than words. But he said only: "I thought you told me they were well."

"Oh—*well*—if that were all . . ."

"And happy as far as you know? They've seemed to me a singularly well matched couple."

"They are—they have been. I'll admit, up to now, Almira's career has been a great satisfaction to me. Of course Sonny's no businessman. His father used to pretend he regretted it, but you can't tell me he'd ever have let him have anything important to do at the office. Oh, no, while he lives Abner will be Kennerley and Company! He's been proud of Sonny in other ways. He loves hearing people say the young Kennerleys are the leaders of Chicago society. (I like it myself; I'm frank about that.) He gives the children anything they want as long as it's grand enough to suit him. The house in Calumet Avenue is twice as big as they needed—and wait till you see the Villa Bellaggio! Looks more like a country club or a fancy summer resort than anything else I can think of. And he's fond of them, too, as far as a cold fish like him can be fond of anyone. He's treated Almira like his own daughter—far better than ever he did poor Corinne. In fact, if only she'd give him an heir, he'd not have a thing to complain of. That's a grief and a grievance . . . *four* little girls! You know how he acts about the Kennerleys, as if they were some kind of royalty . . . and of course it was a blow when Roscoe died so young: he got spinal meningitis away at school and was gone before

Abner could get to him. But, on the whole, much as I dislike him, I'll grant he's been fair to my child."

"Sonny's been a good husband, too," said Ned reflectively. "At least, I've always thought so."

"That's just the trouble." Aunt Lydia dropped the brush and turned to face her nephew. "He's been *too* good. He's overdone his devotion just as he has everything else. Don't forget who his mother was! As far as I can make out, he's had only one object in view for the last nine years, and that's to grant every one of Almira's wishes the minute she expressed it. If she *could* have been spoilt, he'd have done it long ago."

"But then I don't see . . . If Mira's so lucky, why should you mind?"

"Because," replied Aunt Lydia trenchantly, "it can't last. Nothing like that could. As a matter of fact, it's already over."

"What makes you think—"

"Sonny has a mistress."

"Who is she?"

"Her name is Daisy Branson. She's nothing but a common prostitute—a woman from one of those houses over on Dearborn Street—no education or manners or anything."

"Oh, Aunt Lydia, are you sure? It doesn't seem likely—"

"Yes, I'm sure. I wouldn't be telling you if I weren't. Tom and Porter came to me separately, a week or so ago, and said the men at the club were all talking about it and they thought I ought to know. If only they'd spoken sooner! I might have done something then. Sonny met her last year at the races in Louisville—Almira was ill and couldn't go with him. And six months ago he began keeping her regularly: she's got an apartment on Drexel Boulevard, her own carriage and pair, and everything else that goes with it, I guess."

"Does Almira know?"

"She hasn't the slightest idea—that's what's so awful. She's gone right on being as cheerful and unsuspicious as a lamb being led to the slaughter. Oh, when I think—"

256

"But," said Ned slowly, "if she doesn't know now, why need she, ever? I mean—this is a frightful thing to say, Aunt Lydia—but such things do happen every day. Perhaps not so often in Chicago, but half the fellows I know in New York keep women—even the ones who are married—happily married at that. Those affairs don't usually last long enough to be a problem. Sonny will tire of this woman sooner or later and go back to his wife—and Mira'll never guess he's been away."

Aunt Lydia eyed him sombrely.

"That's what you think. That's what I thought, too, at first — what anyone in his senses *would* think if they hadn't to deal with Kennerleys! Sonny wants to marry the creature. . . . No! Don't say 'impossible'—I tell you, *I know!* Porter and Tom both believe so; it's common gossip about town."

"But why? Men don't marry their mistresses. At least," added Ned, blushing suddenly, "not *that* kind of mistress."

"Ah! Normal men don't—but Sonny's not normal. He's been unstable from the start. With that inheritance . . . Poor Corinne, charming as she was, was crazy for years, or next door to it. Sonny's got her charm, and the craziness, too."

Ned said nothing for a minute. It was hard to know *what* to say. The best he could manage at last was: "But even if things are as bad as you fear, I don't see how they could lead to a divorce. You can't get divorced without grounds—and Sonny hasn't any."

"He won't need 'em, with Almira. You know what she's like—you better than anyone, Ned—sweet and dull, without an atom of guile—her father over again! I mean," said Aunt Lydia, the creamy voice thickened a trifle, "if things got so bad that she had to leave her husband for the children's sake, she'd do it without a qualm—even though it broke her heart. And if he wanted his freedom enough to beg her for it, she'd give in, no matter what it cost her. Oh, I know my own child! She's too weak to fight for her rights—I've got to do it for her. And you've got to help me."

After another pause Ned said feebly: "Why, of course, Aunt Lydia, anything I can do . . . but wouldn't Tom or Porter be better? They're Mira's brothers; besides they're much older . . . can speak with more authority . . ."

"My sons," declared Aunt Lydia, with asperity, "haven't, either one of 'em, to my certain knowledge, so much as a shred of tact; I think you'll agree that's what is needed here."

"Or Uncle Rock?" Ned floundered, ready to catch at any straw.

"Too old by far. A man's much more apt to be frank with contemporaries. Anyhow Rock would never be able to do it; I doubt if he could manage to roll the word 'mistress' round his spinsterly tongue."

"Mr. Kennerley, then? He may be old, but he's Sonny's father."

Aunt Lydia lifted her chin.

"I haven't spoken to Abner Kennerley for almost ten years, and I've no intention of beginning *now,* thank you. Besides, he and Sonny have never been intimate. I'd try myself—but a woman's no use in a case like this. And it's out of the question with Isabel here. I'll hardly see the children for weeks, very likely—and before I do it may be too late. But *you* can go where I can't, say what I daren't. Watch your chance during the week-end to get Sonny alone. He's always been fond of you. Don't get angry; that won't do a bit of good. But talk to him sensibly and seriously, and see if you can't persuade him to be sensible and serious, too. So much is at stake—Almira's happiness, the children's—everything we've lived for, really. If you fail, at least you'll have the satisfaction of knowing you did your best. But I feel you won't fail, my dear. Oh, Ned, this is the only thing I've ever asked of you . . ."

Aunt Lydia's voice broke, full of tears; there were tears in her eyes, too, the first she had shed, more than likely, since her husband's death. In silence Ned took her hand and kissed it.

Chapter 2

NED stepped from the last carriage, the parlour car of the five-fifty-five, onto the purplish bricks of the Lake Forest station platform, to find himself in a welter of returning husbands and peering wives who had come to meet them. A long row of horse-drawn vehicles, interspersed with an automobile or two, stood next the platform; at the far end of this Ned presently caught sight of his host in a gig, grasping the reins of a mettlesome sorrel pony.

"Hullo there!" called Sonny, waving his whip in welcome and smiling his flashing white smile. "Forgive me for not getting out; I wasn't sure Dancer would stand; the train always excites him. Mira sent her love and told me to tell you she was sorry she couldn't come, too; the rest of the guests arrived on the four o'clock and she's busy getting 'em settled. Can you manage, old boy? I hope there's room for your bag in the tilbury; I wanted to drive the new French motor-car, but Mira wouldn't let me: she said we'd be sure to break down and have to walk home, and where could she get two men at the last minute to balance her dinner-table? Lord, Ned, but I'm tickled to see you!"

Ned was glad, too. He felt rising within him the same old warm sense of fellowship that was purely instinctive; he and Sonny had never had anything else in common, but it was enough.

They started off at a smart clip; Sonny was perpetually in a hurry. He held the reins easily, scarcely seeming to look where they were going; then turned with another smile to his cousin-in-law and began to inquire minutely into the latter's recent activities, without really listening to the answers.

259

He also offered a summary of his and Almira's part in the current social season, which he characterized blithely as "pretty frantic."

"I thought we'd get some rest when we moved to the country—but not a bit of it! We seem to dine out just as often as in town, and then there are the week-ends as well—jolly good fun, but a little too much on the strenuous side. How Mira copes with it all, I'll never know—but she does: she's a wonder! The house is chock full right now. Papa and Aunt Isabel came out last night, and a raft of people turned up today—God knows why we asked 'em or where they're going to sleep! Celia's here, Ned; she's anxious to see you. And Aunt Isabel's cousins, the Traffords. They seem all right. Then there's the German ambassador, the new one—Graf von und zu Marbach —awful fellow, if you ask me! Gwen Trafford asked if she might bring him. He's got a monocle and a waxed moustache and keeps trying to make love to the women in that silly, vague, continental way they don't seem to mind, don't you know. And I mustn't forget Miss Nella La Touche—did you ever hear such a name? She's what they call an interior decorator—damned if I can tell you exactly what that means! All I am sure of is, she fixed up our house to suit herself and sent me a whacking bill—I could have bought a yacht for half the money! It's a polite form of hold-up, I guess: don't see why Mira couldn't have gone down to Field's and just picked out a few chairs and tables. But I don't care what it costs as long as she's happy. Nella's a horrible bore, though; wants to talk silks and antiques even at dinner; I'll tell Mira not to put her anywhere near you. . . . We're taking the lot down to St. Louis Monday night to see the Fair. Papa has lent me his private car; you'd better come with us, if you've nothing better to do."

Ned replied that Sonny was very kind; he would think it over.

By this time they had left the straggling village behind and were crossing the swampy, willow-dotted meadows of the Skokie Valley. Dancer trotted so fast that Ned was obliged to hold on to his hat. Sonny, however, was an admirable whip, and the fresh breeze was grateful after the stuffy train; it had been another very warm day.

The Kennerleys lived five miles west of Lake Forest: Ned could not afford to lose any time if he meant to obey Aunt Lydia's behest. Somehow he shrank from beginning: the rattling tilbury seemed hardly ideal for an intimate talk; and one couldn't in any case—could one?—start right in raking over the coals of morality a friend one hadn't seen in two whole years.

Salving his conscience by the reflection that doubtless he'd find a better opportunity later, Ned gave himself up to enjoying his drive, meanwhile plying his host with a few questions of a comprehensive nature.

Sonny was cheerily ready to answer, though it could not be claimed that his tongue was expressive. Mira was fine—so were the children, thank goodness! So, on the whole, were Papa and Aunt Isabel; of course the former was not so young as he had been. Celia looked handsome as paint and seemed perfectly bully. . . . No, Longuyon wasn't with her; she'd left him in the East—"Newport, or somewhere, I guess. Good job he didn't come out—can't stand the chap at any price. Have you ever run across him in Europe? . . . Well, you haven't missed a thing. Of all the frog-faced fools! He can't even sit a horse—and his *billiards* . . . !"

All this time Sonny smiled as delightedly as if he were praising his brother-in-law as his greatest friend. Shortly thereafter he turned Dancer into an entrance guarded by pink plaster gateposts and slowed the pony down to a sedate amble on the crushed gravel drive that wound as far as the eye could reach between fields of red clover and sprouting corn. Save for a clump or two of native box-elders the fields were treeless, but the drive was bordered by lines of small elms, their meagre young trunks buttressed by wires against the fierce western winds. "Went in last fall, ten thousand of 'em," Sonny remarked, with a grin. "My landscape man tells me they'll make quite a showing in twenty years!"

Along the way he pointed with his whip to various objects of interest: the hard blue glitter of a little lake (artificial, but stocked with bass and pike—or supposed to be: the swans seemed to gobble up everything but bullheads that weren't fit to eat); the paddocks; the stables, whose gables peered over the crest of a clump of second-growth oaks ("Can't ride half so often as I'd like, and Mira's scared of horses!"); beyond the wood, a spread of lawns; finally, on the slight rise that had to do duty for a hill in pancake-flat Illinois, the tiled roofs and strawberry-mousse walls of the Villa Bellaggio.

The name, Ned felt, should have been a warning. He did not know quite what he had expected: the days of cupolas and bulging front porches were obviously over; nor, perhaps, was it possible now to erect deliberately an overgrown brown or white shingled box, devoid alike of pretentions and period, such as most suburban dwellers had been satisfied with. What kind of architecture *would* suit the Middle West? Certainly nothing could be more lamentably inappropriate than this ponderous Italian pleasure palace, with its frescos and friezes and cypress-lined terraces, set uncompromisingly, defiantly even, under the high, pale glare of the prairie sky.

But there was no time for general conjectures, much less a minute appraisal of details. Sonny had already pulled Dancer up by the rose marble threshold; a waiting groom sprang forward to seize the reins; the front door flew open; and Almira burst out to fling herself in her cousin's arms. "Ned, dear, you've come—I *am* glad!"

Inside, the stony vastness of the entrance hall suggested the lobby of some pluperfect hotel; the butler approaching noiselessly across the deep velvet carpet had precisely the deferential air of a manager preparing to show one up to a luxury suite. But there was nothing either stereotyped or impersonal about Almira's welcome: she tucked her arm in Ned's and, chatting gaily, led him on a whirlwind tour of the splendours of the *piano nobile;* thence upstairs to the nursery wing, all enameled paint and baby-pink-and-blue cretonnes, where the four little Kennerley girls and their nurses lived sealed off, as it were, from adult confusion. Ned shook hands in turn with each of his black-eyed, stolidly cheerful little cousins, trying in vain to recall whether it was Corinne or Lydia who was his god-daughter and agreeing with Almira that the twins, Lucretia and Lucinda, had the Beauchamps nose but Porter hair (not red at all, a clear chestnut shading to auburn). "Mamma pretends to be sorry about it, but I know she's secretly pleased. How did you find her, Ned? I'm a little worried about Mamma; I don't think she's seemed herself since Janet died. I try my best to coax her to come to the country, but she hardly ever will; and she simply *won't* go away for the summer. It's as much as one's life is worth to get her to spend a month at Saratoga or Hot Springs while the servants take their vacations—and I'm sure she puts in most of the time criticizing the food and reading Chicago newspapers!"

Ned's bedroom was so enormous that it quite tired him out travelling to his bathroom and dressing-room as he unpacked and back again. It was replete with every imaginable comfort and convenience. Momentarily he played with the idea of pushing some of the buttons on the switchboard of the house telephone: should he ring up the kitchen for caviar or the stable to order the drag? Or would it be more amusing to try one of the spare-rooms at random and say: "This is Ned Ramsay; who are you?"

He bathed and dressed as slowly as possible, lying for a full twenty minutes in the peach marble tub full of scented hot water (there were four kinds of bath-salts: he tried some of each), and relaxing afterwards, in fresh linen and his light silk dressing-gown, on the brocaded *lit de repos* with his feet on a swansdown coverlet, his eyes resting lazily on the view of the terrace below, the formal gardens beyond it, and, in the distance, the red barns and green pastures of Lake County full in the rays of the setting sun.

No doubt it was all very beautiful, the last word in refinement and taste. The trouble was, it was Nella La Touche's taste. The Villa Bellaggio was purely extraneous; it had no more valid relationship with its owners than with the country they lived in. What was it *for?*—the paneled library of books nobody read; the lacquered Venetian music-room with its harp and its organ and two grand pianos no-one knew how to play; the lake that wasn't fished; the horses that weren't ridden; the roses in the garden one hadn't time to smell! Did all millionaires have to buy the same house and own the same things? Weren't there more diverting ways of spending a fortune? What exactly *would* one do if one were as rich as Sonny Kennerley?

Ned's reveries were interrupted by the dinner gong.

Guests at the villa were wont to assemble in the Winter Garden, a trellised apartment adorned with ferns and ivies and splashing fountains that was, as Sonny observed with some humour, just the spot for a hot summer night. Its three tall windows facing the western glare had been artfully masked by sliding mirrors; iced drinks were being passed on cool silver trays; Illinois and its torrid, devitalizing humidity felt pleasantly remote.

As Ned came in he met Almira, handsome in white satin and the Kennerley diamonds, her hair swept up in a towering pompadour (fashion at last having hit upon a style that became her). True, she seemed to have stepped into her smart gown quite casually; it was as little her personal concern as the Villa Bellaggio; even her jewels appeared like afterthoughts. But her eyes were unclouded; her skin glowed with the rosy, unmistakable tint of health; she looked what Ned felt she was, a thoroughly happy young woman. (Surely Aunt Lydia must have misjudged the case!)

Some of the house party had already come down: Miss La Touche in scarlet and a gold embroidered shawl, toothy and scornful like a chic small llama; Graf von und zu Marbach, bearing the double prepositions as easily as his blond, somewhat ravaged good looks (neither his lisp nor his air of deliberate innocence could conceal the watchful intelligence in his china blue eyes); Reggie Trafford and Gwen, his wife, a colourless couple from Philadelphia, obviously valuable for the primitive but satisfying reason that they *were* from Philadelphia.

Ned was presented to everyone. Fortunately they'd all read, or at least heard about, "Queen Margot," which simplified matters; one had got very tired of being introduced as "the novelist, you know," only to have one's interlocutors murmur: "How interesting! And do tell me, Mr. Ramsay, what have you written?"

The Senior Kennerleys were next to arrive. Mr. Kennerley looked shaky and rather pathetic; his eyes had lost their fire, his voice acquired a hollow, asthmatic note. Mrs. Framingham, on the other hand (how could one remember to call her Mrs. Kennerley?), except for greying hair and the matronly dog-collar of pearls that was almost the badge of her class and age-group, was unchanged. Sharp little women who'd never looked young compensatingly never grew old: Ned could envisage her, all angles and restless acumen, substantially the same at eighty.

Celia was late—after such a long absence perhaps she intended to make an entrance—for the dinner guests were streaming in now, a string of noisy young couples. Now and then one recognized a face: there was Maud Mallard (she'd married Dan Maxwell, hadn't she?), and Florence Harper, who had just returned from a prolonged foreign tour with a husband of sorts. (The young man was said to be the son of a druggist in Chippewa Falls; the name, distressingly, was Dunkelfinger.) And there were Almira's brothers and their wives, a little windblown by the drive up from Winnetka, where the Tom Stacks were spending the night with the Porters. Tom and Carrie, Ned decided, had grown podgy and stodgy with success; but Porter seemed leaner, almost athletic. Maybe he played golf regularly now. . . . As for Fanny, who seized on Ned at once and began talking volubly, she had become the perfect suburban young matron, immersed in her bulbs and her bridge.

By this time the roar had grown deafening—the well known American roar, compounded of alcohol, natural vocal shrill-ness, and the naïve pleasure people felt in meeting their neigh-bours, no matter how familiar. Ned, chatting with Fanny, still kept an eye on the door. He had been looking forward to seeing Celia with mixed emotions. (What would he think of her after all these years? What would she think of *him?*) Suddenly a stir made itself felt amongst the males nearest at hand: as they formed a huddle of heightened interest it was clear that Madame la Duchesse was coming at last.

Just then dinner was announced and the current reversed itself, flowing back from the Winter Garden into the hall and thence to the dining-room, so that all that Ned saw was a slender figure in black in the crowd ahead. In his odd con-fusion of feeling he was almost relieved to see they were not seated next each other: Madame de Longuyon went in with Trafford and had Marbach on her other side, while Ned found himself diagonally across the table between Maud Maxwell and Mrs. Kennerley. Celia waved to him gaily over a mound of orchids as they were taking their places; then the Count claimed her attention and Ned, with a sigh, turned to Aunt Isabel, who began at once on her stepdaughter's praises. . . . Did not the darling look wonderful tonight? How clever of her to wear a plain dark frock and no jewels! The Longuyon emeralds were famous, but beauty like hers needed no enhancement. She was, it went without saying, extravagantly admired in Paris. Oh, the whole story had been a fairytale romance, really! Of course, the dukedom was a Napoleonic creation only—First Empire, fortunately, not Napoléon III— but Longuyon was a charming fellow—delightful in every way—and absolutely devoted to his wife. Had Mr. Ramsay met him abroad? . . . Ah, what a pity! For it was hardly likely he'd venture west this trip. Celia felt that would have been a little too much to expect on his first visit to the States. New York had been doubtless enough of a shock. The tropical heat, too, had overset him—poor dear Pierre! There was nothing like it in France. But he had insisted at once, most unselfishly, that Celia should come out with her father. . . . Such fun to be back in beloved Chicago! Everything precisely the same . . . "though you, dear Mr. Ramsay, have turned, I understand, into a famous author. 'Queen Margot's' on my bed-table this minute . . . plan to read it just as soon as I . . . I suppose this means you will be leaving, too? The East, perhaps, or Europe? . . . Oh, really? You've been living abroad all these years? Strange one never came across . . . No, we're here for a fortnight only, for the dedication of the hospital Abner has given in memory of his wife. Dear Abner, what generosity! It's a marvelous thing for the city. . . . We'd love to settle here, but the climate—so treacherous! And then it is— isn't it? or don't you find it so?—the tiniest bit *borné* socially. . . ."

Ned, meanwhile, sipped his soup and nibbled an olive or two, paying surface heed only to his chattering neighbour as he stared at Celia's delicate profile, which was inclined with an air of receptive interest towards Marbach. (That was one thing, at any rate, life on the continent had taught her: in the old days she'd been as indifferent a listener as the rest of her family.) She was, he decided, as little altered as it was possible for a person to be whom one has not seen for almost a decade. Somehow she had contrived to mature without losing the freshness of youth. The changes one saw were all superficial: she was, of course, a "creation" quite as authentic as her husband's title—her satin-gold locks curled in some subtle and intricate mode that had not yet travelled across the Atlantic; her face and eyes very faintly made up, not that they needed it, but because in France it was the custom to do so; the long, supple lines of her figure presented to their ultimate advantage in a gown at once too simple and too daring to have suited any other woman in the room. Her voice, also, as it reached him in scraps of sentences, sounded slightly exotic: American wives of foreigners, Ned reminded himself, invariably caught some sort of accent sooner or later. (One had known them to begin with experimental enthusiasm even during the engagement.) Still he would have sworn that Celia Kennerley and Celia de Longuyon were one and the same. How he longed for a chance to test his theory! There were courses and courses to sit through yet, worse luck! . . . and here was Maud Maxwell's loud voice breaking in on his thoughts to recall him to duty.

Even when dinner was over the men were expected to sit by themselves for an hour at least over liqueurs and cigars. Ned was frankly tried by these masculine interludes. He greeted Tom and Porter—who clapped him on the back and told him he looked bully: they understood he'd written quite a book—and spoke to one or two other men he knew. After that, there was nothing to do save compose oneself in what one hoped was an intelligent listening attitude and pray for a not too tardy release.

The group tended to centre round Mr. Kennerley—naturally; Ned felt it was not only the latter's age that demanded it. If one's Chicago contemporaries had a trait more salient than the rest, it was their lack of a salient trait. With the exception of Sonny, who was set apart by his good looks and nervous charm, all these young men were exactly alike—round-headed and burly, strident of voice and aggressively cheery. They were hard-working, hard-playing, hard-thinking, hard-drinking, as their fathers had been before them. Many, perhaps, had to work even harder: in a society that failed to recognize the law of primogeniture the great pioneer fortunes were split into sections as their founders disappeared. What they lacked was a sense of adventure, the incentive of knowing the future was theirs to shape as they would. Chicago was "made" now; it could expand, one imagined, indefinitely, but the achievements of its inheritors must follow the patterns their sires had set; the lawless days of invention and experiment were over.

That was a pity: against this amorphous background the figure of Abner Kennerley loomed even larger than when his peers were about him. There he was, just as of old, laying down the law in his querulous way on the sins of the government (did it matter whether the culprit were Cleveland or Roosevelt?) and disposing didactically of whatever war happened to be current: tiresome, opinionated old man! Yet Ned regretted, for the sake of picturesqueness, if nothing else, that the old king must be near the end of his journey; one was sorry, too, that his career could not close amid the scenes that had witnessed its rise. Endowing a hospital was all very well— but why could not Isabel Kennerley see that her husband's one claim to fame was his connection with the city he'd helped to build? Away from it, he'd be just another retired multi-millionaire, a good deal less genial than most; whereas, in Chicago, he was part of the fabric of life for millions who never knew him, assured of some prerogatives of immortality while still comfortably on earth. . . .

"Celia!" said Ned.

"Ned!" said Celia.

They'd wasted no time: as soon as the gentlemen rejoined the ladies they had found each other; then Celia proposed a stroll on the terrace. "I don't know where else we can walk— the wood's full of mosquitoes—and Almira says every time she goes near the lake the swans start to chase her."

Ned felt the terrace would do very well. Now that the sun had set it looked romantically mysterious, with its long rows of cypresses lifting dark fingers against the blue prairie night sky. Celia laid her hand on his arm; they promenaded for a little without speaking. Ned felt elated: her voice might trail a changeling foreign note, but none the less she was *his* Celia still. It was she who broke the silence first: "You tell!"

"No; *you!* I've waited so long to hear. Damned if I thought I'd ever get you away from that blasted lisping German!"

"Poor Marbach!" said Celia. "He's a dreadfully dull man. I've known him for ages. When I was first married he was stationed in Paris, and we knew him later in London, too. Did Aunt Isabel tell you Pierre was first secretary there for two years?"

"I hadn't heard your husband was a diplomat."

"He isn't any more. He didn't like the life; it kept him out of France too much. Pierre is really a farmer at heart. You know what the French are like—it isn't so much the country they love as the fact that it's *theirs*. Properties are their *folie*. We've a place in the Dordogne, and another in Lorraine; and last year Pierre bought a shooting box near Senlis. Papa was very much disappointed; I think he saw us raised in time to all sorts of glittering ambassadorial eminence—with the Longuyon family and the Kennerley money . . ."

"And were you disappointed, too?"

Celia shook her head.

"Not really. Oh, it was fun while it lasted, but I shouldn't care for a career in diplomacy. One's got to be kind to bores, and tactful all day long till one's face is ready to crack with the strain. I don't like people that well."

Ned could believe it; she never had. But when he asked her whether she shared her husband's passion for the country she shook her head again, still more emphatically. "Oh, no, I hate it, except for a week now and then when the weather's quite fine. But I don't have to stay there unless I want to. I do make a point of receiving my mother-in-law—she comes to us for a month every summer. The rest of the time I'm free to go where I like. Pierre usually has the house full of his horrible relations, but he's quite modern—he doesn't expect me to entertain them. I have my own flat in Paris, and a villa in Cimiez; after *Madame la douairière* leaves I do a cure at St. Moritz and then go to Scotland."

"You're happy, then? It's been a success?"

"Very happy," Celia said frankly. "Yes; it's a great success. Pierre is an angel, much better than I deserve. He's got all the money he wants, and the children—it *was* luck, wasn't it, having two boys straight off! And I've got my liberty. It's an excellent arrangement. Why have you never come to see how well it works?"

"I wasn't sure I'd be welcome."

"Nonsense!" cried Celia, with spirit, sounding all of a sudden much less foreign. "You know I'd have loved to see you any time. You've no excuse for ignoring me—you've lived a lot in Europe yourself. Oh, I have your *dossier*—you see, I've been talking to Aunt Isabel, too. Now that I think of it I'm quite annoyed with you."

"My dear Celia," said Ned, "what would have been the good of our meeting? We live in different worlds. What have I to do with villas in Cimiez or shooting boxes in Senlis? I'm a poor devil of a scribbler who's more at home in the Latin Quarter than the drawing-rooms of the Faubourg St. Germain."

"They're on the same side of the river anyhow," objected Celia. "Besides, you're *not* a poor scribbler; Aunt Isabel says you've just written a very successful book. I want to read it, though if it's too clever, I can't promise to understand it. I'm not in the least an intellectual."

"Neither am I. At any rate, I don't feel so anywhere but here."

"Oh, Chicago! What a place! How can you stand it?"

"I love it—in small doses, of course. I couldn't settle. But it's home somehow. Don't you feel that at all?"

"No; not at all. I loathed it when I was a child, and I loathed it after I grew up, and I dare say I'd loathe it yet if I thought I was caught in the trap again. I'm here now only to lend Papa and Aunt Isabel my countenance. She was nervous about meeting people after what's happened; I can't see why. Mamma's been dead so many years now, and Bertie Framingham wasn't a Chicagoan. *That's* a success, too. I must say I underestimated Aunt Isabel in the old days; I never thought she'd have the patience to take Papa on permanently. She's wonderful with him, Ned, and I feel I can't be too grateful—after all, if she didn't look after him, Sonny and I would have to—and I couldn't stand that!"

They had stopped walking by now to lean on the marble balustrade. Celia, who had been gazing peacefully at the mazy dance of the fireflies on the darkling lawn, gave a slight shudder; the translucent eyes went suddenly blank.

"Papa is really an impossible person. He doesn't know it; he doesn't mean to be. But sometimes it's seemed that he can't come close to anyone without blighting their warm human qualities. Look what he did to poor Mamma! And it'd have been the same with me if I hadn't got away. Sonny's a man, of course, though I can't help thinking he'd be twice as much of one if he'd had a different father. Papa kept him under always—he's never allowed him to grow up. . . . But forgive me, Ned. I don't want to talk of sad things when we've just found each other again. You've not told me a single bit about yourself. To begin with, my dear, why have you never married?"

There were, at a moderate estimate, half a dozen good answers to that. Ned selected the one that appeared most appropriate to the time, the place, and the accomplished coquette he divined Celia had grown to be; and the rest of their dialogue proceeded agreeably on conventional lines. When at last they reëntered the house they found the party settled to bridge. It seemed useless to hope for an interview with Sonny tonight; so when Celia, who did not care for cards, dismissed the hovering Count and trailed off to bed with a smile that promised, quite falsely, all things for the morrow, Ned concluded to follow her example.

NED came down to breakfast next day to find all the men assembled except Mr. Kennerley, whose age and infirmities obliged him, albeit unwillingly, to remain in seclusion till noon. Gwen Trafford, wearing a riding habit, was also present, having just returned from a brisk canter over the fields to the Desplaines River; and before the meal was over Miss La Touche wandered in, her small, ugly face as pale as milk in the bright morning light that flooded the dining-room. (She had a trick, one observed, of creeping about the house with an appraising and meditative eye; her air of just not taking down notes on possible *lacunae* in the sumptuous settings of the Villa Bellaggio would have disquieted clients less spectacularly wealthy than the young Abner Kennerleys.)

Ned's intention of waylaying Sonny as they left the table with a plea for a ten-minute chat in the den was frustrated by the latter's plan, immediately set afoot, of a general tour of the premises. This, one supposed, was inevitable: of what use were millionaires' possessions if they could not be shown off? It was a kind of periodic reassurance for their owners, who otherwise might have doubted their value. And, it had to be admitted, Sonny made the process as painless as possible. He literally rushed them through the gardens, the greenhouses, stables, and kennels; even the model dairy, with its rows of fawn purebred Jerseys and glittering modern equipment, was disposed of in a quarter of an hour; he did not seem to know what he had paid for the animals or how the machinery worked, and treated the whole business as a huge joke.

The sole halt of any consequence was made in one of the paddocks, where a miniature grandstand had been erected: here they were bidden to seat themselves, while Sonny's head groom trotted out a series of hackneys and hunters for their inspection. Ned looked, he feared, vacuous; Marbach screwed his monocle firmly into place with a professional manner; the Traffords, true to their Main Line origin, made knowing remarks ("A bit high in the withers," or, "What magnificent hock action!"); and Miss La Touche turned up martyred eyes and prayed for death.

This, too, was merely a transient torture. Once round the ring was enough for Sonny; his clipped "That will do, Dixon," dismissed each glossy prancer in record time; and the party was soon up and away to the lake, where a launch had been ordered to take them to see the new waterlily plantations.

By the time they got back to the house in the sizzling midday heat Almira, in cream lace and an enormous plumed hat, was waiting to marshal her guests for lunch at the club. It took a long time to decide who would go in which carriage; Sonny complicated matters by insisting on driving Ned and Celia in the motor-car, which broke down twice on the way to Onwentsia. Celia sat giggling swathed in veils on the high leather seat, while the men laboured desperately to coax back to life an obstinate magneto.

A large, noisy troop of quite new people had been invited to meet them. Owing to the accident and the number of rounds of drinks that were served it was well past two before they went into table, and after four when they rose. On reaching home most of the ladies retired to their rooms to rest, while Sonny and Reggie Trafford, who was as tireless as his host, got up an impromptu tennis tournament.

After that, everybody bathed and changed; there were more drinks; then into carriages again for a picnic supper. This took place on the shores of yet another lake, oddly enough a natural one, on the western boundaries of the Kennerleys' two thousand acres. "It's quite a jolly spot," Sonny explained; "Mira and I come here with the children when we feel like getting away from things."

Ned could not help recalling Aunt Corinne's idea of a country excursion: the meal was laid on a fine Jacobean table in a stylized rustic pavilion—heavily screened on account of voracious mosquitoes—; there were *pâtés-de-foie gras* and chilled lobster salad washed down by vintage champagne, and such a plethora of disgruntled servants to wait upon them that constant collisions occurred in corners.

A final return to the villa produced more bridge, and some desultory billiards.

Ned collapsed into bed at an early hour, wondering dispiritedly why country life in America seemed organized for the least good of the greatest number, and if it were necessarily true that the larger one's income the higher the incidence of calculated physical displacements.

He went back to town on the morning train in spite of Almira's warm invitation to stay. She and Sonny were also most anxious to have him join them on the trip to St. Louis, but having ascertained that, with the exception of Mr. and Mrs. Kennerley, Senior, the whole party at the villa expected to go, Ned declined on the plea of business engagements: he would see his cousins at the end of the week, when they returned for the opening of the races at Washington Park.

It was a blow to realize that his mission had been a failure; still worse, to have to confess as much to Aunt Lydia, who was markedly unimpressed by his glowing report of her daughter's domestic felicity ("Ah, but don't you see? Almira knows nothing—that's just why I'm worried!"), and remained in a state of brooding unrest.

The private car left on Monday night; on Tuesday morning Ned was called to the telephone by a familiar voice: at the last minute, said Celia, she, too, had decided to stop in Chicago. It was so dreadfully hot and she had seen so many fairs in Paris—they were all alike, really. "I'm at Papa's, you know: won't you come to tea this afternoon?"

Ned went, and spent a pleasant hour in the great golden room that was full of memories for them both. Celia seemed very glad to see him; she clung to him almost wistfully as in her girlhood; the return to the scenes of her past had apparently robbed her of some of the victorious self-assurance she had displayed in Lake Forest.

When they said good-bye they made an engagement to lunch next day and do the pictures at the Art Institute; the day after that, they dined at the Annex and went to "The Wizard of Oz." By Friday it appeared to be understood that they were to spend their free time together: Ned took her to drive in Lincoln Park, and later to row on the little lagoon.

As time passed he became more and more attached: the first feeling of disappointment, that Celia, who had always been to him the incarnation of aloof, intangible romance, should in the end have been satisfied by the flattest kind of worldly success, vanished before the delights of her present company. At all events success had not blinded her: she had achieved balance without pretentiousness, and wisdom without losing her natural charm. She was so frankly what she was —keeping no secrets from her friend, showing a touching faith in his sympathy and discretion—that when she confided, as she ultimately did, that the "liberty" she enjoyed with her husband included freedom from the physical bond, Ned was not really shocked. . . . His grasp of the French moral code had been, up to now, theoretical and literary. The author of

"Queen Margot" knew that most of the men in Pierre de Longuyon's class had mistresses, many of the women took lovers: what mattered to them was the cult of the *foyer,* keeping the home together for the sake of the family; the rest depended on tact and tolerance and taking things as they came.

The transition from comprehension of a general state of affairs to a particular instance of it was made delicately by degrees. Celia announced quite simply on the last afternoon, as Ned paused on his oars to let the boat drift under a screen of drooping willows, that she had engaged rooms at the Annex and meant to move in directly. Life at Papa's was too difficult. . . . Aunt Isabel was a demanding and restless hostess. It would be far more agreeable to be by oneself, in convenient proximity to the down-town shops. . . .

Ned couldn't, and didn't, pretend to misunderstand: the kiss in the cab, on their way home that night through the leafy glades of the park, sealed a bargain as strange as it seemed inevitable. He did not know whether to be happy or unhappy. Part of him mourned the disappearance of his frost princess—never so lost as now, when it looked as if her successor were going to be his. But one *did* lose people, sometimes forever: what could one do but take the new Celia on her own terms, while remaining loyal to the memory of the old?

On Friday the Kennerleys and their guests arrived home from St. Louis. Celia had made arrangements to move to the hotel on Sunday, with her maid and her lap-dog and an impressive number of boxes. She had asked Ned to dine with her that night. They were, however, still separated from what might well be a fateful tryst by Saturday; and on Saturday, June 18, the American Derby was run at Washington Park.

For two decades one of the most famous races in the country, it had lately acquired a poignant interest: since the new law had been passed against betting within the city limits, it seemed more than likely that 1904 would mark the end of the series.

Ned remembered, in other years, seeing Aunt Lydia set forth in festal array with Quentin or Queen and the best victoria; that was one social occasion she made a point of not missing (the summer equivalent of the Charity Ball). How odd it was now for her to show no concern about going! Although the weather was perfect, she had refused several invitations to drive out with friends; and Ned heard her tell Dominique, Friday night after dinner, that she would not be wanting the carriage tomorrow—Simms might have the afternoon off.

Towards the middle of the morning she established herself in the drawing-room window; Ned found her there when he came to say good-bye, her hands lying idle in her lap, her gaze fixed listlessly on the stir of holiday-makers in the street. For once she kissed him without making a pretence at a smile; her air of impenetrable woe cast a cloud on his spirits, which even the prospect of a day spent with Celia was powerless to lift.

Sonny, wearing a grey topper and an Ascot tie, with Gwen Trafford beside him in the driver's seat, held the reins of a fine team of bays; deftly he swung the great black-and-scarlet drag into line on the macadam of Michigan Avenue, already a jumble of coaches and tandem-carts, stanhopes and tilburys, *vis-à-vis* and victorias. Hooves clicked and wheels rumbled, polished mountings of harness flashed in the sun. Ned, on the gammon next to Celia, eyed the prosperous pageant with a touch of queer pride: he was all of a sudden assailed by the emotions of a native Chicagoan, fiercely anxious for his city to measure up to standard for the strangers within its gates.

At the entrance Sonny flicked the bays, who broke into a gallop as they pulled their lumbering burden up the rise of ground to the clubhouse steps. Ned had supposed they were to lunch at the club, but Celia, it seemed, at the last minute had decided it would not do—there were too many bores about; she was not in the mood today for old acquaintances. Accordingly Sonny turned the horses infield, where the footman produced a folding ladder and Carstairs, the portly coachman, assisted the ladies to clamber down from their perch.

From this oval green island the bustle and roar were pleasingly distant, though they had an excellent view of the big redroofed clubhouse across the track with its flying pennants and the bright-coloured blur of the gathering crowd on the porches. The servants made preparations for an *al fresco* meal, while the ladies hoisted parasols and trailed about the lawn in their ribbons and laces and huge feathered hats, chatting with friends from neighbouring coaches (all-a-row like so many grazing prehistoric monsters), and the gentlemen laid private bets with one another and argued whether Highball or Woodson looked a better long shot against the favourite English Lad.

Ned, who knew little about horse racing and cared less, strolled beside Celia, feeling his pleasure doubled because she shared it: from time to time they glanced at each other tenderly, their eyes alight with the promise that their love would be eternal.

Lunch was a cheerful intermezzo, punctuated by jokes and gay little remarks (which to the sensitive ear sounded slightly shopworn, as if they had been used before on similar occasions); then Sonny looked at his watch and declared it was time to go—for Celia had again changed her mind: now nothing would do but to join Papa and Aunt Isabel at the club. Just as the ladies were making ready to climb aloft once more another carriage drove into the field: no coach, but a bright yellow phaëton drawn by a chunky black pony. The reins were held by a young man equally chunky, who was wearing a crimson-and-white striped blazer and a straw hat clapped on the back of his very square head. A cigarette drooped from one corner of the young man's mouth; his face was flushed and his hard button-black eyes partly closed; but Ned was more interested by his companion, a pretty young woman with curly hair, wide-open eyes like a doll's, and a colour as high (if not quite so natural) as her escort's.

The pair were laughing loudly as they reined in the pony; their voices even more than their appearance branded them interlopers in the sacred enclosure. (How had they managed to get in?)

Miss La Touche raised her lorgnette: "What a very odd-looking couple!" And Gwen Trafford smiled across at her husband: "I think they must have started celebrating already —perhaps *they* know who's going to win the Derby—go see if you can get a tip, why don't you, Reggie!"

Ned's amusement vanished when he saw Sonny: the latter had turned a dull red and was biting his lips in an effort to control himself.

"I think, you know, we'd better be moving," was all he could manage to say, in an uncertain voice.

The chunky young man cracked his whip to attract their attention, and the young lady leaned over the side of the phaëton to exclaim with a brilliant smile: "Hello there, dearie —you didn't expect to see me here, did you? Well, to tell you the truth, I hardly expected it myself. I knew you couldn't take me out to the track today, but Dick happened along and coaxed me into coming with him. He's just got back to town from Frisco and he—but I forget, you two don't know each other, do you? Meet my brother, Mr. Richard Branson—Mr. Abner Kennerley, Junior. I won't keep you now, Sonny boy— just wanted to say hello and ta-ta—look me up in the grand-stand later if you have a chance. Hurry up, Dickie; it's time we got going!"

In spite of her raucous laugh the young woman's speaking voice was unexpectedly low and agreeable. That was all she said: she made no attempt to alight from the trap, scarcely even glanced at the little group frozen into immobility on the grass. And as Dickie heeded her command the bright yellow phaëton vanished almost as quickly as it had appeared. But there had been no mistaking that tone of easy proprietorship.

Nella La Touche looked away with a smile and a shrug; Graf von Marbach fiddled helplessly with his eyeglass; Gwen Trafford began talking at random about nothing at all. Sonny started towards his wife with a wretched mumble of "Mira, I swear . . ."

It was Celia who grasped her sister-in-law by the arm—Almira was swaying, ready to faint—and exclaimed briskly: "It's high time *we* were hurrying, too! You know what Aunt Isabel will say if we're not in our places before the first race. Come along, dear!"

The women coalesced round their stricken hostess. Celia half pushed, half carried Almira up onto the gammon, and Sonny, in a daze, returned to his guests and his duty.

If never before, Ned had reason now to bless the brand of good manners peculiar to fashionable folk. It was not all acting either: as far as the Traffords and Marbach and Nella La Touche were concerned, the scene with Miss Branson and her brother had simply not happened. Once he had handed his party over to the care of his father and stepmother Sonny had the grace to disappear; and when he came back after the first race he seemed to have recovered his composure.

It was Almira who caused Ned concern. Pale and shaken, she had spoken scarcely a word since the catastrophe; one felt she was fighting hard to command her emotions, but the effort exhausted her: as the afternoon passed she visibly drooped.

Ned watched her with loving anxiety; he soon saw that Celia was watching her, too; their common solicitude brought them closer than ever. Finally, in the long interval before the race of the day, the latter leaned back to whisper behind her programme: "You'd better take Mira home. It's cruel to keep her here any longer. How shall we manage?"

Ned considered rapidly.

"I suppose there's a train—but hasn't your father a carriage?"

"Of course!" said Celia. "The very thing! I'll just speak a word to Papa—we can say she's a headache—and I must confess the poor darling looks it. He and Aunt Isabel can go back on the drag: I suppose I'll have to stay to look after these tiresome people. Hurry, my dear—now's your chance, while they're all milling about before the race. Ring me up tonight if you can to tell me how things went—and don't forget I expect you tomorrow at seven."

The pair clasped hands like conspirators: Ned felt he could have knelt at his lady's feet.

Almira protested only feebly when the suggestion was broached; she seemed like a frightened child, content to resign herself to the charge of someone she trusted.

On the way home the cousins held hands. They spoke very little: what could they say behind that stiff English back on the box? Ned left Almira at her house in Calumet Avenue, then repaired to his aunt's to make his report.

Aunt Lydia, who was still sitting in the drawing-room window (one could not help wondering if she had ever left it), listened mantled in silence. She appeared neither shocked nor surprised. But when the story was ended she nodded her head several times; and the frightened look in her eyes was more disquieting than that in her daughter's, for it held comprehension as well as alarm: if Aunt Lydia's world had cracked in two, she plainly knew why.

"You see, my dear, I was right, after all," she said. "Things are even worse than I feared—the creature must be horribly sure of herself and her hold over Sonny to risk such a scene. *Now* will you believe me and stop pretending nothing's the matter?"

Ned promised earnestly that he would not let twenty-four hours elapse without making an appointment with the culprit. As things turned out, he had not to take the first step: very early next morning Sonny rang up and begged him to dine at the club.

"It's the only time I have free with this houseful of nincompoops on my hands. We're booked for a man's dinner for Marbach tomorrow night, and Trafford and I are off on Tuesday for a fishing trip in Canada. Please come, Ned—I've *got* to see you alone!"

Ned hesitated, remembering his engagement with Celia. Then conscience, and his attachment to the Stacks, won the victory.

Aunt Lydia's overwhelming relief, the touching reliance she placed on his skill, were almost recompense enough. She departed shortly after breakfast to take the news to Almira, and Ned spent the day wondering what he should say to Sonny and ringing up the Annex at intervals. At first Celia's rooms did not answer; when he finally got through to her maid it was only to learn that Madame la Duchesse had gone to the country with friends and would not be back until dinner time.

There seemed nothing for it save to leave a message of explanation and regrets.

On the way to the club he stopped to order some roses. Across the card that accompanied them he had written: *Terribly disappointed about tonight. Have to see S.—you can guess about what. Longing, my darling, and all my love.*

Chapter 4

THE Chicago Club, which up to now Ned had known only in its rushed midday aspect, all cigar smoke and munching millionaires, was a desert this hot Sunday night. His host had made the gesture of ordering supper served in a private room, but there was no-one about save the waiters and one or two regular residents, old bachelor bores sunk deep in armchairs in the lounge, surrounded by papers that ought, one felt, to be yesterday's.

Sonny looked nervous but resolute as they came to table: as soon as the cherry-stone clams had been whisked away to give place to a mountainous platter of chicken salad he plunged into business.

"Lord, Ned, what a nasty mess! I don't know what you think of me, but I *do* know what I think of myself. Why, I'd give my right hand . . . but it's too late now: the fat's in the fire, I guess."

Ned did not need to ask any questions: the whole story came out pell-mell, uncomplicated by excuses or attempts to disguise the ugliness of the facts. It was true that Sonny had a mistress. It was also true that she lived in a "house"—or, rather, had lived in one: the flat in Drexel Boulevard appeared to be as authentic as the rest of Aunt Lydia's damaging details. But it was *not* true that he wanted to divorce his wife in order to marry Daisy Branson. . . . "Good God, Ned, how could you believe it? How could Aunt Lydia? How could *anyone?* Daisy doesn't mean a thing to me. She's just a distraction—a —a convenience, if you like. Lots of fellows in my position do what I've done. But *I'm* a Kennerley, so the whole world gets to hear about it. Perhaps you don't realize that Mira can't

284

have any more children. I mean, she *mustn't;* Doctor Mallard's forbidden it. I almost lost her last year when the twins were born. Oh, Christ, if I had . . . ! You can't guess what I went through then. Nobody'll ever know. . . . The mischief of it is, Ned,"—beads of sweat were pouring down Sonny's forehead—"Mira's *too* good; she thinks it morally wrong to control the size of your family. All damned nonsense, of course; I could've convinced her in time. Except for that, she's made me perfectly happy. It's been a wonderful nine years—better than anything else I've known—better, even, than I hoped it would be when we married. Mira's my anchor, my compass, my—*everything*, really. . . . I'd rather die than distress her. Please believe me: it's the truth, as sure as I'm sitting here talking to you."

As Sonny paused to mop his brow the waiter appeared with iced coffee. The two young men held themselves in, staring straight ahead, unable to speak a word till the door had shut again. Then Ned said slowly: "I do believe you. But what are you going to do about Miss—ah—Branson? That was all very well as long as Mira didn't know, but after what happened yesterday there's no use pretending "

"By George, I can't imagine what got into Daisy! She's never done a thing like that before. I suppose it was her brother's fault—if that bounder *was* her brother! He was drunk as a lord, wasn't he? And I guess she'd been drinking, too. Oh, after this, she's got to go! Don't think I don't see . . . If there was talk before, there'll be ten times more now. The Maxwells' brake was right next to ours; Maud and Dan must've heard the whole thing. The only way to stop it is to make a clean break."

"Can you do that?"

"Of course I can! I don't care *that* for Daisy and she doesn't care *that* for me. It's been just a business arrangement. She doesn't stand to lose anything by it either. As a matter of fact, she's got her own income already. I settled ten thousand a year on her six months ago. So she's no call to claim I've treated her shabbily. But now it's over between us. She'll see that all right—she'll *have* to see it!"

"Does Mira know what you plan to do?"

"I tried to tell her last night—but she wouldn't listen. The poor darling was awfully upset. She—she locked herself in her room—I haven't seen her since. I tried again this morning, but she still wouldn't let me in. It's the devil of a business, with the house full of people who haven't the decency to take themselves off. I should think they could see they weren't wanted."

"Maybe," Ned suggested, "it would look even worse if they did."

"Maybe. I don't know. All I can think of is Mira, and what I've done to her without meaning to. You've got to help me, Ned. That's why I had to see you tonight. You're closer to Mira than anyone else; you can say things to her that her own mother can't. Go to her tomorrow and tell her what I said. Tell her I care for her and no-one but her—that I'd blow my brains out rather than cause her a moment's unhappiness. Tell her the business with Daisy is finished—that's no lie—it's as good as finished, for I'll never see the little fool again. Tell her—oh, anything you like, just as long as you can persuade her to take me back. You've got to stand by me now. You've always been my best friend. Why, I owe everything to you—if it hadn't been for you, Mira never would've married me—I don't forget that. If you can save me this one more time, I'll be your debtor the rest of my life. You *must* do it, boy—there's nobody else on God's earth who can. Oh, Neddy, I care so much—so much!"

Sonny buried his face in his hands; when he looked up his black eyes were full of tears.

Ned felt painfully embarrassed, as always in the presence of unrestrained emotion. These melodramatics recalled the scenes Aunt Corinne had been wont to make, but there was no mistaking the genuineness of the feeling that underlay them. Besides, one could understand and sympathize with Sonny's plight: the latter had done only what nine-tenths of the young men he knew would have done without giving it a second thought. The trouble was that, as he'd said, the private lives of the Kennerleys could not help becoming public concerns.

In the circumstances Ned felt justified in assuring his friend he would do what he could. "Mind you, I promise nothing." But he would talk to Almira and, if Sonny liked, to Aunt Lydia as well—explain the whole thing as best he was able. All he asked in return was that Sonny should engage to seek an immediate interview with Miss Branson and terminate their relations as he had already proposed to do. "For I've got to be sure, old fellow, that what I am saying is true."

Sonny was ready for anything, amazingly braced by Ned's calm assumption that matters were not past mending. He would get hold of Daisy tonight if he could, or at the latest tomorrow. Depend on it, Ned would have word in the course of the day. . . .

The evening ended quite cheerfully.

Ned refused a lift home on the pretext of wanting a walk. When Sonny had left him he turned north to the Annex and asked for Celia. After a moment the maid's sleepy voice answered: Madame la Duchesse had gone out to dinner—no, she could not say where—no, it was impossible to tell when Madame was likely to reënter.

Strangely downcast, he strolled home along the avenue through the warm grey night. The air was so thick that it seemed to press in upon him, and so humid that even the stars had trouble in shining.

As Ned had expected, Aunt Lydia was waiting for him. She listened with narrowed eyes to his account of the dialogue, and when he had finished gave a long sigh.

"Thank you, my dear; you've managed splendidly; I couldn't

287

ask for more. Let's hope Sonny means what he says—I shan't rest easy, shall you? till we're certain he's rid of the creature. We must pray for the best, Ned; that's all we can do till tomorrow."

The next day, which was hotter than ever, Ned rang up the Annex as soon as he dared after breakfast. This time Madame de Longuyon was at home. Her voice floated over the wire, cool, detached, and faintly amused. (Ned wished he could see her.) But of course she was not angry; she had quite understood about last night and only hoped he had been able to talk some sense into her wretched brother. To tell the truth, she had got back from the country in a state of fatigue so complete that she had gone straight to bed and taken supper on a tray. (The fib about dining out was freely confessed.) "My dear, your awful climate!" said Celia, as though Illinois were some quaint foreign country. "I'd forgotten how fearfully hot it can be. How on earth do you stand it?"

She herself was not going to try very much longer; she would be leaving shortly to join her husband in Newport. Pierre had begun to get lonely; besides, they'd only a fortnight more in the States, and there were still so many places to go, people to see. . . .

Ned felt her a thousand miles away instead of less than two. It seemed as if last week had never been. What was the use in pleading his suit? It was sheer obstinacy that made him refuse to accept his dismissal. She was booked today for both lunch and dinner; the best he could get was a promise to take tea with him tomorrow, if the weather improved.

He rang off with a feeling of utter frustration. It was the past all over again—how would one ever be sure of Celia?

The rest of the day he sat about aimlessly, waiting to hear from Sonny. He did not like to leave the house, for fear the call would come through in his absence. It grew hotter and hotter: the air seemed hard to breathe, exhausted as one imagined the atmosphere on the moon. Driven by a wicked wind from the Southwest, a constant procession of clouds crossed the brazen and lustreless sky. The clouds were edged with violet, thunder rumbled ominously in the distance; but the storm refused to come nearer.

About the middle of the afternoon Sonny called to say he had had trouble in finding Daisy; they were to meet, however, in half an hour at her apartment and go for a drive in the park. "I'll just have time to settle things with her before dashing home to dress for dinner. If I don't call you again, you'll understand why—but don't worry, Ned; it'll all be all right."

Almira came to dine with her mother. Her own house was staffless: owing, she explained, to the heat, Miss La Touche and Gwen Trafford had fled to the Villa Bellaggio; she had sent the servants back, also, except for the kitchenmaid and one of the grooms, and would join the party herself tomorrow as soon as the men had departed for Canada.

She looked pale but composed; her eyes showed traces of recent tears and it was not surprising that she found little to say. Ned, too, felt depressed; save for Aunt Lydia, erect and indomitable at the head of the table, conversation might have flagged more than once.

Just as they were finishing dessert there came a ring at the door—almost shockingly loud in the breathless stillness—and an agitated voice was heard asking for Mrs. Kennerley. Before Dominique had time to appear with the message a young man in livery burst into the dining-room. His face was red and streaming with perspiration; he was gasping painfully and had evidently been running hard.

"Oh, please, ma'am, come quick! They need you at home— something's happened to Mr. Kennerley!"

The man collapsed on a chair; Aunt Lydia turned to him with an imperious question in her eyes. But Almira waited to hear no more. After one agonized look at Ned she picked up her skirts and hatless and heedless, just as she was, hastened out the front door, down the steps to the street, then south along Prairie Avenue, running as she had not run since she was a little girl. Ned followed as fast as he was able. When they reached the Kennerleys' gate they crossed the wide green lawn under the elms and passed through the second gate that led to the grounds of the house on Calumet Avenue.

The door was unlocked and the lights were all lighted in the big round entrance hall. Otherwise everything was as usual, except for the sound of a woman's voice somewhere upstairs, screaming in a meaningless, mechanical way.

The cousins paused for breath; at that moment Doctor Mallard came out of the library, shutting the door behind him.

"Good Lord! Is there no-one to make her shut up? It's bad enough without—"

Then he saw Almira and his expression changed.

"My dear little girl, how did you get here so quickly?"

"Doctor Mallard, what's wrong? Please tell me at once. Is Sonny . . . ?"

Her voice trembled a little, but she had herself well in hand. Doctor Mallard eyed her speculatively, doubtless wondering, with the caution bred of long experience, how best to set about his explanation.

"Almira, I am going to ask you to be very brave. There's been an accident. Sonny's—been shot."

Almira took this without flinching, though her white face turned still whiter.

"Is it serious?"

"I'm afraid so. Very serious. In fact . . ."

Doctor Mallard's voice broke and he put his arm round her shoulder. After all, Ned reflected, he had known her all her life; undoubtedly he'd brought her into the world, like most of the children on Prairie Avenue.

"Is he dead?"

The doctor did not speak; his silence and bowed head were answer enough.

"Let me go to him. No, please—alone."

Almira pushed both men aside and, head high and unfal-
tering of step, went into the library.

As soon as they were by themselves Doctor Mallard told
Ned what he knew. There was not much to tell: he'd been
sitting on his front porch smoking an after-dinner cigar; not
a quarter of an hour ago Sonny's phaëton had been driven up
at a furious pace; Sonny was in it, unconscious, and a young
woman Doctor Mallard had never seen before. William, the
groom, had come running for help; together they'd carried
Sonny into the house; the one maid they'd found on the
premises had taken charge of the young woman, who was far
gone in hysterics. ("We took her upstairs and made her lie
down—but she won't stop shouting long enough to give me
her name or her story. If she don't shut up soon, I'll give her
a sedative—all this will never do!" said poor Doctor Mallard.)

He had seen at once that it was too late to do anything for
Sonny. The boy had been shot through the temple; he must
have died at once, without pain or perhaps even knowing how
it had happened.

"I can't, as I say, get anything out of the girl—and William
wasn't there when the gun went off. All he could tell me was
that he drove Sonny out to call on this young woman, somewhere on Drexel Boulevard; from there they went south to the
park, along the lake shore. He's still too much excited to remember exactly where, but I guess it was a long way out—
no-one's likely to have seen them. After a while Sonny called
to him to stop; they wanted to go for a walk. William says he
didn't notice the gun, but it's Sonny's gun all right—I've seen
it plenty of times. Well, the fellow sat on the box waiting for
them he doesn't know how long it was and Sonny and the
girl went along the beach. They weren't quarrelling, William
claims—as far as he knows, everything was perfectly pleasant
between them. Presently they began taking potshots at some
ducks out on the water; they were laughing about it, he

thinks. He heard two or three separate shots—can't recollect just how many there were—then all of a sudden the young woman was screaming her head off—and there was poor Sonny lying on the sand with a bullet in his brain. William acted pretty smart for a boy of his age: directly he saw it was all over he came straight home instead of going to the hospital, so there's no-one knows anything yet—it gives us a little time to work up a story before the police get hold of it. For it doesn't look good to me, Ned; I never laid eyes on that girl, but I reckon I know who she is—and so do you. We've got to put some sort of front on this for the sake of Almira and the children."

"Where's Mr. Kennerley?" asked Ned.

"He and his wife were dining out on the North Side. Luckily the butler knew where; they've telephoned to him and he's on his way here. But it'll be a few minutes yet before we can expect him. He'll be able to think of something, I imagine. What troubles me most is that I can't be sure it was an accident. Looks like one, of course—seems as if it must have been. Still I don't know . . ."

"It was an accident."

Ned and the doctor wheeled in amazement at the sound of the deep contralto; neither had heard Aunt Lydia come in. She stood in the middle of the room, cloaked and bonneted as though for a party, her round brown eyes fixed on the two men with terrible intensity.

Doctor Mallard started towards his old friend.

"Lydia, I'd give my right hand not to have had this happen to you. It's almost past belief that lightning's struck twice—"

Aunt Lydia waved him away.

"Never mind me; it's Almira who matters. Where is she?"

Doctor Mallard motioned towards the library.

"With her husband. That is . . . you understand, Lydia, it's all over. There's nothing more we can do."

Aunt Lydia nodded.

"I understand. But you're talking through your hat, Jack Mallard, if you think there's nothing to be done. I'll explain what I mean in a moment. First I've got to see Almira."

After she had gone the doctor hurried upstairs to his patient, who was still making a good deal of noise, although the first violence of the spasms had abated.

Ned was left by himself in the stifling, bright, empty hall, to try to grasp as best he could the extent of the calamity that had befallen them. Here, indeed, was a solution to the Stacks' problem as drastic as it was final: how was it possible that Sonny was *dead?* Sonny, with whom he had supped only the night before and talked on the telephone but a few hours ago? The thing was incredible, a horror past bearing. . . . Slowly he began to pace up and down, up and down, unable either to stay still or to think of anything useful to do for the family.

He was still keeping his miserable vigil when Mr. Kennerley arrived. The latter came in alone; Mrs. Kennerley, it appeared, had gone to pieces and been sent home to bed. Ned made his report, while Abner Kennerley listened carefully, in perfect command of himself. He looked dazed, it was true, and had suddenly grown many years older, with sunken cheeks and stooped shoulders. But his mind had not lost its machine-like precision of movement.

"You say no-one knows but ourselves and Jack Mallard, the two servants, and Miss—the Branson woman?"

"Yes, sir—except, of course, Mira and her mother."

"Her mother, eh? Is Lydia Stack—"

"I'm here, Abner."

Aunt Lydia had come out of the library at last.

"Ned, my dear, Almira wants to see you."

When, after the hardest few minutes of his life, Ned returned to the hall he found his aunt and Mr. Kennerley seated side by side on a sofa, talking in low voices. Seeing them thus made him realize that it was very possibly the first time in almost ten years that they had been in the same room together: the bitterness, the discords, that had divided them, were forgotten now. One perceived that they looked at the tragedy in precisely the same way: since Sonny was past help, the one thing that counted was saving appearances. . . .

"No-one knows, then, but the people we've mentioned. Can you trust William?"

"I think so. He's a good lad; I'll make it worth his while . . ."

"There's that woman."

"I know. She's the worst of it. I'll undertake to handle her, though, or my lawyers will. The first thing to do is get her out of the house as fast as we can, and out of town, if possible."

"Then," said Aunt Lydia firmly, "we must say it happened right here at home. Leave out the ride to the park and all. It's much too complicated. Besides, William might get flustered and mention the creature—and where'd we be? Oh, no: Sonny was here in the library, cleaning his gun. He was going on a fishing trip tomorrow, and after all it would be quite natural to take his rifle to Canada, wouldn't it? What worries me most is the newspapers, Abner. You've got to deal with them somehow, make them print what you say."

Mr. Kennerley set his steel jaw.

"If they don't come to heel, they'll lose the biggest advertising account in the city of Chicago."

Aunt Lydia gave him a pale gleam of approval.

"That's right; I know you'll be able to manage. For Almira's sake, and the babies' . . ."

As they continued, haltingly at first, but with increased conviction, to lay their plans to hush up the scandal and make sure everyone was told it was an accident, Ned did not know whom to be sorrier for, the stricken old man or the grim middle-aged woman with terrible eyes. For that was just the trouble: he realized that those two incorrigible materialists did not think for a moment it *was* an accident: they were torn by the blackest suspicions, the cruelest grief. They could not see what Ned had seen so clearly, a few minutes before in the quiet library: poor Sonny had not wanted to die; nor, surely, could Daisy Branson have desired his death, since she had everything to gain by his living. Sonny had been happy, as he'd said; he had won his fight, felt secure at last from the threatening past. The horror was gone; the bullet that put an end to him must have been discharged through one of those awful mischances that made life the haphazard and frightening business it was.

Ned was as certain of this as if his friend had had time to make a deathbed confession in writing; he hoped with all his heart that Almira, too, might be certain. But neither Abner Kennerley nor Lydia Stack would ever be able to believe it.

Epilogue : 1918

S NOW was falling on Prairie Avenue. It had been falling for hours out of a low, windless sky, in which soot had mixed itself so inextricably with the clouds that it was surprising the crystals did not come down black. They frosted the gates and the iron fences, made a whole wide country of the Cobdens' roof across the street, with its winged pigs and grinning gargoyles in high relief against a spotless white desert. What they could not do was hide the gap next door where the Zindersteins' house used to be; that meek pile of rubble looked the uglier, the more desolate, for its dusting of flakes.

Ned, staring at the wintry prospect from Aunt Lydia's chair in the drawing-room window, knew that there were other such gaps all the way up and down on both sides of the avenue. Since the trend to the north had assumed terrifying proportions people were sometimes unable to sell their houses and often chose to tear them down after abandoning them, in order to reduce their taxes. Hardly anybody one knew was left in the old neighbourhood. Almira had been one of the last to go; she had clung, half from habit, half for her mother's sake, to the grey granite palace till the place had to be disposed of for next to nothing (it was now a Home for Inebriates); but even she and her children had been established for at least five years in their comfortable, low-ceilinged flat on the Lake Shore Drive. Tom and Carrie had bought property in Astor Street near the park; the younger generation had moved away in a body, leaving no-one behind save a few obstinate dowagers, hardy enough to survive in their original habitat, but obviously unfit for transplanting.

These relics, who, if sufficiently wealthy and eminent, were dubbed, in the odd, old American fashion, "madams," had developed a marked solidarity: scarcely a day passed that Madam Bunner did not call on Madam Littlefield, or that the pair failed to pay their duty to—Madam Stack? No; not quite: Aunt Lydia, though as rich and respectable as any of the lot, had through sheer force of character escaped the classification. She had fought, too, against being uprooted even more doughtily than the rest. The pleas of her children could not move her: if at last she was quitting the tall yellow house that had been her home for over forty years, it was in spite of herself and for a destination more distant than Chicago's North Side.

Aunt Lydia was dying, at sixty-eight, of the heart ailment she had pretended to suffer from off and on, as a matter of policy, during half of her life. As soon as Tom's telegram had come with the news of the first nearly fatal attack, Ned had hurried on from New York, fearful lest he should arrive too late to say good-bye. Almira had met him at the station that morning with the report that Mamma was conscious, but only just: the doctors felt she could go at any time; on the other hand, she might linger for days. Almira herself had moved down to 1817 to take care of her; it was inconvenient, with the girls expected home from school in less than a week for the Christmas holidays, but anything was better than making that awful long trip twice daily through the snarl of the boulevard traffic. "It takes a good hour, Ned, each way; and then I'd not be easy in my mind—I'd never know when Mamma'd wake and want me."

She had gone upstairs now—after her seizure Aunt Lydia had strangely insisted on being moved to the big front bed-room she had not used since Uncle Hiram's death—to see whether the patient were able to receive a visitor. Ned, waiting restlessly below, was assailed by memories. How much had happened to him—to them all—in the tall yellow house! Often it seemed as if it were the only real thing in his life—or, at any rate, on a plane of reality more solid and satisfying than anything else. Through the vicissitudes and shifting back-grounds of a writer's career, through good times and bad, with-standing even the cataclysmic upheaval of a great world war, it had remained marvelously the same, a set-piece of incal-culable importance. 1817 Prairie Avenue was all the home he'd known in years. Now that he was losing it Ned was filled with sadness—a sadness, frankly, mostly for himself. His cousins, who had stayed in Chicago, could not feel as he did. Tom and Porter had homes and wives of their own, and they and Al-mira had children. Besides, though one couldn't explain it, none of them was so close to their mother as he had been.

For Aunt Lydia herself Ned knew it was best. He had never been able to imagine what she would do if she had to live to be a very old woman; nor, honestly, could one wish her long to outlast the street she had ruled so contentedly.

Almira, plump and prosperous in sables, appeared in the door.

"Mamma's awake, Ned; she's asked for you."

Ned's first feeling, apart from the shock of finding her in an unaccustomed setting, was that Aunt Lydia did not look very ill. Except for her lips, which had a bluish tinge no rouge could disguise, her colour was good; she had never grown wrinkled; her bed-jacket of lime-green silk and lace verged on the coquettish; and a pretty lace cap adorned the red braids that were as carefully dressed as usual.

Her eyes were wide open; when she saw who it was she smiled—and the smile, also, was Aunt Lydia's own.

The nurse bustled forward, professionally cheerful.

"We've just waked up from our nap," she said, in a sugary tone, "and are feeling like a glass of nice, fresh orange-juice. Now, dear, Mr. Ramsay'll sit down in this chair right beside you and I'll be upstairs again in two shakes of a lamb's tail."

Aunt Lydia, without moving her head, managed to throw the young woman in white a glance of strong disfavour.

"You may leave the room, Miss Peterson," she said; "and don't come back till my nephew rings for you."

Miss Peterson made a tittering exit and Aunt Lydia held out her hand—so slowly, so warily, it moved—yet that was not so frightening as her voice, which had lost its timbre: she spoke very clearly, but the volume had dwindled to such a point that one had to bend over the bed to hear what she said.

Ned kissed her: the odour of *violet sec* on the pillow brought back the past with a rush.

"That girl is an utter and absolute fool," said Aunt Lydia, more vigorously. "How are you, Ned? It's good to see you."

"It's good to see *you*, too," said Ned. "I was coming anyhow for Christmas—you hadn't forgotten that, Aunt Lydia? So when Mira told me you weren't well I thought I'd arrive a few days earlier to surprise you."

Aunt Lydia eyed him with satisfaction.

"I'm feeling much better now that you're here. Perhaps I'll fool Jack Mallard yet and be up in time for my New Year's party. He thought I was going to die this week, and I must say I almost agreed with him."

"Now, Mamma," murmured Almira, who had been hovering unhappily in the hall, "you mustn't say such things. Doctor Mallard told me this morning you were getting on very well. If you'll only be patient and not worry too much—"

"Patient? What else can I be, I'd like to know? Go away now, there's a good child, and shut the door after you. I've a great deal to talk over with Ned."

When they were alone, however, she seemed in no hurry to begin.

"So glad you've come," whispered Aunt Lydia. "Don't leave me, will you? Promise, my dear . . ."

"No," said Ned, pressing her hand; "I won't leave you."

Aunt Lydia smiled once more; then the great brown eyes closed and Ned saw that she slept.

From that time on he dedicated himself to his task, refusing to heed Almira's warnings that he would wear himself out. "It's little enough," he told her, "and it's the last thing I can do for your mother, who's done so much for me. After all, why else am I here?"

Aunt Lydia took manifest comfort in her nephew's presence. She seemed stronger if he were near; it was as if he stood between her and the dreadful defencelessness of the gravely ill. She rested more peacefully when her hand was in his; when she woke they would talk together, making the trite, determined little jokes inseparable from the sickroom. Ned often wondered whether she knew she was dying and, if so, how she, who had always been appalled when death came to others, felt about facing her own. At no time that he could remember had she spoken of faith in a future life, nor did she speak of it now. Her references to events in the past were fragmentary, also.

One night she announced without preamble: "I never wanted to marry Abner Kennerley. I could have had him the day after Corinne died—but I didn't want him. Nobody thinks that is true, Ned—but it *is* true. *You* know it is, don't you?" And when Ned had assented she continued emphatically (still in that queer tiny voice): "Meanest man I ever knew! You heard he cut Almira off with a million, didn't you? Just because she hadn't a boy! Except for some measly trust funds for the children, that wretched hospital got it all. Isabel got left out, too," she ruminated, with unmalicious enjoyment. "After she thought she had him where she wanted him. She took to drink before he died; she had to. You couldn't live with Abner Kennerley and not drink. Meanest man I ever knew!"

And she drifted off to sleep.

Another time when the subject recurred, she remarked, *à propos* of Almira's supposed penury: "But she'll be all right. You'll *all* be all right—I've seen to that. Nothing can touch you if you've money in the bank. Remember that always. When I was young sometimes I went hungry for days because my family was too poor to get proper food. I tell you, Ned, I've known what it was to stare through the window at a loaf of bread I'd have given my soul for, and didn't have a nickel in my pocket to buy it with. That was a long time ago . . . a . . . long . . . time . . . ago."

It was the only allusion Ned ever heard her make to her mysterious youth.

Three days after his arrival Aunt Lydia died in her sleep. Her heart just stopped beating; the night nurse in attendance discovered it when she came to take her pulse as a matter of routine. She called Almira and Ned at once, but it was already too late.

There ensued a trying time of commotion, which occupied everyone's thoughts almost, it seemed, to the exclusion of grief. The house became busy with knots of black-clad relatives whispering in corners. The John Stacks and the Harvey Stacks —nobody had laid eyes on them in years—appeared with suspicious speed. *Both* tried to take charge, Cousin Gertrude (Mrs. John) cautioning the family privately against Cousin Penelope (Mrs. Harvey), who ten minutes later returned the compliment in kind. Friends called to leave cards and bouquets; eventually every vase in the pantry was found and filled. An unending stream of letters and telegrams poured in: Carrie and Fanny, as daughters-in-law reckoned one degree removed in their sense of bereavement, assumed responsibility for these. Ned was struck, as messages of condolence from

the grandchildren were read aloud, by the bright tears each
mother reserved for her own offspring's eloquence, whilst
greeting her rival's recitals in stony-eyed silence. Even the
servants—a comparatively new set of stolid Swedes—caught
something of the prevailing excitement and went about looking pleased in a suitably subdued way.

The funeral, which, since Grace Church had burned three
years ago, Almira and her brothers had decided to hold at the
house, was as conventionally smart and well attended as even
Aunt Lydia could have wished. The wide folding doors between bedroom and drawing-room had to be opened to ac-
commodate the crowd. There were expensive singers and
flowers in tasteful profusion. Almira, with her head on
Ned's shoulder, cried softly throughout the service, while
Ned fixed his gaze on the fabulous pall of white orchids in
the window and strove to fix his thoughts on a problem-
atical Hereafter. (What, if there were such a place, could
so mundane and practical a person as Aunt Lydia find to
do in it?)

His most vivid impression was of Uncle Rock sitting trem-
ulously by himself in a corner, bowed to earth by what to him
must be an irreparable loss.

After the return from the cemetery (Oakwoods, not Grace-
land; even in death Aunt Lydia was true to her beloved South
Side), the will was opened and read by Jamie Mallard, who
had lately become Uncle Rock's junior partner. Ned was surprised to find that none of his cousins had the slightest idea
what was in it. He was still more surprised when he learned
he was named as one of the four residuary legatees, being
treated exactly like one of Aunt Lydia's children. It was touching that Tom and Porter and Almira felt this right and
natural; the fact that Carrie and Fanny betrayed a faint tendency to consider the third generation deprived of a part of
their birthright did not distress him unduly.

The estate was much larger than anyone—even her sons in

the business—had supposed. For years Aunt Lydia had spent less than half of her income, the balance being invested in gilt-edged securities that yielded an increasingly handsome return. Yet her official account at the Illinois Trust represented only a fraction of her actual wealth. 1817 had been growing more and more crowded and cluttered; when the contents of the premises were inventoried and appraised the value of the furniture, silver, linen, china, and glass was seen to be staggering.

Nor was this all. During the next few days the heirs were perpetually making fresh discoveries. One drawer in the library desk was filled with cheque-books showing cash balances in various banks nobody knew Aunt Lydia had had dealings with. The bedroom bureau disgorged a nest-egg of Liberty Bonds; the dressing-table, an envelope stuffed with deeds to properties all over the United States. The silver safe on the stairs turned out to be crammed with unset diamonds; even the pantry liquor cabinet held a cache of farm mortgages and several thousand dollars in gold and bills. It was an incredible hoard, hidden away as a bower-bird might hide its treasures, or an enterprising squirrel store up a fantastic provision of nuts for some mythical winter.

To Ned, less concerned than the rest with material objects (how, indeed, should he find room for a tithe of what he'd inherited in the small bachelor flat on Washington Square where he spent his winters?), fell the task of sorting his aunt's personal papers. There were not many: unlike most of her contemporaries she had never kept letters; she had also, one could guess why, ruthlessly destroyed all records of her life before her marriage. Nothing remained to show what Lydia Porter had been; little more to remind one of Lydia Stack.

On the last afternoon before leaving for New York Ned did unearth a small leather notebook, with leaves yellowed by time, in which his aunt had evidently kept an itemized list of cash sums she'd received for investment. Many of the entries were initialled "H.S."; as many more, of later date, bore the

inscription "A.K." Other monograms still further on Ned
might have deciphered had he willed, but he loyally averted
his eyes and consigned the notebook to the flames in Aunt
Lydia's grate: let the past keep its secrets forever.

Having performed this crowning service to her memory, he
gathered up his sheaf of papers and strolled into the drawing-
room, where his cousins were assembled, all the children together (children no longer). Tom sprawled in Uncle Hiram's
old armchair by the fire, smoking a pipe. (How he'd grown
to resemble his father, these last few years!) Almira and her
sisters-in-law, three comfortable middle-aged women, sat in a
row on the sofa, sorting the ultimate oddments of the collection—a trunkful of painted eighteenth-century fans, and such
jewelry as Aunt Lydia had not deemed valuable enough to
lock up in the bank: the corals and crystals, ambers and jades,
were spread on the floor in sparkling confusion. Porter, lean
and balding, at his mother's post in the window, stared out at
the blinding white street; for after a week of dismal weather
Chicago's bright but comfortless winter sun had emerged as
the mercury slid down to zero. Above the mantel Aunt Lydia's
portrait, resplendent in pearls and her best satin gown, presided graciously over the meeting.

Ned handed his bundle to Tom as the eldest: "There you
are, boy; I think you'll find everything in order. There wasn't
so much as I thought there'd be."

"Mother Stack didn't save memorabilia, thank goodness!"
said Carrie. "Do you know, when Aunt Annie died last spring,
it took a month to go through her things—and they found
she'd kept all her cotillion cards and theatre programmes, and
every single Tribune for over fifty years!"

"It's about all your mother *didn't* care about, though," remarked Fanny crisply. "Did I tell you, Porter, I came upon
a whole new shelf of Royal Doulton this morning, in that
cupboard at the top of the kitchen stairs? That makes eighteen
complete dinner-sets—or is it nineteen? I declare I've lost

count. What we'll do with so many . . . And those thirty-foot Italian filet banquet cloths . . . Of course they're perfectly gorgeous; it'd be a crime to cut them up—but who has got a table long enough to use them?"

"Or, for that matter, gives parties any more on such a scale?" said Porter. "Since the war people just don't entertain the way Mamma used to do. Seems to me something's gone out of life that won't ever come back. I'd send all that junk to be auctioned if I were you, girls."

"You wouldn't get much for it," Tom objected. "Not half what it's worth. I've been talking to the fellow at Grant's. . . . If *we* can't use such things, who the dickens else can?"

"Besides," said Almira, in her soft voice, "it would've hurt Mamma so if she'd thought . . . She wanted us to have everything she could leave us, the best of everything. You know that. No children ever had such a mother. All she planned or thought of, really, was for us, even though we didn't guess . . . When I remember now how much we owe her I wish I'd been able to show her more love than I did. I tried to thank her sometimes, but it wasn't easy—she didn't like being thanked. Oh, Mamma was such a good woman!"

Ned's eyes met the painted eyes of the portrait; he fancied they shared a final smile.

For the last time, then, just before sunset, he descended the high flight of steps to walk the length of Aunt Lydia's kingdom. The air was so cold and dry that he gasped as he drew his first breath: this was no day to linger and mourn; Ned stepped smartly over the squeaking, tightly packed snow, trying not to see the sign "Rooms for Rent" in the Cobdens' front window. More houses were gone than he'd thought. There were rubble heaps everywhere; a hairpin factory, long, low, and unutterably dingy, occupied the whole block where the Framinghams' wooden cottage had stood. (The tall yellow house, which nobody wanted, would soon, one surmised, go the way of the rest.) The smoke-blackened elms had been dying out fast. Even Lake Michigan was about to desert its old neighbourhood: Tom had spoken at dinner, only last night, of plans that were afoot to dredge up a whole new strip of parkway beyond the railroad tracks connecting the far South Side with the Loop.

It was a dismal scene, not even dignified in decay; for these buildings had never been intrinsically beautiful, and now that the life that had informed them was gone the shells were painfully ugly, pitiably shrunken. (How had Ned's boyish eyes seen them as immense?)

Here and there a gaunt survivor seemed merely to accentuate the general air of dilapidation and neglect. Ned saw that the Kennerley mansion was standing intact, its baroque roof still a refuge for pigeons, which were huddled amongst the chimneys to escape the wintry blast. The dusty windows reflected a dying gleam of the pale January sun, giving one the grisly illusion that a party was going on inside. (How many years had it been since he'd heard from Celia? That was an episode resolved without climax, curiously complete in its incompleteness. He thought of her now as of someone he'd known on another planet.)

As Ned walked farther south the first faint stirrings of a possible use for all these old memories occurred to him. Never before had he seen his past as literary material. Was it because he'd been too close to the whole thing to get a perspective? Yet, after all, what richer subject could he find? . . . How would one set about it? It shouldn't be too hard to choose the point of attack . . . and a method. (If one wrote about Margot of France as if she were Aunt Lydia Stack, why not reverse the process and write about Aunt Lydia as if she were Margot?)

The prime necessity, it went without saying, would be a clear understanding of the reasons that had led to Prairie Avenue's decline and fall. Why had this pageant, which seemed so substantial, faded so quickly, leaving in truth not a rack behind? Had it happened because the show was purely material? This had been no aristocracy like London's, nor even New York's. Birth and breeding had not counted for much: money was the means, and money the *summum bonum*. . . . There had been others, of course, not a few—good, simple souls like the Mallards, the Bunners—who had played their parts out as if that were all that concerned them. But somehow it was the strong old roosters and their spectacular wives who had set the pace of the piece.

In a way, one saw, since the city would not have been what it was without them, Chicago was their monument—vast and vigorous, rude and crude, its virtues and vices close copies of the virtues and vices of the men who'd made it. Chicago was still there, though the strong old roosters had disappeared, leaving little to show for their efforts but their businesses, which, like Frankenstein's monsters, seemed to have achieved a ruthless life of their own, quite independent of their founders' undistinguished descendants.

Even Aunt Lydia, splendid personification of Prairie Avenue in its palmy days, had vanished: what was left of her now but her bank account, a houseful of loot—and the transient memory of a smile?

Drawing his coat collar higher to ward off the bitter cold, Ned thrust his hands deep in his pockets and strode on in the gathering dusk.